WITH EVERY BREATH

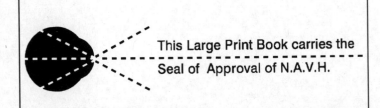

This Large Print Book carries the
Seal of Approval of N.A.V.H.

WITH EVERY BREATH

ELIZABETH CAMDEN

THORNDIKE PRESS

A part of Gale, Cengage Learning

GALE
CENGAGE Learning·

Farmington Hills, Mich • San Francisco • New York • Waterville, Maine
Meriden, Conn • Mason, Ohio • Chicago

Copyright © 2014 by Dorothy Mays.
Scripture quotations are from the King James Version of the Bible.
Thorndike Press, a part of Gale, Cengage Learning.

LIBRARY OF CONGRESS CATALOGING-IN-PUBLICATION DATA

Camden, Elizabeth, 1948–
    With every breath / by Elizabeth Camden. — Large print edition.
        pages ; cm. — (Thorndike Press large print Christian historical fiction)
    ISBN 978-1-4104-7226-7 (hardcover) — ISBN 1-4104-7226-4 (hardcover)
    1. Physicians—Fiction. 2. Women statisticians—Fiction. 3. United
States—Officials and employees—Fiction. 4. Tuberculosis—Research—Fiction.
5. Washington (D.C.)—Social conditions—19th century—Fiction. 6. Large
type books. I. Title.
PS3553.A429W58 2014b
813'.54—dc23   2014024499

Published in 2014 by arrangement with Bethany House Publishers, a division of Baker Publishing Group

Printed in Mexico
1 2 3 4 5 6 7 18 17 16 15 14

For Jane and John Auchter,
my first readers and the best of parents

You gave me a foundation of
love, faith, and inspiration.
I will be forever grateful.

PROLOGUE

Washington, D.C. — 1879

There was only one thing Kate Norton loved more than winning, and that was winning against Trevor McDonough.

Trevor had been her nemesis since the day he arrived at their private academy four years ago. They'd both earned perfect grades throughout school, and for the first time in the history of the academy, there was a tie for valedictorian. Today's grueling academic challenge was the tiebreaker, and a college scholarship rested on the results.

With forty spectators crammed into the classroom, it was warm and crowded, made worse by Kate's tight corset and high-collared blouse. She and Trevor stood at the head of the class as they battled in the spelling portion of the test, which had been dragging on for a mind-numbing forty minutes, and most of the audience was surely hoping either she or Trevor would stumble soon. Kate's father sat in the front row, mopping his brow and looking ready to faint, for Trevor was already ahead in today's competition. This morning he'd won the biology, chemistry, and physics tests, while Kate had won calculus and history. Only spelling and trigonometry remained, and she had to win both if she had a prayer of going to college. Attention turned to Trevor as the headmaster read the next word.

"Mr. McDonough, please spell *abstemious*," the headmaster said. "Abstemious is defined as 'practicing an unusually high level of self-restraint with a lack of joy.' "

Oh, the irony.

Trevor McDonough was the most abstemious person ever born. Kate glanced at him. He stood tall, brooding, and gangly, a swath of black hair tumbling over his forehead and obscuring the sullen darkness of his eyes.

In the front row, Kate's little brother fidgeted and clung to her father's leg. "Hang in there, Tick," she whispered to her six-year-old brother. His real name was Timothy, but the joyfully eager way he clung to everyone had earned him the nickname.

Trevor swallowed hard and asked for the word to be repeated. She had a natural

8

advantage over Trevor in spelling. When he first came to their school, his Scottish accent was so heavy it tricked him into spelling mistakes. He learned quickly, though. Over the years he'd scrutinized the way others spoke and trained himself to speak without a trace of his old accent. She held her breath while Trevor took a stab at the word.

And misspelled it. A jolt of anticipation surged through her.

All she had to do was spell *abstemious* correctly and she would win the spelling test. Tension ratcheted higher. There were forty people gathered on her side of the classroom: her family, her friends from school, and a bunch of people who lived at her family's boardinghouse. Even the postman and the milkman were here to root for her.

On Trevor's side there was but a single person: the coachman who drove him to school each day. Wearing a navy frock coat with gold braids and shiny black boots, the coachman was the best-dressed person in the room.

Trevor had all the advantages stacked on his side. He lived in a mansion and had the best of everything. She didn't know what happened to his parents, but his guardian

9

was a rich senator from Maryland. Trevor probably had his dinner delivered on a silver platter, while Kate spent her evenings juggling serving trays and waiting on the thirty people who lived at the boardinghouse.

"Miss Norton, you must now spell *abstemious.*"

She closed her eyes. *Please . . .*

She spelled the word perfectly, and the crowd burst into cheers as she was declared the winner. Her father vaulted out of his seat and swept her into a bear hug. The school's janitor grinned and clapped her on the back. Tears pricked behind her eyes, and it was hard to breathe.

She mustn't get carried away. She still had to win the trigonometry contest before she would be declared the valedictorian. The next twenty minutes would determine if Kate would go to college or stay working at the boardinghouse.

Not that there was anything wrong with working in a boardinghouse, but she had such dreams. . . .

"You will have twenty minutes to complete the trigonometry equations," the headmaster announced. "The winner of this test will be declared valedictorian and receive a full scholarship for college."

Two chalkboards with squeaky wheels

were rolled into the room, both filled with identical equations. She and Trevor darted to the boards and began tackling the equations at the headmaster's prompting. The only sound in the classroom was the mad clicking of chalk on the slate surface. Kate's mind worked faster than her fingers as she processed the complex stream of mathematical equations, but beside her Trevor wrote just as fast.

Her all-consuming battle with Trevor McDonough began the first day he arrived at their school four years ago. Like a vulture, he immediately spotted her as his only real academic competition. It didn't matter the subject, they competed. Grades were the major thing, but they competed over stupid things too. Who could skip a stone farther. Who could memorize more lines of poetry or hold their breath longer.

The heavy coil of Kate's red hair began sliding down the side of her head, but she couldn't falter now. She needed to complete the equations with a perfect score, and then a college scholarship was hers. Her hand began to shake as she sped toward the end of the final equation.

"Time!" the headmaster called out. He held a stopwatch in his hand and waited for both of them to set their chalk on the trays.

Kate shoved her hair back and glanced at Trevor's equations while he did the same to hers. His black eyes showed no emotion as he scanned her work. Their trigonometry equations looked like ancient hieroglyphics to the untrained eye, yet Kate immediately spotted the two areas where she and Trevor diverged in their methods.

"Please stand back while I score the tests," the headmaster said, the answer key held in his hand. Who was right? She had taken a longer path to arrive at the same destination, but Trevor's work looked tighter, more eloquent.

She glanced at her family in the front row. Her mother had the fingers on both hands crossed, but her father looked ready to start weeping from the stress.

The headmaster finished assessing their work and stepped to the front of the room, a hint of unease in his eyes. Papa came to stand behind her, her mother on the other side.

"It has been a pleasure to have two such academically gifted students over the past four years," the headmaster began. "No matter what their futures hold, I am certain both will enrich our community and go on to great things. However, the school can only endow one student's college education per year. This year, that honor will go to Mr. Trevor McDonough."

The oxygen was sucked out of the room. She felt hot, then dizzy as her father pulled her into a tight hug. "It's okay, baby girl," he murmured, but there was heartbreak in his voice.

It wouldn't be okay. She was going to spend the rest of her life hauling laundry and washing dishes in the boardinghouse. She glared over her father's shoulder at Trevor. He didn't even need this scholarship! He wore a gold watch that probably cost more than her parents earned in a year. The principal walked over to shake Trevor's hand, but no one else did.

The air grew thick as people crowded her, hugging and patting her on the shoulder. She had to think of something to say. She had to pretend that all her wild hopes and ambitions weren't collapsing as she stood there. She forced a smile. "I'll be all right," she said, trying to mean it. Tick nudged through the crowd, his spindly arms reaching out to hug Kate's hips.

"Did you win?" his childish voice chirped as he looked up at her expectantly.

What was she supposed to say? It felt as if she'd let the entire neighborhood down, not just her baby brother, who thought she could do no wrong.

Her mother pulled Tick away. "Hush now," she soothed.

From the corner of her eye, she noticed Trevor leaving the room, the coachman walking a few steps behind him.

"Go congratulate him," her father said. Kate pulled back to see if he was serious. Tired, weary, with grief welling in his eyes, her father nodded. "I know it may be hard for you, but it's the right thing to do. Go shake Trevor's hand and wish him well."

She'd rather stick her hand into a vat of acid. She wished she'd never laid eyes on that joyless, awful boy. Other than being smart, there wasn't a single redeeming feature in Trevor McDonough's entire being. Straightening her shoulders, she followed Trevor out the door and down the hall into the cool spring air. The late afternoon sun was shining, and the sky was a crystalline blue. But the cloudless day only made her feel worse.

"Congratulations, Trevor."

He paused, his face frozen in its typical expressionless stare. His black eyes looked like lumps of coal on his chalky-white face. He finally stepped forward and shook her hand. "Thanks," he muttered before turning away to climb inside the coach. It was lacquered in glossy maroon paint with velvet seats inside.

She watched the horse-drawn carriage roll away, a cloud of dust kicking up from its wheels. No matter how much she disliked him, there was no doubt Trevor McDonough would go on to a dazzling future. He was rich, privileged, and brilliant. Trevor didn't *need* that scholarship, but how strange that when she shook his hand, he was trembling like a mouse trapped in a corner.

She refused to feel sorry for him. He could have made friends if he had tried. If he wasn't so gloomy and hadn't gone out of his way to rebuff every person who tried to be nice to him, he wouldn't have been so ostracized.

To the bottom of her soul, Kate hoped she had just seen the last of the horrible Trevor McDonough.

1

Twelve Years later
Washington, D.C. — 1891

Kate held the letter in her hands. She'd read it so many times over the past week, the words were engraved in her mind, yet she still couldn't understand why a world-renowned doctor would have singled her out to apply for a prestigious position at Washington Memorial Hospital.

Around her, rows of women filled the cavernous room, all of them sitting before tabulating machines. The women busily fed punch cards into the machines, filling the air with the sounds of clicking, humming, and rattling. Kate used to adore her work here at the census bureau. Analyzing data to better understand the world around her had been a joy, the perfect job, and one that drew on her statistical abilities. But that was last year, before the machines invaded the bureau's office.

The machines had put statisticians out of work everywhere. It seemed there was no longer an office in the entire city that didn't have an adding machine or a tabulating mechanism. There was still plenty of statistical forecasting work that needed to be done by people with a good head for numbers, but those jobs went to men.

Men with college degrees.

She pushed the thought away. Tomorrow morning she was going to interview at Washington Memorial Hospital for a position to analyze data and predict trends in health and disease. Never had she wanted a job so badly. It would free her from this beehive and give her the chance to do something meaningful with her brain.

"Are you really going to go through with it?" Betsy Waters asked, leaning over from her tabulating station.

Kate startled and quickly slipped the letter beneath a stack of files. "I've got to," she said in a low voice. "I'll wonder for the rest of my life if I don't."

She still wondered how Dr. T. M. Kendall had learned of her existence. After all, there were dozens of statisticians who had been put out of work when the census became automated, so why did he single her out for an interview?

"I hope Mr. Gertsmann doesn't fire you on the spot," Betsy said. "Last year he fired Letty Smitson just for reading the advertisements for open positions in the Treasury Department."

Kate was well aware of her supervisor's hostility toward any employee who dared to lift her head up and aspire to something outside the beehive. Washington had always been a little unusual in the number of women who were able to find office jobs. Government agencies required an awesome number of clerical workers, and in a small city like Washington, that opened doors for women. Almost a third of the people working in government offices were women, but most were under the thumb of men like Mr. Gertsmann, who greeted Kate's request for three hours of leave with a long, hostile stare.

"I insist on knowing the reason you will miss work in the middle of the week," Mr. Gertsmann said. "Such lack of discipline is not something I will condone without a good explanation."

"Sir, I'm only asking for three hours tomorrow morning. I will be in the office by eleven o'clock." At all costs, she must not let him know she was interviewing for another position or he might fire her then and there.

"I will not allow you to gallivant around this city without knowing your reason for missing work."

"I've worked here for twelve years," Kate said. "In all that time I've only been absent from work once."

"Yes, but that involved an entire week, and you did so without advance warning."

She sucked in a sharp breath. "That was when my husband died! And I didn't receive advance warning the scaffolding he was standing on was going to collapse."

She blinked rapidly. The accident had been four years ago, and Kate hardly ever cried over it anymore, but to have Nathan's death flung at her made her want to break something.

Other women in the office sent her sympathetic glances. Mr. Gertsmann was condescending to all the women in the office, but he always singled her out for the worst of his ire.

"You have no bereavement now, so again I insist on knowing why you plan on missing work."

The clattering of the machines tapered off a little as some in the office started listening in. Given the way the other women in the room glared at him, it was almost surprising that Mr. Gertsmann didn't burst into flame.

"It's a personal matter," she finally answered.

"And is this 'personal matter' in relation to employment at the Washington Memorial Hospital?"

She winced. "How did you know that?"

He yanked a small envelope from his pocket. "Because I've had a request for your references. The newly appointed Dr. T. M. Kendall wishes to know about your vaunted skills as a statistician."

The way he said *statistician* made it sound like a puny and pathetic word. After all, with machines taking over so much of the tabulating work, Mr. Gertsmann thought statisticians ought to be put on the shelf alongside the bow and arrow and everything else that had been rendered useless by modern technology.

"I certainly hope you will find working at the hospital a fulfilling outlet for your ambitions, because I can't imagine employing a woman of questionable loyalty here at the census bureau."

"Are you firing me?" It would be a disaster if she lost this job before securing another. With all the pricey improvements her parents made to the boardinghouse, Kate's income was needed to pay the bank note each month.

Mr. Gertsmann assumed an artificially pleasant tone as he smirked at her. "And if I decide to terminate your employment if you miss work tomorrow morning?"

She had to be smart about this. Mr. Gertsmann was a small man whose ego needed regular tending, and she braced herself to do just that.

"Then naturally I will be here on time," she said calmly. If she had to miss the interview, she would find another way to make contact with Dr. Kendall.

Her conciliatory words had the desired effect. Mr. Gertsmann preened, puffing his chest out and fiddling with the buttons on his vest.

"Excellent," he said. "I am a generous man and will permit you three hours' leave, but I trust this will be the end of your foolish ambitions. Women are ideally suited to the monotony of census work, but if you wish to toy with the fantasy of pursuing a rigorous intellectual position, it will be amusing to watch." He patted her on the shoulder, and she tried not to cringe. "I hope the disappointment is not too great," he added before leaving the room.

"That man makes me long for a bucket of

tar and a sack of feathers," Kate muttered as she returned to her station. She was twenty-nine years old and was dying on the vine at the census bureau. The position at the hospital was a long shot, but she intended to fight hard for it.

"Why does he hate you so much?" Charlie Davis asked as he lounged in the windowsill of the boardinghouse's dining room, his thin frame looking as delicate as a reed. For such a skinny man, he was always voraciously hungry and appeared the moment the scent from her mother's kitchen began percolating through the boardinghouse. With his gray hair immaculately groomed and his neatly clipped mustache, Charlie was like the grandfather she never had, and their daily chat while she set the dinner table had been a ritual since the time Kate was a child.

His question made Kate pause as she retrieved the heavy pewter flatware from the sideboard. "Mr. Gertsmann doesn't like anybody, but one time I stopped a report from going out that had a string of errors in it. A batch of punch cards had been fed into the machine backwards, skewing the data. He ought to have noticed the numbers looked off-kilter, but it slipped past him. I think he was embarrassed I caught it."

"You might have saved his job," Charlie said.

"Maybe." She began laying the plates next. They were large plates, as her mother delivered heaping portions of the best food on the Eastern Seaboard, making their boardinghouse famous among the elected officials in Washington. Most government jobs didn't pay much, and unless the elected officials were independently wealthy, they usually stayed in boardinghouses or hotels whenever Congress was in session.

The dining room was large, with three windows facing H Street and providing a view of the US Capitol building only a few blocks away. The dining room's creamy yellow walls and crown molding was typical of the Federal style that dominated the city. A long table stretched down the center of the room, and Kate had been setting this table each evening from the time she was old enough to be trusted with the crockery.

From behind the swinging door to the kitchen, pots clattered and a kettle whistled. Dinner was at least twenty minutes away, yet the scents of fresh bread and simmering beef were probably tormenting Charlie as badly as a hound tethered just out of reach from a juicy steak. "How about I sneak in the kitchen and see if I can steal a blueberry muffin for you? Mother made them this afternoon."

Charlie's eyes sparkled. "You are an angel of goodness and mercy."

Charlie had lived at their boardinghouse ever since he was elected to Congress thirty-two years ago. He witnessed all her childhood triumphs and tragedies. He taught her to tie her shoelaces and looked the other way when she slid down the polished oak banisters. He listened to her wax ecstatic over her adolescent crush on Nathan Livingston, the funniest boy in school, who could balance a fiddle on the tip of his nose and still look devilishly handsome while he did it. Charlie cheered her on at horseshoe matches and commiserated when she lost the college scholarship to Trevor McDonough. Charlie came to her wedding, and he was a pallbearer at Nathan's funeral only two years later. She would be forever grateful for that. Nathan had always been a little in awe of Charlie Davis and would have been flattered that Pennsylvania's longest-serving congressman did him that final honor.

The aroma of roast beef and simmering onions surrounded Kate as she pushed into the warm kitchen. Steam rose from kettles on the massive cast-iron stove. Kate used a pair of tongs to open the door of the warming compartment. "Please look the other way while I steal a muffin for Charlie."

Her mother didn't turn around from slicing onions into a pan of sizzling butter. "Just *one*," she cautioned. "That Bauman girl is bringing three guests to dinner and gave me only an hour's notice. I ought to start charging Justice Bauman extra for all the mouths they drag in here."

Irene Bauman and her father had been living here the past eight years whenever the Supreme Court was in session. Justice Bauman was a decent man, but his daughter? Kate snatched a muffin and thought about skipping dinner if Irene was going to be there.

No such luck. When Kate returned to the dining room, Irene had plopped down in a chair opposite Charlie, playfully twirling a lock of her honey-blond hair. It was bad enough to watch an eighteen-year-old girl flirt with a man in his sixties, but did she really need to twirl her hair?

"Alms for the hungry," she said, dropping the muffin in Charlie's palm. "If you'll excuse me, I need to starch my dress shirt for tomorrow."

Charlie knew about the interview, of course. It would not surprise her if he'd already put in a good word for her at the hospital, although he denied it. "I've never met this Dr. Kendall fellow," he said. "But if he is half as smart as people say, he'll snap you up immediately."

"I hope you aren't going to wear that boring pinstripe shirt," Irene said. "I'll loan you one of my mutton sleeve blouses, if you like. You would look so much smarter."

Here we go. Why couldn't she and Irene be in the same room for two minutes without the competition beginning? Irene always compared their clothing, their hairstyles, their jewelry. There was nothing Kate loved more than matching wits or skill in a healthy competition, but over fashion? And yet the moment Irene moved into the boardinghouse, the natural rivalry seemed to take root and spring up at the worst times. It reminded Kate of school, when she spent years matching wits against Trevor McDonough. At least Trevor was smart; Irene was a nitwit.

Although she had to admit, Irene's mutton sleeve blouses were spectacular. Would it be so wrong to borrow one? Temptation clawed at her. Just once it would be nice to be as stylishly turned-out as Irene, but Kate couldn't take the bait. If she got this job, Irene would lord it over her for ages, insisting it was her blouse that won Kate the job.

"My pinstripe blouse will be fine." It had gently gathered sleeves and fabulous cuffs that buttoned tightly all the way to her elbows. She loved the dashing feminine appearance the blouse gave her. It was nothing compared to a real mutton sleeve blouse, but it still looked smart.

"Suit yourself," Irene said. "It's such a shame you're interviewing for another job involving math. It must be awful squinting at numbers all day. It will put lines on your face for good."

Charlie winced at the insult, but Kate took it in stride. "Oh, Irene, my face is the place nasty worry lines come to roost for fun."

Kate never worried too much about her appearance. She had a trim, athletic figure from running up and down four flights of stairs to keep the boardinghouse operating, and she never bothered with jewelry or ornamentation. With a wealth of smooth red hair, she simply mounded it atop her head in the Gibson girl style that was becoming so popular.

Kate grabbed a handful of pewter spoons and began laying them alongside the plates. "Who are your guests for dinner this evening? Mother is scrambling to stretch the meal."

"Jenny Fayette and her parents," Irene said while she kept twirling her hair. "I met them at the Smithsonian this morning. Her father is in the navy and his uniform is so dashing. I think he is a captain."

Kate almost dropped the spoons. "Captain Fayette?" she gasped. "Captain Alfred Fayette of the Naval Academy?"

"Do you already know him?" Irene looked mildly disappointed. "I was hoping to surprise everyone with my fancy guests."

Kate didn't have time for explanations; she merely shoved the spoons in Irene's hands. "Here, you finish setting the table. I've got to run."

Kate was breathless by the time she ran to the Marine Barracks on Eighth Street. It was a hot June day, and a stitch clawed at her side while a blister screamed on the back of her heel, but none of that mattered.

Her little brother was going to get into the Naval Academy if she had to pull every string in the city. Tick had dreamed of it ever since he was a child, and last year's rejection was a blow none of them anticipated. No one in her family had gone to college, so how was she to know the application process began so early? Or that they needed letters of support from officers and elected officials?

Tick ended up joining the Marine Corps after finishing school, but Kate wasn't going to let it end there. His letter of rejection encouraged him to apply again, and this time Kate would make sure his application sailed through with a chorus of angels singing his praises. Timothy "Tick" Norton was going to be the first member of their family to graduate from college if it killed her.

The blister got worse as she turned down Eighth Street. It was an older part of the city that hadn't yet been renovated. Washington used to be a small, muddy town, but after the Civil War, money flowed into the city to widen the boulevards, line the streets with trees, and erect elegantly wrought lampposts to illuminate the city. Government buildings were torn down and replaced with palaces of white granite and imposing columns that glittered in the sunlight.

In the southern part of town, the stately government buildings gave way to oak-shaded streets and redbrick walls. Only two blocks north of the US Navy Yard, the Marine Barracks consisted of a long row of buildings with an armory and living quarters. It was impossible to get through the gate this late in the afternoon, but the brick wall was only five feet tall, and with a jump she was able to hoist herself up to brace her elbows on the ledge. Tick was playing a game of dice on a table beneath the thick branches of an oak tree.

"Hey, Tick!" she called. "Get over here!"

Tick whirled around, a grin spreading over his face. With blond hair and sky-blue eyes, Tick had grown into a handsome young man. He was eighteen and already six feet tall, and he wasn't finished growing. Dressed in a plain shirt and brown pants, Tick had changed out of the field uniform he wore during the first part of the day when he served as guard to the surgeon general. His long, loping strides devoured the ground.

"Quit calling me Tick in front of other people," he said as soon as he was opposite her.

"Sorry," she said with a wince. She had been trying to quit, but he'd been Tick since she'd changed his diapers and taught him how to walk. With her mother cooking and cleaning for thirty boarders, Kate practically raised Tick, and she'd loved every minute of it. She was eleven when he was born, and he was the best gift any girl ever had. She loved his soft baby smell and the drooly smile he gave her every morning when she lifted him from the cradle. Later, he clung to her like a tick she could never shake, hanging on to her leg as she walked around the house. Whenever she came into his line of sight, he would launch himself across the room and straight into her arms.

"Listen," she whispered. "Captain Fayette from the Naval Academy is coming to dinner tonight. Change into your dress uniform and get back to the house. This is too good an opportunity to miss."

"Tonight? I can't leave without permission. There are rules about things like that."

"If your mother was dying from a heart attack this very moment, don't tell me you couldn't figure out a way to get home. Now go ask for permission. And quick. Dinner begins in fifteen minutes."

Tick shifted. "This isn't exactly a life-or-death thing, Kate. I don't want to get a reputation for slacking off."

She wanted to leap over the wall and shake some sense into him. "But this is a perfect opportunity. You're acting like I want this more than you."

Tick didn't answer her right away. He glanced back at the others playing dice beneath the tree, then back at her. "Of course I want it, but I have a good position here. I can't risk it to go chasing after another."

What he said made sense. After all, wasn't she risking her job at the census bureau by chasing after a long-shot position at the hospital? Kate was a risk taker, while Tick had always been more cautious.

She dropped back down to her side of the wall, brushing the grit from her elbows. "Okay, I get it," she conceded.

Tick reached a hand over the wall to grab her shoulder. "Thanks for coming, Kate. If Captain Fayette comes again, let me know and I'll try to get time off, okay?"

She nodded, hoping the disappointment wasn't showing on her face. "Deal."

"And good luck on the job interview tomorrow," Tick said. "The surgeon general has been trying for years to lure Dr. Kendall to Washington, so working for him would be a real coup."

Tick meant the words kindly, but they just ratcheted Kate's anxiety higher. A man of Dr. Kendall's sterling reputation would surely have his pick of applicants, and the odds of her getting the job were slim. Still, she had to try.

The blister cut into her heel as she began walking home. Two blocks ahead of her a horse-drawn streetcar was picking up passengers. For five cents she could ride home in time to help serve dinner. If she hurried, she could catch it before it set off at a brisk trot up Virginia Avenue.

Or she could race it home.

She suppressed a grin as she hiked up her skirts and made a dash down the street. The streetcar had a good head start on her, but she could still beat it home if she pulled out all the stops. She sprang over curbs and around pedestrians, gaining a few yards with each block. The blister was forgotten. All that mattered was drawing up alongside the streetcar and passing it and reaching the front stoop of her house in first place.

The thrill of competition surged in her veins. Pitting her will and stamina against the horse gave her something to strive for, to battle and win.

After all, there was nothing she liked better than winning.

2

The hospital was an imposing Gothic building at the end of New Hampshire Avenue. With five stories of dark red brick, two massive corner turrets, and large windows sparkling in the morning sunlight, it looked stately and rich resting amidst the leafy neighborhood.

Kate smoothed her skirt as she descended from the streetcar. Her freshly starched pinstripe blouse was tucked into a slim charcoal-gray skirt, and she hoped she looked more confident than she felt.

What did she know about medicine? Statistics came naturally to her, but she wished she wasn't such a novice when it came to medicine. The female clerk who greeted visitors in the receiving area was impressed when Kate asked to meet with Dr. Kendall.

"Such a handsome man, that one!" she cooed. It seemed a little odd for a gray-haired matron to be gushing over a man. "I declare, I think all the nurses are carrying a torch for that man. They all stare after him as he walks down the hallways, and they're forever bringing him cookies and sweets."

If anyone ever brought Mr. Gertsmann cookies, Kate would suspect they had been laced with strychnine.

The clerk must have noticed Kate's confused expression. "Not that Dr. Kendall ever encourages them," she rushed to add. "Oh my, no. A more proper man you'll never meet. If you wait on the bench outside the conference room on the fourth floor, I'll let him know you have arrived."

Kate followed the directions. Although the front lobby had been grand and imposing, the hallways were lined with cold sage-green tiles. Her footsteps echoed off the tile, and the medicinal scent of carbolic acid made her nose twitch.

The wall outside the conference room displayed the diplomas and awards won by the hospital's doctors. A half dozen of the framed commendations were dedicated to Dr. T. M. Kendall, and they came from research clinics all over the world. Her brow rose in surprise when she saw Louis Pasteur's signature under an award for research in bacteriology.

She plopped down on the bench, dazzled by all the activity in the hall. Orderlies wheeled patients on gurneys while nurses carried trays of medicine. Kate wondered if she would be required to dress like them if she took a position here. The nurses' uniforms were distinctive with nipped-in waistlines, white aprons, and little folded caps on their heads.

At the end of the hall she spotted a tall, dark-haired man coming her way. He must be a doctor, for he was dressed differently from everyone else, in a formal black suit and tie, a starched collar, and a fine serge vest. Everything was covered by a white lab coat, a stethoscope draped over one shoulder. He must be Dr. Kendall, for he locked gazes and headed toward her, his lab coat flaring out as he strode down the long hallway.

She smoothed a strand of hair and wished she'd borrowed Irene's fancy blouse after all.

It was easy to see why the nurses would be attracted to Dr. Kendall. He was a handsome man, though with such an austere face. She'd find him attractive too, if he didn't remind her so much of . . .

No. It couldn't be.

She blinked and stared hard as he drew

closer. He had the same dark eyes, the same humorless expression on his lean, handsome face.

She shot to her feet. "Trevor McDonough!"

If he was surprised to see her, he gave no indication, his expression blank. "Hello, Kate."

"What are you doing here? I thought I was to meet with Dr. Kendall."

"I'm Dr. Kendall. I changed my last name when I went to college."

She was flabbergasted. "Why would you do such a thing?"

"You changed *your* name."

"I was married!"

"Yes, I heard about that. My condolences." Not a flicker of emotion crossed his face. A fence post showed more emotion than his stern features.

Trevor unlocked the conference room door and gestured for her to go inside. Kate stepped into the room, the warm wood paneling and book-lined walls a welcome change after the cold severity of the hallway.

Trevor didn't look like a gangly boy anymore. When they were in school, his clothes hung on his skinny frame like a scarecrow. He was still lean, but he looked taller, more fit. The underfed pasty-faced boy was gone. Trevor had a finely molded face with sharp cheekbones, a long blade of a nose, and flashing dark eyes. But there wasn't a hint of a smile on that straight mouth of his. Never in a million years would she have expected Trevor to grow into such a fine-looking man.

She could see why the nurses would be impressed, which was a horrifying thought. It was like becoming accustomed to an annoying weasel that pestered your garden, then one day noticing it had transformed into a handsome prince.

Trevor McDonough was no prince. He might have grown into a handsome man, but he still had that awful killjoy look on his face. Nothing had changed.

"Why the new name?" she asked.

Trevor tossed a file on the large conference table in the center of the room, then rifled through his pockets until he found a pencil. He motioned for her to sit. "We're not here to talk about my personal life. I need to find out if you have the qualifications for the statistician job."

This was a waste of time. Working for Trevor McDonough would be impossible. He would have her squashed under his thumb even more tightly than Mr. Gertsmann. At least she was smarter than Mr. Gertsmann and could outmaneuver him with ease. That wouldn't be the case with Trevor.

"I know you have the mathematical ability for the position," he continued, "but this is no ordinary statistician's job. We will be working with terminal patients, and that requires a certain mettle. I am measuring the effect of a new serum to see if it can strengthen the blood of patients suffering from tuberculosis. I need someone to analyze hundreds of data points and run the necessary calculations."

Despite herself, she was intrigued. The noise from the hallway faded as she leaned forward to catch every word Trevor spoke.

"Tuberculosis is a dangerous disease," he said. "Some people have qualms about being around infected patients. Do you have a good understanding of what tuberculosis is?"

She had to confess she did not. Over the next ten minutes her blood ran cold as Trevor explained the disease. There were lots of other names for it: consumption, the white plague, the white death. It occurred when bacteria took root in the human lung and began multiplying like mad. Scar tissue developed, creating lesions that stiffened and bled when the patient coughed. The lung tissue was gradually destroyed by cavities that filled with fluid and blood, making it hard to get enough oxygen and sapping the strength of the victim. From there the bacteria could seep into the bloodstream, crippling bones and infecting the heart, kidneys, even the brain.

Kate had always feared illness. Ever since two of her brothers died from diphtheria, she'd been haunted by the prospect of death. There had been four children in the Norton family. She was the oldest, and then Carl and Jamie, with Tick being the youngest. When she was fifteen, diphtheria descended on their neighborhood, clobbering all three of her brothers. Those awful weeks were seared into her memory. Kate had tried to nurse her brothers, but she was a disaster, always starting to weep as she coaxed broth down their throats. One morning she awoke to find Carl's bed empty and was told he'd died during the night. Jamie died two hours later. Kate went numb, but she bawled for an hour when Tick's fever finally broke and she knew he was going to make it. Nursing her dying brothers had been harrowing, but Nathan's death was even worse. The first warning of trouble came when a police officer knocked on their

41

door. . . .

She shook off the memory. If the position here was confined to mathematics, she wouldn't have to worry about more people dying on her. "Would I need to help care for the patients?"

"Not as a nurse, but you would be with me as I examine them to record their data. You would be in daily contact with the patients."

"I've never been very good around sick people."

"Perhaps you'd like to hear what Mr. Gertsmann had to say about your qualifications. Let's have a look, shall we?" Trevor's face remained blank as he removed a small envelope from his breast pocket. The paper crackled as he extracted the letter, his voice cool as he read the words. " 'Mrs. Livingston is a diligent worker, but one who thinks far too highly of her intellectual skills. You will find her to be arrogant and contentious with her superiors. The only capacity for which I can recommend her is in a clerical position in which she is given no responsibilities that would reinforce her negative tendencies.' "

Kate was speechless. She wanted to lunge across the table and tear the offending letter to shreds. But then with a flick of his wrist,

Trevor tossed the note in the trash can.

"I doubt you will find other employment as long as the eloquent Mr. Gertsmann is writing your reference," Trevor said dryly. He straightened and continued to outline the position as though that note hadn't just soured the air. "So you will be required to work with tubercular patients. There is no cure for the disease, but I am determined to find one. I am trying to stop it from infecting vital organs once it's in the bloodstream. I need to measure how the serum I developed affects the proliferation of the bacillus."

This was going to be a challenge. Trevor was still a cold fish and would be hard to work for. At least fish had hearts beating somewhere in their cold-blooded bodies. With Trevor she couldn't be certain. For twelve years she'd carried the image of Trevor as he beat her that final day in the classroom, his face as disinterested as if he'd just tied his shoelaces.

"I always wondered something," Kate began hesitantly. Trevor cocked a brow but said nothing. She braced herself and asked the question that had nagged at her for twelve years. "Why did you fight to win that scholarship when you knew it was my only chance to go to college? When you were being driven around town in a fancy carriage and had gold cuff links, why did you do that?"

"I wanted the money."

She choked on her own breath. "Your family was rolling in money! You had tailor-made clothes imported from Scotland. Your own carriage."

"You asked a question, and I answered it honestly." There wasn't the slightest trace of appeasement in his voice or compassion on his face.

"Why did you change your name?"

"Do you want the job or not? If you do, I'll expect you to be here at nine o'clock on Monday morning." His voice was as flat and detached as though they were discussing the weather. Even the way he held himself seemed remote. He sat stiffly in the chair without touching the armrests or the back.

She would never land another job as long as Mr. Gertsmann was her supervisor at the census bureau. Trevor's job sounded important and challenging, but a niggling suspicion took root in her mind. Maybe Trevor was doing this just to get her under his thumb. Back when they were in school, they waged a full-bore battle against each other with every scrap of intelligence they could gather. Sometimes she won, sometimes he did, but they always began the day on an equal footing. That wouldn't be the case if she worked for him. He could grind her nose into the dust every day if he wanted.

"Why would you want *me* for this job?" she pressed. "I have no medical background, and there are plenty of people in this city who are skilled in statistics."

"I can teach you the medical knowledge you need," he said. "What I'm looking for is a lot harder to find. A cure for tuberculosis is nowhere in sight, but with God's help I *will* find a cure. It's going to take decades and promises to be a long, brutal slog, but I will get there in the end."

Trevor leaned forward. He wasn't a cold, emotionless man anymore. A spark of electricity flashed in his eyes and transformed his entire face. Urgency and excitement simmered just beneath the surface, seeping into his voice.

"I'm going to need help, and I need someone who is *fearless*. Someone who isn't afraid to stand up to dragons and battle them day after day. Our results may not show promise for years. Our patients will die. There will be days when you feel so beaten down you'll want to crawl home and give up. But I'll need you to get up, dust yourself off, and be ready to wage battle the next day." He locked eyes with her. "I need someone who wants to win as badly as I do. *That* is why I want you for this job."

The passion in his voice made her rock back in her chair. It made perfect sense. Blindingly beautiful, perfect sense. She had always been at odds with Trevor, but what if they joined forces? What if they funneled all of that competitive drive toward the same goal, throwing every ounce of their combined passion at one of the world's deadliest diseases? Trevor rolled a pencil between impatient fingers as he looked at her with that curious gleam still burning in his eyes.

"What of it, Kate? Can I convince you to tear yourself from the joys at the census bureau and take up the crusade against tuberculosis?"

Working for Trevor would be a gamble, but every instinct urged her to take the chance. Though putting faith in her old nemesis was risky and frightening, she wanted this job and was never one to back away from a challenge. "All right, Trevor. I'll work with you."

A tiny smile flickered over Trevor's face before he reverted to his chilly demeanor. He opened a file and withdrew a page. "Here's an announcement that will appear in tomorrow's *Washington Post*. Please review it for accuracy."

Kate took the paper and read.

Mrs. Katherine Livingston has accepted a position at Washington Memorial Hospital as statistical forecaster for the Tubercular Research Clinic. Inquiries regarding the data collected in the study may be directed to her at the hospital's main office.

She was shocked. "Why on earth would you do this?"

"Public perception is vitally important in this sort of research. We won't ever make a move in the clinic without keeping the public informed. They can turn against you quickly. People fear tuberculosis like it's a modern-day plague. We are rarely popular with the local community."

She held up the page. "And you think this will help?"

"It can't hurt. It will appear in tomorrow's paper."

"You were awfully confident of my response. What if I had said no?"

He flipped open another file and began making notes, his pencil scratching in the silence. "Then I would withdraw the announcement. But you've never struck me as a foolish person. Impulsive and overly emotional sometimes, but never foolish."

He was baiting her, yet Kate refused to fall into the trap. It would be better to score a point. She affected a casual tone.

"If you really want to make an impression on the public, you ought to get an announcement in the *Congressional Record*. It is circulated all over the world and has a cachet no mere newspaper can wield. I can arrange for an announcement if you'd like."

"You could do that?" Trevor looked impressed.

Anything spoken on the floor of Congress was submitted to the *Congressional Record,* but members of Congress could also slip in announcements, and there was a good chance Charlie Davis would do it for her.

"Of course," she said.

Trevor leaned back in his chair, wiggling a pencil between nervous fingers as he considered her. She could see the thoughts spinning in his head as he weighed a response. He shifted in his seat and began tapping his foot, growing more frustrated by the second. "Okay, I have to admit, that's pretty good," he finally said.

She tried not to preen, but these little victories over Trevor were so rare it was hard not to savor them.

"Coming from you, I'll consider that a

compliment, Trevor."

His expression stiffened. "That's fine, but when we're working around other people, you will need to call me Dr. Kendall."

"You can't be serious."

He didn't even look up from his file as he began collecting papers. "I'm entirely serious. It is my legal name and it's important to keep a professional distance, so you'll need to call me Dr. Kendall like every other employee in this hospital."

He seemed determined to hide why he'd changed his name, but she would figure it out in short order. Besides, she had no desire to advertise their long association to anyone else working in the hospital.

"I'll see you Monday morning, Dr. Kendall."

3

She didn't even bother to return to the census bureau. Instead she headed straight home, where Charlie Davis reclined on the sofa in the front parlor with his feet propped on a stool, reading the morning newspaper. As she shut the door, he dropped the paper and rolled into a sitting position.

"How did it go?" A chicken potpie dish, scraped clean, sat on the table beside him. Kate picked it up, as well as the plate that once held muffins and fresh fruit.

"I got the job," she said as she carried the plates into the kitchen.

Her mother dropped the lid over a kettle. "You did?" Her face lit up as if she were about to levitate. Charlie followed her, batting aside the swinging doors as he followed her into the kitchen.

"You did?" Charlie asked. "Why then do you sound so tense?"

Kate folded her arms and tried to keep

the shaking from her voice. "I'll be working for Trevor McDonough."

Her mother gasped. "The horrible Trevor McDonough? *That* Trevor McDonough?"

"The very same. Except now he's calling himself Trevor Kendall, and he won't explain why he changed his name."

Charlie and her mother exchanged glances. "That does seem a little odd," Charlie conceded.

"That boy was always so strange," her mother said. "I don't like the idea of you working for him. Not one bit." The light had faded from her eyes as she picked up a knife to slice carrots. Her mother never forgave Trevor for snatching that scholarship, and if he was smart, he would never set foot in this house. Her mother knew how to hold on to a grudge, and she was fierce in protecting her cubs.

Charlie was more generous. "I always thought you and Trevor McDonough were destined to be either mortal enemies or the very best of friends. You're too alike to be anything else."

Her mother dropped the knife. "Kate is nothing like that horrid boy! Everyone likes Kate. She is always smiling and helpful. If that McDonough boy ever smiled, it would crack his face into pieces. I doubt he has a friend in the world."

Kate grabbed an apple and leaned against the counter, a long-buried memory rising to the surface.

There was only one time Kate tried to befriend Trevor. It was shortly after he'd arrived at their school, and his Scottish accent was so thick it made him a target for mocking. If Kate had been on the receiving end of that kind of teasing, she would have laughed and corrected their accents, trilling her words in a lovely Scottish brogue until she forced them to laugh alongside her. Not Trevor. He just withdrew even more. While most students played games during their lunch break, Trevor walked off behind the school to stare moodily into the distance. If he hadn't been so unfriendly, people would have invited him to play, but Trevor made it tough. One day Kate persuaded Nathan to ask Trevor to join a game of kickball with the rest of the boys. Nathan was the friendliest person ever born, but when he invited Trevor to the game, Trevor just glared at Nathan and stormed off behind the school.

Nathan looked at Kate and shrugged before joining the other boys. Kate was mortified on Nathan's behalf, but she'd seen enough temper tantrums from her little brothers to know hurt feelings when she saw them.

She followed Trevor around the back of the school. He was sitting on the ground, gangly legs sprawled before him, with his head braced in his hands as he stared at the dirt. "Why are you so unhappy?" she asked.

He startled, scrambling to his feet. Had he been crying? It was impossible to tell because before she could get a good look, he kicked dirt at her. "I'm not unhappy," he said and then ran off into the woods.

They didn't see him at school for the rest of the week. He must have caught trouble for it at home, because after that, Senator Campbell's fancy carriage arrived every morning to drop Trevor off and retrieve him at the end of the day. Everyone knew that Trevor's guardian was the senator from Maryland, and that bought him a certain level of respect. His academic brilliance was another point in his favor. But during the entire four years of school, Trevor never made a single friend.

Her mother loaded a plate with fresh bread and a thick wedge of smoked Gouda cheese. "Fetch the kettle," she said. "We need to talk about this."

Ten minutes later they were at the dining table. They had been joined by Sergey Zomohkov, a diplomat from Russia who had been living with them for the past three months. Mr. Zomohkov rarely rose before noon, but he and his wife usually stayed awake until at least two o'clock in the morning.

"The job sounds perfect," Kate said. "I'll finally have a chance to do something really important. It means working for Trevor, but I am used to dealing with cold fish. I've prepared fresh herrings for the past decade."

Her mother looked ready to pull her hair out. "But you will be quitting a safe job to work for a man you barely know."

Of course, Kate *did* know Trevor. He was so tightly stitched she was surprised he didn't squeak when he walked, yet there was no denying he was the smartest person she'd ever met. And in a strange way, she enjoyed their rivalry at school. Just knowing Trevor was in the classroom made her try harder, study longer. Already she could feel the anticipation to test her skills against him rising to the surface.

The Russian diplomat smacked his hand on the table, rattling the china. "Why does this old rival want to work with you?" he demanded. "Maybe now that you are a widow, he hankers for you?"

Kate shuddered. "I will need a bucket of

bleach to scrub that mental image from my mind."

"Why else would a man want a woman to work in his office?" Mr. Zomohkov asked. "Men have desires. Men have —"

"Stop!" Kate pleaded. The last thing she wanted polluting her mind was Trevor's manly desires. The very idea made her shudder.

Her mother nodded. "Mr. Zomohkov is right. There is something odd about Trevor McDonough . . . or whatever he is calling himself these days. He's always been peculiar."

She could not quite believe it, but she was going to defend Trevor. "Tick says the surgeon general knows Trevor. That he spent years trying to lure him to Washington. Apparently, Trevor is a very famous medical researcher."

She was about to tell them about the fancy awards Trevor had hanging on the wall in the hospital, but the diplomat's wife made her appearance. She was a large woman, with a triple strand of pearls around her thick neck, even at noon. The woman smiled and nodded at everyone, her pin curls bobbing with each nod. She didn't speak a lick of English, which made dining a challenge, but her husband was always willing to translate for her.

No translation was necessary, though, as Mr. Zomohkov rose and embraced his wife. He growled something in Russian and kissed his wife on the lips. Twice. He also swatted her on the behind and flashed her a lusty grin, which Mrs. Zomohkov returned.

Customs must be very different in Russia, for these two engaged in open affection with each other each time Mrs. Zomohkov made her appearance. Kissing, hugging, and murmuring words that brought a flush to the Russian woman's cheeks. Though their blatant affection sometimes bordered on embarrassing, Kate thought it rather charming. Except it made her miss Nathan. It had been four years since he died, and the ache of loneliness was getting worse instead of better. At least she was finally able to listen to fiddle music without dissolving into tears. Nathan was a carpenter by trade, but he loved the fiddle and played it whenever they wished to celebrate. Birthdays. Inaugurations. The first sight of tulips in the spring. When Mama made an apple pie. Really any excuse was good enough for him to break out his fiddle. They had been so happy together. . . .

Her mother set a tray of pastries before Mrs. Zomohkov, then launched into another tirade against Trevor. "That boy has nothing but vinegar in his veins. The sour will spread to anyone standing next to him. It's not safe, you working for that man."

"Life is never safe," Charlie said. "Tell us, what is it Trevor will be having you do?"

Trevor's face, tense with barely contained energy, flashed before her. *I need someone who wants to win as badly as I do.*" Just remembering the intensity vibrating in his voice made her heart race a little faster.

"He's testing a new serum that might stop a lung disease from spreading to other organs in the body. If it works, it will prolong the patient's life."

"What kind of disease?" Mr. Zomohkov asked.

"Tuberculosis. He only takes the very worst cases."

The diplomat reared back. Turning to his wife, he unleashed a spiel in Russian. Mrs. Zomohkov gasped and shot to her feet, tipping over her teacup. Kate tossed a napkin over the spreading stain, but Mrs. Zomohkov was shrieking in Russian and gesturing like a madwoman.

The diplomat finally persuaded his wife to stop yelling, but not before she grabbed her pastries and fled upstairs.

"What do you know of tuberculosis?" Mr.

Zomohkov demanded.

Kate looked around the room and all the faces staring at her, awaiting an answer. "Trevor explained the disease to me. It sounds horrible, but he is determined to find a cure."

"There is no cure for tuberculosis," Mr. Zomohkov pronounced. "Only misery and death. It spreads from person to person and leaves people twisted and crippled and dead. It is a dangerous disease, Mrs. Livingston. You will be playing with fire if you tamper with it."

He stormed off to follow his wife, and Kate was left to wonder if he was right to be so afraid of the disease.

It was the first question she asked Trevor on Monday morning. She arrived at the conference room promptly at nine o'clock to find the large table covered with stacks of paper. Once again, Trevor was wearing a black suit with a vest and tie beneath his white lab coat, a stethoscope clamped around his neck.

"Of course it is dangerous," Trevor said. "I told you that."

"Is it frightening enough to send a woman shrieking from the room at the very mention of it?"

The clock on the conference room wall ticked out a steady beat as Trevor contemplated her with that expressionless stare of his. "She is a wise woman. Tuberculosis ought to strike fear in the heart of anyone who works with it. All my employees are tested each month to ensure they have not contracted the bacillus. I'll need you to provide me with a sputum sample as soon as we go upstairs."

Heat stained her cheeks. She'd happily go through the rest of her life without mentioning the word *sputum* in polite company. "Isn't that overreacting?" Kate asked.

"If we catch the disease early, there is a chance at recovery."

"How good of a chance?"

"Almost none, so try not to get it." He continued to sort his papers as though she were going to be satisfied with that horrific assessment.

"Is that your best scientific opinion? You want me to risk my life over a flippant response like that?"

His face softened just a trace. "Only around ten percent of people who get tuberculosis will survive. We are beginning to believe that moving to climates with high, dry air is the best chance for a cure. People who go to such settings can double their

odds of survival, but tuberculosis is still usually a death sentence. You will need to be
scrupulous about following the safety rules
while you are here."

He went on to describe how the disease
was contracted by inhaling the bacillus.
Victims of tuberculosis were often seized
with uncontrollable fits of coughing, during
which moisture from their lungs sprayed
into the air. The most common way for the
disease to spread was to inhale air near an
infected person who had been coughing.

"I insist you wear a mask whenever you
are near the patients. If you follow the rules,
you will be fine. Come on, let me show you
the ward."

Kate followed him up the narrow staircase
to the top floor. She'd never been in a
hospital clinic and didn't know what to
expect, but it seemed remarkably homey.
The entrance had a sitting area tucked into
the semicircle of a turret. An assortment of
comfortable chairs, a sofa, and a small table
filled the cozy space. Beneath the window
were a set of bookshelves crammed with
reading material. Cotton drapes on either
side of the window billowed forward in a
gentle breeze.

"Tuberculosis spreads in cramped, poorly
ventilated quarters," Trevor explained. "The

more fresh air we can keep in the ward, the better. It will get chilly in the winter, but the fresh air is good for the patients. Here's a mask. Keep it with you from now on and always wear it in the wards."

The other side of the reception area had a nurses' station with a single desk and filing cabinets, all behind an oak counter. The nurse at the desk was a dark-haired matron wearing a starched uniform with one of those funny little caps. Kate nodded and smiled to her, but Trevor didn't bother to introduce Kate as he strode down the hallway.

Kate scurried to keep up. "It would be nice to be introduced to people. I'm new here, and it seems a basic courtesy."

Trevor shrugged as he opened the door to the ward and gestured her inside. It was a spacious room with huge windows on one wall and rows of beds on the opposite side, all filled with patients. They were all women, and a few turned to look as Kate entered the room. Others were reading, and some still slept.

"Everyone, this is Kate Livingston. She will be helping me to gather data." Trevor looked at her. "Happy?"

She smiled. "You are as warm and friendly as I remember."

61

A thin girl in the bed nearest to Kate started snickering. "You tell it to him, ma'am," she said with approval in her voice. Kate thought the girl was going to laugh, but instead the child was racked with a deep, scratchy fit of coughing.

Trevor tied a mask over his face and motioned for Kate to do the same. The heat of her breath felt strange against her face as she tied it on. The damp warmth was uncomfortable, but she dared not take the mask off.

The girl struggled to heave in a lungful of air while she reached for a mask on the small metal table beside her bed. It sounded like she had gravel rattling in her lungs.

Trevor took a seat on the chair beside the girl's bed, then motioned for Kate to come closer. Seeing him with the lower half of his face covered by the white cotton mask underscored the danger of her new position. Had the Russian diplomat's wife been right to run screaming from the room at the mere mention of the disease?

Trevor shot her an impatient glower and beckoned her again. She took a tiny step forward but couldn't make her other leg move. It was as if her feet had taken root in the cold linoleum floor. That poor, sweet child . . . but Kate dared not get any closer.

An invisible weight kept her frozen in place.

"It's all right," Trevor said. "This patient is not currently contagious, but I insist all coughing patients use a mask until the seizures pass, whether they're contagious or not."

He went on to explain that patients were not usually contagious, that only when the bacillus morphed into a particular stage did it have the ability to infect others, and he carefully monitored each patient's health daily. The employees always knew which patients were contagious.

She could see little of Trevor's expression behind his mask, but his voice was typically clinical. He motioned again for her to draw closer. Kate forced her legs to move, praying that Trevor was right about what he said. She was unable to meet the girl's eyes. What must the child think of her?

"My name is Kate," she said, silently asking the girl's forgiveness for her hesitation.

"Hi, Kate. I'm Hannah Wexler." If the girl resented the way Kate behaved, she gave no indication. Kate looked directly at the girl. Beneath Hannah's chalk-white skin, a tracery of blue veins fanned across her face.

"Pull up a chair, Kate. I'll show you how I gather data and track the results."

Curiosity nudged away the fear as Kate

took a seat in a plain metal chair beside Trevor, who grabbed a chart hanging from the end of Hannah's bed. "This is patient 27F62. That means she's the twenty-seventh female patient admitted to the study, and her birth year is 1862. All the patients are filed under their numbers. As I scan data, it's easier for me to place their relevant details when referring to them by their numbers. Lean forward, please."

Trevor pressed his stethoscope against the girl's back and closed his eyes to listen, but all Kate could think was that she and the child were the same age. If Hannah was born in 1862, that made her twenty-nine, just like Kate. The girl looked so wasted away and tiny, as though she hadn't even reached puberty yet.

Trevor explained that the first thing he did each morning was to listen to all the patients' lungs and take their temperatures. All patients were to drink a vial of the serum Trevor was hoping could slow the progress of the disease, and two hours later Trevor would draw samples of blood and saliva for testing. The samples were sent to the laboratory for analysis, and the results sent to Kate to calculate the effect of the serum.

Trevor gestured to a column of numbers on Hannah's chart. "This is where we track her weight, temperature, white blood cell count, and the levels of iron in her blood. So 27F is doing comparatively well in the past few weeks."

"*Are* you feeling better, 27F?" Kate asked Hannah. "I can't help but wonder what it feels like to be referred to as a number. If it is in any way a life-affirming practice, perhaps I can get a number too."

Hannah smothered a laugh. "We're all used to Dr. Kendall and his strange ways. Besides, I'd rather deal with Dr. Kendall than the undertaker," she said with a wink.

Kate blanched. Had she understood the girl correctly? This sort of gallows humor seemed shocking, but perhaps it was the way the patients coped with their condition.

As they progressed through the ward, Trevor examined one patient after another, all of whom he referred to by their patient numbers. There were fifteen patients in the room, and one empty bed. On their eighth patient, Trevor turned the chart over to her and instructed her to begin writing down the data.

It felt good to handle numbers again, and she was eager to learn how to interpret all this data. She closed the manila folder of the last female patient and followed Trevor out of the room. The male patients lived in an identical ward across the hall. She thought they were going into the men's ward next, but Trevor reached behind her to close the door to the female ward with a smack.

"Do you know why bed number nine is empty?"

Kate gave him a blank look. Trevor tugged his mask down to dangle around his neck and continued, "It's empty because 23F died on Tuesday. I will have another patient take her place as soon as I find one who meets the criteria for this study, and that patient will also be referred to by her number. Trust me, it will be easier for you to think of a patient as 27F rather than Hannah Wexler."

"But she's a human being, not a number."

Trevor gave her a wintery smile. "This may be difficult for you to accept, but there are areas where I have far more insight than you. Treating dying patients is one of them. Every person you just met will be dead within a year. They won't be among the lucky ten percent who can hope for a cure because their cases are too advanced. All I can do is buy them a few more months and the satisfaction of knowing their participation in this study may someday lead to a cure. They will all die, and they know it. It will be easier if you refrain from becoming friendly with them. Don't ask after their children. Don't look them in the eyes or encourage pointless conversation. They are research subjects, not friends."

There might be a grain of truth to what he said, but did he have to be so stone-faced? "Trevor, you are the most cold-blooded person I've ever met. I'll bet you need to sun yourself on a rock to generate body heat."

His face remained stoic as he grabbed a set of blank forms from a wall bin. "We do the same procedure for the male patients," he said, then pushed open the door and strode into the men's ward, where all sixteen beds were filled.

The men ranged in age from a boy of sixteen to a man of fifty. Some of them didn't appear to be all that sick, while others looked like skeletons. One man was so weak he couldn't sit up on his own. Trevor helped peel him up from the mattress so that the patient sagged over, then Trevor pressed the flat disk of his stethoscope at various spots on the man's back. When instructed to take a breath, the man's eyes darkened in pain. The ridge of his spinal column was so prominent it tented up the back of his nightshirt. As Trevor helped the man lie back down, she wondered if it hurt to lie on a spine that exposed. His name was Ephraim Montgomery, and agony distorted every line of his face. Despite his emaciated frame, he had wide shoulders and broad hands. It would not surprise her if Mr. Montgomery had once been a carpenter or a longshoreman. He was probably once a strong man who could have hauled twice his own weight. Now he could not sit up without help.

"Kate?"

She shook herself. Trevor had been feeding her data while she stared at the dying man. "I'm sorry, could you repeat that?"

He did, but Kate's fingers trembled as she recorded the data. When her husband died, it had been quick. One moment Nathan was framing the fifth floor of a new office building, and the next moment the scaffolding beneath him collapsed. She was told he'd died before they even got him out from under the rubble. She prayed it was so, that he never suffered agony or knew what was happening. Ephraim Montgomery knew exactly what was happening to him, and the resignation in his eyes made her want to weep.

When they'd finished their rounds, Trevor showed her to the office they would share, a rectangular room with two desks in it. She hadn't realized she would be working so closely with him. Trevor's desk was placed beneath a window overlooking the wooded area behind the hospital. The smaller desk was on the other side, with a worktable in the middle of the room. One wall was lined with wooden filing cabinets.

"We will be sharing this office for as long as you are employed here," Trevor said. "I won't feed the rumor mills, so the door must always remain open."

"Certainly." It would be mortifying if anyone imagined she and Trevor were up to no good behind a closed door.

She tugged the mask off her face, relieved to feel cool air on her skin again. "Why do you only take dying patients? Why don't you take people who might be cured?"

Trevor pulled out his desk chair and sat. "Tuberculosis starts in the lungs. It's possible to live for decades so long as it remains confined in the lungs, but if it gets into the blood it can spread to other organs, and people die fast. All our patients have it in their blood, which means it's likely to infect their organs soon. The serum I give them is rich in nutrients, and I'm hoping it will strengthen their blood enough to help slow the spread to the organs. I estimate it buys the patients an extra six months of life."

"What's in the serum?"

"It's a concentration of beef bone marrow and minerals, all distilled into a cod-liver-oil base. The patients drink it twice a day."

Kate wrinkled her nose. "Cod liver oil is disgusting. Can't you mix it into something like honey or tea?"

"Cod liver oil has a high concentration of nutritious properties. If the patients don't like it, they can go somewhere else to die."

She smiled tightly. "There's that warm-hearted man I've always admired."

He handed her a file. "Henry Harris is the laboratory assistant who analyzes the samples. Have him show you around the rest of the clinic. And give him a sputum sample while you're at it. He will be testing you monthly, so get used to it. I may have time to be back later this afternoon. If not, I will see you tomorrow morning at nine o'clock."

"You're leaving?" It was her first day and she was already completely overwhelmed.

Trevor hung his lab coat on a hook beside the door. "You'd be surprised how much time sunning myself on that rock requires."

He left the room without looking back.

Henry Harris was a mighty bull of a man.

He wasn't fat; rather, he gave the impression of a solid wall of muscle. He literally had no neck. His massive shoulders sloped toward a broad face that looked like a gentle giant.

"Princeton football, national champions, 1878!" he introduced himself with pride.

"Congratulations," Kate said as she shook his hand. The center of the lab was dominated by a long table with a black countertop, topped with a series of sleek microscopes arrayed like soldiers lined up for battle. Shelves loaded with dark bottles and empty glass beakers covered the walls of the lab. It was Henry's job to evaluate the samples taken from the patients, and afterward the data would be passed to Kate for analysis.

"I've got the best job here," Henry said, hunching over a microscope. His beefy hands looked too large to manipulate the tiny dials and wheels of the microscope. "I look at the blood and saliva samples and track the numbers. You would not believe the things you can see under a microscope. It's like a whole world of tiny cells and weird creatures."

He showed Kate how to look into the eyepiece and rotate the dial until the sample under the glass zoomed into focus. He was right! "Is it only because these people have tuberculosis that all these little things are living in their saliva?"

Henry reached behind him and grabbed a glass plate and slid it into position beneath the column of the microscope. "Have a look at this one. This sample came from Nurse Ackerman, and you'll see hers doesn't look much different, except there are no little cells that look like purple grains of rice. If those little purple tubes show up in your sample . . . well, I guess it's best not to think of it. Just wear your mask when you're around the patients, all right?"

Henry showed her the rest of the clinic. There were three washrooms: one for the male patients, another for the female patients, and a third for the staff. Apparently even sharing wash facilities with the patients carried the risk of infection, since a damp hand towel could carry live bacillus for hours.

A staff table was behind the nurses' station. "We eat all our meals here," Henry said. "We get the same thing the patients eat. The patients have a hard time keeping on weight, and Dr. Kendall feeds them like royalty. Beef, milk, and eggs at every meal. Hot chocolate. Cheese. And desserts."

Perhaps this explained Henry's immense size.

At noon an army of young women arrived, pushing carts loaded with covered trays. Wearing pale pink uniforms with white aprons, these women were at the lowest rung of the hospital-staff ladder. The attendants delivered meals, changed linens, and bathed patients. Each of them donned a white cotton mask before entering the wards to distribute the meals. The orderlies were men who did the heavy lifting and transporting of patients.

It didn't take long to learn the hierarchy at the hospital. The female attendants and male orderlies were at the bottom. Then came the nurses with their light gray dresses and starchy white aprons and caps. The laboratory staff was somewhat higher. And at the very top were the doctors, who strode about the halls like lords of the manor.

Kate joined Henry at the staff table for lunch. Nurse Ackerman staffed the nurses' station at the front of the clinic, and Henry had already warned Kate that the woman was as cheerful as a rainy day. Nurse Ackerman wore her severe dark hair slicked tightly back, her only ornamentation two gold rings hanging from a chain around her neck.

"My husbands, may God rest their souls,"

the nurse said as she cleared the staff table in preparation for lunch. "I was widowed when I was twenty-nine, and then again at forty-three."

Nathan's death had knocked Kate beneath a suffocating avalanche that took years to lift. She couldn't imagine enduring that tragedy twice, and she sent Nurse Ackerman a sympathetic look. For a moment she saw the gleam of remembered pain surface in the nurse's dark eyes. A moment of shared understanding. Only women who'd endured the tragedy of widowhood could understand the hollow ache of such loss.

A pretty young attendant wheeled the meal cart toward them, setting covered plates on the staff table. After trays were delivered, the attendant held a final tray out.

"Dr. Kendall isn't here?" The disappointment in the girl's voice was comical.

"Go on with you, Jenny," Nurse Ackerman scowled. "Dr. Kendall doesn't have time for the likes of you."

Jenny rolled her eyes as she put Trevor's plate back on the empty meal cart. "I just like looking at him," she said. "I dare not get too close or I'd probably get frostbite."

Kate hid her smile as the young woman left. It was nice to know she wasn't the only one who thought Trevor could use a blast of human warmth to melt the ice off him.

4

Trevor strode down the tree-shaded lane on a residential street in Georgetown, hoping to finish his business quickly, then get back to the hospital while there was still daylight. Kate found his departure in the middle of the day appalling, but he had no intention of explaining himself. He was a private man, and Kate was far too nosy. Even when they were in school, she was always nagging him and asking pushy questions. Once Kate picked up a scent, she would chase it like a bloodhound until she ran it to the ground and dragged out all the answers.

It was one of the things he liked about her.

He pushed thoughts of Kate from his mind. The battle he was about to fight was too important to lose. He walked down the sidewalk set close against a row of tidy town houses until he reached the last house on the row and rapped softly on the door.

"Mrs. Kendall?"

He had a key, but would only let himself in if she were asleep. He could hear her shuffling around inside, which was a good thing. He wanted her awake and alert for the battle he intended to finally win.

The dead bolt turned, but a chain prevented the door from opening more than a couple of inches, so he tilted his head so he could wink at her through the opening. "It's just me, Mrs. Kendall."

The old woman smiled and closed the door to release the chain. "Trevor, dear! I've been making a nice hot custard for you. Come inside."

Her white hair was braided into a tidy coil around the back of her head. When he was a boy, he was always amazed at how Mrs. Kendall could engineer her hair into that perfect coil. Her face was now wrinkled and spotted with age, her eyes tired, her back stooped . . . but that fastidious hair was exactly the same. It was a good sign.

"Tea?" she asked.

"Yes, please." He didn't really want any, but Mrs. Kendall loved to fuss over him. It was why she still insisted on making custard every time he came over. He wanted to tell her not to bother, because it took at least an hour of standing over a stove to make, but work was important for a woman like her. If she lost her sense of purpose, she would decline even faster.

He scanned the room. It was a generous space with a kitchen along the side and a bedroom off the parlor. He was pleased to see she had the window cracked.

"I brought you some raspberries," he said, setting them on the small dining table. She sucked in a breath, a little life sparkling behind her faded blue eyes.

"Oh, heavens, I hope it was not too much bother."

"Not at all." He had them shipped from Philadelphia, but she didn't need to know that. As soon as she set a glass of tea before him, he motioned for her to sit.

"Let's get the business over with first," he said. He handed her a piece of paper. "Cough and spit."

Her cough didn't sound good. It was rasping and wet, but at least there was no blood on the paper she handed him. Without letting any sign show on his face, he swiped a glass slide over the paper, wrapped the plate in a handkerchief, and slipped it into his coat pocket.

"Any problems I should know about?" He held his breath, waiting for the answer, but she brushed the question away.

"Just the same old things," she said, drifting over to the stove, where the custard simmered over a low flame. A warm vanilla scent filled the room as she stirred, awakening painful childhood memories.

Mrs. Kendall knew all his secrets. To this day he kept everything about his past carefully guarded, and Mrs. Kendall was the only person in the world who knew his full story. She taught him how to cover his tracks and protect himself. During those awful years when he first came to America, she had been his savior. To the rest of the world she was only the head housekeeper in Senator Campbell's household, but for him she had wings and a halo.

And he wanted to return the favor.

"There is a new tuberculosis sanitarium opening at Saranac Lake in upstate New York. I can make arrangements for you to have a private room and the best care available."

The scrape of the wooden spoon on the bottom of the pot did not break tempo. "But my home is right here."

"There is no chance of a cure for you here. The humidity is too hard on your lungs, and you will die if you remain here. You need the thin, dry air of the mountains."

"And all those people you've got up on

the fifth floor of that hospital? Is that what you tell them? There is no hope?"

His patients were too far gone to have any hope for a cure. Even under the best conditions, only a tiny fraction of people who traveled to remote sanitariums in the mountains were cured, and that only happened after years of complete rest.

"I can't save those people, but I can try to save you," he said. "Your lungs are getting weaker. You will die if you stay here."

"I'll die if I leave my home," she retorted.

"Please don't say that. They have quality facilities up there, and I'll make sure they treat you well."

She moved the custard to the back burner, then came to sit in the chair opposite him. She was wheezing as she plopped onto the chair. "My daughter is here in Washington. My church is here. This is my home, and these people mean something to me. It will take a cannon to get me out."

That was the thing about Mrs. Kendall. She might look like a sweet old grandmother, but she was as crafty, determined, and downright stubborn as any person he ever met. Half his techniques for staying one step ahead of the dragons that chased him all his life had been learned from her.

He folded his arms across his chest and

narrowed his gaze. "Genghis Khan could have used you when he was rounding up the Mongol hordes." He would give anything if he could save Mrs. Kendall, but he wasn't going to win this battle today. To the bottom of his soul he wished he could return the favor she had done for him, but that was going to take a miracle.

Then again, Trevor had never shied away from wishing for miracles.

The first thing he saw on returning to the hospital was Kate Livingston playing with a mangy dog on the front steps, dangling a twig just above the dog's snout, and it seemed delighted to play along. He'd seen that dog around in recent weeks but always ignored it. Then he noticed the empty lunch box beside her.

"Please tell me you haven't been feeding that dog."

Kate didn't even glance his way as she continued to dangle the twig. "Of course I fed her. I didn't realize the hospital provided our meals, and this dog looked hungry."

The last thing they needed was a vagrant dog loitering outside the hospital, but to his horror it seemed to have lost interest in Kate and began nudging a wet snout on his pant leg. He took a step back, but the iron railing kept him trapped from retreating much farther. He leaned an elbow against the railing and glared down at the dog.

"She likes you," Kate giggled. The dog left strands of yellow hair on his wool trousers, and swiping only moved them around. This was a mess.

"Dogs carry vermin, scabies, and three kinds of skin rot. This one has bad breath." But the mutt wagged its tail furiously as it explored his shoe and then darted up to lick his hand. He rubbed it on his vest. Everything would need to be laundered now.

"You haven't been around animals enough to get comfortable with them," Kate said.

"Nonsense, I grew up on a farm. Animals are food, not friends."

"Really?" She tilted her head up at him. "Was that in Scotland?"

He clamped his mouth shut, wishing he could call the words back. Now she was probably going to start pestering him with a barrage of questions he had no intention of answering. Scotland was the last thing he wanted to talk about. He needed to change the subject.

"What are you doing outside? It's the middle of the day, and I thought you had statistics to calculate."

"Henry won't have the data ready until

late this afternoon. I had nothing to do, so I gossiped with your nurse for another hour. Do you know she scans all the newspapers, looking for mention of you?"

"Of course. That's one of the things I pay her for."

"Honestly, Trevor, that seems extraordinarily vain, even for you."

He couldn't expect her to understand the importance of a doctor's reputation in the field of medical research. Funding from research institutes depended on his reputation, and with a disease like tuberculosis, it didn't take much to stir up public fear.

"I need to know what people are saying about me. The more positive publicity I garner, the better my odds of securing additional funding."

Kate coaxed the dog away from his shoe and gave it a hearty scratching behind both ears. "Then you ought to be delighted, because she found a big story about you in today's *Washington Post.*"

"What did it say?"

"I have no idea. Before I could read it, a nurse from downstairs brought you a basket of ginger cookies. She was very disappointed you weren't there. The poor girl looked like Napoleon after being trounced at Waterloo. You have a very devoted following."

He wished the nurses would stop fussing over him. It was embarrassing, and he never knew what he was supposed to say to them.

"Come on, I need to see that article." Without waiting, he vaulted up the remaining steps two at a time. "Be sure to scrub your hands," he tossed out over his shoulder. "We'll be lucky if we both aren't dead from the plague after touching that mutt."

Kate reached the front door before him. "I'll race you to the top."

She darted in front of him, pushed through the door, and scurried down the hall to the stairwell. No fair! The blasted mutt was making a nuisance of itself by darting around his knees, and it took an extra five seconds to make sure the dog didn't get inside the building. Still, he wasn't going to let Kate beat him in a footrace.

He knew a back way. The far side of the hospital had a service staircase, but the extra time to get there was worth it. The back staircase had no doors between each floor and was usually empty. He rushed up the stairs, his steps echoing up the cavernous space. Kate was going to be completely bogged down by a crush of people on the public staircase. He grinned as he cleared the second floor and launched up the third set of stairs.

He was out of breath by the time he burst through the rear entrance to the clinic, his lungs heaving. He was desperate for a drink of water. He paused, adjusting his vest and tugging his tie straight before approaching the nurses' station at the end of the hall.

There was no sign of her.

He hid his smile and strode to the front counter, nodding to Nurse Ackerman and grabbing a ginger cookie from a basket. He affected a casual pose as he leaned against the counter, struggling to control his breathing. It wouldn't do to look winded after his mad dash up the stairs.

He heard her clattering up the stairs before she flung the door open with a bang. Kate staggered in, her coil of heavy red hair lopsided and slipping down the side of her head in a haphazard tangle.

"You must have cheated!" she said, dragging air into her lungs. "Is there an elevator in this building?"

He raised a brow and looked at the nurse. "Is there an elevator in this building, Nurse Ackerman?"

"No, sir."

It was hard to keep his breathing steady, but he did. "Sorry, Kate, no elevator. It seems someone has been getting soft over the years. Ginger cookie?"

She was still panting when she reached for the pitcher on the counter and poured herself a tall glass of water. She set the pitcher down with a thud. "You are the worst human being on the planet," she muttered, then gulped the water.

"So I've been told." He turned to Nurse Ackerman. "You found an article in today's newspaper?"

Nurse Ackerman looked uneasy. She cleared her throat and didn't meet his eyes. "Yes, sir."

The newspaper was folded open to expose the story. He took it to the sitting area, wishing for a glass of water too, but he could wait until after Kate left.

The headline was a shock.

Quack Remedies Applied in Washington Tubercular Ward

His muscles tensed as he scanned the article. It mentioned the serum patients were given to drink. It lulled them into complacency but offered no hope for a cure. It mentioned the high death rate of his patients.

Of course he had a high death rate! He only accepted terminal cases!

His teeth clenched as he continued scanning the article. Nothing written here was technically wrong, but it put the worst possible implication on everything he did at the clinic. The article was anonymous, but he would find out who wrote it. If he had to tear the newspaper building apart brick by brick, he'd find out who wrote this article and why.

"What does it say?" Kate asked. "You look like you just ate some bad fish."

He wanted to tell her it was none of her business, but that wasn't true. Every person who worked in this ward was his responsibility, and they needed to know what was going on. In all likelihood there was a scandal-mongering journalist on the loose who might be pestering the staff for information.

"Someone has begun to resent the clinic." He handed Kate the newspaper, then poured himself a glass of water. He could feel Nurse Ackerman's eyes on him while he drank. Setting the glass down on the counter, he clenched his fists and stared moodily at the remnants of lunch on the staff table. He'd need to hound the attendants about cleaning up faster. He'd tolerate no unsanitary conditions in this clinic.

"Is any of this true?" Kate's voice was thin and wobbly.

"It's *all* true; it simply throws the worst

possible light on what I'm doing. This kind of article is just an attempt to get the hospital to evict me and close down the study."

Nurse Ackerman rose to her feet, fear on her face. "Can they do that?"

"I've paid in advance for the floor for the next two years. There's no need to fear for your job." He could see the confusion on Kate's face and rushed to explain. "I don't work for the hospital. I lease this space and pay all the employee salaries. The food. Every drop of medicine. This ward is not at the mercy of the hospital and never will be."

He meant the words to be reassuring, but it seemed to have the opposite effect. Kate's eyes narrowed as she looked around the ward, then back at him. "You're paying for all this? Out of your own pocket?"

"Yes." After all, some good ought to come from the fortune that had been dumped in his lap.

Kate's mouth thinned, and she looked ready to snap. "I thought you said you were poor, that you needed money."

"When did I say that?"

"The day you won that scholarship!" She was shaking now, her voice shrill.

"Please keep your voice down. This is a hospital, and there are patients on the other side of that wall."

She stepped closer and leaned in, speaking in a fierce whisper. "That scholarship was the only chance I had for college, and you didn't even need the money."

"I can't believe you're bringing up ancient history." He picked up the newspaper from where she'd tossed it on the nurses' counter. The first order of business was to find out who wrote the article. This kind of bad news could spread unless it was killed quickly.

"It isn't ancient history for me." Her voice vibrated with quiet rage. "Can't you at least look at me when you talk?"

"Not when you're being overwrought and foolish."

"Tell me the truth. Why did you take that scholarship when you didn't need the money?"

He could tell her the truth, but that would only open up a whole slew of questions he couldn't discuss, so he attacked where she was most vulnerable. "What was I supposed to do, stand aside and let you win?"

She flinched a little but didn't back down. "Just that one time, it would have been the decent thing to do, Trevor. The *human* thing."

He needed to get away from her. The last thing he wanted was for Kate to quit over some old grudge, but he couldn't waste time pacifying her.

"I suggest you take the rest of the day off and think about how you can relegate what happened to the past. It's over, Kate. If you still want this job, please be here at nine o'clock tomorrow morning."

He didn't look back as he walked down the hall and closed his office door behind him.

The following morning, Trevor behaved as if Kate's outburst had never occurred, for which she was grateful. The challenge of this new position was too exhilarating to quit over an old grudge.

Over the coming weeks they slipped into a routine. Every morning they made the rounds as Trevor performed a quick examination of each patient while Kate recorded the data. Trevor took blood and sputum samples and sent them to Henry in the lab for testing. The results landed on Kate's desk, where she tabulated the new findings against each patient's previous data.

It didn't take long for Kate to notice the trends in patient numbers. She was no physician, but the count of tuberculosis cells in Hannah Wexler's samples was declining while the hemoglobin in her blood improved.

"That's a good thing, right?" she asked Trevor.

"It's too early to tell," Trevor said, but the flare of satisfaction in his eyes was obvious as he studied Hannah's chart. "The numbers need to maintain this trend for at least three months before I'll be convinced the serum is working, but this is a good sign. Very good."

He flipped the chart closed and passed it back. Kate hid her smile and resumed her work on the other side of the office. This was exactly the kind of challenging, meaningful work she had always hoped to find. Who cared if she had to put up with Trevor and his fussy ways?

And he wasn't all that bad. He could be prickly, demanding, and his scrupulous insistence for cleanliness bordered on the ridiculous, but they worked together with the speed and precision of a finely tuned clock. She loved watching him work. He was so intense about the way he threw himself into whatever he was doing, and there was something very attractive about that kind of enthusiasm.

After a few weeks, Trevor trusted her to go to the surgeon general's medical library to scan the new journals for anything relating to blood and nutrition. One day she discovered an entire issue of the *New York Medical Journal* devoted to recent discoveries in blood research. She pleaded with the librarian to allow her to take it out and show Trevor. Taking the current issue out of the library was forbidden, but after promising the librarian a free week of dinner at her mother's table, Kate had the prized journal in her hand. She couldn't wait to show it to Trevor and was practically skipping as she dashed up the hospital steps.

Kate passed through the clinic doors to see one of the pretty blond attendants flirting with Trevor. The girl sent him a dazzling smile, and Trevor seemed unusually kind as he smiled down at her. A cart loaded with covered lunch trays sat neglected a few feet away. The attendant was Bridget Kelly, whose fine blue eyes sparkled whenever Trevor stepped into her line of sight.

"In Ireland I'd be freezing my bum off every morning," she said in her pretty little Irish accent. "At least here they don't make me go milk the cow before the sun is even up."

"Just one cow?" Trevor asked. "In Scotland I had to milk all four of the cows on our farm."

Trevor's Scottish accent was back in full force, making her inexplicably angry. While she was squinting over medical journals and cutting deals with librarians, he was flirting with a fetching Irish milkmaid. Bridget reached out and squeezed Trevor on the arm.

"With that arm? I don't believe it."

Kate had never milked a cow in her life, but suddenly she wanted to find one and milk it better, faster, and more thoroughly than Bridget Kelly's wildest fantasies. She jerked the ties of her cloak free and pulled it off.

"If you're homesick for milking cows rather than delivering meals to the dying, maybe you could go help Butch Muchalski at his dairy on Tenth Street."

Trevor's brows raised in surprise. "Good afternoon, Kate." His thick brogue was gone, which annoyed her even more.

"I thought you might like to see the most recent issue of the *New York Medical Journal.* Apparently other doctors are trying similar techniques for strengthening the blood." She handed the journal over. A flash of gratitude transformed Trevor's face, but Kate was too busy scrutinizing Bridget to savor the moment. A flush heated Bridget's face as she reached for the cart.

"I'll get these plates served right away," Bridget said, her voice charming as she pushed the cart away. "Please help yourself to some ginger cookies. I brought them for everyone."

Kate waited until Bridget was gone before swiveling a glare at Trevor. "I thought you didn't flirt with the help."

"I was just being polite. I remember how hard it is to be a stranger in a new country." Trevor grabbed a lab coat from the hook and headed toward their office.

The comment made her feel even lower. No one had been very nice to Trevor when he arrived at their school. Not that he made it easy, but she always felt a little bad about the way people teased him for his accent. In hindsight, she wished she'd made a stronger effort to befriend him.

Why had she been so irrational about Bridget Kelly? Kate had no claim to Trevor. They had developed a friendship since she began working here, but she had no business interfering if he wanted to flirt with a pretty girl.

Nathan had been gone for four years, and the loneliness was getting harder to bear. She had loved him, mourned him, and would always cherish the memories of their two years together. But she didn't want to be a widow for the rest of her life.

She glowered down the hall at Trevor's stiff back as he strode into their office.

It would be a terrible idea. Unthinkable. Trevor was forbidden fruit, and she mustn't let herself think of him as anything else.

It was late in the day when Trevor noticed the broken spirometer on the floor. He went into the darkened supply closet to reach for another box of cotton swabs when he heard the crunching of glass beneath his shoe. Fumbling for the chain, he tugged on the single light bulb to show the apparatus he used for measuring lung capacity broken on the floor.

"Nurse Ackerman, do you know who has been in the supply closet today?"

She didn't. Nor did any of the orderlies or female attendants he questioned. None of the patients had a key to the closet, so they were surely blameless.

With his entire staff lined up outside the supply closet, Trevor scanned their faces. "Look, accidents happen," he said tersely. "No one is in danger of having their pay docked, but I need to know when equipment has been damaged. If a patient was in distress and I didn't have ready access to the proper equipment, it could be a dangerous situation. I don't want any more such occurrences," he warned.

But this wasn't the first time. An expensive set of scalpels had disappeared from the clinic. He thought he must have misplaced them and they would soon surface, but they never did. And last week he sensed someone had been in his office during the overnight hours. His chair was at an odd angle, and something simply seemed off. It could have been the janitorial staff, but the vague feeling of unease remained.

He stayed late that night to change the lock on the front of the clinic. It was going to incense the hospital's superintendent, but Trevor was paying good money for the use of this floor, and security was important. He squatted on the floor and tried for the third time to wriggle the new lock into place.

"Blast it," he muttered as the pliers slipped off the bolt cylinder, and the new lock mechanism clattered to the floor. He yanked his hand away and sucked on the drop of blood where the pliers nipped him. One would think a man who could remove an appendix and stitch a patient back together ought to be able to replace a door lock.

He glanced behind him. Two female attendants giggled in the corner as they pretended not to watch him make a fool of himself. It was embarrassing, but he wasn't going to let an audience dissuade him from changing the lock. He was fairly certain someone had been prowling in his supply closet, and he was going to put a stop to it.

Changing the lock took longer than expected, and the sun had gone down by the time Trevor arrived at the southeast side of town. He headed straight for the seediest part of the riverside, where the dank scent of rotting wood permeated the air. Most respectable people had fled the streets by this time of night, but there were plenty of sailors, troublemakers, and prostitutes loitering along the wharves. He scanned the crowds, looking for a distinctive wiry frame.

Oskar found him first. *"Gibt es die verrückt* doctor." *There's the crazy doctor.* Oskar's voice cut through the cackling of two women arguing over a coil of discarded rope. Trevor strode toward Oskar, answering in the same language.

"Hello, my crazy friend." The stench coming off Oskar was unbelievable, like he had been sleeping in a cask used to marinate fish. "Do you still have a place to live?" Trevor asked.

Oskar nodded. "A room above the cannery. You?"

"A room above the railroad station,"

Trevor replied.

One of the tragedies of tuberculosis was that as victims became too sick to keep working, many lost the ability to pay rent or get decent food. Unless there was family willing to take them in, they found themselves on the street, where their condition deteriorated even faster. Oskar's luck was unlikely to hold much longer. He was getting too sick to keep working, and when that happened, he would probably be sleeping on the streets.

"Here, you will be in need of this," Trevor said as he passed a bottle of his serum into Oskar's hand, who slipped it into his pocket before any of the others loitering along the docks could see. These transactions were no one's business, and it would only cause trouble for Oskar if people learned why they met.

"Have you seen anyone new I should know about?" Trevor asked.

Oskar unscrewed the bottle and took a swig, his face twisting in distaste as he got the oil down. "There is a new whore working a few blocks down. Curly hair. Bad teeth."

Trevor nodded and set off in the direction Oskar pointed, scanning the crowds as he went. Even in the dim light, he was good at spotting the kinds of people he searched for. The hollowed-out cheekbones and sunken eyes. The ghostly translucent skin that stretched across prominent bones. There were thousands of consumptives in the city, and most of them had nowhere to go.

It didn't take long to spot the woman Oskar mentioned. The way she leaned against a lamppost could be mistaken for a suggestive pose, but Trevor knew the look of exhaustion on her sickly white skin.

When he approached her, she tried to stand a little straighter as she reached out to stroke his shoulder. He covered her hand with his own.

"I just want to talk."

She winked and laughed. "Okay, one of those," she said. Her laugh held a distinctive rattle in her lungs. Her clothing looked clean, so in all likelihood she still had a place to sleep.

"Do you have any children?" Trevor asked.

"Heavens, no. I'm only eighteen."

She looked forty, but Trevor supposed she might still be in her twenties. Tuberculosis tended to age a person.

"If you do have children, it is important not to cough around them. The sickness in your lungs can be spread. Sleep with the windows open."

The woman pushed away from the lamp-post and pressed her body against him. "I said I don't have children." Her laugh was throaty, and her hands roamed his back. Trevor turned his face to the side, wishing for a mask, but there was no way he could earn the trust of these people if he pulled a mask out before speaking with them. He managed to disengage from the woman's wandering hands, then reached into his coat for another bottle of serum.

"This is a medicine that may help you. It doesn't taste good, but you won't be so hungry after you take a swig. Once in the morning and once at night."

She looked at it skeptically, the cloudy yellow oil glowing in the gaslight. This woman had no reason to trust strangers. It was impossible to know what had driven her to the streets, but she was a human being who had pain in her lungs and little kindness in her life. He knew that but for the grace of God he might have been in a situation as desperate as hers, and he would do his best for her.

Trevor pressed the bottle into her palm, holding her wasted hand and looking deep into her eyes. He told her honestly that he could not promise the medicine would cure her lungs, but it would improve her overall health.

"Is it going to cost me anything?"

He shook his head. "I'll be by every few weeks with more. What is your child's name?"

"Luke," she admitted. "Just like the saint."

He gave her a sad smile. "Drink the oil and sleep with your windows open," he said softly. "Do it for Saint Luke. He deserves it."

5

Kate grew to love her job more with each passing week, but as spring turned into summer, more hostile stories appeared in local newspapers about Trevor's clinic. Two articles spoke of the dangers of having so many consumptives housed in a densely populated section of the city, while the third suggested Trevor was swindling patients of their life savings.

The charge made Kate fume. She still wasn't precisely sure where Trevor got the money to fund the clinic, but it wasn't from the patients. Trevor didn't charge them a dime to live there, and all of them had been destitute when they were accepted into the study. It was frustrating watching him become a punching bag in the newspapers, but every time she suggested he go on the offensive, he merely glowered at her.

"I have the backing of the surgeon general," he snapped. "No muckraking journalist can get me out of this hospital."

Which was a good thing, because Kate loved her new job, even when Trevor was a bottomless well of frustration.

As the weeks slipped by, she completely ignored his advice not to befriend the patients. Never had she seen people so desperate for simple human companionship until she began working at the clinic.

One afternoon she was twenty minutes late turning in her statistical report because she had been tempted into helping Ethel Gordon share in her infant granddaughter's baptism. Ethel was too sick to attend the church ceremony, but her daughter desperately wanted Ethel to see her only grandchild dressed in the family's antique baptismal gown. A group of the healthier patients gathered in the sitting area, everyone dutifully wearing their masks, to see the little baby dressed in yards of white cotton embellished with handmade lace. The mother held the baby up from behind the nurses' counter, waving the chubby little fist at the assembled patients on the other side of the room.

It was one of the most moving things Kate had experienced in years, yet it made her late getting her report in to Trevor. Trevor was sitting at his desk when she rushed the report over to him.

"Why is this late?" he demanded.

Kate slid into her desk chair. "Because it was biologically impossible to tear myself away from the sight of that precious infant," she said. "There wasn't a dry eye in the sitting area. If you could have seen the way Ethel's face lit up, even you would have been moved. When we got that baby into the baptismal gown, she looked as sweet and precious as a little princess."

"No baby is a princess. I heard the squalling from down the hall. I would appreciate it if you tried harder to rein in your overwrought, womanly emotions." He turned back to reading a medical journal.

"These overwrought, womanly hands are going to strangle you if the hectoring from your side of the office doesn't stop."

Despite Trevor's quirks, it was actually pretty fun working with him. The sheer challenge of calculating huge sets of data and extrapolating the results was so gratifying. Every day she held her breath, hoping to see the numbers turn in a way that would indicate the bacillus was declining, or at least holding steady. Ephraim Montgomery's numbers got worse every day, but most of the others were holding their own. Hannah Wexler was actually showing *improve-*

ment in her blood.

"You are not to breathe a word about that to her," Trevor warned. "She is a terminal patient, and telling her about the improvement in her blood will not cure the disease in her lungs; it will only raise her hopes. This is a stay of execution, not a cure."

Kate was getting used to Trevor's blunt language and refused to let his severity upset her. He still referred to patients by their numbers rather than their names, continually warning Kate against her chatting with them.

She ignored him. She noticed that a group of about ten patients gathered in the sitting area each day before dinner to read aloud from a novel. Most of the patients became breathless after reading only a few minutes, so the book was passed among the handful who could read, with long breaks while the readers caught their breath.

"Would you mind if I read to them?" Kate asked Trevor one day as he studied slides under the microscope. "I don't mind staying after my shift to read a little each day."

"They're patients, not friends, Kate."

She lifted her chin. "And I think it would do these *patients* good to have someone read to them, rather than add stress to their already diminished lung capacity."

"Suit yourself."

The first day she approached the group, one of the older gentlemen waved a finger at her. "You can't sit with us until you mask up," he said.

His name was Leonard Wilkes, and he had been a sailor in the Merchant Marine until his illness was discovered and he was put off the ship at an island in Bermuda. It took almost two months for his coughing to go into remission so he could fake health and board another ship home. He was forty-three but looked sixty.

Kate dutifully donned her mask, then picked up a battered copy of *The Adventures of Tom Sawyer*. Most of the patients walked to the sitting area on their own steam, while Ephraim Montgomery had to be helped into a wheelchair pushed by one of the nurses. Sometimes he slumped over in the middle of her reading. The first time he did so, she looked over to Leonard.

"Should I wake him up?" she whispered.

Leonard shook his head. "It happens. Just keep reading."

The other patients agreed, so Kate continued. As time went on, she got to understand more about the patients who chose to gather for the reading group. It was hard for people to be confined in a sick ward, and gathering with others for a story gave them an hour to escape into the worlds created by Jane Austen or Charles Dickens. A favorite of the group was any book by Mark Twain.

"Do you suppose Mr. Twain will write another sequel to *Tom Sawyer*?" Hannah Wexler asked. "*Huckleberry Finn* was so good, and he ought to do another."

"Maybe we should write a letter and ask about plans for a sequel," Kate suggested.

"Could we really do that?"

"I don't see why not."

Leonard Wilkes perked up. "Tell him the request comes from a bunch of patients dying in a tubercular ward. That ought to light a fire under him!"

He snickered, and Hannah joined him in a guilty chuckle. This sort of gallows humor always made Kate wince. What kind of person would she be if she joined in their laughter? And yet it was common for the patients to jest about their illness. Yesterday Leonard joked that Dr. Kendall's serum was so awful he was likely to die from the taste before tuberculosis got him.

"Very well, it is resolved," Kate said. "I will draft a letter to Mr. Twain and will circulate it among the patients for anyone who wishes to sign."

When the letter was written, she donned

her mask and brought it to every patient in the ward for their signature. As she approached Ephraim Montgomery's bed, his ghastly pallor and sunken eyes made it look as though he were already dead, but the slow, shallow breaths indicated he was only sleeping. She tiptoed past to the next patient.

"Can't I sign?" Ephraim wheezed.

Kate froze. "I'm sorry, I thought you were asleep."

Ephraim struggled to rise. His hand trembled, making his signature scrawl across the bottom of the page. "Tell him to hurry," he said with a resigned smile.

Her vision blurred with a sheen of tears. Her nose twitched, and the back of her throat hurt as she collected the last of the signatures in the men's ward. She dashed back to the office, reaching for a handkerchief and blowing her nose, smothering an ungainly sob in the soft cotton fabric.

"No sniveling, Kate."

Trevor didn't even look up from his desk. Temptation clawed at her to ball up the handkerchief and throw it at him, but that would only prove that he was right about how draining it was to make friends with these people. She folded the handkerchief and slid it back into the top drawer.

"Just a bit of hay fever," she sniffed.

Mercifully he didn't argue with her. If she were a better Christian, she wouldn't find dealing with death so difficult. Why was it easy for her to believe in a loving God but still be terrified of watching people die? She hadn't handled Nathan's death well. Even four years after the accident, she still wrestled with questions and doubts about why such a healthy, cheerful man had been snatched away so early. She prayed, she sought counsel, but still she questioned. So far there'd been no answers to soothe her apprehension, only the looming fear that such a tragedy might someday overwhelm her again.

No city in the country was more eager for news than Washington, D.C. Journalists tracked each morsel of gossip flowing out of Capitol Hill, rushing to be the first to get the story into print. Political news was a major staple around the boardinghouse dining table, and this morning was no different. Kate startled when she saw the newspaper's headline.

President Harrison Threatens to Send Marines to Chile.

"What?" Kate gasped. "Why is the president mad at Chile?"

"He's not," Harvey Goldstein said as he cut into his morning omelet. Harvey was a reporter for the *New York Times* and always had his ear to the ground. "The British are supporting rebels in Chile and are sending them aid. Rumor has it President Harrison is likely to retaliate by sending the marines to the other side." The reporter glanced over at Charlie. "What's the word in Congress on that?"

One of the benefits of living at the Norton Boardinghouse was hearing political gossip before it leaked into the newspapers. It was the reason journalists liked living there. Charlie considered the question carefully before answering.

"The president is still licking his wounds for sending the marines to Argentina last year. It will be a gamble to intervene down south again."

The talk was enough to give Kate an upset stomach for the entire day at the hospital. They couldn't send Tick to the wilds of South America over some silly quarrel with the British, could they? True, he was assigned to the surgeon general, but if the country engaged in a military intervention, anything could happen and Tick could find himself on a battlefield.

It was hard to concentrate on her statistics

with her mind wracked with worry. Especially since Trevor wouldn't stop fiddling with his pencil. From the other side of the office he kept rapping his pencil on his desk as he read a medical journal.

"Could you please stop that incessant tapping?"

The noise stopped, but a few minutes later he was back at it.

"Trevor!"

It stopped again. "Sorry," he said dryly. "I find the amount of frilly knickknacks suddenly populating my work space brings out my old nervous habits."

Kate glanced at the two potted plants and the lace doilies on the table. They made the place look much nicer, but Trevor grunted when he saw them. "Dust collectors," he muttered under his breath, but he hadn't asked her to remove them.

The moment it was five o'clock, Kate went tearing across town to the Marine Barracks and was able to coax Tick out to dinner at a local pub. No sooner had they sat down than she broached the topic.

"About Chile," she began.

Tick interrupted her before she could even start. "If they call us up, I'm going."

"But surely that's not what you want!" She would think of something, pull a string

111

somewhere to get him out of it.

"No one wants to go, but if it happens, it happens. Besides, it wouldn't be so bad to see something of the world."

"Something like rebels armed with British rifles and grenades? Or the opportunity to catch cholera and malaria? Or how about another round of diphtheria?"

"Kate, I can't live my life in the shadow of your fears. I'm sorry about what happened to Carl and Jamie, but you can't keep me wrapped up in cotton for the rest of my life."

Was she so obvious? Watching Carl and then Jamie die from diphtheria haunted her for years, and surely it was natural to protect her only surviving brother.

Natural but not wise. Her father had been warning Kate to quit hovering over Tick so much, but she couldn't bear any more loss in her life. Nathan's death only reinforced all her old fears about how fleeting life could be.

"Do you ever think about them?" she asked. "Carl and Jamie?"

Tick's smile was sad as he held a cup of coffee between his hands. "I don't really remember them. I was only four when it happened, remember?"

"Right. I feel so helpless," she mumbled. "You could get shipped off to fight some war we don't care about. Trevor has been getting horrible stories written about him in the newspapers, and I haven't been a lick of help getting them stopped. I want to *fix* things so all this won't happen."

Tick's eyes twinkled, and he drew a long sip of coffee. "Poor Kate . . . wanting to run the world and yet no one will let her."

She kicked him under the table, but before he could respond, a musician in the corner of the pub picked up a fiddle and began playing a tune.

Kate stiffened. Tick shot to his feet and said, "I'll go ask him to stop."

He was gone before she could say anything. For years the sound of a fiddle was enough to reduce Kate to tears. The bright, lively music would always remind her of Nathan, but her heart had mended. Now the sound of a fiddle only brought a gentle rush of bittersweet memories. The music lurched to a halt in the corner while Tick leaned over to whisper to the fiddler.

"He'll hold off until we leave," Tick said after he returned to her side, looking down with concern in his somber blue eyes. "You okay?"

She stood and impulsively kissed each of his cheeks.

"Kate," he said in a warning growl.

113

"Sorry!" she said, smiling. When he was little, she used to pinch his cheeks and kiss his face silly, but for his sixteenth birthday she promised she would quit. Sometimes she still slipped up, though.

"You're not sorry at all." He wiped his face but was grinning as he escorted her out the door.

A veil of low-hanging clouds cast the morning into faint shades of gray. A storm was brewing, and the electricity in the air stretched Trevor's nerves even tighter as he strode to the hospital, the summons burning in his pocket.

In a perfect world he would never need to deal with another hospital administrator as long as he lived. The people who ran hospitals were rarely men of medicine, and Frederick Lambrecht was no exception. The hospital's superintendent was nothing more than a bureaucrat who quibbled over the cost of test tubes or the expense of feeding dying patients in a tubercular ward. Every time Trevor was pulled away to go blather with some hospital administrator, he was losing research time when he could be making headway against the disease that was killing thousands of people each year.

He went through the administrative wing,

rapped on the superintendent's door, and entered without waiting for a reply. He would waste no time on niceties.

"I pay the food bill for the patients out of my own pocket," Trevor said as he slapped a grocer's bill on Mr. Lambrecht's spacious walnut desk. If the administrator was so concerned about costs, perhaps he could swap that gleaming antique desk for a plain oak desk like Trevor used. The velvet draperies and silk rug also had no place in a hospital concerned with trimming costs.

Mr. Lambrecht pushed the invoices back toward Trevor. "I am well aware of your generosity in supplying beef and dairy to the patients," he said. "But the food is cooked in hospital kitchens, using hospital staff, and served by hospital attendants. None of this comes cheaply. Why can't your patients eat the same food all the other patients receive?"

"A carefully controlled diet is part of my study," he replied. "The patients do better when they keep weight on."

"Then I insist you help fund the added kitchen expense. When I agreed to take this study, I was assured the hospital would incur no additional expense."

Trevor glared. Frederick Lambrecht never "agreed" to take this study. He grudgingly accepted the tubercular clinic on his hospital's fifth floor because the surgeon general insisted on it. The hospital was funded on federal dollars and was therefore obliged to accept government directives in matters of public health.

Nevertheless, the complaint was valid. Trevor's demands for his patients' diet were exacting, and the lead cook had been amazed when Trevor outlined the high volume he expected the kitchen to deliver. He did some quick mental calculations.

"I am willing to fund an additional cook to supplement the kitchen staff," he conceded.

"And the attendants?"

"Forget it. I see those women loitering in the halls without enough to do as it is." Clusters of them giggled in the hallway whenever he walked past. Lately one of them had taken to slipping him notes in the hallway. It was awkward and he wished they would stop.

"Your patients have been making heavy use of hospital supplies. The amount we spend on soap has soared."

Trevor rocked back in his seat. "Soap? You're begrudging my patients *soap*? What kind of doctor would I be if I didn't insist on cleanliness?"

Mr. Lambrecht narrowed his eyes. "That brings me to my next topic. I'm sure the articles appearing in various Washington newspapers have not escaped your notice. The words *quack* and *disgrace* were never used in relation to this hospital before you arrived."

The barb hurt. Nothing in his professional career infuriated him as much as those vile articles, but he would not waste his time by placating idiots. "It's just a bunch of muck-raking journalists who want to whip up paranoia to sell newspapers."

"Perhaps, but the publicity is damaging the hospital, and I want it stopped."

"And how do you propose I do that? I've already demanded a retraction, and they haven't done so. If you have another suggestion, I would welcome it."

"I'm not interested in cleaning up your scandal," Mr. Lambrecht snapped. "If you can't maintain a respectable reputation, I want you out. You can take your patients and move elsewhere."

"I would like to see you explain that to the surgeon general."

"Don't be so sure you have the surgeon general's full support," Mr. Lambrecht said. "No politician likes to see this sort of scandal splashed across the newspapers."

"Barrow is a man of science. He's a doctor, not a politician."

"That's where you're wrong," said Mr. Lambrecht. "No man that high in the government is immune from politics, and trust me, he's angry about these reports. If there is one more damaging article in the newspapers, I'm taking my complaints to the surgeon general. And then I want you out of the hospital."

On that refreshing note, Trevor grabbed the food invoices on the desk and stormed from the office. Few doctors wanted to be associated with tuberculosis, as there was no glamour or prestige in curing a disease that primarily afflicted the poor and uneducated. The surgeon general was different, though. Soldiers and sailors lived in cramped quarters that mimicked the conditions of the urban tenements, so he had a vested interest in funding Trevor's work. But apparently even the surgeon general had a limited supply of patience.

The meeting with the hospital's superintendent made Trevor late for work, and it was raining outside, which only added to the ominous sense of foreboding that had been plaguing him for months.

Kate was already at her desk, contemplating a tableful of numbers. She wore a starched collar with a slim black tie tucked into her vest, her red-gold hair neatly coiled atop her head. By heaven, was there anything more attractive than watching a pretty woman tackle a thorny mathematical equation?

"Good morning, Kate. If you looked any smarter, I'd fear you were after my position."

She didn't look up from her paper work. "Trevor, if you don't rein in that ego, I will be forced to have you deported back to Scotland. They do that for disagreeable aliens."

"Your threats are as terrifying as a newborn kitten." He fought back the smile that threatened to emerge. No matter how miserable his morning, all he had to do was walk within ten feet of Kate and listen to her sling an insult at him and he felt better.

"Patient rounds in ten minutes," he said, snapping up his stethoscope from the desk. He needed to keep pretending Kate was just another employee. It had been getting harder to ignore the electricity that hummed between them, but he would do it.

Because if Kate knew all the dark secrets he carried, she would faint from the shock of it.

6

Kate found Trevor the most fascinating and frustrating man she'd ever known. Far from being the dull, one-dimensional person she once assumed him to be, he had the strangest quirks. Although the patients loathed the vile concoction of cod liver oil steeped with the bone marrow he required them to drink, Trevor willingly swallowed a dose each day.

"The patients whine about the taste all the time," Trevor said. "I'm trying to prove to them it's not that bad." He poured a healthy dose of the cloudy yellow liquid into a shot glass and tossed it back without flinching.

"I can't even bear to *smell* it," Kate said while suppressing a shudder.

"The Vikings used to swear cod liver oil sustained their strength on long ocean voyages. Come on, have a glass."

She lifted her chin. "I'd like to believe that

medical science has progressed since the Vikings stormed the globe."

He had other odd practices. Trevor was always the first to arrive in the morning and the last to leave at night, though sometimes he disappeared for hours in the middle of the day. "I'm on the roof," he would tell Nurse Ackerman before leaving the clinic.

"What does Dr. Kendall do on the roof?" Kate asked the nurse.

"Lord only knows," Nurse Ackerman replied gloomily. "Something dire, I'm sure."

Not that Kate had time to worry about what Trevor was up to on the roof. What she really wanted to know was why he'd changed his name.

Each time she asked him about it, he stonewalled her, so she had taken to poking around the hospital, looking for clues. She studied every framed certificate, diploma, and award on the wall outside the conference room. He graduated from Harvard with a medical degree when he was only twenty-two. Then he spent several years with the world-renowned Dr. Robert Koch, studying tuberculosis in Berlin. He also did research in Paris at the Pasteur Institute.

Strangely there were two years during which he had no diplomas or awards. She would be tempted to think that perhaps he'd been doing something fun or interesting with his life, except this was Trevor. The man didn't have a recreational impulse in his entire body.

She asked him about those missing two years one afternoon when she was helping him file expense reports in the hospital's administrative office on the first floor. "Had you finally had enough of work and took time to sit back and enjoy your vast wealth? Play golf with the robber barons?" He didn't look up as he slotted a folder into the dense drawer of files.

"Yes, Kate, I was playing golf with the Vanderbilts. When will you have the projections for the white blood cell counts completed?"

It was typical of the way he brushed her off, but she enjoyed the challenge. The more he evaded, the more determined she became. "I notice your Scottish accent is almost completely gone. We could barely understand you when you first showed up at school. What part of Scotland are you from?"

"The part where people mind their own business." The filing drawer thumped as he closed it. She followed him back upstairs to the office they shared. Before they reached the office, Nurse Ackerman intercepted them. "Doctor, there has been another mention in the newspaper."

"Another article?"

Nurse Ackerman had a distinctly uncomfortable look on her face. She shifted from foot to foot and swallowed before answering. "Not really an article. More of a picture, sir."

He snatched the newspaper from the nurse's hand. Even from a few feet away, Kate could see what looked like one of those obnoxious political cartoons. A gangly man dressed in black clothes had a grotesque grin as he waved a syringe in the air while tap-dancing in a graveyard. *Dr. Death Strikes Again,* the caption read.

Kate grimaced. Even for someone with no feelings, that had to hurt. But Trevor's face was like stone as he folded the newspaper and tucked it under his arm. "Kate, go back to finishing the files."

"I thought you wanted the projections for the white blood cells."

"Later." He turned and stalked down the hallway. After exchanging a brief look of commiseration with Nurse Ackerman, she followed him. The office door was closed. She rapped on the door and entered without waiting for permission.

"What's going on?" she asked.

Trevor was sitting at his desk, elbows braced on the armrests, his hands steepled before him. He stared out the window and didn't respond to her question.

How precisely did you ask a man why he was so hated? Trevor could be blunt, unfriendly, and rude, but this level of disparagement went beyond a personal tiff. A respectable newspaper would not be running these articles unless there was something behind them.

She stepped farther into the office. "Trevor?"

"Kate, we're not going to discuss this."

The legs of her desk chair scraped the floor as she dragged it over to Trevor's side of the office. She took a seat close beside him, letting him know she didn't intend to let this drop. "I think the employees are entitled to know why someone is calling you 'Dr. Death' and writing ugly stories about the clinic."

He whirled to face her, and she blanched at the anger on his face. She held up her hands. "I don't believe a word of it, but burying our heads in the sand won't make the problem go away. Have you spoken with the journalist who is writing the stories?"

"Yes. He won't reveal who's passing

information on to him. Some sort of non-sense about protecting his sources. It's probably just a bunch of paranoid people threatened by my work. It won't be the first time doctors studying contagious diseases are vilified. I've already demanded a retraction from the editors at the *Post.*"

"Demanded?" That sounded like Trevor. Clearly it wasn't working or they would not have printed that cartoon today. "Who did you speak with?"

"The clerk in the front of the building. He said the editor wasn't available."

"Not available to angry people who barge in and demand retractions. There are better ways to go about this sort of thing."

"And what would the dauntless Katherine Livingston recommend?"

She ignored the sarcasm in his voice and chewed the side of her thumbnail as she analyzed the problem. This needed to be handled carefully. She didn't know anyone at the *Washington Post,* but she knew plenty of other people in high places. A lifetime of serving people at her mother's dinner table had earned her that.

"Honey catches more flies than vinegar, and you seem to drink vinegar by the gallon," she said. "It wouldn't kill you to actually smile now and again. Or get to know some of the right people."

He stiffened, and the air grew even frostier. "I've never been impressed by people who make friends to oil their way to the top."

That statement explained so much, and Kate fought to keep her voice pleasant. "You're asking the local people to support a clinic that treats a horrifying, contagious disease in the middle of their neighborhood. You need to build friendships and alliances, and I can help you with that. Come to my mother's house for dinner. She serves lots of important people who work at different places throughout the city. Congressmen, ambassadors, trade officials. If I work very hard, I might be able to persuade her to serve a standoffish doctor who seems to delight in offending people."

He folded his arms across his chest, lowered his chin, and glared at her. A muscle twitched in his cheek, but he didn't deny the truth of what she said. If this was just about Trevor, she wouldn't subject her mother to his company, but across the hall there were thirty-two people who needed him. Those people needed a champion, and she needed to prop Trevor up to assume that role before his reputation was in shreds.

She bumped up the pressure. "My mother

is the best cook in Washington. She serves a Brunswick stew so tender it will melt in your mouth. The scent fills the neighborhood, and people would sell their firstborn child to get a place at her table."

"And these are the sort of people you think will improve my reputation?"

She wanted to smack him, but this argument was too important to lose. "Dinner is served at six o'clock. Come to the Norton Boardinghouse on H Street, and be nice for once. Don't ask for a newspaper editor's head on a platter. It's important to establish friendships before calling in favors."

"It sounds like a colossal waste of time."

"Six o'clock. Tonight."

He shook his head. "No good. I am assisting Dr. Flynn with a pulmonary surgery this afternoon. I can't be there before seven."

She returned to her desk and opened a file of hemoglobin statistics. "Take the green streetcar line to H Street. Come late if you must, but I *will* see you at dinner tonight."

7

Trevor held on to the worn leather strap as the streetcar pulled near H Street. The streetcar was nearly empty at this time of the evening, but he preferred to stand when he was nervous. The surgery took longer than planned, but the patient was doing well. Surgery was an intellectual challenge he enjoyed, and it was so much easier than making chitchat like Kate wanted him to do tonight.

But she was right. He needed allies, because the situation was a lot worse than Kate knew. In addition to the negative coverage in the newspapers, he had been getting threatening letters delivered to his home address. The newspaper articles were tame compared with the virulence in the letters he received at home. And those anonymous letters were written by someone who knew a great deal about his personal history, mentioning too many private details for it to be a coincidence. Whoever was behind this campaign was not so much afraid of tuberculosis as someone who despised him. Someone who wanted to see him ruined.

He tightened his fist around the strap. Medicine was the only thing he had in the world. He had devoted his life to cramming his head with every scrap of medical knowledge he could dig up. He'd risked his life in the relentless quest to find, tackle, and slay the dragon of tuberculosis.

When the streetcar slowed to a halt, Trevor sprang to the ground, wondering how long Kate expected him to play nice at dinner. He'd been in surgery for three hours, on top of a long day at the clinic, and all he really wanted now was to collapse in bed.

Kate lived on a nice street lined with white granite buildings and a row of trees along the walkways. Elegant black lampposts were already illuminated, sending a warm glow along the boulevard. The Norton Boarding-house was a four-story town house with bow windows and shiny black shutters. Lights illuminated the first floor, and lively conversation leaked from behind the front door.

Was he supposed to knock? He rapped, but when there was no response he opened the door and stepped inside.

The aroma of simmering beef and warm apple cider surrounded him. He followed the boisterous voices to an oversized dining room crammed with people. A group of men in one corner had pulled their chairs to the side with their heads in earnest conversation. Others sat at the table, enjoying huge slabs of apple pie while a man with a thick accent recounted witnessing the coronation of the Russian czar. There was no sign of Kate.

He stood awkwardly in the entrance of the dining room. It was warm in here, and he didn't know what to do with his hands. What a mistake it was to come here.

A pretty blond girl spotted him and sprang to her feet. "You must be Dr. Kendall!"

The conversation sputtered to a halt, and twenty heads swiveled toward him. The girl wended her way around the table and held both hands before her.

"Kate is still helping in the kitchen, but she told me to be on the lookout for you. I'm Irene Bauman." She inclined her head to one of the men clustered at the far end of the room. "That's my father with the white mustache in the corner. He's a justice on the Supreme Court!"

What precisely was he supposed to say to

that? He cleared his throat and shifted. "Very nice." Maybe he should make a point of telling the judge this country needed better laws to keep vicious newspaper reporters on a leash.

The girl tugged his arm and dragged him toward the table. "We saved a seat for you. This is Tom Wilkerson; he works at the Patent Office. And Charlie Davis, congressman from Pennsylvania. And this is Harvey Goldstein; he's a journalist for the *New York Times*." The formalities continued until she must have introduced twelve people, all of whom were blurring in his mind.

"You came!"

Finally Kate made an appearance, and relief trickled through him. She held pots of tea in both hands, double doors swinging closed behind her. She handed the teapots to a serving girl and then hurried around the table to greet him.

"I was afraid you wouldn't make it," she said.

"The surgery took longer than expected. A resection of an upper lobe on the lung. It's a tricky operation."

Strange, for she really did look happy to see him. She guided him to a chair and told the pretty blond girl to stop clinging to him. Then Kate left to get him a bowl of Brunswick stew, which was good because he was famished. When she set the bowl before him, he almost wept from the aroma. The first bite was an explosion of flavor, shredded beef in a sauce that was both spicy and sweet.

Everyone else had already finished their meal and was jabbering away, but he was eating and therefore spared from having to make conversation other than an occasional nod. It was always such a challenge to think of things to say with strangers, but he liked listening to Kate talk with the people crammed around the table. The way she bantered and sparred kept everyone on their toes. The man from Russia complained that the newly installed hot water tank was inadequate.

"It is functioning perfectly well," Kate explained. "My father spent a fortune getting that piping installed, but there is only about fifteen minutes' worth of hot water at a time. That's the way the system is designed to work."

The Russian wasn't satisfied, and finally Kate dragged him away to show him the size of the water tank. The blond girl immediately filled the vacant chair beside him.

"I think it is so exciting that you're a doctor," she breathed. "The doctor we use is probably ninety years old and no fun at all. I'll bet you're so much smarter."

He wanted to say that many of the smartest people in the world were old men, and some of the silliest were teenaged girls with sparkly bows in their hair, but Kate would probably say that was rude, and so he refrained.

"My hands are always cold," the girl said with her breathy voice. "Is that normal?" She laid a chilly finger on his wrist, then traced the back of his hand.

He cleared his throat and pulled his arm away. "Cold hands are generally no cause for concern."

"But my feet are always cold too." There was a rustling of silk as the girl fidgeted in her seat. Something brushed his leg, and the unmistakable feel of icy toes slid beneath the hem of his pants, nudging at his ankle with her bare toes.

"See? Is that normal?"

There was nothing normal about this girl. He slid to the far side of his chair, but there wasn't much room to escape. It was bad enough when the nurses trailed him around the hospital, but this girl was pestering him only five yards away from her own father! He glanced over at the man in the corner, still arguing politics with the others, and wondered how he could get away from this girl.

The double doors swung open, and a matron with fading auburn hair and the demeanor of Attila the Hun stood at the head of the table. Kate's mother?

"Final call," she barked. "Anyone caught in the kitchen after closing can expect a beheading. Who wants something else to eat?"

Now he knew where Kate got her bossiness. The congressman raised his hand and politely asked for more stew. A few men wanted refills of their tea. Mrs. Norton nodded her head and then pinned him with a pointed stare.

"You! I'm bringing you a slice of pie, because you're too thin to be operating on people when you look like a bean pole. And then we're going to talk. Irene, get your hands off Dr. Kendall before you're arrested for indecency."

Mrs. Norton went back to the kitchen, and dinner started breaking up as people began drifting away. Irene pouted and moved to the far end of the table, but as the volume in the room dwindled, the congressman from Pennsylvania seemed interested in a conversation.

"Kate tells me you lived with Senator

Campbell when you were growing up."

He stiffened, fiddling with his fork. "I did, yes."

"I met Senator Campbell during my first term in Congress. We served on the committee for the well-being of the war veterans. Campbell always showed great compassion to the wounded veterans."

Trevor nodded, scrambling to turn the conversation to anything else. Senator Campbell showed more compassion for his racehorses than anyone living under his roof, including his wife and children. Certainly the man had no interest in the Scottish stray who had been foisted on him.

Mercifully, Mrs. Norton arrived with more food. The apple pie looked delicious, but he'd lost his appetite. Kate drifted back into the room but without the Russian diplomat in tow.

"I've just spent the last ten minutes trying to explain the laws of physics to Mr. Zomohkov. He won't believe that modern plumbing must still obey the limits of heat transfer. He wants an endless supply of hot water."

Mrs. Norton took the seat directly across from him and poured herself a cup of tea. "My husband took out a loan of three thousand dollars to supply this house with hot water and modern toilets, and look what we get."

"You get the eternal gratitude of your most devoted boarders," Charlie Davis said. "Back to Senator Campbell. What was it like growing up in his household? I gather that mansion on Lafayette Square is quite the showplace."

Mrs. Norton's hawklike gaze was fixed on him over the rim of her cup, waiting for an answer. Even Kate set down her fork to listen.

"Yes, it was a nice home." It ought to be, given the fortune his father had paid Senator Campbell to take an unwanted child off his hands.

"He was your guardian, right?" Charlie asked. "I suspect you had a front-row seat for the politics of this city."

Trevor saw the senator no more than once or twice a month, which was fine with both of them. It was Mrs. Kendall who raised him and taught him what he needed to know to survive in the world.

He speared the pie with his fork and took a bite. It could have been sawdust for all the attention he paid it. "Very fine pie."

Kate cleared her throat and plastered an agreeable expression on her face. "Dr. Kendall has been doing such interesting research. I'm sure he has so much to share if he could just get to know a few more people in the city," she said tightly, then kicked him under the table. "Why don't you tell us about your innovative techniques for finding a cure for tuberculosis?"

Did she really think going through these little pleasantries was an effective technique for silencing the *Washington Post*? Or figuring out who was sending him those revolting letters?

"I can't imagine anyone wants to hear about tuberculosis," he said. "Not at dinnertime." The conversation came to a thudding halt, but even he knew that lung cavitation or infected corpuscles rarely made for good dinner talk.

"So why did you change your name?" Mrs. Norton asked, her voice blunt. "McDonough is a perfectly fine name, and it seems strange to change it. Not normal."

A bite of pie lodged in the back of his throat, and he reached for his glass to wash it down. He maintained a carefully blank look. He didn't want anyone to know the question had flustered him. "I changed it when I began college," he said simply.

"Yes, but *why*?"

The annoying blond girl perked up and leaned forward. "You changed your name? How exciting! I'll bet there's a terribly romantic reason why. You *must* tell us!"

It was hot in here, and everyone in the room was looking at him. Why did all these strangers feel entitled to snoop into his private business? He set his fork down, pushed back from the table, and stood.

"Thank you for dinner." He left without looking back.

8

Kate set off for the hospital the next morning ready for a fight. It was one thing for Trevor to be rude to her, but she wouldn't tolerate it toward her mother or the others at the boardinghouse. He embarrassed her horribly by his behavior. She tried to apologize on his behalf, mentioning the stress he was under because of those awful newspaper stories, but her mother remained unmoved.

"I still haven't forgiven him for grabbing that scholarship out of your hands. That man is as cold as a salamander. Always was, always will be."

Kate stepped off the streetcar at the hospital stop and saw Trevor on the front stairs, the big stray dog wagging her tail and bumping her muzzle against him. Trevor wore a sour expression as he tried to nudge the dog off the steps.

"Good morning, Trevor. Making more

friends?"

The lines around his mouth tensed. "Kate, you need to back off. So does your mother. She was very rude last night."

"She asked you a polite question! So did Charlie Davis. You practically bit their heads off. The whole purpose was for you to try to be friendly and build up goodwill, so you'll have community leaders on your side."

"They weren't on my side; they were down my throat and in my private business. That adolescent hoyden was up my pant leg with her chilly toes."

"I refuse to believe anyone on earth is chillier than you."

The bickering continued all the way up the stairs and into the clinic. "Kate, we're not going to discuss this." The door banged open and Nurse Ackerman jumped, then rose to her feet.

"You have a visitor, sir. Mr. Tobias Jones, from the Board of Commissioners."

Kate followed the nurse's gaze to see a bullnecked man waiting in the sitting area. Her mouth went dry. This couldn't be good. The District of Columbia was unlike any other city in the country. It was overseen by the federal government, but since Congress had little interest in municipal affairs, the city's real power was in the hands of a three-member Board of Commissioners. Tobias Jones was the president of the board, and together with the other two appointed officials they ruled over this city with the power of monarchs.

And Trevor was a walking disaster in dealing with people. If Mr. Jones was here about the newspaper articles, Trevor was going to be surly and defensive, which was not the way to talk to a powerful politician.

"Dr. Kendall?" Mr. Jones asked. He carried a stack of newspapers, the top one folded open to the grotesque cartoon of Trevor dancing in a graveyard.

"Yes, I'm Dr. Kendall." Trevor saw the cartoon as well, and his voice was sharp.

"I'd like to speak with you about some recent articles appearing in the *Washington Post*. The people of this city have legitimate concerns about what is going on in this clinic."

"That's ridiculous," Trevor snapped. "As is the trash appearing in the newspaper. The residents of this city can't catch tuberculosis from patients quietly minding their own business on the fifth floor of a hospital clinic. Any reporter who can't grasp that shouldn't be trusted with paper and ink."

Mr. Jones sucked in a breath, puffing his

chest out like an angry bull getting ready to charge. Trevor needed saving, so Kate stepped forward.

"Louis Pasteur's theories on anthrax were initially met with great suspicion," she said. "I suppose it's natural for people to fear what they don't understand."

"Is that what's happening here?" Mr. Jones's eyes narrowed as he studied her. "Just a group of paranoid journalists whipping up fear?"

This needed to be handled carefully, and she scrambled for every tidbit Charlie Davis ever taught her for winning the goodwill of politicians. The most important was to use flattery based on fact.

"People once lived in mind-numbing fear of smallpox before a vaccine was tested and proven effective," she continued. "That wouldn't have happened but for a handful of doctors who braved the protests and rioters who wanted to banish them from the land." She leaned forward to place a hand on Mr. Jones's arm and added in a conspiratorial voice, "Did you know Benjamin Franklin helped turn public opinion on that one? Once he was convinced of the value of the smallpox vaccine, he published a great many articles in support of it. I think it's one of the reasons history remembers Benjamin Franklin so fondly. He was a forward-thinking man, a politician who wasn't afraid to stand up for what was right."

"Indeed," Mr. Jones said, a little ire fading from his tone.

"Would you like a tour of the wards?" she asked. "I'm so proud we've been able to offer treatment to some of the poorest people of the city — all free of charge, thanks to Dr. Kendall. I would be happy to show you the clinic and perhaps even introduce a few patients." It was impossible to look at the wasted bodies of people in the final stages of tuberculosis and not feel compassion.

Mr. Jones was hesitant. Who wouldn't be after the barrage of articles whipping up fear about tubercular contagion? Just then the door burst open, and the morning brigade of attendants arrived, wheeling carts stacked with breakfast trays. Kate dashed to the nearest cart and lifted the lid. The scent of bacon, cheese omelets, and warm cranberry muffins filled the air.

"Have you had breakfast?" she asked. "We feed the patients like royalty here, but there's always some left over for the staff. Can I offer you anything?"

"Thank you, but I've already eaten," Mr. Jones said.

Kate replaced the lid. All three of the

young ladies were dressed in their tailored pink gowns, with white aprons and folded caps perched atop their heads. Kate stood beside the smallest of them, a birdlike girl who barely reached her shoulder.

"This is Jenny Bell," Kate said. "This is her first position and she's already doing so well. How old are you, Jenny?"

"Seventeen, ma'am."

"Seventeen and already taking on such a responsible job. The patients adore her because she's always so cheerful first thing in the morning."

Jenny flushed. "Thank you, ma'am." Jenny put on her mask, then wheeled her cart down the hall.

Kate reached for a spare mask and extended it to Tobias Jones. "Would you like to meet the patients? This is a good time because they will all be awake as the young ladies distribute breakfast."

A spark of amusement gleamed in Trevor's eyes as he understood Kate's point. If three teenaged girls weren't afraid to walk among the afflicted, what sort of man would Mr. Jones be if he refused?

Mr. Jones took the mask and followed Kate to the wards. Mercifully, Trevor let her take the lead in showing the facility. She introduced a handful of the patients, trading quips and political gossip. It was clear the patients were friendly with her, well fed, and provided with clean and comfortable quarters. No helpless victims of quack medicine in sight.

Before Mr. Jones left, he said the oddest thing to Trevor. "I understand the press sometimes enjoys stirring up a bit of panic, but that doesn't mean I'll turn a blind eye if you let standards slip. We are not in the Himalayas here."

Kate turned her attention to Trevor the moment the door closed behind the commissioner. "The Himalayas?"

"It's nothing," Trevor said as he stalked away, but his look of seething annoyance was unmistakable.

She would need to file the Himalaya Mountains away with the growing list of Trevor's oddities.

That mention of the Himalayas was driving Kate insane.

She'd seen the diplomas and awards that indicated Trevor had traveled widely throughout Europe, but the Himalayas? Wasn't that in India? The Himalaya Mountains summoned images of rugged climbers and dusty, windswept mountain passes, not the fastidious Dr. Kendall, who washed his hands both before and after his meals.

Naturally, when she asked him about it, he was as closemouthed as ever. "I've always admired how the Indian people respect other people's privacy," Trevor said. "So rare in this world."

No amount of prying could coax any insight from him, but it made Kate determined to find out more. Her opportunity came one morning when an orderly from downstairs came bursting into the clinic.

"Dr. Kendall is needed in surgery right away. A railway worker got too close to the crane hook, and it tore his stomach open. His insides are all on the outside now. Dr. Flynn wants Dr. Kendall to assist."

Trevor heard and was already shrugging into a lab coat.

Kate felt a little weak in the knees. She couldn't imagine what it must take to handle a man's intestines, but Trevor was unflappable as he followed the orderly out the door. Maybe it was good that Trevor was so cold. If anyone would have a steady hand under such circumstances, it would be a man with no heart.

There was little for her to do until Trevor examined the patients and provided her with a new set of data to analyze. It gave her a perfect opportunity to snoop into his private life. She glanced around the clinic, noting two patients playing checkers in the sitting area, and another woman reading. They were far enough away not to hear whispers, so Kate drew a chair up close to the nurses' station. It was time to pick Nurse Ackerman's brain.

"Do you know why Dr. Kendall was in India?"

"No. I didn't realize he had been."

Kate tried not to let her disappointment show. There were so many things about Trevor that were a mystery. "Does he have any family at all? Any friends?"

"Not that I know of. We have to beat the young nurses off him with a stick, but he never shows the slightest interest in any of them."

That seemed odd. Trevor was a handsome man, and as far as she knew, he had never been married or even courted a girl. It was disturbing, but she had to admit he was a very attractive man. If she didn't know him so well, she might even be one of those silly girls fawning over him.

He was the complete opposite of Nathan. Her husband had been a laughing man who flirted with everyone, but especially her. Whatever emotion Nathan was feeling was written plainly on his face for all to see.

Trevor was different. Austere and reserved, she wondered what it would be like to peek beneath that shell. Trevor wasn't emotionless. Oh no. She'd caught glimpses of a mighty passion simmering beneath the surface, but he always held it so tightly locked down. Restrained. What would it be like to tear away his stern outer layer and see that smoldering emotion unleashed?

She shook herself. This was *Trevor* she was thinking about, and she ought to be horrified to be contemplating such things.

"Where does he live?" she asked Nurse Ackerman, who must know because there were times when he needed to be summoned for an emergency.

"That's the strange thing. He has a room over the central train station. We told him it was a terrible place to live, because the racket of those trains never stops, but he said it was a decent room that leases very cheaply. Dr. Flynn helped him move in, and he says the man lives like a monk."

That did seem odd. If Trevor was so wealthy, why did he scrimp like that?

Trevor was bound to be occupied in surgery for hours, which meant she had the office to herself. She drifted back to her desk. Taking out a sheet of paper, she made a list of all the places and dates where she knew Trevor had been. She traced him through Harvard, his years of research in Germany and Paris, and then back for additional research studies in Baltimore and Philadelphia.

Where was he from 1887 to 1888? There were no newspaper clippings, no awards or diplomas. It seemed strange for him to disappear so completely from the world of medical research.

Her gaze trailed to the row of filing cabinets that covered one side of their office. She only used the last set of drawers to file patient statistics. Most of the others were stuffed with files from Trevor's earlier studies. She had no business poking through those drawers, but temptation clawed at her. All she wanted was to know if any of those files corresponded with the years she couldn't account for Trevor's whereabouts.

The drawers were organized in chronological sequence, yet not a single file dated to 1887 or 1888. The file closest to Trevor's desk was locked, with a shiny silver lock at the top that kept all the drawers fastened tight. She gave each drawer a tug just to be sure. She'd bet the shirt off her back there was something in these drawers about the missing two years.

There were more certificates and awards

on the board outside the conference room downstairs. Grabbing a pad of paper, she dashed downstairs to examine the board, looking in vain for mention of anyplace Trevor might have been during 1887–88.

There was nothing. She stared at the collection of awards and certificates. Where was he during those years?

"I've been looking for you." Trevor's voice cut through the bustle of the hallway. "You're needed upstairs. We're late in gathering data." Trevor looked exhausted, and she remembered where he had spent the last several hours.

"How did the surgery go?"

"He's alive, but infection is going to be a problem. I doubt he'll make it. What were you doing down here?"

"Snooping around into your past."

One corner of his mouth tilted up in something that looked like it wanted to become a smile. "Learn anything interesting?"

"Where were you in 1887 and 1888?"

The smile vanished. "That's really none of your business, Kate."

"India? I'm guessing you were in India."

"What makes you say that?"

"Tobias Jones mentioned the Himalayas. Your penchant for seeing your name in print let me trace where you've been for most of the last twelve years, all except those missing two years." Another thought captured her. "Maybe you were doing something terribly un-Trevor-like and were out having fun. Living with the Gypsies or exploring the romantic streets of Paris."

"Kate, you need to drop it."

"There's that charming man we all know so well. I thought you were likely to bite Tobias Jones's head off the other morning, and the man has more power in this city than the pharaohs of Egypt."

"I have no interest in licking the boots of government officials. Come on, we're late."

She wanted to point out how close he had been to alienating a potential ally, but he was already walking down the hall. How typical.

"Why can't we ever have a real conversation?" she asked as she trailed after him. "How am I supposed to know what question is going to set you off?"

"Here's an idea," he said tightly. "How about we limit our conversation to issues pertaining to tuberculosis and the treatment of our patients? Would that be a good starting point?"

"It would be if we both lacked an ounce of natural curiosity or basic human warmth." He opened the stairwell door and started clomping up the stairs. By heaven, she was getting tired of speaking to the back of his head. "Is this how they teach people to treat one another in the Himalayas? Or Scotland? Or wherever you're supposedly from?"

"I'm not listening to you, Kate." He strode into the clinic, swinging the door so hard it smacked the opposite wall. Trevor liked to run and hide at the first hint of confrontation, but she wasn't letting him escape this time. He was stalking down the hallway like a fox seeking shelter in its hole. He reached their office and tried to slam the door, but her foot blocked it.

Trevor whirled around and smacked both his hands high on the doorframe, blocking her entrance. "Go get the files to collect data," he snapped. She ducked beneath his arm and slipped into the office.

"Not until you agree to come back to my house for dinner and behave like a normal human being. One with a pulse."

A glint of amusement flickered in his eyes, and she could tell he was struggling not to smile. It was kind of fun arguing with Trevor. It always had been.

She grabbed a note card and a fountain pen from her desk. "You need to write my mother a note and politely ask to be invited back to dinner."

"Don't take offense, but I see no point in trying to win the approval of your mother. I'd have better luck wrangling with a saber-toothed tiger. If you don't go start gathering data, I'll begin searching for a more competent assistant."

"Ha! As if anyone else would put up with you. Besides, I am the best thing that ever happened to this office."

"Your modesty is a constant source of inspiration for us all," he said.

"Where were you those two years?"

"Minding my own business. A sadly lost virtue for a category of people named Kate Livingston."

It was almost two o'clock and they were badly behind schedule. As much as she wanted to keep probing, her first priority had to be the daily collection of patient data. She scooped up a handful of patient charts. "Don't think I'm letting this drop."

"I pray nightly for all manner of impossible dreams. I shall add 'you letting it drop' to the list."

She was grinning as she followed him. How come the things that used to infuriate her about Trevor now made her laugh? His prickly demeanor and fastidious grooming.

The austere bearing that hid a wickedly dry sense of humor. Had he been this funny back in school and she failed to notice?

She followed him down the hall to the men's ward, waiting while he shrugged into a fresh lab coat and clamped a stethoscope around his neck. There were a lot of things she had failed to notice about Trevor until recently. Like the way emotion simmered in his dark eyes when he was passionate about something. Like how his entire face became quietly animated as he studied a problem. There was something immensely attractive about that quiet, smoldering intelligence.

She needed to guard against the peculiar magnetism that hummed between them, because giving in to this infatuation with Trevor would be the worst sort of foolishness. He would probably brush her off the way he did all the other nurses who hankered after him, and it would be mortifying. She and Trevor had developed a real friendship, and it would be at risk the moment he sensed she had a romantic interest in him.

But she had to work alongside him every day, and it was getting harder to pretend she didn't long for more.

Trevor's habit of disappearing up to the roof most afternoons continued. He always informed Nurse Ackerman of where he would be but refused to tell Kate what he was doing up there. Honestly, Trevor was more closemouthed than a clam at low tide.

What was he doing up there? At first she thought he might be escaping to smoke a pipe, as tobacco was strictly forbidden in the tubercular wards, but he never smelled of smoke when he returned. And quite frankly she couldn't imagine anyone as fastidious as Trevor inhaling smoky air into his lungs.

One bright August day her curiosity got the better of her, and she decided to follow him. The staircase leading to the roof was so narrow, she had to gather her skirts and turn sideways as she climbed. A rickety door led to the outside. She twisted the knob slowly, careful not to make any sound as she opened the door and stepped outside.

The asphalt on the rooftop was cracked and buckled, with weeds growing in the gaps. Chimney stacks and terra cotta ventilation pipes dotted the huge space, which was almost two acres wide. The entire roof was surrounded by a low brick wall. A nice breeze tugged at her hair, smelling fresh and clean as she looked out over the treetops.

Where was Trevor? She tiptoed so as not to give herself away. Moving a little farther, she saw his boots sticking out from behind a chimney stack. Was he lying down?

She skirted more until she could see the rest of him. She gasped. He was half naked!

Trevor was lying on a full-length chaise, without a shirt and basking in the sun. He shot upright when he heard her gasp.

"What are you doing up here?" he asked.

"What am *I* doing? I'm not the one who's half naked on the roof!"

Now she knew why Trevor was no longer the pale ghost he'd been back in their school days. He was baking in the sun every day. Kate turned away, a flush heating her checks. Never in her wildest dreams had she ever wanted to see Trevor McDonough without a shirt.

He didn't seem too happy about it either. From the corner of her eye she saw him tugging his shirt on with jerky motions. "Am I needed downstairs?"

"No."

"Then why are you up here?"

"I was curious. Are you decent?"

"As much as I ever am."

She turned with caution. He was still sitting on the chaise, hastily fastening the buttons on his shirt. But the collar was still open, revealing the tanned skin on his neck and the top of his chest. A healthy flush stained his cheeks, but he didn't look angry, only a little embarrassed. She risked a jab.

"So. You really do sun yourself on a rock to generate body heat."

The glint of amusement was back. "Whenever the sun is bright. I obviously need a lot of it."

"Why?" She was genuinely intrigued. While the roof was a barren, inhospitable two acres of asphalt, the breeze was fresh and the view of the treetops soothing.

"I think there may be a medicinal value in sunlight," Trevor said. "I'm running a test."

"On yourself?"

"It wouldn't be the first time. I'm trying to refrain from eating beef but see if I can duplicate the same medicinal qualities in my blood by lying in the sun."

"Now, that is beyond foolish."

"Children with rickets can be healed by a sunlight regimen. Patients who suffer from nerve disorders also seem to benefit. I have been toying with the idea of testing it on tuberculosis."

She drew a step closer. Trevor nudged a wooden footstool toward her and gestured for her to sit. "All over the world, doctors are experimenting with sanitariums in the mountains. The idea is that the dry, clear air of the mountains may provide the proper conditions for the lungs to heal."

She sat and arranged her skirts around her as Trevor described the theory behind the mountaintop-sanitarium treatment.

"The sanitariums only accept early cases when people can still hope for a cure," Trevor continued. "You've seen the patients I care for. They are destitute. The sanitariums are expensive, and the likelihood of a cure is low, but what if . . ." Trevor leaned forward, and his voice thickened with intensity. "What if it isn't the quality of the air, but the *sunlight* that is curing them? It's a free treatment anyone in the world can afford. No need to move to another part of the country for years, no doctors or expensive sanitariums draining a family's life savings. Don't you see the possibility, Kate? The potential is too great to ignore. I have to try."

Her fingers curled along the rim of her seat. When Trevor was flushed with excitement like this, he was irresistibly attractive. She tore her gaze away to glance around the roof. "Are you thinking of testing it here?"

Trevor stood, excitement gleaming on his face. "Follow me, and I'll show you what I'm planning."

Turrets on either side of the hospital

bracketed the space, with two acres of flat asphalt stretched between. He pointed to the far side of the roof. "I want to re-pave that area with tile for the wheelchairs. Something will need to be done for the drainage, but I'll hire an architect for that. The biggest challenge will be constructing an elevator to get the patients up here."

Kate walked to the chest-high wall surrounding the roof. From this vantage point she could see all the way to the US Capitol. How clean the city looked from up here. She closed her eyes to savor the cool breeze on her face. It was soothing merely being up here.

"Do you think it's an insane idea?" Trevor asked. The caution in his voice startled her. He was actually holding his breath as he awaited her answer.

"It's nice up here," she said. "I expect the patients will like it as well."

Trevor moved to stand beside her, bracing his hands on the wall and gazing out toward the horizon. "You have no idea how badly I want to find a cure. Sometimes I snap awake in the middle of the night with ideas. Theories. Prayers." Longing was carved into every line of his face.

"When I first started researching this disease, it was a time of such hope. Dr. Brehmer had just discovered how to isolate the tuberculosis cell. After hundreds of years of speculation, we *finally* knew how it spread. Everyone was convinced we were on the cusp of finding the cure. I woke up each morning with such hope, I couldn't wait to run to the laboratory. Literally run. I thought if I wanted something badly enough, worked and prayed hard enough, it was bound to come true. I would pay any price. Make any sacrifice."

Trevor's hands clenched the brick wall so hard his knuckles went white. He dipped his head, and his voice grew soft. "When I was finishing my studies at Harvard, the janitor who cleaned the laboratories came to me and begged for help. He had two children he believed had consumption, but no money for a doctor. I agreed to treat them for free. The look on that man's face . . ."

Anguish clogged Trevor's voice, and he swallowed hard. "It was the first time anyone ever looked at me with that terrible combination of hope and desperation. He was frantic to save his children, and I was convinced I could do it. I thought . . ." His voice trailed off. The hope on his face drained away and he shook his head.

"What happened?" she asked.

He drew a breath to speak, but then must have thought better of it because he turned and headed for the doorway leading downstairs. "Forget it. It doesn't matter."

She grabbed his elbow to stop him from reaching to door. "Trevor, what happened?"

She wasn't certain why it was so necessary that she know what happened all those years ago, but Trevor was becoming very important to her, and she was desperate to understand him better. When he tried to pull away from her, she tightened her grip.

"Tell me," she said. "Please, I need to understand."

At last, he conceded and turned to brace his hands atop the wall, staring out over the treetops.

"They were twins," he finally said, as though the words had to be dragged from him. "They were only twelve years old . . . Jack and Amy Collison. Everything about their home was designed to foster tuberculosis. The whole family shared the same sleeping room, with the windows closed because they thought the night air was dangerous. Jack and Amy showed immediate improvement as soon as I got their father to keep the windows open and improve their diet. After that, everyone in the family looked at me like I was a savior. I let myself become close to them. I celebrated their thirteenth birthday with the family. I went to Sunday services with them. Jack's wildest dream was to climb to the top of Jay Peak in the Green Mountains, and I promised that when he could blow into a spirometer long enough to keep a ball suspended in the chamber for twenty seconds, I would take them. I worked so hard to get them both healthy. Jack practiced blowing into that stupid device for months, but it worked. His lungs got stronger, and I knew if they could climb to the top of that mountain, there was nothing that could stop us."

Once Trevor began talking, the story began flowing out of him, as if the memories had been bottled up for so long that they could no longer be contained. His face took on a faraway look, and it was easy to get caught up in the elation that lay just beneath his words.

"You can't imagine what that day was like," he said. "Jack was grinning the whole way up the mountain. When Amy grew tired, I carried her on my back. We kept climbing, and when we got to the crest of the mountain . . . sometimes in life you know when you're in a perfect moment, and that was one of them. When we got there, the air was sweet and clean. The wind, the sky, the sheer exhilaration . . . I felt that if I reached my hand out, I could touch God himself. It was *that* pure. As long as I live, I will remember that moment of blinding joy. I felt a calling and knew what I was destined to do with the rest of my life. I broke down and wept. So did Jack and Amy. I clung to those children and *knew* I would cure them. The whole world spread out below us, and I vowed to find a cure for tuberculosis or die trying. I wanted it too badly to fail."

His voice began to quiver. "Of course, I *did* fail. It almost destroyed me when Amy died, and then Jack less than a year later. I loved every member of that family, but I won't ever make that mistake again. My spirit almost broke, and I had to learn different ways of working with patients."

He turned to face her. "I know the people at the hospital think I'm cold. I know using patient numbers seems heartless, but I won't be able to last in this job if I do it any other way. You can't imagine the misery I've seen. I'm human. I feel. And it hurts every time I lose a patient."

The exhaustion in his voice was staggering. He looked beaten and drained as he braced himself against the wall. "Dreams are hard," he said. "You work toward them, struggle and sacrifice, but that doesn't

163

always mean you will get there. I used to believe if I wanted something badly enough, I was destined to win it so long as I never gave up trying. Now I'm not so sure. I don't know if I'll be able to cure this disease, and I don't know how to handle that."

There was a hollow look in his eyes, and Kate ached to reach out and hold him, but he hadn't stopped talking.

"Most people with this disease are too poor to afford a sanitarium, but if they can be treated with sunlight? I've got to try, Kate. I know whoever dares to suggest sunlight might be a cure is opening himself up to ridicule." His face darkened, and she knew he was remembering the scathing articles in the *Washington Post*. "They'll probably call me a quack, a charlatan."

"Nobody who knows you thinks that," she said.

A look of surprise crossed his face. Strange, but before this afternoon, she never realized how much her opinion mattered to Trevor. He shook off the fog of old memories, and excitement flushed his face. "I've already had an architect make a preliminary draft for the renovation," Trevor said. "Come on, let me show you."

She followed him downstairs. The tubercular ward seemed dim after the splendor

164

on the rooftop, but his excitement was infectious. While Trevor fetched the architectural plans, Kate went to his desk to clear some space. Her eye was caught by a simple note in the center of his desk.

I remember.

Those were the only two words on the note. *I remember.* Before she could process what the strange note meant, Trevor arrived with the plans, beaming with suppressed excitement until he saw the note.

"What's this?" he asked and picked up the two-word note.

"I have no idea." They were going to need space and light to see the plans properly. She was about to move his pencil cup aside when little silver balls strewn across his desk caught her eye. She squinted. Sunlight glinted on their surface, perfectly round little globs not much bigger than kernels of corn. She reached out to touch one and it jiggled, quivering in the sun, even after she took her finger away.

Trevor dropped the papers and sucked in a fierce breath.

"Don't touch it!" he shouted. His arm cut into her middle as he hauled her backward, then dragged her out of the office and toward the nurses' station. He plunged her hand into a pitcher of water.

"What are you doing?" she gasped. The water was freezing, and it hurt.

He dragged her hand out and scrubbed it with a handkerchief in rough, painful swipes. He threw the handkerchief on the floor. "Dump out that water and throw the pitcher away," he said to Nurse Ackerman. "Throw out the handkerchief as well, but be careful. Don't let it get on your skin."

He went back into his office, Kate close behind. Trevor stared at the trembling little globs of silver, horror on his face.

"What are they?" she asked.

"Mercury." He swallowed hard, then grabbed a pencil and nudged one of the silver balls. It wobbled and merged with another, making a larger glob of shimmering silver.

The mercury was all over his desk, his chair, scattered around the floor. She glanced around the room. Her desk was clean, as was the rest of the office.

"Let's get out of here." Trevor's hand clamped around her arm and propelled her out of the office.

He rapped out a series of questions to Nurse Ackerman. Had she seen anyone in his office today? Was there any sign of a break-in? The nurse didn't see anyone suspicious, but four attendants had delivered the meals, and an orderly took a patient downstairs for a dental treatment. The mail clerk had been here, and a janitor and plumber to tighten some pipes.

"We need to get security in the ward," Trevor said. He dragged a hand though his hair. "I'll pay to have a guard here around the clock."

Kate didn't know much about mercury, but it must be dangerous because Trevor was flustered, and it took a lot to fluster Trevor. Sweat beaded up on his forehead, and he was struggling to control his breathing.

"I can help you clean it up," she whispered.

"No," he said brusquely. "I know how to handle mercury and will be the only one to clean it up. I'm going downstairs to arrange for a security guard, but no one is to go into my office. You may as well go home. I don't want you back in the office today."

After Trevor dismissed her, Kate waited on the steps of the hospital, playing with the mangy dog she'd named Princess. Though a homely creature, the mutt was sweet tempered, and Kate slipped the dog a piece of her lunch every day.

She was glad for the dog's company,

because quite frankly she was frightened. She didn't understand how serious this was until she saw how the hospital staff reacted to news of the mercury splashed across Trevor's desk. Guards were positioned at the front and rear doors of the clinic. Two police officers arrived to interview the staff. Kate stopped by the medical reading room and learned that mercury was a toxic element that could be dangerous even from touching. It was probably her imagination, but the tip of her finger where she'd touched one of the silver globs seemed to tingle.

She would tolerate no more of Trevor's evasiveness. He wasn't leaving the building without telling her what had sparked this rash of bad publicity. And he surely knew whoever wrote the chilling note, *I remember.*

She hugged the dog. "You need a bath, Princess," she whispered. Maybe she would take the dog home for a quick scrub. Her parents forbade pets in the boardinghouse, so it would have to be done quickly.

"Please tell me you haven't been feeding that dog again." Trevor stood on the step above her. There were shadows under his eyes, and for the first time she noticed lines on his face. He must be exhausted.

"Trevor, I need to know what's going on."

He darted down the stairs without looking at her. "This doesn't concern you."

"It most certainly does." His long legs devoured space, and she had to run to keep up with him. "The book I consulted says mercury is a poison, and someone dumped it all over *our* office." The sun was beginning to slip behind the trees, casting long shadows. It was a warm August evening, but she still felt chilly.

"They're mad at me, not you."

"Who's doing this?"

A muscle worked in his jaw, yet he kept striding forward, his eyes angry. "I don't know."

"But you do know *why.*"

He didn't deny it. The sidewalk was dense with pedestrians, and Trevor wasn't about to spill his secrets out in the open. Trying to keep up with him was like swimming upstream, angling around a paper boy and a vendor pushing a coffee cart.

A churchyard and cemetery was on their right, bordered by a low brick wall. As they passed the gate, she grabbed Trevor's arm and steered him inside. He didn't resist, but his glower could scorch her skin.

"Why is this happening, Trevor? I can't help unless I know."

His fists were clenched. Scanning the churchyard, he nodded to a bench in the

169

corner. "We won't be overheard in the far side of the yard."

They moved to a stone bench in the corner, where it was cool under a couple of shade trees. The cold of the bench penetrated through her skirts. Anxiety made her hands clammy, and she blew on them to generate some warmth.

"Five years ago I conducted a study using mercury to treat tuberculosis," Trevor began. "It was not a success."

She gasped and dropped her hands. "Mercury? But mercury is a —"

"Poison. Yes, I know. It's also been proven to be highly effective in treating certain diseases, and in a test tube it kills tuberculosis. It was effective in rabbits as well."

So many of the treatments for tuberculosis were barbaric, but Trevor never endorsed any of them. At least until today, when she heard about the mercury.

He went on to explain that he'd prepared a mercury solution that was then injected beneath the skin, where it would slowly leach into the patient's system. While his patients showed an immediate decline in their levels of bacillus, all six of them died anyway.

"Mercury poisoning is not an easy way to die," he said. "It attacks the central nervous system, and patients lose control of their limbs. They shake uncontrollably. And their vision and hearing shut down."

The anguish in his voice shredded her. He struggled to control his breathing as he continued, "The patients were terminally ill and knew the risks, but they were willing to take a chance. I thought it might be a real cure. Not a treatment, a *cure.* Other doctors had tried it and reported improvement, but no one had been cured yet. I was determined to find the right dosage that would kill the disease but not the patient. I had to guess, and I guessed wrong."

Never had she seen a person so badly in need of comfort, but she feared Trevor would fling her away if she tried.

Let him try, for she wasn't running away. She laid a hand on his shoulder. He was trembling but didn't let it show. It made her ache how tightly contained he was, even as he was in misery.

"You can't blame yourself for this. You didn't know," she whispered.

He straightened and took a deep breath. "Yes, well. Someone clearly remembers and wants to be sure I'm unable to continue working in this field."

"Perhaps a family member of one of the patients?"

He nodded. "It seems the logical place to start looking. In the meantime, I need to hire guards for around-the-clock security at the clinic."

"Can't the hospital provide that?"

"The superintendent won't pay for it. I hate to squander research dollars on it, but I can't afford another disaster."

This was typical Trevor, refusing to reach out for help. "The marines provide guard services at all the navy hospitals. My little brother guards the office of the surgeon general. Since you're conducting this study at the behest of the surgeon general, I expect the military might provide security."

For the first time, Trevor perked up. "They would do that?"

"It couldn't hurt to ask. Wait . . . *I'll* ask. I don't want you making a hash out of this."

A ghost of a smile hovered on his mouth. "Are you suggesting you're better at dealing with people than I am?"

She stood and shook out her skirt. "Trevor, on any given day you might beat me in trigonometry. Or chemistry. Or a footrace. On very rare occasions you will beat me in a spelling contest. But you will never, not even on your best day, beat me in the category of basic human warmth."

Amusement lurked in his dark eyes.

"You're probably right." He stood and, to her great surprise, took her hand and kissed the back of it. "Thanks, Kate."

Then he let go of her hand and sauntered off in that long-legged stride of his. The spot where his lips had touched her hand tingled during the entire walk home.

9

Getting away from the hospital was always tricky, but Trevor got another doctor to take patient samples for the next few days while he braced himself to reopen old wounds. The ache of regret churned through him as he stared out the window of the rumbling train on his way to Baltimore.

The Baltimore study was the worst catastrophe of his career. No one in the medical field blamed him for what happened. After all, the careful administration of toxic substances had proven the most effective form of treatment for many of the world's most virulent diseases. When it worked, the public rejoiced and hailed the miracles of modern science. But sometimes experiments failed, and the mercury study was a torment he'd carry for the rest of his life. He dutifully published the results in the medical literature and then hoped to close the book on it for the rest of his life.

I remember.

Whoever wrote that note and spilled the mercury in his office wanted to make it impossible for him to forget. His old hospital was the first place to start looking. Maybe Trevor had never been good at making friends, but he was a master at reading emotions. He was on the hunt for someone who had difficulty meeting his eyes, whose muscles stiffened when they saw him, or who acted unnaturally bright.

The familiar scents of carbolic acid and floor wax greeted him as he stepped into the hospital. The nurses and orderlies seemed surprised but welcoming when they saw him. Even the doctors gathered in the staff area were cordial, inviting him to stay for a lunch.

A handful of his former associates were no longer here. Henry Harris had followed him to serve as his lab assistant in Washington. His data analyst, Andrew Doyle, had gone on to medical school at Harvard. One of his nurses married and moved to Ohio. All the others who assisted in the study were still here and seemed to welcome his visit. He merely smiled faintly in return, his spirits sinking lower as the day wore on.

The trip to the hospital was disappointing, as the next days were going to rip open every old wound as he visited the family members of the six people who'd died in the Baltimore study.

The meeting with Michael McCusker's family was typical. The family still lived in a badly ventilated two-room apartment over a tanning factory. Mrs. McCusker had been left with four children when her husband died, and she began weeping when she saw him.

"The Lord was ready for him," she said as she brought Trevor a glass of cool tea to the table. The glass didn't look too clean, and from the look of the teenaged daughter who was tatting lace in the corner, at least one of the McCusker children had an active case of tuberculosis. Trevor casually rolled the glass between his fingers rather than risk a drink.

"Can you wait until my youngest gets back from school? He was just a tyke when you met him before, and I want to show him off to you."

Looking into the face of Mike McCusker's widow was torture, and every impulse in him wanted to flee, but he owed it to the woman. He spent the next hour listening to her son recite poetry, then helped her repair the leaky pipe beneath her kitchen sink.

He learned two things from the meeting.

Two of the children in the McCusker household already had tuberculosis and didn't know it, and they bore him no ill will for what happened five years ago.

Meetings with the other families were also fruitless. If any of these people resented him, he hadn't been able to spot it. His failure to identify a suspect meant he would need to hire a private investigator before returning home. Washington was an easy train ride from Baltimore, and if anyone associated with his old research study was making regular trips to the city, Trevor needed to know. It was going to cost a fortune to hire someone to monitor the situation, but what else could he do?

It was ridiculous how much pride Kate felt after securing guard coverage for the clinic. On Tick's advice she made an appointment to speak with the commanding officer at the Marine Barracks. She pointed out that Trevor had been recruited by the surgeon general to lead the study, and the government surely had an interest in ensuring the integrity of the research. The commanding officer agreed to provide coverage for three eight-hour shifts per day until the situation was resolved.

She couldn't wait to tell Trevor. He'd been

gone for three days now, and she was counting the hours until he got back so she could share the good news. Something about the way he took her hand and pressed a kiss on the back of it had captured her imagination. In a good way. It was such an affectionate, gallant thing to do.

It was getting harder not to think about Trevor. Maybe she'd been starved of affection for too long, but every time he stepped within her line of vision, her heart sped up. Those dark good looks, the fierce intelligence, the humor that lurked just beneath the surface. She loved working alongside him. He respected her and gave her the best job imaginable. Maybe that was why she was so eager to help him by securing the guard for the hospital.

She was delighted when the marines assigned Tick to serve as one of the guards. Five days a week he would stand guard at the tubercular ward from four o'clock in the morning until noon.

"Be sure to wear your mask if you're ever near the patients," she cautioned him. "I'll never forgive myself if you get infected with this disease."

"Stop mothering me, Kate," he said as he took his position near the back door. "I understood Nurse Ackerman's instructions perfectly well, and you don't need to breathe down my neck."

She winced a little. "Yes, of course," she murmured before heading back to the office. Tick was two inches taller than she, with wide shoulders, a strong back, and sandy-blond hair that had been trimmed to military precision. He wore his light brown field uniform with a pressed shirt and tie. He looked like a man to the outside world, but she still saw traces of the towheaded toddler who followed her around the boardinghouse, always begging for a hug.

Nurse Ackerman knocked on the door, a newspaper in her hand. "Another article for Dr. Kendall to see when he returns," she said.

Kate wanted to snatch the newspaper from the nurse's hands and rip it to shreds. Did Nurse Ackerman really need to keep tormenting him with every single article? Trevor already knew he had a problem and was doing everything to root it out. Kate pinched the skin between her eyes.

"I'll make sure he sees it," she said wearily. Nurse Ackerman was only following Trevor's orders, but this bombardment in the press was awful.

Just knowing the guards were here was reassuring, because the threat was no longer just hostile articles in the newspaper. Someone had infiltrated her office and splashed mercury on Trevor's desk. Dozens of people walked in and out of the wards each day, and Kate hated the feeling of suspicion that seized her each time an unfamiliar face entered the clinic. Even with Tick and the other marines standing guard, Kate couldn't shake the crawling suspicion that someone was watching her.

It wasn't safe here.

Trevor rode back into Washington on the morning train, bracing himself for the accumulation of work after a three-day absence. The backlog at the hospital would be bad, but more than anything, he dreaded what he might find at home.

The situation was far worse than anyone knew. The newspaper articles were distressing enough, but they paled in comparison to the vile letters he received at home. Always anonymous, always seething with rage.

He was tired and grubby from the three days in Baltimore, and he needed to stop off at home for a change of clothing before heading to the hospital. He battled a sense of unease as he climbed the staircase to the boarding rooms over the railway station.

The rooms were cheap, as few people wanted to live above the racket of a train station, but Trevor had always been good at sectioning off his mind to ignore distractions. Besides, his inborn sense of Scottish thrift saw this inexpensive room as perfectly fine for his modest needs.

The row of brass mail compartments gleamed at the end of the dimly lit hall. He clenched the mail key as he approached his box and drew a steadying breath. The hate-filled letters usually arrived weekly, and he was overdue.

He unlocked the small compartment and leaned down to pull out two medical journals and a single letter. He held his breath as he looked at the letter, relief flooding him as soon as he recognized the handwriting.

It appeared his father might finally be offering a tiny concession. The mighty Neill McDonough had acknowledged Trevor's new name on the envelope.

Perhaps it was petty to have returned all the previous letters addressed to Trevor McDonough. He wasn't interested in anything his father had to say and had simply scrawled *No such person at this address* on the dozens of letters he'd received over the years. They were sent unopened back to Scotland.

This letter was addressed to Trevor Mc-
Donough, care of Dr. T. M. Kendall.

Trevor tucked the medical journals and
the envelope under his arm as he strolled to
the end of the hall and let himself into his
room. The only furniture was a bed pushed
against a wall, a chest of drawers, and a
table weighed down with stacks of medical
journals. A washroom at the other end of
the hall was shared by all the tenants, and
there was no need for a kitchen. He took all
his meals at the hospital.

He tossed the journals on the table and
carried the letter with him as he plopped on
the bed. Should he open it? He stared out
the window overlooking the railroad tracks,
an oncoming train rumbling this way. By
the time the train arrived, he would make
his decision.

There was nothing left for him in Scotland. Opening this letter would stir a flood
of painful memories, and he didn't trust
anything his father had to say.

The train drew closer, reverberating with
a wall of expanding noise as the engine car
barreled down the tracks. He could return
this letter like all the others and let his
father know he intended to abide by the
horrible bargain they struck when he was
only thirteen years old.

Or he could forgive his father.

He gave a bitter laugh. His father didn't want to be forgiven; he probably only wanted to draw Trevor back into some scheme of self-aggrandizement.

The window glass rattled as the train came to a halt at the station, its brakes shrieking, steam escaping the boilers. It was time to make his decision.

He opened the letter.

His father's firm handwriting filled two sides of a single page of linen paper embossed with the McDonough coat of arms. But it was the photograph that caught his attention. It showed three children standing beside their parents. A man with a heavy mustache, and the woman with . . .

He closed his eyes, never imagining his father could be quite this cruel.

It was Deirdre. The last time he saw her, they were both thirteen years old. He knew she had married, of course. And he was glad for her. What kind of jealous, bitter man would he be if he had wished spinsterhood on a girl he once adored?

"Please don't leave," Deirdre wept as she clung to him. "I'll love you forever. I'll wait forever!"

She had waited four years, and then she married a wool merchant from the village.

He hadn't thought of Deirdre in years. As much as it hurt when he left home, their relationship had been little more than two lonely children who found each other on the windswept moors and dreamed about the possibility of escape. He was glad it appeared Deirdre finally did escape.

He carried the picture to the window, tilting it to see the image better. A rush of satisfaction surged through him at the sight of all those healthy children. They had shoes made of good leather, no scuffs. Deirdre wore a lace collar and a pearl brooch pinned to her bodice. She looked very prosperous for the daughter of a sheepherder. She looked happy.

Good. The wool merchant was a fine provider and gave her things Trevor could never have afforded had he remained in Scotland. That first year away from Deirdre had been hard, but over the years the ache had eased.

Now he dreamed of a very different sort of woman. Not so much a girl to ease his loneliness, but a woman of fire. One who was a challenge. A joy.

He had always liked Kate. Back in school, he loved competing with her, even though she was too enraptured with Nathan Livingston for Trevor to harbor any foolish romantic fantasies. Nathan was perfect for Kate. The two of them were always laughing. Cheerful. People flocked around them because their sunny disposition seemed contagious.

Nathan was dead now, but that didn't mean Trevor was free to start yearning after Kate. She was so far out of his reach, she may as well live in the stratosphere. And if she knew all his secrets, she'd probably run screaming for the hills.

He pushed the thought away and picked up his father's letter, propping his hip on the windowsill to catch the weak light filtering through the overcast sky. His eyes widened as he read.

Well, well, well.

It appeared even the all-powerful Neill McDonough couldn't control the world. Trevor tossed the letter in the trash can and shook his head in disbelief. He would never allow himself to be drawn back into his father's glittering world. When he was thirteen he came to an agreement with his father, one that still carried the taint of shame and betrayal. They had struck a bargain, and Trevor had no intention of letting his father back out of it now.

How could a wound still feel so raw after all these years? With clinical detachment he locked the memories away and left in the direction of the hospital. He had three days of accumulated work to tackle, but all he could see when he walked into the clinic was a huge vase of lemon-yellow begonias dominating the nurses' station. He had no doubt who'd brought them in.

"Kate, get those flowers off the counter," he barked. "They're dust collectors and are sucking up the oxygen."

Kate leapt up from where she was finishing her lunch at the staff table. "Every window on this floor is open and we're flooded with fresh air. These flowers are bringing a little bit of sunshine into a sadly grim environment."

Trevor glared at the flowers hard enough for them to wilt, but Kate probably had a point. She was good at thinking of little things to make life better for the patients.

"I want them out the instant they start attracting vermin."

"The only thing that might attract vermin is the rancid expression on your face," she said. "I was having a brilliant morning until you came in to sour the air."

"Ah, well. We are born to suffer." He fought to keep the laughter from his voice. The trip to Baltimore had been a failure. He had a headache from the clattering train and was no closer to figuring out who was trying to destroy him. But within seconds of being in Kate's company, his mood had brightened. How could she have this effect on him? He'd want to shake her if he didn't like her so much.

And that was a problem. He was coming to like Kate Livingston far too much.

"I thought you might like to know I secured the services of the marines to guard the clinic," she said casually, gesturing to a uniformed soldier standing guard at the rear entrance. "They've already begun their rotation."

Trevor nearly choked. He'd forgotten Kate's boast about obtaining coverage from the government, but the marine guarding the rear entrance proved the truth of her words. Without thinking, he scooped her into a bear hug. "You're a miracle worker."

She was grinning as she disengaged herself from him. "I won't let you forget you said that, but it would be best if you didn't manhandle me in front of my brother. Private Norton covers the early shift, and he's very protective of me."

Trevor glanced at the young man with sandy hair and smiling blue eyes. The soldier placed his hand on his service revolver. "I'll probably have to challenge you to a duel if you touch my sister again." He cleared his throat and resumed his military stance. "Sir."

Trevor turned back to Kate. Ever since they were thirteen she had been surprising him with her cleverness and determination.

"Thanks, Kate," he said casually before heading to his office. "One of these days I'll remember to quit underestimating you."

Because quite frankly he needed all the help he could get in tracking down the low-life rat trying to destroy him. When Trevor was a boy, he helped round up the lambs on the neighboring farm every spring. It always seemed those lambs knew they were targeted for slaughter. He felt like one of those lambs now — knowing something bad was looming on the horizon but unable to find the source of the danger.

10

A storm had been brewing for days, burying the city beneath a blanket of steel-gray clouds. Several times this morning, pinpricks of rain spattered against the windows, although now it was turning into a healthy downpour.

Kate propped her hip against Trevor's empty desk, mesmerized by the droplets of rain as they rolled and fell from the waxy leaves of the maple tree outside the window. Anything to get her mind off what was happening to Trevor. He hadn't told her where he was going this morning, but she'd seen the appointment with a lawyer on his office calendar. It surely had something to do with the continuing harassment in the newspapers.

The details reported in the papers were eerily accurate. Kate burrowed deeper into her shawl, the dank chill penetrating the fabric. It felt like someone was watching their every move, but the faceless tormentor remained in the shadows, just out of sight.

There was a quick knock on her open door. "The attendants are bringing lunch in, ma'am."

"Thank you, Private Norton," she said, then winked at him for good measure.

While Tick maintained a military demeanor during the hours he was on duty at the hospital, he made fast friends with Henry Harris, their bullnecked laboratory assistant. Henry shared Tick's passion for football and also joined them at the staff table for meals. The attendants delivered covered trays for the staff, and it felt odd to have a meal served to her for a change. Kate waited while Bridget Kelly, the Irish attendant, set down trays of beef stew and warm rolls.

Henry eyed Bridget as she wheeled the empty cart out of the room. Never had she seen such a hungry look on a man's face. It would be a relief if Bridget took a fancy to Henry, anything to stop the girl from flirting with Trevor.

"She's very pretty," Kate said as she slathered butter on a roll.

Henry's face flushed bright red. "As if she could ever tear her eyes off Dr. Kendall long enough to notice a man like me. I'm as wide

190

as I am tall. If any of the nurses ever looked at me and giggled the way they do for Dr. Kendall, I'd worry my trousers weren't buttoned properly."

"Miss Kelly?" Tick asked. "I think she's very nice. She tries to tease me when she wheels in the breakfast carts. Every morning she comes right up to my face and says 'boo!' but I always keep looking straight ahead. Except for this morning. I looked at her and said 'boo' back. She nearly jumped out of her shoes. I can see why you would fancy her."

Henry seemed as sullen as the low rumbles of thunder outside the window. He didn't look up as he pushed food around on his plate with a fork. "This sort of thing happens all the time in hospitals. We work long hours. I never see anyone except for the ladies here."

A heavy crash of thunder shook the windows and caused the lights to flicker. Kate held her breath, but after a moment the flickering stopped and the warm illumination filled the room again.

Henry motioned them closer and said in a low voice, "At least I never fell in love with a patient. One of the lab assistants in Baltimore fell in love with a young lady who died of tuberculosis. Dr. Kendall was grooming him to go into medical school, but Andrew Doyle fell in love with a patient and wouldn't leave her side. It was horrible. Rose, I think her name was. She got weaker and weaker, and I thought Andrew was going to follow her into the grave."

Kate remembered the feeling. How many months had she lived in a fog after Nathan died? It had only been within the last year that she could listen to fiddle music without dissolving into tears. She glanced at Nurse Ackerman, wincing at the way the older woman played with the two wedding rings hanging from a chain around her neck. Nurse Ackerman had been widowed twice and surely knew better than any of them the pain of loss.

Tick seemed unaware of the woman's distress. "What happened to Mr. Doyle?" he asked.

"Oh, the girl died, and Dr. Kendall finally nudged Andrew into medical school. Harvard, I think."

Nurse Ackerman pushed away from the table. "If Dr. Kendall finds you gossiping like a passel of magpies, he'll have you all fired."

The storm was finally unleashing, with steady rivulets of water running down the windowpanes. It seemed to get chillier as damp air penetrated the walls. A white flash of lightning lit up the sky, followed by another crash of thunder directly overhead.

The room was plunged into darkness, with only the silhouettes of her companions visible. Kate made her way to the bow window in the turret alcove, bracing her hands on the ledge of a bookshelf as she looked outside.

Strange, the lights on the other floors of the hospital were still on.

"Kate, go check on the women's ward," Nurse Ackerman said. "I'll check to make sure the men are all right. Henry, go downstairs and see what can be done about restoring the lights."

Walking slowly, Kate went to the female ward, hearing the clatter of metal trays as the women fumbled in the darkness. With their wall of windows facing west, it was even darker here.

"Is everyone okay?" Kate asked.

"Margaret flinched with that last clap of thunder," someone replied. "Her tray's all over the floor."

By the time Kate got the patients settled and the spilled tray cleaned up, the storm's ferocity had eased. There was no sign of Henry or Tick, but a glance out the window showed the other hospital floors still illuminated. It seemed they were the only floor to have lost electricity.

Tick's face was grim when he entered the ward ten minutes later. "Someone has tampered with the electrical wires," he said.

Trevor was stunned when he returned from his meeting with his lawyer to be greeted by a clinic lit with kerosene lanterns and no electricity. An electrical expert was already on hand to inspect the wiring.

"Looks like you've got rats," the electrician said, squatting near the place where the fifth floor's wiring originated. Sure enough, the layer of cotton-braided insulation had been gnawed through, exposing the bare wire and making it vulnerable. The cotton was coated with paraffin, which might be attractive to rats, but there had never been any sign of rodents on this floor.

"The exposed wires must have picked up the extra charge in the air from the lightning and overwhelmed the circuit. I won't touch it until the storm's fully passed."

This was going to cost a sizable amount to repair, and it would provide more fuel for Superintendent Lambrecht's hostility toward the clinic. Trevor shook his head. Maybe rats destroyed the wiring, but more than likely it was whoever was trying to ruin him.

"How long ago did the damage to the insulation occur?"

"Hard to say," the electrician replied. "It could've been last year, could've been last night."

Trevor changed the lock on the clinic's door two weeks ago, and during that time there had been no more suspicious activity inside the clinic. In all likelihood, the sabotage to the wires occurred before he changed the locks, and it took the storm to trigger the electrical failure.

What kind of fool tampered with electricity? Did someone hate him enough to risk electrocution just to damage Trevor's reputation? Then again, maybe Trevor was growing paranoid and this was only a simple infestation of rats.

No. He didn't believe it for a second. His enemy was growing craftier by the day, evidenced by the envelope that arrived in his mail two days ago. The envelope was stuffed with clippings from medical journals. The articles had yellowed with age but were all on the same topic: doctors who'd been censured, reprimanded, or had their licenses to practice medicine revoked. Two of the doctors had eventually been convicted of manslaughter and sent to prison.

It was those articles that had prompted Trevor to hire a lawyer. He hated squandering funds on legal fees, but he had no choice. It was now obvious that his enemy wanted to destroy Trevor's medical career and see him sent to prison for what happened in Baltimore.

As expected, Lambrecht used what happened with the electrical wiring to try to evict Trevor from the hospital.

"Rats?" the superintendent sputtered. "If word of *rats* in this hospital gets into the press, we won't have another paying customer for the next decade. I want you *out.* I don't care that you have the support of the surgeon general. Nowhere in our agreement did I consent to having my building infested and destroyed. I'm beginning eviction procedures immediately."

Which required another visit to Trevor's lawyer. This time, though, he brought Tick Norton to the meeting. Kate's younger brother had keen insight, and Trevor wanted one of the marine guards brought into the loop about the details of the investigation.

Wearing his fatigues and an awestruck expression, Tick looked around the attorney's ornate office in wonder. "Do lawyers really make this kind of money?" he whispered.

"*Other* people make this kind of money. Lawyers are just good at figuring out how to siphon a piece of it their way."

Sometimes it was hard to remember that Tick was only eighteen and had never set foot outside of Washington. With his strong frame and quick mind, Tick seemed far more mature, but his look of wide-eyed innocence as he gaped at the office reminded Trevor of a scrawny lad from Scotland who'd once been equally dazzled a long time ago.

His lawyer, Edward Frontera, entered the office. With horn-rimmed glasses that matched his jet-black hair, Mr. Frontera plopped a file down on the conference table.

"Well?" Trevor demanded.

"The contract the hospital signed with the surgeon general is airtight. They can't boot you out without the surgeon general's consent."

"And they won't get that," Trevor asserted.

"Unless your license to practice medicine is revoked. If you lose your license, the contract is rendered null and void."

Trevor had already begun a battle plan to protect his medical license. An attempt to revoke his license would take months and was not his immediate concern. The eviction could happen at the end of the month, less than three weeks away, and his research would be scuttled in midstream. While the lawyer outlined the various ways the hospital administration could attack him, Tick picked up a stack of the anonymous letters and flipped through them. All of the hostile letters had been turned over to his lawyer for safekeeping. Trevor clenched his fists. It was mortifying to have a young man he respected read such slander.

"I don't think whoever sent these letters lives in Baltimore," Tick said as he held a note aloft. "This paper was purchased at Steigler's shop on Twenty-Third Street. You can see the watermark when you hold it to the light."

Trevor rocked back in his chair, stunned by his own stupidity. He'd blindly assumed his tormentor hailed from Baltimore since it was apparent the mercury study had been the catalyst of this mess. Washington was such a quick trip from Baltimore by train, and he'd assumed that whoever was behind this was slipping into town to do his dirty work, then disappearing back home an hour later.

"If the culprit is someone who lives in

Washington, your lab assistant is the most likely suspect," his lawyer said. "Does Mr. Harris have any reason to hold a grudge against you?"

"Henry Harris gets steaming mad every time Harvard beats Princeton in football," Trevor said. "Aside from that, he's the most placid person I know."

Tick shifted in his chair, looking a little seasick. "I think he's jealous of you. There's a girl who serves meals. Bridget Kelly, the Irish girl. He likes her, but he thinks she's got her cap set on you."

Trevor had to consider the possibility that this had nothing to do with the disastrous mercury study, and if anyone could manufacture a convincing false lead pointing to the Baltimore study, it would be Henry Harris. Henry was beside him through every month of that ill-fated study.

"Men can do foolish things when a woman is in the equation," Mr. Frontera said.

Trevor fiddled with a pencil, twirling it as he thought. "Keep an eye on him," he said to Tick. "I don't think Henry has anything to do with this, but I can't afford to overlook him."

Mr. Frontera made note of Henry's name. "Is there anyone else who would like to see you driven out of business?"

If Trevor widened the circle of suspects to people outside of the Baltimore study, he needed to include his father. It was revolting to even consider the possibility, but this wouldn't be the first time the almighty Neill McDonough played dirty to get what he wanted.

"My father would like me to quit medicine," he said reluctantly.

If his lawyer was surprised, he carefully concealed it. "And does your father live in the area?"

"He lives in Scotland but travels to Washington often. I received a letter this week that indicates he's been in America within the past few months."

He felt guilty adding his father's name to the list of possible suspects, but it had to be done. His father couldn't have gleaned enough inside information about the mercury study to mastermind this campaign of vilification, but money could buy a lot. His father was determined to get Trevor back to Scotland, and Neill McDonough rarely failed at anything he put his hand to. A few thousand dollars placed in the right hands could buy all manner of bad publicity or the revelation of old secrets.

And Trevor had firsthand experience of

how cold his father could be when on a mission.

11

In the coming weeks, Kate found a haven from the hostile forces weighing on Trevor by escaping with him up to the roof of the hospital.

Those stolen hours were always the best part of her day. They never spoke of the mercury or the ongoing harassment. The roof was a sanctuary, where they spent hours talking of nothing more important than novels or local gossip. She loved those halcyon hours basking in the sun, even if Trevor's idea about sunlight as a medical cure was probably pure nonsense.

One early September afternoon she perched on a stool and challenged him about his theory.

"People have been living beneath the sun for thousands of years," she said. "If the sun has therapeutic value, why are we still getting sick from a multitude of diseases?"

Trevor lay sprawled on the lounge, his

shirt hanging open and his eyes closed as he listened. He gave a wry grin at her comment, then turned his head to lock gazes with her. His confident gleam gave warning that she was about to be eviscerated by a brilliant counterargument.

To her surprise, he said nothing as he propped himself on an elbow. His dark eyes slid down her neck and then to her shoulder. She became mildly uncomfortable as his scrutiny tracked across the front of her snugly fitted bodice, slowly traveling all the way down to the neatly pleated cuff at her wrist. Then he took in the length of her skirt until his gaze reached the leather tips of her boots.

"Kate," he said in a silky voice, "except for a few square inches on your face and hands, you're completely blocked from the sun and have been from the time you were an infant in diapers. I rest my case."

He rolled onto his back, closed his eyes, and tilted his face back toward the sun. He was right, blast it. Her clothing prevented the tiniest hint of sunlight from touching most of her body.

Quite the contrast to Trevor, who lounged with his shirt unbuttoned to expose his bronzed chest to the sun. She supposed it was scandalous to sit beside a man so scantily clothed, but for heaven's sake she was no blushing maiden who would faint at the sight of a man's chest.

Trevor seemed different up here. Relaxed. Normally he was so tightly stitched, but she was glad he felt open enough to allow her to see him this way. She glanced around the rooftop, a niggling suspicion creeping through her mind. Even Trevor would not be so audacious . . .

She cleared her throat. "Are you proposing our patients will be disrobed while they're taking your sunlight cure?"

A wicked grin was his only response.

"Trevor McDonough!"

"Kendall."

"Don't quibble with me. You can't permit men and women to mingle together while half naked up here. The hospital will shut you down. Mr. Lambrecht and the rest of the board will have a fit of apoplexy."

Trevor was nonchalant as he explained his plan. He would construct a partition to divide the male and female areas. The women would wear shifts, leaving their shoulders, arms, and the lower portions of their legs exposed to the sun. The men could bathe in the sun without shirts on, and an attendant would be on duty at all times. The attendant would supposedly be

204

there to provide services to the patients, but the real purpose would be to ensure against accusations of impropriety.

He rolled into an upright position, swinging his legs around so that he could sit facing her. His unbuttoned shirt dangled open and he looked flush with excitement. "I have to try, Kate. I won't let the prudes of the city turn me away from this idea."

She didn't want to talk about tuberculosis anymore. The words of Charlie Davis came to mind. *"I always thought you and Trevor McDonough were destined to be either mortal enemies or the very best of friends. You're too alike to be anything else."*

It seemed Charlie was right, but how was she to let Trevor know she was interested in him? He probably thought she was still mourning Nathan, but these days all Kate could think about was the subtle dry humor Trevor wielded. His passionate commitment to a noble cause. The ardor lurking just beneath the surface, which he kept so restrained.

"Have you ever fancied a girl?" The question popped out before she could call it back. She turned to face him, watching as he stared at the cracked asphalt between his feet, rubbing his jaw. He took so long to reply, she wondered if he'd heard the question.

Finally he looked up. "There was a girl in Scotland. Deirdre Sinclair. She lived on the farm next to ours. We grew up together, and I always assumed we would get married someday. But things didn't work out that way."

"Has there been no one else?" These were terribly personal questions, but Trevor never volunteered information about himself, and the only way she would learn the answers was to press him.

And she desperately needed to know.

He started buttoning his shirt again, and this time the flush on his face didn't look like it came from the sun. "Not really. I've always been immersed in my work, and there hasn't been time for . . . that sort of thing."

Trevor looked so isolated as he sat there, his face pensive and somber. She knew what it felt like to be alone. Even though she was surrounded by family and people at the boardinghouse, there was a special sort of ache that came from being without a partner. She'd been living with that ache for the past four years, and now she was ready to move on. Nathan had been the love of her youth. He was funny and charming, and she adored him. Would he have grown into a man of gravity and stature? She would never know, and yet a fascinating, challenging, and impressive man was before her. When she was with Trevor, everything was more vibrant, as if the air carried an electrical charge.

"Nathan died four years ago," she said quietly. Her knees were only inches from his, and she had to clench her hands to stop from reaching out to him. "At first I didn't think I would ever be able to look at another man. I was wrong."

She looked straight at Trevor. He looked like a starving man standing before a banquet. His eyes glittered. He leaned forward a few inches, and she held her breath. All he had to do was to reach out and bridge the few inches between them, and she would leap into his arms.

Please, Trevor. We could be so good together. . . .

Trevor jerked away and snuffed out the hungry expression on his face. He stood, turning from her as he tucked the ends of his shirt back into his trousers, then reached for his vest and coat. "Yes, well." He cleared his throat as he slung the rest of his clothes over his arm. "I'd best get back to work. Henry should have the report on the hemoglobin count by now."

He brushed past her and walked to the doorway without a backward glance.

In the following days, Trevor retreated behind his typically frosty demeanor. He made no mention of her mortifying advance on the rooftop, for which she was grateful. But did he have to act as if all trace of normal human warmth in his body had been surgically removed?

He was curt with Nurse Ackerman, he quit sharing meals with them at the lunch table, and he could barely look at her during their rounds. The last straw came late one afternoon when she was reading to the patients. There had been no response from their letter to Mark Twain, and with no sequel to *Tom Sawyer* in sight, Kate began reading *Wuthering Heights* to the group. All the regulars attended the readings, although Margaret Longmire, or patient 18F in Trevor's horrible code, was too frail to walk and had to be wheeled into the sitting area.

Kate was just about to start chapter three when Trevor strode into the clinic. "What is 18F doing out of the ward?" he demanded of Nurse Ackerman.

It was Kate's idea to wheel Margaret out, and she was prepared to take the blame if it was a problem. She stood. "I've been reading *Wuthering Heights* to some of the patients. They all seem to enjoy it."

He grabbed a file from the nurses' station and scanned the chart. "What a stupid book. Cathy dies, and Heathcliff goes crazy. A pointless waste of time." He walked toward their office without even looking up from his chart.

Kate closed the book with a snap. "I'll be back," she muttered, and stormed after Trevor.

He seemed surprised when she burst into their office.

"Just when I think you might not be solid ice right down to your core, you always have to prove me wrong. Why did you just do that?"

"Do what?"

"Spoil the end of the book!"

"Because it's a stupid novel. Melodramatic drivel."

She slammed the office door, not caring about Trevor's fussy rules for propriety. She was quite certain he wouldn't want the royal scolding she was about to deliver overheard by all the patients.

"Let me be very clear," she said in a firm voice. "Maybe you never learned decent manners in Scotland or India or wherever you supposedly grew up, but it isn't too late to learn them now. The press, the hospital administration, and most of the elected officials in this city would like to see the last of you. It is time to work on becoming a warm-blooded human being. It will be a struggle, but you need to try. You are coming to dinner at my mother's house tonight, and you will comport yourself with manners and respect."

"I'll do no such thing. The new issue of *Hemoglobin Research* just arrived, and I intend to read it tonight."

There had to be a tiny speck of humanity buried under that block of ice. She'd seen it in the churchyard. She'd seen it on the rooftop. Trevor had a heart that bled and ached and longed to cure the disease that was killing thirty-two people on the other side of this wall. Unless he could drag it out and let the rest of the world see it, he would continue to burn bridges wherever he went.

"Let me repeat myself. You *will* come to dinner tonight. You *will* be polite. You need allies in this war, and you've never bothered to collect any. I cannot fight for these people if you won't. You said you wanted someone willing to help you slay dragons. Why am I the only one making an effort to do it?"

She was yelling now, but it seemed to be

the only way to break through to him. He looked stunned by her statement. He tilted his head to the side and wrinkled his brow the way he always did when he was deep in thought. She moved in for the kill.

"Six o'clock at my parents' house. And don't you dare be late this time."

There was a long pause, and then a gleam of respect lit his eyes as he contemplated her, a smile hovering around his mouth. "Okay," he finally said.

She smoothed a wayward strand of hair back from her forehead, straightened her blouse, and opened the door to leave.

Six of the patients huddled around the door, eavesdropping. Given the guilty looks on their faces, they must have heard every word. "Score two points for Kate Livingston," Leonard Wilkes said loud enough for Trevor to hear.

Trevor had gone back to scowling when she closed the door.

Trevor arrived for dinner ten minutes early and brought a bouquet of daisies for the table. He was a perfect gentleman as Kate reintroduced him to a handful of the boarders who sat near him at the crowded dining table.

Kate asked her mother to be on good

behavior too, so the main topic of conversation at dinner was the possibility that former President Cleveland might try to recapture the White House next year. When the conversation turned to Trevor's work, he was equally polite, even when Mrs. Zomohkov started raising the alarm about tuberculosis. Kate spoke no Russian, but the disgust in Mrs. Zomohkov's tone was blatant. Her husband cleared his throat and dabbed his mouth before providing the translation.

"My wife is concerned about the poor and wonders if they are more prone to the ravages of the disease?"

This showed that Mr. Zomohkov had perfected the art of diplomacy. Given Mrs. Zomohkov's rancid expression, Kate was fairly certain his wife had spoken more colorful words about contagious disease among the poor.

Trevor's reply was tactful. "The poor are more likely to contract the disease because they live in crowded tenements, but it can strike anyone, anywhere. Soldiers and sailors are especially vulnerable, because they live in tight quarters." He then looked directly at Mrs. Zomohkov and said gently, "I will find a cure someday. And when I do, it will protect you, and your children, and all your friends from a disease that can strike any one of us. We are all in this together."

They waited while her husband translated. There was a hint of a thaw as the tension in Mrs. Zomohkov's shoulders eased, but displeasure kept her mouth frozen in distaste. Then Trevor surprised them all.

"Sprechen sie Deutsch?"

"Ja," Mrs. Zomohkov said. A spiel of foreign words then passed between the pair. They were speaking in German? Some of the newspaper clippings mentioned that Trevor had spent a number of years studying at the University of Vienna. Trevor grinned as he leaned forward and whispered something to Mrs. Zomohkov, who began giggling like a schoolgirl.

There was something oddly attractive about watching Trevor converse in a foreign language. Where had Trevor learned German well enough to study abroad?

After a few minutes, Trevor leaned back in his seat. "Forgive us," he said to everyone. "Mrs. Zomohkov and I were reminiscing about the Vienna Opera House. I was privileged to hear the great Russian composer Tchaikovsky perform there."

Mrs. Zomohkov kept smiling and nodding as Trevor spoke, even after the conversation turned to modern music and whether the city of Washington would ever open its own performance hall.

Later, Kate handed Trevor his jacket and walked him to the front door. As Trevor slipped into his jacket, he gave her a slight grin.

"One dragon down," he whispered before he left.

12

After the evening Trevor charmed Mrs. Zomohkov, he began coming to dinner regularly, and Kate was thrilled by his progress toward becoming a warm-blooded creature. In the weeks that followed, he grew more relaxed among the boisterous crowd. One night Tom Wilkerson from the Patent Office amused them all by describing an invention designed to exercise overweight house cats. As he spoke, Kate became strangely mesmerized watching Trevor.

Still wearing his vest but with his collar loosened and his cuffs rolled up, he listened politely while absently fiddling with his empty teacup. She asked if he wanted a refill. His eyes were warm as he shook his head and went back to listening about the cat exerciser, a half smile on his face while running his thumb along the rim of his cup in a slow, lazy motion. Those hands could perform surgery. Manipulate the dials of a microscope. Trevor's intelligence had always fascinated her, but when he looked relaxed like this . . . well, all the inappropriate fantasies she'd been nurturing about him came roaring back to life.

But he could still turn on a dime.

The morning Ephraim Montgomery died, she got a glimpse of the old Trevor in all his glory. It was the first time a patient died since Kate had begun work at the clinic, and she was upset. She stood in the doorway of the men's ward, watching Trevor make notations on Mr. Montgomery's chart. Two hospital orderlies rolled Mr. Montgomery's bed down the aisle and out the door, leaving a wide gap in the tidy row of beds. Ephraim Montgomery had been some woman's son, or husband, or brother.

An ungainly sob escaped as she stared at the empty spot in the ward. From across the room, Trevor glared at her. He flipped the chart closed and stalked down the aisle toward her.

"Outside," he snapped.

She couldn't meet his eyes as she followed him. He pulled the door to the ward shut and towered over her. "Don't you dare turn into a blubbering idiot in front of the patients. If you can't hold it together, go home. Don't you have any idea how scared they are?"

"Who wouldn't be?" Kate said in a shaky voice.

Trevor looked like he wanted to shake her. "You're part of the staff here, and that means they look to you for courage. For strength. At the very least, they look to you for the hope that death is not some awful finality of nothingness. Existence doesn't end with death, and when you blubber like that it saps their confidence. Find your backbone. Have the fortitude to stand up and fight. That's what I hired you for."

He turned his back and followed Mr. Montgomery's bed out of the clinic without a backward glance.

Kate hung her head. She had a stomachache and a headache, and sometimes Trevor made her brain want to explode. The worst part was that he was right. Her inability to reconcile herself to death was surely the biggest moral failing of her life.

All of these patients knew they were going to die soon. She was starting to understand what Trevor meant when he warned her they would be bruised and broken on a daily basis as they battled this disease. They would be beaten down time and again, but tomorrow morning she had to get up and face the day with renewed strength.

"He's wrong, you know."

She whirled around. Leonard Wilkes was sitting in the turret alcove, gentle sympathy on his wasted face. Leonard was always the patient most likely to make a macabre joke about death, so the compassion on his face took her by surprise. She sniffled and adjusted her collar.

"Who's wrong?"

"Dr. Kendall. Oh, he's right that we're all in God's hands, whether here on earth or on our journey to the other side, but there's no shame in grieving. It's normal. Grief freshens our perspective on life; it helps us appreciate the blessings we've been showered with. 'Weeping may endure for a night, but joy cometh in the morning.' You're doing fine, Mrs. Livingston."

She didn't feel fine. She could accept everything Jesus said about faith and the afterlife, so why did she have such an irrational terror of watching people die? Why did she gnash her teeth over what happened to her baby brothers and to Nathan? What happened to them was so unfair. She still couldn't understand how a loving God could snatch children away for no apparent reason, or make Ephraim Montgomery suffer such a lingering and horrible death.

And she felt small and mean for those

thoughts. A better person would not question God like this.

She managed a smile for Mr. Wilkes, but as the day wore on she felt worse both in body and mind. It was a glorious autumn day, but she wanted just to crawl into bed and stay there. Instead she pulled out the chart of statistical calculations. She had plenty of work to do and would not give Trevor the satisfaction of seeing her run away.

"Trevor, you could be a little nicer to me."

Kate's voice smacked him in the face as he returned to their office after completing Ephraim Montgomery's autopsy, where he had a view of how tuberculosis ravaged the liver, stomach, and intestinal tract. Kate's declaration caught him by surprise, even though he supposed he'd been tough on her this morning. But losing patients was always disastrous for him, ripping a tiny piece of his armor away. If he gave in and wallowed in emotion like Kate, he would never survive.

"Why should I?" He tugged off his lab coat and hung it on a hook near the door. "You knew this job was going to be a challenge when you accepted the position."

"Because I have a normal human heart

that bleeds and hurts when someone dies. I can't shut off my feelings the way you can." There was no accusation in her voice, just a deep aching pain of bewilderment. "When I was fifteen, two of my brothers died from diphtheria."

He remembered. An announcement had been made at their school to explain Kate's absence, and everyone rallied around her to offer support when she finally returned. Trevor watched from a distance, unsure how to respond. Kate had been shattered by the loss, and for months she was a mere shadow of the girl who usually competed with him so fiercely.

"I always wondered what they would be like if they'd been given the chance to grow up," she continued. "Carl was only twelve, and Jamie ten, when they died. Whenever I hear a boy singing, I remember Jamie. He used to sing his lungs out in the washroom, because he loved the way it echoed off the tile. And then Mama would come running and tell him to shush, that he was waking up the boarders. I wonder if Carl would still be a sore loser over chess." She doubled over in her chair, her breathing ragged as she battled tears. "I wish I'd let him win sometimes. I should have done that . . . I was older than him, and I should have let him win every game we ever played. I wish I'd bought Jamie that stupid toy train for his birthday, even though it cost too much. He wanted it so badly, and he went to his grave without ever playing with a decent train set. Will this never stop hurting?"

Trevor went to stand next to her. His hand hovered just above her head. He wished he could pick up the grief that weighed on her spirit and carry it for her.

She straightened, turning her tear-stained face to him with a flicker of hope in her eyes. "That's why I want Tick to go to the Naval Academy. It's safer for officers, and I can't bear the thought of Tick going into harm's way. I'd rather he become a rag-picker than a soldier on the front line."

He noticed how she hovered over Tick. Everyone noticed. He dragged his desk chair across the room to sit beside her. Their knees were practically touching. He leaned down so he could look her directly in the eyes.

"Men are different from women," he said. "We want to conquer things, whether it's a foreign enemy or a microscopic germ we can't even see. If you try to protect us from that, we'll begin to die. Tick isn't destined to become a ragpicker, and you know that." A strand of her hair was stuck to her face, and he reached out to tuck it back. "Don't try to stop Tick from following his dreams, wherever they may lead."

She pulled back in her chair, looking tired and defeated. "The thought of Tick dying has always scared me to pieces. I didn't realize how hard it was going to be to work here. I barely knew Ephraim Montgomery, but I've been a watering pot all day. I think maybe I don't belong here."

A shaft of fear seized him. "Don't talk like that. You're strong enough to handle this." It startled him to realize how quickly he'd come to need Kate, to depend on her.

"I don't feel strong. I feel weak and brittle, and sometimes I just need someone to lean on. I don't think I can keep doing a job where all these people will keep dying." Two big tears slid down Kate's cheeks.

Trevor sighed. He knew she was keeping the boardinghouse afloat with her wages. She'd pulled strings to get Tick assigned to the hospital. After a long day dealing with terminally ill patients, she helped serve dozens of people at the boardinghouse with an endless stream of good humor. And this morning, when she showed the first hint of weakness in a job most people would loathe, he called her a blubbering idiot.

"You can't quit, Kate. I was wrong this

morning when I said you needed to toughen up. I sought you out for this job because you are fierce. Because I've traveled all over the world, and you're the only one who ever prodded, challenged, and inspired me."

Inspired. It was such a puny word to describe what she did for him. She made him want to call down the moon, to grapple with whirlwinds, to slay dragons.

He took her hands, squeezing them and looking in her eyes again. "I want you beside me, shoulder to shoulder. We've got months and years and maybe decades of slogging through this before we will find a cure. That's how it is in medicine. I would give my right arm to make it otherwise, but there are no shortcuts. It's going to be a long, hard ride. That's why I need you with me."

She watched him with a combination of hope and fear. "Trevor, do you ever still think of Deirdre?"

Where had that come from? He hated talking about Scotland, or anything about his past, yet he couldn't keep pushing Kate away. He cared about her too much.

"No. I hardly ever think of Deirdre." It was the truth. Deirdre seemed such a pale long-ago memory compared to the fiery, blazing glory of the woman who held his hands so tightly.

"You have no idea how much I resented you back in school," Kate said with a watery laugh. "I used to think of you as 'the horrible Trevor McDonough,' and yet now I think you are one of the finest people I've ever known. And if you don't think of Deirdre anymore . . ." Her thumb trailed across the back of his hand, and he held his breath. "I want you to know I think of you a lot. Pretty much all the time."

He knew exactly what she was driving at, and he wanted it so badly it was hard not to lunge across the few inches that separated them. He wanted more from Kate Livingston than she could possibly imagine . . . but she didn't know him. Not really.

"Kate, I'm not a good bet."

She stiffened. "Why not?" She withdrew her hands, leaving a cold void between them. "Does this have something to do with why you changed your name? Or those missing two years? Were you in prison or something?"

"Oh, for pity's sake," he muttered. He pushed his chair back and stood. This was a mistake. If she knew the truth about those two missing years . . . well, it was far worse than prison, and Kate deserved much better than someone like him. She deserved a hero. He was nothing but a man in a white lab coat who pinned his hopes on a long-shot cure based on cod liver oil and sunlight.

"Why won't you talk to me?" she pressed. "Why do you have to keep everything locked down so tightly? I won't bite, Trevor."

"You're already biting. I need you to stop."

He crossed the office to his desk, yanking out drawers to look for the rubber stamp he needed to finalize Ephraim Montgomery's death certificate. It was time to shut these inconvenient feelings off and get back to work. Toying with the attraction that simmered between them was dangerous. He needed to revert back to the professionalism that worked so well.

"I think I should go home," Kate said weakly.

His fist tightened around the stamp, but he couldn't turn around to look at her. "I won't listen to any nonsense about you quitting."

"I just don't feel well," she said. "I want to go home."

He couldn't keep driving her this way if he wanted her to stay. "Go then. I expect you back here tomorrow morning at nine o'clock."

She didn't say a word as she left and closed the door behind her.

13

Kate had never felt so strangely horrible in her life. Her stomach ached, her head pounded, and she wanted to draw and quarter Trevor.

How mortifying to be rejected by him. *Twice.* She hadn't been discouraged after that first overture when he clammed up on the rooftop. She didn't expect the famously reticent Trevor McDonough to fly into her arms at the first hint of affection. He would need to become accustomed to the idea, and that was why she bided her time.

But there was no mistaking that yesterday he had flat-out rejected her. He had plenty of time to process her statement on the roof, and he clearly wanted nothing to do with her.

She dreaded Trevor's arrival to the office, even though she doubted he would acknowledge their odd conversation or change his behavior in any way.

Which was why she was surprised at how uncomfortable he seemed when he finally arrived, almost two hours late for work. She was at her desk, tabulating yesterday's statistics, when she felt a presence behind her. Trevor stood in the doorway.

"Is there something you need?" she asked.

"I was wondering if you could come with me on a call after work today."

"A call? What does that mean?"

He cleared his throat and stared at a spot somewhere over her left shoulder. "A friend of mine would like to meet you. She's very ill and can't travel, so I'm hoping you will come to her home this afternoon. It won't take long."

She had a stomachache and didn't feel like doing anything other than going home and curling up in bed. "I don't know, Trevor." It seemed churlish to refuse when he'd been so good about coming to her house for dinner over the past few weeks.

"I wouldn't ask, but Mrs. Kendall has been declining fast and —"

"Mrs. Kendall?" The name made her sit up straight.

He moved to his desk, where he began tidying stacks of papers. He still wouldn't look at her. "She has tuberculosis," he said. "She's survived the disease longer than anyone I know. I make house calls for her."

"I notice you and Mrs. Kendall share the same last name. Dare I hope there is a connection?"

His mouth thinned. He looked like he would rather have a tooth pulled than provide an answer, but she wasn't going to budge until he did. He folded his arms across his chest and stared over her left shoulder again. "Yes, there's a connection. Mrs. Kendall was the housekeeper in Senator Campbell's house. I met her when I was thirteen years old."

"Right after you arrived from Scotland?"

"Yes."

"Why did you change your name to match hers?"

He met her eyes. Sometimes Trevor could look like that wounded boy she once knew on the playground, and now was one of those times. He looked away again before speaking.

"I never had much of a relationship with my father. He sent me to America when I became inconvenient, and Mrs. Kendall was the only person in this country who seemed to care if I lived or died. She meant a lot to me. Still does."

Trevor was inconvenient to his father? *Inconvenient?* She wanted to ask him what he meant by such an odd statement, but he was still struggling to find words and she dared not interrupt him.

"During those years in school, Mrs. Kendall was the only one I could talk to, and I told her about you. She always wanted to know what was happening at school. The only thing I cared about was making good grades, and since you were the measuring stick I used to judge myself by, we ended up talking about you a lot."

Strange, because it had been the same for her. She used to tear her hair out every time Trevor bested her in a competition, and her parents always heard about those Herculean battles with "the horrible Trevor McDonough."

"Anyway, Mrs. Kendall is dying," Trevor continued. "I don't know how much longer she has, but probably not more than a few weeks. When she heard I hired you to work at the clinic, she asked to meet you." An ironic smile flitted across his mouth. "And I'm afraid I've never been able to deny Mrs. Kendall anything. So I would be very grateful if you could pay a visit with me. If today won't work, perhaps another day, but it will need to be soon."

"All right," she said.

She would be there if she had to walk

every step of the way.

They took a streetcar all the way to Georgetown. Unless Mrs. Kendall was independently wealthy, Kate suspected Trevor was
probably footing the bill for the town house.

"You won't need a mask," Trevor said as
they walked the final block alongside a row
of leafy trees. "I tested Mrs. Kendall this
morning, and she isn't contagious. She will
probably offer vanilla custard. It doesn't
hold a candle to your mother's cooking, but
please accept. You can bet she spent most of
the afternoon making it."

As they approached Mrs. Kendall's door,
Kate heard voices from inside. A lot of
voices. She thought they would be visiting a
woman on her deathbed, but the rumble of
laughter and good cheer from inside was
unmistakable.

Trevor looked equally confused as he
rapped on the door.

A second later, the door was flung open
by a matronly woman with frizzy orange
hair. "Trevor!" she squealed and drew him
into a hearty hug. He looked awkward as he
submitted to the embrace, but she released
him quickly. "You must be Kate," she said
in a rush. "You can't imagine how much we
all heard about you when we were growing

230

up. Come in, come in."

There were at least a dozen people crowded into the apartment that smelled of warm vanilla and spiced tea.

"It looks like we've just stumbled into a reunion of Senator Campbell's household staff," Trevor said. "Sorry about this, Kate, I didn't expect it."

A handsome older gentleman wearing a tweed vest stepped forward. "Allow me to make the introductions, Mrs. Livingston," he said in a voice that sounded like it belonged on a Shakespearean stage. "I am Marcus Coburn. I was the butler in Senator Campbell's house for twelve years. This is Mary Hatch; she was a parlormaid. And her sister, Alice, who did the laundry. The good-looking fellow in the corner is Martin Harkin; he was in charge of the stables."

Kate's eyes widened in surprise. Martin Harkin was the coachman who drove Trevor to school every day. He winked at her in recognition, and she smiled back. But the butler hadn't stopped with the introductions. He nodded at the woman with orange hair who'd opened the door. "That's Nellie Kendall, Mrs. Kendall's daughter. She helped with the cooking."

There were other introductions Kate struggled to hold straight in her head. How

231

amazing to see Trevor surrounded by so
many people eager to see him. He always
kept himself so aloof at the hospital — not
that he was terribly different here. He was
taciturn as he guided her through the crush
of people to a frail woman sitting at the
kitchen table, an impressive braid coiled
around the back of her head like a crown.

"Kate, this is Mrs. Kendall. She was the
housekeeper for Senator Campbell during
the twenty-four years he was in office, and
is no doubt responsible for this hullabaloo."

Mrs. Kendall tilted her head to get a good
look. "So you're the woman who tormented
my poor boy all those years." The woman's
eyes sparkled as she said it. Kate sat in the
chair beside Mrs. Kendall. It was hard for a
frail person to keep her neck turned like
that, and it was Mrs. Kendall she'd come to
see.

"I never thought of Trevor as a poor boy,
but I confess to keeping him tormented. He
returned the favor with equal fire."

Her comment was greeted with a roar of
laughter. "Good for you, Kate!" someone
called from the other side of the room. A
plate of warm vanilla custard was placed
before her, and the others began gathering
around the table.

She scanned the group, all of whom

seemed flush with good cheer. One of the men had a flask and added a little fortification to the spiced tea. The flask was offered to Trevor, who declined with typical reserve.

"So all of you knew Trevor as he was growing up?" she asked. If so, this place would be a gold mine of information.

The woman with frizzy orange hair nodded her head. "Except back then we called him Trevor *McDonough*. Now that Mother has taken him under her wing, does that make us brother and sister, Trevor?"

"You were always as annoying as any sister could be," Trevor said dryly.

"I'm taking that as a compliment!"

He winked at her. "I meant it as one."

Kate was breathless to hear more about why Trevor changed his name, but the conversation flew so rapidly, making it impossible to stay on the topic.

"Hey, do you remember the time Trevor challenged Martin to see who could haul more coal in from the shed?"

"I won," Martin said proudly.

"I was only thirteen and you were eighteen," Trevor protested with a smile. "Of course you won."

Mrs. Kendall buried her head in her hands. "The whole servants' wing was a disaster. Coal dust tracked everywhere, and the two of you were as filthy as coal miners."

She met Trevor's gaze, and he gave a little shrug. How easily she could imagine him challenging an older boy to a competition, even for something as pointless as carrying buckets of coal.

Other memories were tossed around, and Kate realized this was a sort of family reunion. A couple of the women bragged about their babies, and the men swapped stories of old times. Trevor seemed to be included in most of the stories. From what Kate gleaned of the conversation, it seemed he ate in the servants' wing and caroused with them. As the guests started breaking up into smaller groups, Kate stayed beside Mrs. Kendall. For some reason, the old housekeeper had made a point of wanting to meet her.

"Trevor tells me you were quite a cook," Kate said. "That your vanilla custard is world famous."

"Bah." Mrs. Kendall waved the comment away. "My cooking is marginal at best. I wanted to meet the girl who kept Trevor on his toes all those years. And who interested him enough to come looking for her more than a decade later."

Heat gathered in her cheeks. Four months

ago she would have cringed in horror at any suggestion that Trevor might be interested in her, but now she couldn't stop the reckless fantasies of sharing something more than an office with him. Apparently his interest was limited to her mathematical abilities.

"He told me he wanted me on his team because I am as competitive as he is," she said.

"Is *that* what he said?" Mrs. Kendall drawled. She laughed a little, and it ended in a raspy cough.

"Why? Did he tell you something different?"

Mrs. Kendall shook her head. "That boy has always been closemouthed about himself. You have to read the tea leaves with Trevor."

Kate would never have a better opportunity than right now to get a peek at Trevor's mysterious past. He was deep in conversation with a few of the other men. Or rather, he was listening as the other men talked. Trevor was always more of a listener, silently gathering information and filing it away in that awesome mind of his.

"Senator Campbell was Trevor's guardian," Kate began, "but it seems he was closer to the servants than to the senator's family. Or his own, for that matter."

"True enough."

"Why is that? It seems so strange for a man to ship his son off . . ." Kate let the sentence trail away. She knew virtually nothing about why Trevor came to America or why his father thought him "inconvenient."

Mrs. Kendall laid a hand on Kate's knee. "Trevor arrived to us with more burdens than any thirteen-year-old should carry. And they aren't my business to discuss." The old woman's eyes were kind and her hand frail, but the message in her tone was clear. Mrs. Kendall would defend Trevor's privacy with her dying breath.

"This has been so much fun," one of the former parlormaids said. "We should get together for Christmas."

Mrs. Kendall gave a noncommittal shrug. Trevor stiffened, and her daughter's face crumpled. If Trevor was correct, Mrs. Kendall wouldn't be here for Christmas this year. No one else, though, seemed to be aware of the old housekeeper's deteriorating condition.

"It was a real shame when the senator lost his reelection and the house was sold," the old butler said. "Christmas was never the same after that."

The mood dampened as those gathered

around shook their heads. Kate was accustomed to seeing people come and go through Washington after each election, but it never occurred to her that an entire household like Senator Campbell's would be disbanded because of a failed election. These people seemed as tightly bound as any family.

Mrs. Kendall's daughter leaned forward with a mischievous hint in her voice. "Of course, nothing will ever outshine the year Trevor's father pulled out all the stops for Christmas dinner." The comment was greeted with a round of laughter.

"What did Trevor's father do that year?" Kate asked. Another chorus of laughter rippled through the servants, although Trevor's face darkened and he withdrew even further.

Lettie Kendall noticed and grabbed Trevor's shoulders. "Never let it be said that Mr. McDonough didn't want his boy to have a fine Christmas dinner! I thought Mr. Coburn would faint when a sailor walked that lumbering Black Angus steer down the streets of Washington straight to our front door."

"His father sent a live *steer*?"

"A Black Angus steer," the butler confirmed. "The finest breed of cattle in all of

Scotland. But that wasn't all. He sent smoked salmon and jars of honey from a monastery in Spain. There were wild truffles and candied ginger, but the best part was that he sent a French chef to prepare everything and make a chocolate torte fit for a king. And a case of single malt Scotch whiskey. Now, *that* was a fine Christmas dinner."

"Senator Campbell sent a bottle of the whiskey to the servants' wing," Martin said. "Nothing ever tasted so fine. Spoiled me for life, that Christmas did."

Lettie chimed in with her own memories of the legendary Christmas dinner. Kate's chest tightened, and the room suddenly seemed too warm. This spectacular dinner was showered on a boy who claimed he needed money for college, who fought for a scholarship that was Kate's only means of bettering herself, while he gorged on a chocolate torte prepared by a chef imported from France. Her stomachache had gotten worse and she just wanted to go home, but the stories continued.

"What about his sixteenth birthday," Martin said. "What was that fancy book your father sent you?" Trevor shifted awkwardly while everyone in the room waited for him to respond.

"It was a book of Shakespeare's plays," he finally said.

"But there was something special about it. It had a fancy name," the butler said. "A first file? A first . . ." He snapped his fingers, trying to remember.

"A first folio?" Kate asked.

"That was it! A first folio."

If she weren't surrounded by a dozen people, she would have lunged across the room and strangled Trevor. Instead she picked up a paper napkin and began fanning herself.

Trevor didn't need money for college. He'd won that scholarship just to prove that he could.

As the reunion dragged on, Kate thought the evening would never end.

Trevor was silent as he walked beside her to the streetcar stop. There was plenty of time for him to offer an explanation about his shockingly extravagant life, but he said nothing. The street was deserted, their footsteps echoing on the walkway. She waited until they arrived at the vacant bench, where the streetcar would stop.

"A first folio?" she finally burst out.

Trevor's jaw tightened, but again he said nothing as he stared at the horse-drawn streetcar rolling toward them. He ought to be embarrassed! What kind of man gave a sixteen-year-old boy one of the most valuable books ever printed? The first edition of Shakespeare's plays had been published in the seventeenth century and was sought after by collectors all over the world.

The streetcar came to a stop before them. Trevor stepped aboard and paid a coin for them both, and she followed him down the narrow aisle. The streetcar was crowded with only one seat left open. Trevor offered it to her, then turned to grasp the hand strap above, standing stiffly beside her as the streetcar jerked into motion.

"How many first folios are still in existence?" she fired at him.

"I have no idea. A thousand or so."

"Two hundred twenty-eight," she corrected. "I remember from high school literature class. You were sitting only two desks away and heard it too. You sat there like a dolt and didn't even bother mentioning to the class that you owned one!"

"It was no one's business," Trevor said.

"You always had to be the best in everything. Why didn't you bring that book in so we could all be dazzled by your riches?" She was being unfair but didn't care. There was so much about Trevor that drove her mad.

"And a Black Angus steer! What's wrong with plain old American beef?"

"Kate, please shut up," Trevor muttered.

Other people in the streetcar were looking at them, but she had nothing to be ashamed of. She hadn't snatched a scholarship out of the hands of a poor classmate. "Do you still have it? The first folio?"

"I sold it at an auction."

That must have brought a pretty penny. Tears pricked the back of her eyes. Trevor was rich, but he didn't like her enough in school to let her win that scholarship. And he didn't like her enough now to think of her as anything but a statistical assistant. When the streetcar drew near her stop, Trevor guided her to the front.

"You don't need to walk me home," she said. It meant he would need to wait another thirty minutes to catch the next streetcar to take him across town.

"It's no bother."

She felt too lousy to argue with him. And ashamed of herself for getting angry over a twelve-year-old grievance.

The blow Trevor dealt her had been delivered by an awkward eighteen-year-old boy who never knew how to do anything other than compete. Here she was acting like an angry brat instead of a grown

241

woman. She knew better. It was time to let this go.

Aside from his appalling manners, at his heart Trevor had been immensely decent to her since the moment she met him again four months ago. He paid her a generous salary and treated her with respect. He welcomed her on to his team, and even if he didn't return her affection, she shouldn't hold it against him.

"Can you slow down a little?" she asked. "I feel really rotten."

His steps slowed. Was she angry with him over the scholarship or was this because he didn't return the romantic sentiment that was growing and blossoming by the day? Trevor was the first man to spark interest in her since Nathan died. She constantly wondered what it would be like if they became real partners, sharing their lives. Became man and wife. She wondered what Trevor would be like as a husband, what he would be like as a father.

When they came to the front door of the boardinghouse, she turned to him. "I'm sorry I groused at you. You didn't deserve it and I'm sorry."

Standing in the gathering darkness, with his face cast in shadow and the hint of a smile on his mouth, Trevor was possibly the handsomest man she'd ever seen. It had nothing to do with his good looks and everything to do with his calm, fierce intelligence. The respect he had for their teamwork. The way electricity sparked in the air when he was close.

"We were head-to-head until that final trigonometry equation," he said. "You would have beaten me if the principal had judged on speed rather than method of calculation. It was a coin toss. I think he tipped it to me because he was reluctant to give the scholarship to a girl."

Deep down inside, Kate always suspected the same. Although women were regularly being accepted into college today, twelve years ago it would have been unusual. At that time, Trevor would have had a better chance to put his degree to meaningful work. For Trevor, his willingness to acknowledge the headmaster's bias was quite a concession.

"I really hate it when you're right," she said with a reluctant smile.

He touched the side of her face. "You were a match for me. I was always right about that."

Her cheek burned where he'd touched her. Without saying anything more, he turned to walk back to the streetcar stop.

She wanted to call him back but forced herself to hold the iron railing to stop from lunging after him. The metal cut into her palm as she watched him fade into the mist.

14

Trevor sat at his desk, staring at the maple tree outside his office window and the first hint of scarlet tinting the leaves. Normally the sight of this tree was soothing, but today he clenched his fists as he prepared to write another check to the private investigator. It was infuriating to keep throwing money away in search of the coward behind the campaign to destroy him, but it needed to be done. The tip of his fountain pen scratched in the silence as he wrote the check.

His lawyer arranged for a private detective in Baltimore to track down those associated with the Baltimore study whom Trevor had been unable to find. Two of the nurses had married and moved away. One of the doctors had relocated to another hospital in New Jersey, and his assistant was in medical school at Harvard. All of them would need to be found and interviewed.

A heavy sigh came from Kate's side of the office. She was curled over her desk, eyes closed, looking like she was about to fall asleep.

"You all right over there?"

She looked up at him. "I must have eaten something bad." Even from across the room he could see a fine sheen of perspiration on her skin, and it was chilly in the office today.

"If you have a fever, I want you to go home."

"I'll be okay. If I show up at home before lunch, my mother will put me to work in the laundry."

"Fair enough."

Nurse Ackerman brought him the mail, including a stack of the daily newspapers. "Any more newspaper articles?" he asked, holding his breath.

"Not this morning. Just a few letters and a medical journal. And a letter for Kate."

The muscles in his neck eased. He hadn't even realized how tense he was until Nurse Ackerman assured him there were no articles today criticizing his work. Which was pathetic. He had a twenty-four-hour stay of execution, but the waiting game would begin again tomorrow morning. Kate ripped open the top of her envelope with hasty fingers. What a ragged mess she made of the envelope, but she was never overly tidy.

Kate hissed and recoiled, shooting to her feet as a pair of photographs fell on the floor at her feet. "This is disgusting," she gasped.

He darted to her side and stiffened when he saw the top photograph. It showed a man, naked from the waist up as he sat on an examining table, his spinal column twisted from the ravages of tuberculosis.

The second photograph was the nude corpse of a woman on a mortuary slab. The sores on her skin were testament to advanced tuberculosis. He recognized the woman. She was one of his patients from Baltimore.

Two words were scrawled on the back of the photograph: *I remember.*

"Who would send me such a horrible thing?" Kate asked.

Someone who was tired of attacking him personally and was now reaching out to torment his staff. Before Trevor could answer, Kate clamped a hand over her mouth and ran from the room.

He was sickened too. This had to end. He would hire however many investigators it took to find out who was behind these revolting messages. He would place men at the post office, plant someone at the newspapers. He would protect his people from the vendetta launched against him. Kate deserved that much.

It wasn't like Kate to run away from things. She was more likely to face a problem than run away from it. Something was wrong, and he rushed into the hall. "Where did she go?" he asked Nurse Ackerman.

"The washroom. It looked like she was going to be sick."

He went to the washroom door and knocked loudly. "Kate?"

Retching sounds came from behind the door. Dry heaves, as though she'd already thrown up whatever was bad in her stomach. He knocked again, but there was no answer and the door was locked.

He reached in his pocket for the key, unlocked the door, and stepped inside. She was kneeling on the floor, curled over the toilet. "How long have you been sick?"

"A couple of days," she said on a ragged breath. "I don't know. It's been a while."

She made no protest as he walked farther into the room and pressed his hand to her forehead. She was scorching hot.

"Can you sit up straight?" he asked.

"Not really. It hurts." She braced both hands on her thighs and pushed up a few inches, then stopped. "Trevor, it really hurts."

"I want you to stay here while I have an orderly bring a stretcher."

She laughed a little. "I'm not *that* sick."

"Humor me."

She didn't argue with him as he sent Nurse Ackerman to get a stretcher. Sometimes it was better to err on the side of caution. Hopefully this was nothing, but if Kate had what he suspected and he didn't act fast, she could be dead before the end of the week.

The way Trevor reverted to his cold, impassive demeanor frightened her. She had been carried on a stretcher to an examining room on the third floor of the hospital. A nurse took notes as Trevor examined her. Lying curled up on her side with a thermometer in her mouth, Trevor asked her to roll over onto her back.

"It will hurt if I do."

"It won't kill you. Now, over you go."

Slowly she rolled over. She wanted to throw up again, except her stomach was already empty. Trevor extracted the thermometer, his face emotionless as he took the reading. It felt awful to have him standing over her.

His voice was firm and professional as he pressed on the side of her stomach. "Does that hurt?"

"A little, yes."

He moved to the other side. "How about that?"

She screamed. Tears streaked from her eyes, dry heaves once again racking her body.

The nurse waited with her while Trevor stepped into the hallway. She heard him speaking to someone, but their voices were too muffled to understand. This was ridiculous. She never got sick. If someone could just take her home, she would lie in bed until this awful feeling passed.

Shuffling footsteps approached the table and Trevor was standing over her again. There was another man, whose white beard made him look like Santa Claus. Trevor introduced him as Dr. Schrader.

"Kate, we think you have appendicitis. The appendix is a small organ at the bottom of the large intestine, and yours is infected. Sometimes it will go away on its own, sometimes it won't. Yours is pretty bad."

Dr. Schrader moved into view. "We have to take it out, Mrs. Livingston. It's not a difficult operation, but we will have to put you under while we do it."

An operation? It was unthinkable. To lie

down and let someone cut her open and poke around in her insides . . . no. "I don't need an operation. I'll be fine."

"Kate, you won't be fine," Trevor said firmly. "Your appendix is acutely inflamed, and that means the infection is getting very bad. If the appendix ruptures, it will spread the infection through your entire body. And then there's nothing we can do." He said the words in that flat, dispassionate manner that always got under her skin. Looking her in the eyes, he continued, "Do you understand what I'm saying? You will die, Kate. If your appendix ruptures before we get it out, you'll die."

She couldn't make this decision alone. She needed to talk to her parents. "I want to go home. Tomorrow we can talk about it again if I still feel this bad."

"I'm not making myself clear," Trevor said. "We need to operate right away. Your appendix could rupture at any moment, and the longer we wait, the greater the risk. Do you understand?"

"I want to talk to Tick."

Trevor nodded. "He's right outside. We've already briefed him on your condition."

Trevor and the other doctor left the room, and Kate pushed herself into a sitting position on the examining table. Tick stepped into the room, looking as white as a ghost as he twisted his cap in his hands. But the moment he saw her, he plastered a grin on his face.

"Look at you, grabbing all the attention," he said in an artificially bright tone. "All the patients upstairs are talking about you." He took her hand, his fingers cold. "I hear you've got quite a case. Good thing we have a couple of doctors on hand who can fix you up, right?"

"Don't you see what they want to do?" She wished her voice didn't shake so badly, but how could she stay calm when every muscle in her body trembled? "Tick, I don't want to do it. I want to go home to bed."

"Come on, Kate. You're the bravest person I know."

"Not when it comes to this. I just want to go home. Will you take me?"

Tick drew a steadying breath. "Look, you aren't thinking clearly right now. Trevor said it's an easy surgery, but that you're as good as dead if they don't get that thing out before it bursts. Don't go getting soft and stupid on me now. Everyone needs you too much."

And then she saw the fear behind his wide blue eyes. He was putting on a brave show, but he was scared too. She couldn't abandon

Tick. He needed her, and she'd do anything for him.

She nodded. "Okay, I'll do it."

After Tick left to tell Trevor the news, Kate closed her eyes and prayed harder than ever before.

It was just her luck that the hospital's chief surgeon was in Boston for a conference and wouldn't return until next week. That meant Trevor would be operating on her.

She lay on a table, her shoulder blades hard against its surface. Trevor stood on the far side of the room, arranging silvery pieces of equipment that flashed in the lamplight as he set them on a nearby tray.

"Have you ever done one of these before?" she asked him.

Trevor rolled the tray next to her and the table. "Plenty, ever since my third year of medical school."

"But Dr. Flynn is the expert, isn't he? Maybe we should wait for him to come back from Boston?"

"Kate, I know what I'm doing. Try to relax. It's going to be okay."

She supposed she trusted Trevor as much as anyone to do this. Dr. Schrader was somewhere behind her head, preparing a mixture of ether and chloroform, which he said would make her sleep so deeply she wouldn't feel a thing. She didn't really believe it. She saw the scalpel Trevor had been cleaning, and there was no way it could slice into her without her feeling pain.

The wheels of Dr. Schrader's chair rolled closer to her head, and the sharp odor of carbolic acid surrounded her. "You'll be sure I'm all the way asleep before Trevor starts cutting?"

"I promise. Don't worry, I'm an old pro at this."

And then Trevor was standing over her, a mask dangling around his neck. She clenched her hands around the edges of the table. "If this doesn't work out, please tell my parents and Tick that I love them."

Mercifully he spared her the arrogant attitude. "Of course," Trevor said softly.

"Tick's application for the Naval Academy is due the last week in January. Will you make sure he gets it in on time?"

Trevor nodded.

"They want letters of recommendation. It would be great if you could write him one."

"I can do that. Anything else?"

She closed her eyes. *The Lord is my shepherd; I shall not want. He maketh me to lie down in green pastures . . ."* She drew a blank and scrambled for more words from the Psalm. She couldn't even remember the Lord's Prayer. This was it then. "I'm ready," she managed to say.

Trevor nodded to Dr. Schrader, who pressed a white cloth over her nose and mouth. What an awful smell. The last thing she saw was Trevor drawing up his mask to cover his face.

15

It always took a long time for the effects of ether to wear off. Patients could be groggy for hours, and they needed someone to sit with them to ensure they didn't try to get up or tear at their bandages. Usually a nurse was assigned that duty, but Trevor had sent her away hours ago. Kate didn't know any of the nurses on this floor, and he didn't want her surrounded by strangers. He was exhausted and so full of relief that he felt like a limp rag, but he couldn't leave her side. Sitting in a hard chair pulled up close to Kate's bed was the only place in the world he wanted to be.

She'd been drifting in and out for a while now, sometimes muttering a few words, other times able to converse quite lucidly, but he knew she would forget everything when she finally emerged from the anesthesia. Patients never remembered what they'd rambled while under the effects of ether.

For hours he'd been stroking her hair back from her forehead, watching little emotions flit across her beautifully molded face as she slept.

She turned her head and opened her eyes, staring up at him. He drew the chair a little closer and leaned forward. "How are you feeling, princess?"

"Princess is my dog."

"The mutt that loiters on the hospital's front steps?"

"Mmmm."

How typical of Kate to bestow such a noble name on a mangy dog. "I fed her for you. She looked hungry, and I figured you'd want me to."

"Good," she murmured, then drifted off again.

He would do anything for Kate. She had no idea how much she meant to him during their years in school. The hours competing with her were the only times he remembered being happy during those miserable years. For a few hours every day he could forget the lousy hand of cards life had dealt him and just be a normal boy who liked a pretty girl.

Nathan Livingston didn't bother him. He knew Kate adored Nathan and would probably marry him someday, which was fine because Nathan was a decent guy. Trevor never aspired to Kate in that way. She was way out of his reach, but he relished the sheer joy of competing with her, even if it was something as stupid as who could skip a stone farther. Kate was always so fierce, never giving him an inch, and he liked that about her. Even now he liked that about her. Listening to the scratch of her pencil in the office as they both plugged away at their research. Watching her take notes as he read statistics to her. Watching the way her red hair caught the sunlight.

Kate stirred again. "Are you going to be here when I wake up for real?"

"You'll go back to disliking me when you wake up for real."

She chuckled. "I wouldn't be so sure of that."

She turned her head away and started humming a nonsensical little tune. What he wouldn't give to have a woman like this in his life. Kate was a once-in-a-lifetime woman. If he were a normal man like Nathan, he would have been able to compete for her. Court her by bringing her flowers or maybe one of those boxes of chocolates they sold in the fancier stores. But he wasn't normal, and never could be. If Kate had any idea of who he really was, she would want nothing to do with him.

Kate rolled her head back, still looking a little drunk on ether. "All the nurses like you," she said.

"They don't know me. I try to scare them off, but nothing works."

"You have a dimple when you smile. Right there." She stabbed a finger in the air, almost poking him in the eye before he grabbed her hand, tucking it back beneath the sheet. "Why haven't I ever noticed it before?"

Because he never had much to smile about.

"Am I going to have a scar?" She pulled up the bedsheet to look. He grabbed her hands again and placed them back at her sides.

"Careful, Kate. I put in a beautiful line of perfect stitches. If you ruin them, I'm putting them back in without anesthesia."

"I can see your dimple again. You shouldn't smile when you threaten me. I'll bet I can sew better than you."

"I have a very steady hand. My stitching is flawless."

Her head lolled to the side, and her breathing became deep and regular. A moment later, she started muttering to herself. "Trevor McDonough," she murmured.

"Who would have imagined I'd fall in love with the horrible Trevor McDonough."

The smile fell from his face. If Kate truly loved him, it would be unbearable to be around her. He would never be free to marry, but if he were . . . well, Kate had always been the finest woman he knew.

"Trevor McDonough," she mumbled again. "I've gone silly and stupid over Trevor McDonough. It's so embarrassing."

He closed his eyes, letting his fingers stroke her silky hair. Sometimes his longing for Kate was so great he didn't know if he could draw another breath. There were times in the office when he ached to drag her into his arms, to hold her close and tell her how he really felt about her.

He continued stroking her hair, just for a few more seconds. This was going to be the last time he ever set a finger on Kate Livingston. She was going to forget everything about this conversation, and tomorrow things would go back to the way they had always been. He drank in the sight of her. She was sunlight and energy and hope, and yet he needed to get away from her. He loved her too much to let these feelings get out of control.

He withdrew his hand. "I'm going to ask the nurse to sit with you for a while. Her name is Esther, and she'll take good care of you."

But Kate had already fallen back asleep. He placed a gentle kiss on her forehead before leaving the room.

16

Kate was warned that her biggest risk following surgery was the danger of infection, so she was allowed no visitors. Aside from the nurse who delivered her meals, Trevor was the only person she saw, and he was lousy company.

He came in twice a day to look at her incision and check for infection. The tentative friendship they had before her surgery vanished behind his ironclad shell. He held his chart before him like a shield whenever he came to examine her, using the same clinical demeanor he had with the patients upstairs as he took her temperature and checked her pulse. At any moment she expected him to start referring to her by a number. Couldn't he at least meet her eyes when he walked into her room? The man had as much passion as a potted plant.

Being an invalid was lethally dull, but three days after the surgery she was beginning to feel human again. The nurse propped some pillows behind her back, so she could sit upright and try to engage Trevor in conversation.

"I hope you've been to the boardinghouse for dinner. After saving my life, I expect my mother will shower you with rose petals and kill the fatted calf."

He didn't bother to reply as he made notes on his chart.

"Trevor!"

"Please keep your voice down," he said calmly. "I'm three feet away and my hearing is excellent."

"Then tell me you've been going to dinner and making friends. You need allies. There's a new man boarding with us, and he works at the Justice Department. He would be a good person to know."

Trevor replaced his pencil in the pocket of his lab coat. "I've no interest in cultivating friendships with government bureaucrats. They're cold-blooded vultures without a speck of human compassion."

Like someone else I know. "Trevor, I know it can be hard to pretend you have an actual beating heart beneath that lab coat, but you were making progress before I got sick. I hope we don't have to do remedial therapy."

Paying no attention to what she said, he

turned to leave. "Your parents are waiting outside. I said they could visit. Do you want to see them or should I send them away?"

"Why didn't you tell me?" She tried to rise, but Trevor's hand shot out and held her in place. After assuring him she would remain in bed, Trevor left the room.

A minute later her parents peeked in the door.

"It's okay. I'm not going to break," she said with a smile.

The door opened wide, and her mother burst into tears. Her father's eyes didn't look too dry either. They stood at the foot of her bed, looking as if they'd like to pounce on her, but they obeyed the rules to keep their distance. Her mother dried her eyes. "I would've had to kill that horrible man if any harm came to you."

Kate tried not to laugh; her stomach was still too tender. "You'll have to get in line. I think half the patients want to kill him over the cod liver oil he makes them drink."

Her parents weren't allowed to touch her. Instead they sat on stiff-backed chairs on the opposite side of the room, looking out of place and ill at ease in the stark hospital setting.

"How's everything at home?" she asked.

There was an awkward pause before her

mother jumped in to reply. "Fine," she said brightly. "Everything is fine."

But it wasn't fine. She could tell by the glances that flew between her parents, and the way her father's hands clenched and flexed.

"What's wrong? Is someone sick?"

"No one is sick except you, Kate," her father said with too cheerful a smile.

"Tick? Is Tick all right? I haven't seen him since the surgery."

"Tick is fine," her mother soothed.

"What about Charlie? He always gets a cold this time of year."

"Charlie is fine and kicking up a ruckus on the floor of Congress," her father said.

Kate ran through the names of all the other boarders, but her parents were determined to assure her everything was perfectly fine and she shouldn't worry her head for a single second. Still, she knew something was wrong.

They left after their allotted one-hour visit, but when Tick came later that afternoon, she wasn't about to tolerate being brushed off. Still wearing his uniform after completing his shift at the clinic, Tick's handsome face was bursting with excitement at seeing her again. She would have none of it.

"What's going on at home?" she demanded. "And don't try to deny it, because I can tell when Dad is lying, and he lied through his teeth all during their visit this morning."

Tick sat in the same hard-backed chair on the far side of the room, rubbing his hands on his thighs and looking like misery itself. "We aren't supposed to talk about it until you're feeling better."

"I'm feeling better. Talk."

Tick continued to hedge, but when she threatened to get out of bed to shake him, he finally relented.

"It seems having the guards stationed in the hospital scared away whoever planted the mercury. There hasn't been any more trouble upstairs, but now they're planting stuff at our boardinghouse."

She was dumbstruck, and her blood ran cold as Tick provided the details. Two days ago the cleaning girl took a load of sheets down to the first floor to launder them. She found a box filled with thin glass plates in the washtub. At first she didn't know what to make of them, but their father did.

They were medical slides, filled with samples of diseased lung tissue. A label attached to each slide was coded with the same numbering system Trevor used for his patients.

They called the police immediately. Trevor came to the house to examine the slides and confirmed they were human tissue samples common in medical research. The glass plates were the same type used in his Baltimore study, although Trevor said the slides were new, not six years old.

The police took the slides away and questioned every person living in the house. No one had noticed anything unusual or spotted a stranger in the house, but with so many people coming and going, it would have been easy for someone to slip inside without attracting attention.

Mr. Zomohkov and his wife both moved out the following day.

"They had already paid through the end of the month and wanted their money back," Tick said. "Mrs. Zomohkov is convinced the slides were soaked in tuberculosis germs, even though Trevor said the slides weren't dangerous. Even so, Father gave them their money back. I doubt we'll be seeing them again."

Their boardinghouse built its reputation on her mother's fabulous cooking and the powerful network of alliances that could be found around their dining room table. She clutched the sheets, feeling suddenly cold.

Surely a single incident wouldn't ruin a reputation that took more than a decade to build, could it?

"I have permission from my commanding officer to begin spending the night at home," Tick continued. "A couple of other guys from the barracks are donating their spare time to keep an eye on the house when I can't be there. Nice to have friends, you know? Besides, Mom's cooking is much better than what they feed us at the barracks."

Kate sagged against the pillows. This was all her fault. She had brought this trouble to their home. Whoever was out to ruin Trevor was now polluting her own home and trying to drag her parents down as well.

"They've picked the wrong house to attack," she said, her voice vibrating with anger.

She almost bit Trevor's head off when he came in to check on her later that afternoon. "When were you going to tell me what has been going on at home?"

He continued scanning her chart with the detached expression she knew so well. "We have a team from the local police department investigating the incident, three private investigators, and the US Marines on the case. There's nothing you can do that isn't already well covered. I need you to calm down."

"Believe me, I've tried!"

"Try harder." He flipped her chart closed and headed for the door.

"If you walk out that door, I'm following you."

He froze. Every line of his back went rigid as he gripped the doorknob. Slowly he turned to face her, his face looking as if it were carved from stone. "If you try to get out of bed, we have straitjackets."

She threw a pillow at him.

He caught it, but the pillow messed up the alignment of his tie and vest, and his perfectly groomed hair was knocked into disarray. He looked stunned, like no one had ever thrown a pillow at him and he didn't know what he was supposed to do with it. Finally a little starch went out of his spine, and he dragged a chair to the bedside and sat, the pillow resting in his lap. He scrubbed a hand over his face and swallowed hard.

"Kate, I'm sorry about what's happened," he said, staring at the floor. "I've dragged your family into this whole disgusting mess, and I swear to you I will find out what's going on. Just give me some time."

He told her that his private investigators

in Baltimore had already interviewed the hospital staff and most of the family members of the patients involved in the mercury study, and they could find no evidence that any of them harbored a grudge against him.

"Is it possible this has nothing to do with the mercury study?" she asked. "Is there someone else you offended over the years?" He glowered, but she rushed to explain. "Look, most of your life is an open book, because you can't resist seeing your name in the newspaper. But right after that mercury study in Baltimore, you were missing for two years. Where were you?"

He sighed. "Not that again."

"Maybe all this is related to what you were doing during those two years?"

"Nice try, but I can assure you it does not."

She wanted to jump out of the bed and shake him, but even pushing herself higher against the pillows made her abdomen ache. She straightened the sheets over her lap and adjusted her nightgown.

"Why are you so secretive about that time? Maybe you were a lush and spent two years drunk under a coconut tree?" His withering glare was answer enough, but she decided to keep digging. "Or you were robbing banks out west somewhere. Why don't you just tell me where you were?"

"Kate, I've been conducting the study upstairs and doing your share of the statistical work for the past three days. I really don't have time for nonsense."

"You don't have to be so frosty."

A memory kept tugging on the fringes of her mind. Trevor drawn up close to her bedside, leaning over her with a wistful smile, stroking her hair as if he couldn't bear to tear himself away. Surely that was just a dream? His face had been gentle as he leaned over her. Maybe the drugs had fed her overactive imagination, because the man who comforted her in those strange, hazy hours had all the warmth and tenderness of the world blazing in his eyes. It was hard to look at Trevor without remembering that man. He'd been so gentle. Still teasing and overbearing, but also kind and patient and . . . loving.

A nurse tapped on the open door and then pushed a metal cart with Kate's evening meal into the room. One wheel wobbled and squeaked, while her stomach growled in anticipation. As the cart came closer, she sighed as she smelled beef broth. They'd given her nothing but clear broth for days, and she was famished.

Sometimes it was so much fun to tease

Trevor, especially when he was acting all formal and professional. She needed to crack through that reserved demeanor and find the passionate man who loved nothing more than matching wits with her.

"What's wrong with the kitchen in this hospital? Can't you do better than beef broth?"

"You could probably handle something a little heavier," Trevor said. "What are you hungry for?"

"Black Angus steer," she said without missing a beat, but she spoiled the effect when a giggle escaped.

"You are really pushing it, woman," he said. He looked at the nurse. "You can give her some oatmeal with a little milk. Let me know if she gives you any trouble and I'll get that straitjacket."

It had been almost twenty years since Trevor handled a shotgun, but his old training picking off rats at his mother's farm came in useful today.

Joseph Barrow, the surgeon general for the navy, asked Trevor to accompany him to the country for a day of shooting clay pigeons. Why a grown man would find pleasure standing in a field, getting chewed on by gnats while shooting a piece of clay launched from a spring-loaded trap was beyond him. Shooting the varmints off his mother's patch of land served a purpose, but today's outing seemed entirely pointless. The weight of a shotgun against his shoulder brought back old unwelcome memories of another life in Scotland, but his muscles remembered how to cock and angle the gun to trace the flying clay disk until it slowed near the top of its arch. He squeezed off a round.

"Well done," Barrow said as the clay disk shattered and fell to the ground. He nodded to the young marine at the trap to launch another clay pigeon.

How much longer was he going to have to do this? It was obvious why the surgeon general had dragged him out here. For whatever reason, men liked to do business on golf courses or hunting fields, which was a colossal waste of time.

"What's the state of the nonsense with the *Washington Post*?" Barrow asked as he knelt to reload.

Trevor clenched his teeth, feeding another round into the shotgun's chamber. "No progress," he replied. "They gave me a lot of blather about freedom of the press. It seems more like 'freedom to slander' to me."

"Hmmm," said Barrow. He stood with his

freshly reloaded shotgun and nodded to the marine to release another clay pigeon. Trevor winced at the loud blast and watched the clean hit shatter the target to pieces. The acrid scent of gunpowder tinged the air. "I'm going to need you to do better, Dr. Kendall."

"I've been informed that murdering the editor of the newspaper is not an option."

Barrow affected a polite smile as he rested the butt of the shotgun on the ground and turned to Trevor. "Pity. Nevertheless, I'm starting to take heat for this, and I don't like it."

"I don't like it either. I don't like that these people will do anything to drive me out of the hospital. I don't intend to let them win."

"Fine," Barrow snapped. "But get on with it. The newspaper articles are bad enough, but what happened last weekend at that boardinghouse went beyond the pale."

Trevor shook his head. He'd hoped that incident would have escaped the surgeon general's notice, but apparently the man had his ear to the ground. Barrow was still on his rant.

"The president is gearing up to ship the marines to Chile, and I've got enough on my hands without this drivel about an

274

incompetent doctor on my payroll. Find out who's behind the rumors. I don't care how you do it, but get it done. Otherwise you'll need to clear out of the hospital and find another source of funding. I can't have this sort of thing stinking up my reputation."

Trevor blinked at the steel in the man's voice. For over a decade the surgeon general had done nothing but lavish praise and funding on Trevor's research, and now his career was threatened because of a *journalist*?

His lawyer had effectively squashed Superintendent Lambrecht's attempt to get Trevor evicted from the hospital, but if the surgeon general pulled his support, Trevor's last line of defense would be gone.

The image of Jack and Amy standing beside him on the crest of that mountaintop rose in his mind. Their memory fueled him through sleepless nights, propelled him through docksides and whorehouses and tenements on a quest to find and help other suffering people.

But not if he was driven out of his profession by a bitter coward who didn't even have the spine to face him. He hoisted the shotgun to his shoulder.

"I'll put a stop to it," he said.

■ ■ ■ ■

Kate came home a week following her surgery. A temporary sickroom had been arranged in the front parlor because her mother didn't want Kate on the fourth floor where there was no water closet or anyone to hear her call for help. Tick helped Kate get situated on the sofa, and her mother brought a little bell to ring if she needed anything.

During the day, the house emptied as most of the boarders headed off to work. Kate had nothing to do but worry over who planted those revolting slides in their house and why. She spent hours gazing out the front window to watch passersby on the street, paying extra attention when one of them paused before their house or seemed to linger for no apparent reason. She didn't like being this paranoid, but there was no doubt that someone had slipped inside and escaped notice once before, and she wasn't going to let it happen again.

Irene Bauman often flitted around, bored out of her mind. For the first time, Kate realized half of Irene's problems probably stemmed from having nothing to do all day but ogle the male population of the city.

Near dinnertime people began returning home. Charlie Davis presented her with a big bouquet of flowers, and Justice Bauman brought a jar of candied orange slices.

Kate wasn't allowed to sit at the dinner table, so she ate her bowl of oatmeal in exile on the parlor sofa. The rumble of hearty conversation from the dining room made her feel deserted, and watching pedestrians outside on the street made her sense of isolation even worse. A man hefted a toddler high against his chest with one arm and held his wife's hand with the other. A couple of children tossed a ball to each other. And in the distance . . .

Was that Trevor headed their way? In the dim twilight she could see his tall frame, his dark wool coat flaring out behind him, and a medical bag in one hand. Such a typically dour expression on his face. She smiled as his footsteps thudded on the landing, wishing her heart wouldn't speed up so much at the sight of him. He walked in without knocking and spotted her on the sofa.

"I don't make house calls very often," he said as he walked into the room and set his bag down.

"I hope this isn't going to cost extra."

"It's going to cost whatever your mother is serving for dinner." He didn't crack a smile as he pulled up a footstool, reached for her hand, and started taking her pulse. "Feeling better today?"

"I'm fine, but I hope you don't let dinner go to your head. Everyone has been singing your praises all afternoon. Even Mother is willing to concede your brilliance, which is a shame because you've already got such a problem with your ego."

He studied his watch as he continued taking her pulse. "Don't be bitter, Kate. Besides, after that surgery, I'll bet you're glad I was always better than you in biology."

"That's not true!"

"In four years of school, I had better grades in biology three times, and we tied once." Trevor pulled a thermometer from his bag and shook it before placing it under her tongue.

He had her there, but she didn't intend to concede. She shifted the thermometer to the side. "Any luck with the investigation?"

His mouth thinned. "I spoke to a couple of investigators today. They're looking at professional rivals — people I beat out for a grant or funding, which is nonsense, because medical rivals don't get ahead by firing low blows like this. I'm sure this is related to the mercury study."

"Or it could be related to those missing

two years." She removed the thermometer from her mouth. "Is that when you were having a passionate affair with an opera singer? Or an actress?"

"Oh, for pity's sake . . ."

She couldn't resist digging. "Or ran off with Gypsies? Or went digging for gold in California?" She pushed herself a little higher on the sofa. She had been deliberately goading him with ridiculous theories but gasped when a terrible thought seized her.

"Were you married? Do you have a wife and family stashed somewhere?"

A burst of laughter escaped him. "Is that what you think?"

Given the way he laughed, it did seem pretty foolish. It was impossible to imagine the dry, upright Dr. Kendall getting soft and romantic over a woman, but when he smiled like that, there was a dimple on the side of his face. Why had she never noticed it before?

The dimple triggered a memory . . . Trevor smiling down on her with tenderness, his gaze soft as he cared for her. He'd been so gentle, so loving . . .

Raucous laughter sounded from the dining room, and they both startled.

She glanced away and forced a lightness

into her tone. "Whatever you were doing couldn't have been that bad. And it might help us figure out who hates you enough to want to bring you down. The way you clam up whenever I mention it makes me think there's something I need to know. Where were you, Trevor?"

"I was minding my own business," he snapped. The temporary reprieve evaporated, and the arctic blizzard returned. He dumped the file in her lap. "I'm hungry. You can record your own temperature reading. You know how." He then turned and headed toward the dining room.

So grouchy! Not that Trevor was ever a bundle of sweetness, but they had a very nice understanding before the surgery, even if he had resisted her advances. It was embarrassing how much she enjoyed his company and looked forward to working alongside him.

For some reason he held himself aloof from her. She absently twirled the thermometer, rolling the hard glass tube beneath her tongue. Why was he so reticent about his past, and about those two years in particular? She leaned her head back against the pillow and racked her brain for everything she knew about Trevor.

His father was wealthy, but Trevor disliked

280

him enough to shed the McDonough name. Trevor had been sent to America to be raised by a guardian, yet his father cared enough to send a Black Angus steer at Christmas and a priceless book of Shakespeare's plays as a birthday present. Was his father still alive? Maybe she could ask Tick for his help in figuring this out. Tick was quite clever at solving problems, and she was desperate enough to recruit him to the cause.

Because someone from Trevor's past wanted to ruin a very fine man, and she wasn't going to stand to the side while it happened.

17

The enforced rest felt good at first, but after three days on the parlor sofa, Kate was ready for a change of atmosphere. Though she was well enough to return to her own bedroom, spending the entire day alone upstairs seemed too dreary for words, so she remained in the parlor. Besides, this gave her a chance to keep an extra set of eyes on the security of the boardinghouse, because they were no closer to finding whoever planted the medical slides.

Irene Bauman was on hand to keep Kate company. She let Irene model her latest clothing purchases and listened to the girl prattle on about the clerk at the general store, whom she was convinced fancied her. So did the assistant at the post office, and a young lawyer at her father's office. It seemed the entire male population of Washington carried a torch for her. It was a wonder the nation hadn't ground to a halt in the wake of Irene's staggering appeal.

One of Tick's friends from the marines, Corporal Stephen Lad, was spending a few hours every day at the boardinghouse to make sure there was no more trouble. So far, almost a dozen men had taken turns covering the hours until Tick could return from his duties at the hospital and take over. It must be very dull, and sometimes they volunteered to do a few chores to keep themselves busy.

This afternoon Corporal Lad was helping her father repair a loose drainpipe at the back of the house. Irene perched on the footstool and leaned closer to whisper, "When I passed Corporal Lad this morning, he made facial advances toward me."

"Facial advances?"

Irene nodded. "You know, following me with his eyes, smiling without smiling. Men do that to women they find attractive."

"Oh, Irene . . ." Sometimes the girl simply left Kate speechless. She couldn't wait until Trevor gave her the go-ahead to return to work.

"I wonder what those policemen are doing outside?" Irene said.

Kate swiveled to look out the front window. Sure enough, there were four police officers walking toward the house. A moment later their footsteps sounded on the front steps. "Go get my father, quick," Kate said.

This was what happened when Nathan was killed. Her heart raced, and her lungs seized up. This could be about Tick. Or Trevor . . .

Kate hurried to the front door, yanking it open to see all four police officers gathered on the front stoop. "Yes?"

"Good afternoon, ma'am. I'm Officer Rycroft of the Washington Police Department. We have a warrant to search these premises."

A wave of dizziness passed over her. "A warrant?"

"What's all this about?" Her father came striding in from the rear of the house, Corporal Lad right behind him. Kate moved back to clutch at the banister, trying to process what was happening as the other police officers pushed inside and began spreading throughout the ground floor of the boardinghouse.

"We have reason to believe tainted medical samples may be hidden in the house."

"Someone planted medical trash here last week," her father said, looking ready to explode. "We had nothing to do with that."

The officer looked uncomfortable. "I'm

aware of the case. We've had an anonymous tip about serious misconduct, and given what was found last week, a judge has signed a warrant to search the property."

The strength left her knees as Kate sank down onto the stairs, one hand clinging to the banister. Her father continued to deny they had done anything wrong, but the policemen were already going in and out of rooms. It felt like a violation as one of them opened the drawers of the dining room bureau, rummaging through the cutlery with a loud jangle. One officer mounted the staircase.

"You can't go up there," her father said. "Those rooms are occupied by people who pay good money for their privacy. Business people! Congressmen!"

"Our warrant covers the entire house, including all the individual rooms."

The color drained from her father's face. This was a disaster. Footsteps thudded on the staircase and on the floor above them. The officers were respectful, but this was awful.

And it was all her fault. If she hadn't gone to work for Trevor, none of this would be happening. The Zomohkovs already left because of this, and now surely there would be others who felt compelled to leave. Her father plopped down on the stair beside her and slung an arm around her waist. "Don't you worry," he said in a low voice.

But she did worry. As the afternoon dragged on, the boarders began returning home. Charlie Davis looked up the staircase in bewilderment when he wasn't allowed to go to his room. He agreed to wait outside until the search was finished.

Tom Wilkerson from the Patent Office was less congenial. "I have confidential paper work in my room," he said. "This is an outrage!"

Kate wasn't sure if he was yelling at the police officer or her father. Either way, she prayed the police would finish their work and get out so this mortifying incident could be over. It was after five o'clock and the rush of people returning home would begin soon.

"Found something, Sergeant," a voice called from high on the fourth floor. "It was in Mrs. Livingston's closet, on the top shelf."

She sucked in a breath. Her own bedroom? She hadn't been upstairs since before her surgery, but she had nothing to hide in her room.

Kate moved off the staircase as an officer carried a large box down the steps, holding it far from his body as though the contents revolted him. She'd never seen it before!

"What's inside?" the sergeant demanded.

Kate held her breath. The police officer tipped it forward so they could see.

Inside the box were more slides of medical waste and half-empty vials of mercury.

This box was worse than before. The lung tissue and mercury were bad enough, but most damaging was the paper work. Kate recognized the papers instantly because they were the same forms she used for the current study that measured the saturation of nutrients in the patients' blood — except these forms tracked mercury.

One set of files reported mercury dosages and effects on the patients, but there was an identical file that reported an entirely different set of statistics. Statistics that indicated tremendous improvement in the patients' health.

"It looks like Dr. Kendall was faking his results and hiding the evidence in Mrs. Livingston's room," the police officer said.

"That's absurd," Kate said. Yet it was easy to see how someone who didn't know Trevor might come to believe such a thing. The names and dates on both files were identical, the dosage of mercury the same.

Only the conclusions were wildly different, and that pointed to a clear-cut case of medical fraud.

She didn't need a lawyer to tell her where this was leading. They suspected Trevor of falsifying his research and hiding the evidence in her house. Officers interviewed some of the boarders, wanting to know how often Dr. Kendall had been to their house and if he had ever been caught prowling around the upper floors.

Tick arrived home, pushing through a throng of people gathered outside. He pulled her aside, concern in his eyes. "Don't say anything," he warned. "They may try to implicate you in something, and you're under no obligation to speak with them."

"Someone is trying to frame Trevor," she whispered.

Tick frowned. "This house has been under constant guard since that first box was found. My guess is the second box was planted in your room the same time they put the one in the washroom. When no one found it, they sent an anonymous letter to the police to prompt a more thorough search."

Her hands went clammy. It wouldn't be long before whoever was doing this would try to draw an association between her and

Trevor. After Trevor began dining with them, their friendship was common knowledge. What better way to damage Trevor than to imply he was hiding evidence of fraudulent research at the house of an associate?

Tick pulled the draperies aside and eyed the people on the street. "It looks like some reporters have arrived."

The breath left her in a rush. Trevor was already taking a beating in the newspapers, and this was going to launch a frenzy. He didn't deserve this. She felt tired and weak as she returned to sit on the stairs, leaning her cheek against the cool wood of the newel-post.

Trevor arrived a few minutes later. His face was white with anger as he shoved through the onlookers clustered on the sidewalk. He spotted her on the staircase and headed straight to her.

Leaning over, he said in a low voice, "Are you all right?" His eyes darted over her face, and he reached out to cup the curve of her jaw. Concern simmered in his gaze. A lump formed in her throat because the first question he asked was about her.

"I'm fine, but I don't understand why this is happening."

He nodded brusquely. "I don't either, but

I'm going to find out." He strode away to speak with the sergeant in charge. Behind her, she could hear the harsh tone of one of their boarders, who demanded a refund of his money.

"I won't stay in a house where disease is rampant," the boarder said.

Justice Bauman perked up. "See here, is there any danger of that filth infecting the inhabitants of this house? I have my daughter's well-being to consider."

Silence descended on the parlor, and everyone looked at Trevor. "No one can catch tuberculosis from what's in that box," he said. "It doesn't work that way."

"How can you tell?" a boarder said. "It appears as though you haven't had much success curing those people at the hospital."

Trevor looked like he wanted to strangle the man, but he wisely decided not to engage. Justice Bauman was talking to a policeman on the landing, and a few minutes later the police allowed the boarders to return to their rooms.

But the damage had been done.

By the end of the evening, eight of their boarders informed her father they were moving elsewhere. In ten days the payment on their mortgage was due, and their ability to pay it was dwindling by the hour.

Kate was unable to sleep as she lay on the sofa and stared out at the starlit night. Trevor was so passionate in seeking a cure for tuberculosis, but he was out of his league now. While she wasn't sure how to handle things either, her sitting on this sofa and doing nothing was getting them nowhere. If Trevor couldn't solve the problem, then she would.

At half past three in the morning she heard Tick stirring abovestairs, preparing for his four o'clock shift at the hospital. She was dressed and waiting when he came downstairs.

"I'm coming with you," she said.

"No, you're not," he replied, keeping his voice to a whisper. "You're going back to bed." They had been trained since childhood to keep quiet until all the boarders were awake.

She took a step toward him and fastened the ties of her cloak. "First of all, I have a sofa, not a bed. And I'm not setting foot in my bedroom until we figure out what's going on. I need to go to the hospital with you."

"I don't think that's a good idea."

She pulled up the hood of her cloak. "The surgery was ten days ago. I'm perfectly fine now, and I need time in the office without Trevor breathing down my neck." When Tick still looked uncomfortable, she redoubled her efforts. "Trevor is the most closemouthed and stubborn man alive. He won't reveal anything of his past to me, and you can be certain he hasn't been forthcoming with the police either. I need to find out where he was during a two-year period in his past. I think it's the source of all these troubles."

Tick finally relented, and by four o'clock they were at the hospital. No one was about the place this early in the morning, their footsteps echoing in the darkened hallways. After Tick switched positions with the marine who stood the night guard, Kate unlocked the door to the office she shared with Trevor.

She swallowed back a lump of guilt as she sat in Trevor's chair, telling herself if he weren't so secretive she wouldn't be forced to invade his privacy this way. Her heart pounding, she slid open the top drawer.

A tray of pencils, a pair of scissors, some paper clips, and a slim medical dictionary. The rest of the drawers were equally devoid of personal details. She turned in the chair, thinking . . .

The locked file was surely her best clue for wherever he was during the years 1887–88. Another search of Trevor's desk failed to turn up the key. She ran her hands along the underside of the drawers to see if perhaps the key had been secured there. But after ten minutes of searching, she was certain there was no key in his desk.

Then it came to her. Tick knew how to pick a lock. They had used his skills more than once when boarders had accidentally locked themselves out of a room. She tipped her head outside the office door and saw him standing guard at the back entrance. She smiled, and he gave her a brisk nod in reply.

"Good morning, ma'am," he said before riveting his eyes straight ahead.

She loved it when he put on his grown-up façade. "Tick, I need a favor."

He glared at her.

She cleared her throat and tried again. "Private Norton, I need assistance in the office."

He glanced up and down the halls. All was still except for the night nurse, who was paging through a vaudeville magazine at the front of the clinic. He reluctantly followed her into the office.

She gestured to the locked file drawer beside Trevor's desk. "I need you to pick the lock on that drawer," she said.

"Forget it."

"It's not like I'm ransacking his files for fun. I just need to find out where he was during those two years. I think it may be behind what's happening at the boarding-house."

"Trevor doesn't think so. If he did, he would tell us."

"Can you be sure about that?"

Tick looked back at her, indecision on his face.

She pressed her case. "Our parents owe a payment to the bank on the first of the month, and we just lost a third of our boarders. More people are likely to leave today. We can't afford not to open that drawer."

"I don't have anything to pick it with."

"This is a hospital ward. I'll get you whatever you need." A quick look in the supply closet found some of those shiny metal tools Trevor used to poke and prod the patients. She stood over Tick as he squatted down by the drawer, carefully fitting a slim pick into the lock and lifting it open. The drawer slid open silently.

"Now get out of here," Kate whispered.

She closed the office door behind Tick, then returned to the file cabinet. All the drawers were empty except the bottom one, which was dense with the same sort of medical files in the other drawers. Scooting off the chair, she knelt on the floor, pulled the bottom drawer out farther, and read the only name printed on all the file tabs.

Trevor McDonough.

She sucked in a breath. With trembling fingers she rifled through the files. Some were faded and creased with age, others crisp and new, but each file was labeled with a year.

She grabbed one of the older files and flipped it open to see a medical chart inside. She scanned the columns and the numbers, a wave of dizziness crashing in as she realized what she was looking at.

No. Please no, not this . . . not Trevor. But she knew what the charts meant.

Trevor had tuberculosis.

He had sixteen years of records to document his illness. She slammed the drawer shut, a scream tearing from her throat, its echo crashing through the silence of the night.

Tick burst through the door. "What's wrong?"

She knelt on the floor, clinging to the cold

metal drawer handle, unable to lift her head. Tick hunkered down beside her, his hand on her shoulder. "Are you hurt?"

Her heart had just been torn in half, but that wasn't what he was asking. Her chest hurt so bad it was hard to even draw a breath. "I'm okay," she whispered.

Everything finally made sense. Why Trevor held her at arm's length. Why he was so dejected and aloof and so sickly white when they were in school. Why he drank the same medicine he gave the patients.

"I need to get you off the floor. This can't be good for you."

Tick lifted her up and guided her into Trevor's chair. Gently he tilted her chin with his hand so he could look her in the eyes. "Should I get a doctor? You don't look so good."

"It's all right," she mumbled. "People who don't want the truth shouldn't go rummaging through locked drawers. That's all."

"What did you find?"

She found that she was falling in love with another man who was destined for an early grave. "It has nothing to do with what's happening at home. It's none of my business. I'm sorry I looked."

"Do you want me to send for Trevor?"

Another teardrop plopped onto her lap,

and she swiped at her face. "No. I'll be all right."

But she wouldn't be all right. All summer she had been battling an irrational attraction to Trevor, and she had been losing. Beneath his aloof demeanor he had an immense zeal for life. He kept it tightly under wraps, but she had seen it . . . on the rooftop, in the lab, even when he caught her gaze across the dinner table there was an answering flare of awareness before he could snuff it out. They both felt it, but now she understood why he'd been too honorable to act on it.

A few weeks ago she had sat in this very office, laying her heart at his feet. He looked desperate for her, but he pulled away. *"Kate, I'm not a good bet,"* he'd told her.

Now she understood what he meant by those words.

18

Ever since he was a boy, Trevor did his best strategizing while walking. Whether it was hiking through the misty Scottish highlands or the glittering streets of Berlin, a vigorous full-bodied stride was the best way for him to tackle a problem. It helped to burn off the tension so that he could focus all his attention on the perplexing problem at hand.

Bypassing the morning streetcar, he walked to the hospital as he obsessed over who could be trying to destroy him. It was bad enough when he was the target, but the image of Kate with her shattered expression — sitting there on the staircase of her parents' boardinghouse as the police searched their home — had haunted him all night.

Once inside the hospital, he vaulted up the stairs two at a time and then burst through the door to the clinic, strode down the hall, and flung open his office door.

What was Kate doing here? Why was she sitting at his desk?

The chair squeaked as she swiveled the seat to face him. Her face was pale and tear-stained. His breath left him in a rush when he saw the file on her lap. He sagged against the doorframe.

"Oh, Kate, I wish you hadn't seen that."

Her lower lip wobbled, and tears pooled in the bottoms of her eyes. "Why didn't you tell me?"

Because tuberculosis was such a foul, horrible disease, and he didn't want anyone treating him differently because of it. From the day he first met her, Kate had relentlessly teased, tormented, and challenged him. Since they began working together, she looked at him with excitement. With admiration. With the spirited joy of competition. He didn't want those things to be replaced by pity.

"You don't seem sick," she whispered. "You aren't like the patients in the ward. I don't understand."

He didn't either. There were so many things about tuberculosis that were still a mystery. He closed the door so they could speak privately, then grabbed her desk chair and pulled it across the room to sit next to her. It hurt to look at the despair in her face.

"Talk," she ordered.

That made him smile. How typically Kate. She always confronted problems head on, while he buried them, kept them hidden under layers of secrecy. It was easier to solve problems on his own without entangling others, while she wanted to spill them to the world.

"I was diagnosed when I was thirteen," he said.

"Was that why your father sent you away?"

His laugh came out harsh, but he quickly stifled it. "No, it had nothing to do with that." His thirteenth year was the most miserable of his life, beginning with his being placed on a ship and sent away from Deirdre and every other person he knew in the world, and then just a week later to be clobbered with the news of a terminal disease.

"I was on the ship headed for Washington when my cough became so bad the ship's doctor wanted to see me. He said I had all the symptoms of tuberculosis and told me I probably had two, maybe three years to live."

He didn't tell Kate how the doctor had ordered him to stay in his cabin and keep away from others. That if he coughed on others or became friendly with them, it was

300

as good as sharing his terminal disease.

"When I arrived at Senator Campbell's house, I didn't tell anyone. The ship's doctor warned me they might turn me out of the house if they suspected. I couldn't go home to my father, and I didn't know a single person in America, so I stayed quiet. I hated it, but I had nowhere else to go and I was afraid. Mrs. Kendall figured it out pretty fast. She recognized the rattle in my lungs because she'd been battling the same disease."

Mrs. Kendall backed up what the ship's doctor said. She had been keeping her disease a secret too, for what logical man would let a tubercular woman supervise his kitchen if he knew? Or welcome a sick boy into his home? Mrs. Kendall taught him how to hide when the coughing seized him, how to get sunlight to offset the tubercular pallor. She taught him to drink honeyed tea by the gallon to ward off the fits of coughing. But the most important thing she provided was a person for him to confide in. They were two people who shared a terrible secret. In his desperate and storm-tossed world, Mrs. Kendall became his safe harbor.

School was a special blend of torture and release. All the other kids were normal and happy, but he couldn't befriend any of them, because if he started coughing it would put them in danger. They were always laughing and cheerful. It hurt to be around them when his world was so bleak. But Kate was different. He didn't need to befriend Kate to compete with her. For a few hours each day he was released from worrying about the plague growing in his lungs and could indulge in the thrill of matching his wits against the smartest girl he ever met.

"After a few years, I started feeling better. Mrs. Kendall swore it was her cooking. She always made me eat second helpings of beef and milk. She insisted it was good for tuberculosis. I ate because it was hard to keep weight on. Senator Campbell used to joke about his soaring grocery bill. He must have written something to my father, because that was the month the Black Angus steer was delivered."

Kate winced. "I'm so sorry I teased you about that."

He clasped his hand over hers. Her hand was so slim in his palm, and he traced his thumb over the back of it. "Don't worry about it, Kate. Anyway, I think there was some truth to Mrs. Kendall's idea about diet. When I left for college, my lungs were clear. I went to a specialist in Boston, and he said I showed no signs of tuberculosis. I was finally able to gain some weight, and my skin started to hold its color. My strength returned. During those years I felt . . ."

It wouldn't be fair to tell Kate what going to Harvard felt like. The return of his health at the same time he was able to bask in the joy of rigorous academic study was exhilarating. He was among the tiny fraction of tubercular patients who'd been liberated from a death sentence. The world stretched out before him like an endless feast of learning, discovery, and opportunity. It was as if every blessing in the world had been simultaneously showered on him.

"Are you . . . ?" Kate's words were hesitant. "Are you cured?"

How was he to answer that? It would be so easy to lie to her, to tell her what she wanted to hear so she could put this horror behind her and never worry about it again. He couldn't bear to look at her as hope faded from her face. He turned to stare at a sparrow flitting in the tree outside his window. Anything rather than look at the heartbreak in Kate's eyes.

"For a while I was convinced I was cured," he said. "When tuberculosis is confined to the lungs, sometimes it simply disappears.

It only happens about ten percent of the time. We don't know why or what causes some people to spontaneously heal, but I thanked God that I seemed to be one of them."

And during those years he became obsessed with finding a cure. He attacked the problem by seeking out the best scientists in the world to share their research. He observed at clinics and universities and then launched trial programs of his own.

"I treated the worst cases," he continued. "For eight years I was around patients whose lungs were infected with a massive degree of tuberculosis. I quit wearing a mask, even when I was working with patients I knew were at the contagious stage of the disease. For eight years I checked myself, and for eight years I was clean."

Kate stiffened beside him. He didn't want to proceed with the story, but he had to. He sent her a reluctant smile. "As you know, I can sometimes be a little arrogant."

"A bit, yes." She gave a sniffle and waited for him to continue.

"I started to wonder why I hadn't been re-infected, especially since I spent so many years around infected people. Was it possible that once a person survived tuberculosis, they acquired some sort of immunity?

Smallpox works that way."

For over a century, people had been safely receiving the smallpox vaccination by having a tiny dose of the disease injected under their skin. After battling a mild, localized infection, they were immune for the rest of their lives. If there was a chance to develop a similar vaccine for tuberculosis, it would be a godsend, but he needed more information.

"I wanted to know if I was immune from ever getting tuberculosis again. This isn't the sort of thing I could test on a volunteer. I had to test it on myself."

"Oh, Trevor . . ." She whispered his name, and never had he heard such agony carried on a single word. She knew exactly where this was leading.

"I collected a sample of live tuberculosis bacillus and prepared to expose myself to it. I spent the night before on my knees at a church, praying with every ounce of strength I had. Then I had a doctor in Boston help me with the injection. He shot the bacillus into my left bronchial tube, the passage that leads directly to the lung. And then I waited."

It didn't take long to know his experiment had been a failure.

"Six days later I tested positive for tuberculosis."

Tears coursed down the side of Kate's face. How badly he wanted to assure her that everything would be well, that there was no need to cry over him. But he couldn't lie to her.

"I followed the best medical advice to cure it, and all the experts believed that the highest, thinnest air in the world was my best chance of beating the disease. Dr. Brehmer cured himself of tuberculosis by living in the Himalayas. That was how I got to India. I spent two years in a sanitarium high up in the mountains. Even then some doctors were speculating about the value of the sun. So I lay out in the open, wearing nothing but my skivvies every day for two years. It was freezing cold, but I got used to it. I drank straight cod liver oil and ate as much meat as I could get my hands on. And by the time I left, I was cured. That was three years ago. I'm one of the few people in the world to have beaten the disease twice."

"Do you still have it?"

Today he was healthy, but tomorrow? His immune system had already taken quite a beating, and his odds of surviving another attack were slim.

"I test myself every week. My lungs are clear, and they have been for three years.

Sometimes the bacillus can lay dormant for years before roaring back to life, so I don't know what my future holds. I still drink the cod liver oil and lie in the sun. I figure my odds of it coming back someday are pretty good, but I just don't know."

This wasn't the kind of information he wanted to share with anyone, certainly not a person he cared for. In a tiny corner of his soul he always harbored a wild, irrational hope about Kate, but first those dreams were killed by his disease, and then there was Nathan. During his school years he never tormented himself with romantic fantasies of Kate. Besides, the opportunity to compete with her was all he really needed.

All that was different now. Kate was free, and she sensed the electricity between them. Now that she understood why he'd always held himself aloof from her, a kernel of hope began to emerge. Like a small flame that was allowed more fuel, it began to glow and burn brighter. Most women would run screaming from him, but Kate? She was a risk taker. There was never a challenge Kate didn't want to beat down and tackle until she got exactly what she wanted.

He picked up the files resting on her lap and set them on the desk. He drew his chair closer and reached for her hand. "Kate, look at me," he said.

Her chin was still pointing down, but her eyes came up to meet his. Her expression nearly drove the breath from him. How could she wear her feelings so openly and still function?

"So now you know. I've never let myself get close to a woman because I'm not a good long-term bet. But I care for you. I've *always* cared for you." Without asking permission, he reached up behind her neck to stroke the heavy coil of her hair. He leaned forward, giving her plenty of time to pull away if she chose.

She didn't.

He kissed her softly on the mouth. Nothing had ever felt more right or natural than kissing Kate, and she didn't pull away from him. She leaned toward him and kissed him back.

Emotion surged through him, but he leaned back in his chair and forced his face to remain blank. Whatever Kate decided to do in the next few seconds would change the course of his life. She stared at her lap, her hand nervously twitching inside his palm. Then she pulled away.

Kate would not look at him as she scooped his medical files from the desk and carried them back to the filing cabinet. She knelt on the floor and shoved the files back into the lowest drawer. She sighed, holding on to the open file drawer as though she couldn't sit upright without its support. Every muscle in her body was rigid, but her head hung low like the blossom of a flower whose stem sagged under its weight. She refused to look at him.

"I've already buried one man I loved," she said in a whisper. "I don't think I can do it again."

The flame of hope flickered out. Her words were a blow, but he didn't let it show on his face. He swallowed hard before answering. How quickly dreams could shrivel and vanish, like autumn leaves that skittered away on a gust of wind.

"I kind of thought you might say that."

Her tears started rolling again as she turned to look at him. "Trevor, I'm sorry. I'm so sorry . . ."

It was easy to pretend he wasn't hurting. He'd been doing it his whole life. "Don't worry about it, Kate. I've known since I was thirteen I should never get too close to a woman." He went over to where she knelt on the hard floor. "Let me help you up. You're barely out of a sickbed."

She sniffled. "I could race you down the

stairs and beat you out the front door."

It was a lie, but he let her win this one.

They were going to have to pretend this conversation had never happened. It was sure to be torture, but he would do it. He'd rather have whatever tiny piece of Kate he could get than see her leave the hospital.

"I have a stack of reports that need to be analyzed," he said in a neutral voice. "I've arranged them in order of priority. I would appreciate it if you could have them done by the end of the week."

"Of course," she said, and he breathed a sigh of gratitude.

With every ounce of his heart and soul, he wanted Kate as more than a colleague. He wanted her as a woman, as a wife, as someone he could hold long into the night and the first thing every morning. It was an insane hope that he was foolish to even toy with, but he could settle for remaining her friend. He was light-headed with relief when she took the stack of reports to her desk. She was going to stay.

Hiring Kate was the best thing he'd done in his professional career, and he could handle anything so long as she didn't leave him.

19

Trevor went back to work at his desk as though nothing had happened, and Kate tried to do the same, but after two hours she'd been unable to finish a complete set of calculations. It was as if her brain had splintered into a dozen pieces, none of which could function together. She wanted to cling to Trevor and weep at his terrible news, yet at the same time the logical piece of her brain was terrified because Trevor's missing two years had nothing to do with the harassment at her parents' boarding-house. She was no closer to discovering who was launching this hideous crusade against a man she'd come to love.

Her breathing became ragged again and she sniffled.

"Quit crying, Kate."

Trevor's voice from the other side of their office was flat, and he didn't look up from the document he was writing as he spoke.

She whirled in her chair to face him.

"I don't know how you can pretend nothing has changed," she said. "How can you just sit there and go on like everything's fine?"

"Because nothing has changed," he asserted calmly. "My health is exactly the same as it was this time yesterday, we both have a backlog of work to process, and you have no interest in anything beyond a platonic relationship. Therefore, nothing has changed. Any sniveling from your side of the office is a pointless waste of time."

She sighed. It wasn't true; everything *had* changed. If he'd made such a ridiculous comment yesterday, she would have teased him about being a lifeless block of ice, but that seemed only cruel now.

Nurse Ackerman tapped on the door. "A message arrived for you, Dr. Kendall."

A quiver of anxiety trickled through her. Ever since those ominous notes began arriving, any unexpected message set her on edge. Trevor scanned the message, his mouth compressing into a hard line.

"What's wrong?" she asked.

"I need to meet with the surgeon general. He heard about the raid last night. I expect he's going to demand my resignation." He grabbed his briefcase and began stuffing files inside it.

"You don't really believe that, do you?"

"I didn't believe the police would ransack your parents' house, but they did."

He slammed in and out of the filing cabinet, making a racket while he pulled every file related to the mercury study. He glanced over at her. "And I want you to go home. You're overly emotional and not yet ready to be around the patients."

"I'm healthy as a horse."

"Doctor's orders, Kate," he said before storming out of the office.

Trevor walked to the surgeon general's office. It would be faster to take a streetcar, but he felt no obligation to rush across town like a disgraced schoolboy summoned to the principal's office. Besides, Trevor needed time to think, and he couldn't do that while being jostled about with a crush of people on the streetcar.

He could take anything so long as Kate didn't leave him. For a glorious moment this morning, he thought she might welcome him into her life as a man who was desperately in love with her. In that fraction of a moment he was almost blinded by joy. These last few months had been the most exhilarating of his life, and it was due to

Kate being by his side.

But if a platonic relationship was all he could have with Kate, he would accept it. He'd held his breath all morning, fearing that at any moment she would push away from her desk and say she could no longer cope with the sorrow that came with this job.

And now he had the surgeon general wanting to tear a piece of him as well. He'd battle this storm just like all the others. The memory of Jack and Amy Collison rose again in his mind. How foolishly optimistic he'd been when he believed he could heal those two children. Maybe all doctors grieved the most when their first patient died, but Jack and Amy had been more to him than that. The anguish of their deaths taught him to keep his guard up around all future patients, but their memory still burned brightly enough to keep fueling his quest. They would be forever young in his mind, and he could not shake the sensation that they would approve of his determination to keep fighting.

Trevor climbed the concrete steps leading up to the brick fortress, prepared for battle.

He got one. Sitting behind his grand desk in full military uniform, Barrow's eyes were like flint.

"For the first time since I've taken office, I've had the muckrakers penning scurrilous stories about me because of this tuberculosis debacle, and I've had to defend myself to the War Department. I hired you to find a cure for our sailors and soldiers. What's this I hear about you consorting with pickpockets and prostitutes?"

That was surprising. Trevor had been distributing his serum to the underbelly of Washington ever since arriving to the city last year, but apparently someone was now watching him and carrying tales to the surgeon general.

"I distribute medicine to them. No one else in the city seems interested in their well-being."

"Well, it looks bad. You're a man of science, working in an outstanding medical facility, and you shouldn't be out slumming with the dregs of society. And all this on top of the mercury debacle. I won't permit my reputation to continue taking a beating. I'm assigning a new doctor to lead the study, one with a spotless reputation. In three weeks, Dr. Michael Wells will be taking over the study."

Trevor reeled back in his chair. "Michael Wells? He has a spotless reputation because he's an infant!"

"He's twenty-two years old, the same age you were when you began practicing medicine. He will complete his medical internship in three weeks, and after that he's taking over your study. I want you out of the office before he arrives."

Michael Wells was a promising young man whose interest in tubercular research had caused them to cross paths several times over the past few years. That didn't mean Trevor intended to turn over his research to the boy. It took years of working with tubercular patients to sense the quirks and fluctuations of the disease, and he had no intention of turning the helm of his ship over to an untested boy who was just learning the ropes.

"You can't fire me," Trevor snapped. "I'm paying for the study from my own funds."

"It was my influence that persuaded the Washington Memorial Hospital to open one of their floors to you. I'm withdrawing my patronage, and you've got three weeks to clear out. Your patients and your staff may stay, but you need to go."

Trevor flexed and clenched his fingers, wishing he had a pencil to fiddle with. "What does Michael Wells have to say about this? I can't believe he would support my removal."

"Since the navy paid for Dr. Wells's education, it hardly matters if the move has his approval. He has agreed to take over the study."

Trevor stood, bracing his hands on the edge of Barrow's desk to lean over and glare down at the man. "Removing me might spare your reputation in the newspapers. Maybe it will please the government bureaucrats you bow down before, but what about the men in the ships? In the army barracks? What is your obligation to defend them when compared with your own reputation?"

He straightened and stalked over to the door. He swallowed back the anger and turned to face Barrow once more. The man was a doctor, and yet he cared more for his reputation than the lives of those who were falling victim to the most insidious disease in centuries.

"I could take lessons from you in safeguarding my reputation. Had I gone into surgery or the university, I would have garnered far more glory. Both would have been safer and more prestigious, but I chose a disease of the poor, of the immigrants and prostitutes and factory workers. *Of the soldier.* And I will keep fighting for them, even if you won't."

The slamming of the door gave him a

temporary surge of satisfaction, but it couldn't solve the problem. In three weeks he would be ousted from the study, unless he could solve the mystery of who wanted to destroy him.

For two days the newspapers were full of lurid details about the raid at her parents' house. Kate's mouth went dry when her name was splashed across the pages, noting the "special friendship" she shared with Dr. Kendall and the fact that the damning box of medical records was found in her bedroom. Some of the newspapers even printed the names of prominent boarders who were forced to loiter on the street as their private rooms were searched.

What a disaster. The only glimmer of hope came from the *New York Times.* That wasn't surprising, since Harvey Goldstein, a journalist working for the *Times,* was a boarder at her parents' house, and he'd gotten to know Trevor through the dinners at her mother's table. His article was the first to suggest the hostility was a result of a paranoia whipped up by people afraid of a contagious disease they didn't understand.

Amazingly, the next day the local newspapers sheathed their claws as well. Kate couldn't resist gloating when Trevor arrived at the office.

"You see? Your friendship with Harvey Goldstein brought a fair newspaper article in New York and prompted the other papers to soften their tone. You should listen to me more often."

Trevor sat at his desk and pinched the skin on the bridge of his nose. "Kate, your voice is already burned like acid into my frontal cortex." He rummaged through his medical bag, then rolled his office chair to her side of the office, holding a thin stick with a cotton swab at the end. "It's time for your monthly check. Open wide."

She opened her mouth, holding her breath as Trevor swiped the back of her throat with the dry cotton swab. It always felt so awful to have that stick down her throat, but it only lasted a moment.

Immediately after swiping Kate's sample onto a glass slide, Trevor repeated the procedure for himself. He slipped both slides into labeled envelopes and carried them to the laboratory for Henry to test.

A shaft of anxiety pierced her. Trevor's immune system was different from hers. He was more vulnerable to catching the disease, and the knowledge that Henry was about to look at Trevor's sample set her nerves on edge.

"I need to make a house call," Trevor said, grabbing his overcoat. He didn't say whom he was going to see, but when he slipped a mask into his pocket, she had a suspicion.

"Mrs. Kendall?"

Trevor nodded.

"I thought you said she wasn't contagious?" Kate always found it strange the way patients suffering from tuberculosis could go through long dormant periods when they were incapable of spreading the disease, but then it could morph into a highly contagious germ capable of spreading by a single sneeze.

"Last week she became contagious again," Trevor said bluntly.

Kate bolted to her feet. "And you're still willing to treat her?"

"Yes, Kate. I'll treat any patient who needs my help, whether contagious or not."

After he left the office, slamming the door behind him, Kate put a hand to her forehead. Her head had begun pounding. Trevor tested himself every week, even as he marched off to treat a woman who could be infecting him. Only ten yards away, Henry was examining the slides collected from the employees at the clinic.

She couldn't bear waiting any longer. Rising from her chair, she walked over to the laboratory. Henry's nose was buried in the *Washington Post,* and she had to call his name three times before he jerked his attention to her.

"Sorry, Kate," he mumbled as he pushed the paper away. "The Princeton football season isn't going well, and their upcoming schedule doesn't look promising." Henry's greatest pride in life still seemed hinged on the three years he played football for Princeton. Kate wished she had nothing more serious to worry over than football scores.

"I was hoping to learn the results of my lab test."

"I'll have a look right now," he said, then reached for the sample with her name on it. He opened the slide and used an eyedropper to plop a single bead of purple dye onto the sample. If any tubercular bacillus lurked on that slide, the dye would make it easier to see. Henry pushed the slide into place under the microscope and adjusted the lens to the proper angle.

"You're all clear," he said.

Kate pasted a tight smile on her face. "Could you test Dr. Kendall's sample as well? He would like to know."

Henry looked confused. She'd never made such a request in the past. After a moment, he shrugged and repeated the same procedure for Trevor's slide. It seemed Henry took forever as he adjusted the dial, twisting it forward and back as he studied the sample. His face contorted while he squinted through the eyepiece.

Kate held her breath. Maybe Trevor had lied about his health. Maybe that was why he was so comfortable treating patients who were contagious, because if he already had the disease again, it wouldn't really matter, would it? Her mouth went dry as Henry straightened.

"His sample is clean too," he said simply.

Relief at hearing the news almost made her dizzy.

She returned to her office and plunked down at her desk, turning to look at Trevor's empty chair. She was trembling. Was she going to hold her breath each time she saw him carry his slide to the lab for testing? The last few days they had done nothing but squabble over petty things rather than discuss the real issues that lay between them. He nagged her to use a letter opener to open her correspondence rather than ripping it open like she always did. She criticized the way he incessantly rapped his pencil while he was reading. It even annoyed her the way he wasted time by washing his hands both before and after each meal.

Working alongside him had been easier when she didn't know he returned her feelings. When he kissed her that morning, it had been the most tender, heartbreaking moment of her life. She wanted to hold and comfort him. She wanted to lean against him and have him tell her that everything would be all right, that her fears were baseless.

But her fears were not baseless, and nothing Trevor could say would convince her otherwise. At this very moment he was tending a woman whose breath contained a germ that could kill him. How could he risk his life like that?

She rose from her chair. It was time to save Trevor from himself.

The library of the surgeon general was housed in a grand building on the National Mall. Located only a stone's throw from the Smithsonian, the towering building was a fortress of red brick and classical lines. In addition to the medical library, the building housed the Army Medical Museum, a research wing, and the office of the surgeon general.

And today Kate intended to use all those facilities to get answers to her questions. Pestering Trevor for more insight into his condition had been hopeless. *"Short of removing my left lung and slicing it open for a public viewing, I have no way of knowing if there's any permanent damage,"* he'd said when she tried to glean more insight into his condition.

The surgeon general's medical library was her best bet to find out what Trevor was up against. The cavernous space of the library soared three stories high, with books stacked to the ceiling. Rows of narrow metal walkways and staircases were used for accessing books on the upper levels. The rest of the floor space was dominated by oversized worktables. But the best resource in the room was the librarian.

In addition to being a librarian, Louis Spiegel was a medical doctor. With a thick mustache and rectangular spectacles, Dr. Spiegel was patient and helpful, though the knowledge he imparted made Kate's blood run cold. He guided her to the other side of the building, where the medical museum housed thousands of specimens and the odor of formaldehyde tinged the air. The librarian showed her cross sections of healthy pink lung tissue compared with tubercular lungs. The damaged lungs looked as if filled with pockets of brown grit. Bulging white scar tissue surrounded each of the cavities. No wonder the patients at the hospital were so short of breath.

"If someone survived tuberculosis, are they at greater risk of contracting it again?"

Dr. Spiegel gestured to the sample of ravaged lung tissue. "Someone whose lungs once looked like that would have greater difficulty throwing off the disease again. I'm afraid there are too few people who have survived it for us to have much insight."

He accompanied her back to the library, where they spent an hour poring over the medical literature. Pride rushed through her when they stumbled across a number of articles written by Trevor, although there were plenty of other articles that underscored the grim prognosis of what they were battling. There was no cure in sight. Doctors hadn't even begun to understand the disease, and everyone was blindly groping in the dark.

Then she stumbled across an article that made her want to tear her hair out because of how stupid she had been. She held the journal up so that Dr. Spiegel could read the title. "Is this true?" she asked.

"I haven't read the article, but it certainly seems like common sense."

If Trevor were here, she'd be tempted to throw the journal at his head. The article spoke of the dangers faced by doctors and nurses who treated tubercular patients. It stated that medical professionals faced far greater risk of contagion than the general population. It recommended medical personnel with compromised lung health be assigned duties where they had no contact with tubercular patients.

Why was Trevor continuing to work with people who could infect him? Surely Nurse Ackerman or Henry could draw those samples, so Trevor didn't have to be in personal contact with the patients. *She* would take the samples if it would keep Trevor safe. His commitment to finding a cure was admirable, but every day he set foot inside the clinic was a danger to him. Trevor was smart enough to work in any medical field he chose. He could teach at a college or pick another disease to study. He didn't *have* to work with tuberculosis.

She sat back in the chair, staring out the window at the sunlight glinting through the trees. She would simply have to persuade Trevor to abandon tuberculosis in favor of a safer career. If he would be willing to do that . . .

A whole new world of hope began unfolding inside her. They would be so good together. Every day would be filled with the joy of working alongside a man who challenged, excited, and thrilled her. She loved him. She loved his intelligence and his commitment to medicine. His heroism and his humor and the way his eyes came alive when he looked at her. Yes, he might be stricken with tuberculosis again, but so could any person. If he would take reasonable precautions, she could be brave enough to risk a life beside him. As soon as he shifted into a different line of medical research, there would be nothing standing in their way.

Trevor's brilliance and passion for medicine were too valuable to waste on the front line of the battle against tuberculosis — not when there was a whole world of medical discovery just waiting for the right person to take up the calling. He could study cancer or diseases of the heart. There were so many other paths he could take, all of them important and in need of further research.

Her biggest challenge was going to be convincing Trevor of that fact.

Trevor's eyes were grainy from lack of sleep as he stepped off the streetcar and headed toward the hospital. He'd spent most of the night before on the southeast side of town, distributing serum to the people who had probably never seen a doctor in their lives. Or in Barrow's charming turn of phrase, Trevor had been "slumming with the dregs of society." He didn't care what others thought of the people he treated. They had pain in their lungs and little kindness in their lives. He had firsthand experience with the agony of tuberculosis and wouldn't turn his back on anyone who suffered with it.

After a sleepless night, he spent the morning at his lawyer's office, gearing up for a legal battle against the surgeon general. It promised to be an ugly fight. The surgeon general secured the hospital space using money awarded to the navy from the Pasteur Institute. That grant had been awarded in Trevor's name, not the surgeon general's. If the government yanked Trevor's privileges from the hospital, Trevor would retaliate by demanding a return of the Pasteur money. It was sure to be a difficult and frustrating legal quagmire.

It was going to be a long day. Hopefully he could get his hands on the patients' charts and scan them without having to see Kate. Being around her was a sweet kind of torture he didn't have the strength to face today. She'd picked a fight with him each time he'd seen her in the past few days. He knew exactly what was happening, for he did the same thing when upset. It was easier to lash out and attack rather than surrender to the heartache. His entire thirteenth year he'd been sullen and angry at the world.

Unfortunately, she was waiting for him the moment he stepped onto the fifth floor.

"Trevor!" she said brightly, tugging off her mask and striding toward him with a smile that was almost blinding. She'd been playing checkers with a few of the patients in the sitting area but sprang to her feet the moment he walked through the door. How pretty she looked, wearing one of those puffy-sleeved blouses tucked into a slim black skirt. Yet it was her face that captivated him. Her cheeks glowed with health, and her eyes looked as excited as a child on Christmas morning.

He was immediately suspicious. Kate had nothing to be that cheerful about, and she was too clever by half. He glanced up and down the hallway to see if there was anyone she was performing for. Aside from the patients playing checkers and the ever-present Nurse Ackerman, they were alone.

"What can I do for you, Kate?" he asked, trying to inject a little energy into his voice. Actually it wasn't that hard. Sometimes just being near her made his world lighter.

She drew to a halt a few feet from him, her hands clasped before her. "I have an idea," she whispered. "Can I show you something?"

Whatever had put that sparkle in her eyes was something he wanted to see. Kate always had that quality about her, going back to when they were in school together. She could find the silver lining in any cloudy day. He was irresistibly curious as he trailed after her to the sitting area, where she picked up a medical journal, opened it to a marked page, and held it before him.

He was stunned when he saw the subject of the article. Had she dared show this to anyone else at the clinic? He didn't even want to discuss it within earshot of his employees or the patients. Flipping the journal closed, he rolled it into a tube and used it to point to the door.

"Outside," he ordered. Anger lent him strength as he barged out the door and down the stairs.

"Did you know about that?" Kate asked in a breathless voice while she followed him downstairs. "Your odds for contracting tuberculosis shoot way up from working so closely with infected people, and I can't imagine why you're continuing to do it."

Her voice echoed in the stairwell. Just

what doctors and nurses wanted to dwell on — the elevated risk of contracting the fatal disease killing their patients.

"Please remain silent until we get to the conference room," he said in his detached voice. He kept his mouth clamped shut while proceeding down the crowded hallway, Kate still trailing after him.

"I know you're an intelligent man. So I don't understand why you, of all people, would put yourself at such risk."

Kate didn't seem capable of holding her tongue, and the conference room was at the other end of the building. In frustration, he grabbed her arm and hauled her inside the linen storage closet. The scent of bleach rose from the stacks of neatly folded sheets on the shelves. He fumbled for the chain attached to a single light bulb overhead, tugging on it, then slammed the door shut. Crammed with shelving, the storage closet was cramped for two people, but he didn't want Kate yammering in the hallway. Everyone in the hospital was already aware of the elevated risk regarding contagious disease, and her waving that article around was pointless and unkind.

Standing only inches from her, he said, "I once injected myself with live tuberculosis cells, and you don't think I'm willing to risk my life to find a cure for this disease?"

"Now that you know you aren't immune, why are you still here?" She didn't even wait for an answer as hope began blooming on her face again. "Trevor, I care for you. I've tried to fight it because, well, you're the horrible Trevor McDonough and I've perfected the art of resenting you over the years."

He battled a reluctant smile, for the affection blazing in her eyes robbed her words of any sting. His heart turned over as she took his hands, clasping them in the little bit of space between where they stood. Her voice was so tender and fragile he could barely hear it.

"I think we might have a future together," she whispered. "I know the world is not a safe place, and I can accept that. It nearly killed me when Nathan died, but I'm willing to take a risk on you."

Hope flared to life. If Kate were willing to join her life with his, it would be as if a gust of wind had filled his sails, lifting him higher and farther than he ever thought possible. She was the spark that had always been missing in his life.

He couldn't stop himself. He wrapped his arms around the small of her back and hoisted her in the air. She clung to his shoulders as her feet left the floor, and the beginnings of an impossible dream began taking shape inside him.

"Do you mean that?" he asked, holding his breath. He held her so high that he had to look up at her.

The way she smiled down at him was glorious. "I do. I love you. I want to share my life with you." She lowered her face to kiss him. He couldn't believe it. Kate was in his arms and raining kisses on him. She was smiling so wide she could barely land a kiss on his mouth. He dragged her tightly into his arms, holding her close and kissing her back with all the love rushing through his veins.

When he set her down, his arm bumped against the shelf and the medical journal came tumbling down, landing on the concrete floor with a splat. He glanced at the journal, then back at Kate.

"Why did you show me that article?" A dark thread of suspicion took root. Kate looked hesitant but kept smiling as she smoothed the lapels of his jacket and moved to straighten his tie. He liked the feel of her hands on him, but he reached out to still them. She was up to something.

"When I first learned about your battle with tuberculosis," she said, "I assumed it meant you were destined to get it again, and then you would die and I'd be alone. The article confirms that you're at a much higher risk every day you continue to treat patients with tuberculosis. But, Trevor, if you switch fields, you're at no elevated risk! The article says doctors who don't treat infectious patients are much safer. You could go into surgery. Or fix broken bones. Or teach —"

He rocked back, bumping against the shelving behind him. "But I'm called to treat tuberculosis, to find a cure for it."

"Trevor, think! There are other things you could do in medicine where you would be safer."

She was so naïve. There was no place he could run where he would be isolated from people who carried the disease. He would never know precisely how he contracted tuberculosis the first time, but it wasn't in a hospital. The odds were he'd gotten it from his mother. He remembered the sound of her cough, and in her final months her handkerchief was always dotted with blood. He would be lulling Kate into a false sense of security if she believed quitting this work would make him safe.

"Kate, I could get tuberculosis from sitting next to an infected person on the streetcar. From sitting next to someone at your mother's dining table. You need to understand that."

"But why increase your risk? Once you set foot into the ward, you risk your life with every breath you take. That's a choice, Trevor."

"Yes, and it's my choice." How could he explain it to her? He had a unique perspective on the horrors of this disease. Already he could feel Kate slipping away from him, unless he could make her understand. He tilted her chin up to him.

"I feel called to treat this disease, Kate. Do you understand what I'm saying? I believe there's a reason I've been able to survive it twice. I think God wants me right here in this hospital, doing everything I can to try to figure this thing out. I'm one of a few doctors alive who has experienced everything my patients endure and is still willing to share the same space with them. I know the pain of feeling my lungs stiffen with scar tissue, to feel like I'm drowning inside my own body. I know how it saps the energy from my limbs and spirit. And I feel called to do something about it. God wants me in this battle, and I won't run away. Please don't ask that of me."

"I *am* asking it." Kate pulled back from him, until she collided with the shelving behind her. "I understand there are no guarantees in life. Either one of us could fall down the stairs and die today. But you don't need to take pointless risks. The only way we can make a life together is if you quit studying patients with tuberculosis."

Her voice was pure steel. It was the old Kate, the Kate who battled for what she wanted and almost always got it. She wanted him to quit. The surgeon general wanted him to quit so that a man scarcely older than Tick could take over. It was hard to keep standing upright as the pain ripped through him, closing up his throat and making his voice tight with frustration.

"Two minutes ago I was happier than I'd ever been when you said you'd share your life with me." She winced, but he would not stop. "You give with one hand, and then take away with the other."

"You don't need to yell, Trevor."

The linen closet was small, and he could probably be heard outside, but he didn't care. Frustration was breaking his control, and years of anguish came roaring out.

"Do you know how long I've wanted you? You're like sunlight and water and air to me. All you need do is walk across my line of sight and my whole world lights up."

"You love your crusade more than you

love me," Kate said, her lips trembling. "You'll kill yourself! You'll die because you're too arrogant to think another doctor could work with those patients as well as you." She stepped forward, bumping against him and grabbing the lapels of his coat. "Please . . . we could be so good together."

He pulled away. "Don't touch me, Kate. Don't come near me. I love you, but you don't know the meaning of the word. You only love when it's easy, when there are no storm clouds on the horizon."

"Trevor, I'm afraid."

"Of course you're afraid!" he shouted. "Do you imagine for one second that I'm not? But I won't give in to it. I would lay down my life for you. I would lay down my life for any one of the thirty-two people lying in those beds upstairs, and I won't turn my back on them. If I run away from what I've been fighting for all my life, *then* I begin dying. *Then* my purpose will be over."

She flinched and began straightening her shirt. "I've got to get out of here."

"Don't go."

She twisted away to fumble with the doorknob. He tried to turn her to face him.

"Kate, don't go, please. Stay and fight this out."

She shook him off and fled from the closet

as though it were on fire. He braced his hands on the doorframe, watching her dart around the people in the hallway. He wanted to run after her, drag her back into the closet, and plead with her to stay. He gripped the edges of the doorframe so hard it cut into his hands. His tie was askew, and he could tell by the way people looked at him that he was a disheveled mess.

What had come over him? He wasn't the kind of man to yell and storm and rage. All his life he'd kept such emotions clamped tightly inside, but Kate had unlocked that lid and they came thundering out.

He wanted her back. He wanted to look at her every day in their office and as they made their rounds in the hospital. He wanted to come home to her at night and watch her unwind that coil of her hair by the light of the fire.

Yet he knew from the moment he crested the top of a mountain with two dying children by his side what he was destined to do with his life. He would give anything if he could have Kate alongside him, but he was prepared to finish the journey alone before he would abandon his quest.

Kate couldn't return to work with tears streaming down her face and her heart splitting into pieces. Instead she ran to the churchyard two miles away, where Nathan was buried. By the time she arrived there, she'd composed herself and wasn't sniveling like a baby anymore.

She'd never seen Trevor so angry or even imagined he had it in him. Nathan never yelled at her. They'd been so young and never had any real problems in their life together.

"You only love when it's easy," Trevor had accused.

Was he right? She and Nathan never had any problems other than the frustration of saving enough money to find a place of their own to live. When they found nothing they could afford, they laughed and made do in Kate's tiny bedroom in the boardinghouse. If Nathan had lived longer, surely they would have been tested by life's challenges, but yes, her life with Nathan had been easy. Was she brave enough to love when it was hard?

The iron latch on the cemetery gate was cold as she lifted it and stepped into the walled yard. Right now Nathan was the only person she could talk to. She couldn't even bawl on her mother's shoulder, because Trevor asked her not to tell anyone of his condition. People weren't meant to carry terrible secrets alone. Maybe Trevor had mastered that skill, but she hadn't. Her boots wobbled on the path rutted by the roots of silver maples, until she stood before Nathan's final resting spot.

"Look at you," she murmured, leaning down to brush away the dried leaves that mounded up at the base of his headstone. She yanked a few clumps of weeds and tossed them aside. "I'm sorry I haven't been better about visiting. I have a new job and it has been . . . well, it's much better than my job at the census bureau." The lump in her throat made it hard to keep talking. She brushed the grit from her hands and tried again. "You remember Trevor McDonough, don't you? It turns out he's really something extraordinary. Who would have guessed it?"

It felt odd rambling to Nathan about a new man, but who else could she talk to? They had never spoken about such things, but she was certain Nathan would hope for her to remarry someday. If she'd been the one to die early, she would have wanted Nathan to find a good woman to marry.

She knelt down on the grass, clinging to Nathan's stone as she closed her eyes and prayed. *Dear Lord, am I making the right decision? Trevor needs someone to help him, but I don't think he's doing the right thing by risk-*

ing his life. I don't think I have the strength to support him. I don't think I can go through this again. What is it you want me to do?

There was no answer except the wind rustling in the trees overhead. Chilly air seeped through her cloak, and she pulled it tighter. She stood and looked across at the two square stones marking Carl's and Jamie's resting spots. Only their initials were carved into the stones. Her parents had been too poor to afford proper stones when they died, and afterward Kate had grown attached to these simple markers and didn't want to change them.

Why had God given her parents these two boys if they were going to die so early? They never had a chance to leave their marks on the world. Tick didn't even remember them anymore. Aside from Kate and her parents, there was no one else to remember Carl or Jamie Norton.

Surely it was a blessing that no one could see into the future. She couldn't have borne the agony of knowing what would happen to Nathan or her brothers. It would have been a constant sword hovering over her head, clouding her every hour with them. She was grateful she hadn't known what life had in store for them. With Trevor, she knew.

Fresh grief washed through her. She wasn't sorry she'd been blessed with Nathan or her brothers, but she'd never willingly invite this sort of misery back into her life. She hoped one day she would find another man to love, but it could not be Trevor McDonough.

She would have to quit her position at the hospital. It would be impossible to sit only a few feet away from him every day. To hold her breath every Monday while Henry tested Trevor's slide, waiting to learn if this was the week he had finally contracted the disease again.

She would need to find another position, for her parents depended on her income, especially since almost half of their boarders had left, and finding the money for the bank note at the end of the month was going to be dicey.

It didn't matter how much she loved working alongside Trevor. She pushed herself to her feet. There was no point dwelling on it. She knew what needed to be done.

Trevor wasn't going to take the news of her resignation well. Kate lay awake most of the night as she mustered the strength to walk away from the best job she ever had. Each time she tried to talk herself into staying, she remembered waiting in the doorway of the laboratory as Henry checked Trevor's slide. She couldn't endure that every week for the rest of her life, not when Trevor was choosing to put himself into the path of an oncoming train. How could she have children with a man who wouldn't take reasonable precautions? A man who loved his job more than he loved his wife?

Her note of resignation weighed heavily in her skirt pocket as she climbed the stairs to the hospital's top floor the next morning. She dreaded giving it to Trevor. Resting her hand on the door to their office, she murmured a prayer for strength, then walked inside.

Trevor's chair was empty.

"I believe he's up on the roof, ma'am," Tick said from his post by the rear entrance.

It was a sunny day but a chilly one. Would Trevor really be lying in the sun on such a day? But he did in the Himalayas, which surely was more uncomfortable than autumn in Washington. And if sunlight had medicinal benefits, she wanted him outside soaking up every moment of it.

She let herself onto the roof. Trevor was fully clothed, an open notebook resting on the ledge of a nearby brick wall. It was the first time she'd seen him since their encounter in the linen closet, and she braced herself.

"What are you doing up here?"

"I'm writing notes for the architect. I want this space ready for patients by the spring."

He didn't look at her as he spoke, his tone calm and professional. Cold. A few months ago she would have mistaken that behavior as detached, but now she knew better. His knuckles were white and his jaw clenched. Trevor was barely hanging on. She walked to stand beside him.

"I need to give you this," she said gently.

"What is it?" He glanced at the note, refusing to take it.

"I need to resign, Trevor. You know why."

He finally looked up at her, and this time his eyes were furious. "I never took you for a quitter, Kate." He dropped his pencil and folded his arms across his chest.

"Fine, I'm a quitter. You win. Is that what you wanted to hear?"

"Trust me, I don't feel like I'm winning right now." He turned from her to brace his hands on the edge of the wall, gripping it as he looked out over the treetops. His shoulders rose and fell with the strength of his breath, and then he sagged. When he spoke again, his voice sounded drained.

"Why are you giving up so easily?" he asked. "We've got a future worth having. A future filled with hope and passion and accomplishment."

"With fear and a dying husband."

He smacked his hand against the side of the brick wall. "I love you." He turned to her, his face full of longing. "I love your fire and intelligence and your humor. I love the way you never back down from a challenge. Don't let me down now, Kate."

"You don't even love me enough to tell me why you changed your name."

He gave a bitter laugh. "Is that all it would take? Fine. I changed my name because I despise my father and I want nothing to do with him. That's not the reason you're running away. Don't try to pin this on me."

The wind tugged at her hair, and a chill raced through her body. She turned away from the anger simmering in his eyes.

"You're right. I'm running away because I can't stand by and watch you kill yourself trying to cure tuberculosis. I understand you're a competitive person, and once you start a race it's hard to back out, but there are other challenges in medicine you could tackle. Why does it have to be this one?"

"Because I have been called. I've known it since the day I climbed to the top of a mountain with two children destined to die from this disease. I can't refuse that call. Never. Not even if it costs me the woman I love."

He strode to the door and headed downstairs without looking back. He still hadn't taken the note from her hands.

She followed him down, surprised to see Nurse Ackerman waiting for them at the base of the staircase.

"A message has arrived for you, Dr. Kendall. It's urgent."

Trevor's back stiffened. How she hated that her nerves seized up every time Trevor opened his mail. It would help if the private detectives he hired had made the least bit of progress in discovering who'd polluted her home with that foul medical waste, but they had learned nothing.

Trevor scanned the message, and his shoulders sagged.

Only for a moment. Then he straightened and headed toward their office without a word. She exchanged a nervous glance with Tick and Nurse Ackerman, both of whom shrugged in bewilderment.

She followed Trevor into their office, watching as he banged in and out of drawers, stuffing a bag with equipment.

"What's wrong, Trevor?"

He swallowed hard and grabbed his wool overcoat from the hook. "Mrs. Kendall is dying," he replied. "Her daughter asked me to come at once. I'll stay with her until she passes. Then I'll be back to talk to the architects about the roof." He finished packing his medical bag, his face closed and somber, the corners of his mouth turned down.

Mrs. Kendall was the closest thing to a family Trevor had left. Kate could only imagine the pain he must be feeling, but in typical Trevor fashion he was icily silent.

"If there's anything I can do —"

"I don't need anything."

She wanted to shake him. Was it possible Trevor never learned to ask for help? If he was banished from his home for some mysterious reason when he was only thirteen, perhaps he never had someone to lean on in a time of need.

"I know you don't *need* my help, but I want you to have it if it will make these next few days any easier."

He froze in the doorway. All Kate could see was the back of his overcoat and his dark head, but the tension in his entire body was obvious. He was so alone. All his life Trevor had been alone. Now she was leaving him as well, and Mrs. Kendall would be gone soon.

He turned, and she could see the hard-set line of his profile. "The only thing I really need is a competent assistant. I don't have time to search for your replacement. You can help by placing an advertisement in the appropriate places and interviewing the qualified applicants."

"You want *me* to do that?"

Trevor nodded on his way to the door. "You know the position better than anyone. Get someone on board right away. The sooner you're gone, the better."

20

Kate was busier than ever in the days that followed. Dr. Schrader, the one who reminded her of Santa Claus, filled in for Trevor to examine the patients each day and collect the data. She dutifully processed the statistics and filed them for Trevor's review when he got back.

In Trevor's absence she handled the appointment with architect Clifford Watson to explain the plans for expanding the clinic onto the roof. Kate knew exactly what Trevor wanted done, and she showed Mr. Watson the rooftop space. With a neatly groomed beard and warm brown eyes, the architect was enthusiastic as he scanned the roof.

"We can build a windscreen on the eastern side to make it more pleasant for the patients," he offered.

"Probably a good thing," Kate said as she burrowed a little deeper into her cloak. The

October air was chilly, and it was always breezy up here. After showing the architect the roof, she escorted Mr. Watson to the staff table. He spread out a large piece of drafting paper and began sketching potential plans. His expert hands were swift as they filled the page with possibilities.

"We will need to have an elevator installed, as some of the patients will be too weak to climb the stairs," Kate said. Was this something Trevor could afford? It was always such a mystery about where he got his money. He seemed so frugal in his personal life, but his generosity toward the clinic made her suspect he had a bottomless bank account somewhere.

"I can draw up a proposal with an elevator, and one without," Mr. Watson said. "It will certainly be the biggest expense of the project."

Kate pointed to a blank space. "Trevor would like to install some sort of heating mechanism here. He thinks this will buy the patients a few more months during the colder seasons."

"I'll make a note of it," Mr. Watson said. He cleared his throat and adjusted his tie. "Forgive me, Mrs. Livingston. I cannot help but notice you do not wear a wedding ring."

Feeling embarrassed, she nodded and

said, "I'm a widow."

"Ah." And with that simple word she felt the atmosphere shift. "My condolences. It was a recent event?"

"Four years ago. Can we discuss the options for supplying power to the heater? I don't know if gas or coal would be more efficient."

Anything rather than discuss her widowhood or romantic availability. Trevor owned her heart right now. Someday, after she was no longer working here at the hospital, perhaps she'd be free to look at another man that way, but not now.

The worst part of her day was reviewing the applications that flooded in for her job. Letters of interest began the day after she placed the advertisement, and each one of them hurt as she reviewed the letters. All of the men applying for the job had college degrees, and most of them had experience with laboratory research. It made her appreciate just how big a risk Trevor took when he'd hired her. She put aside the applications from the people who should be brought in to interview.

The third day of Trevor's absence, she arrived at work to see that Tick wasn't at his post. Neither was Nurse Ackerman. She looked over to an attendant who was preparing to wheel a breakfast cart into the men's ward.

"Where is everyone?" she asked.

The attendant lowered her voice to a whisper. "One of the young ladies died last night. Miss Wexler."

"No!" The world tilted, and Kate grabbed on to the back of a chair to steady herself. It wasn't possible. Hannah had been doing so well, and her blood counts were strong. Poor, sweet Hannah Wexler . . . the very first patient she'd met here. Kate swallowed hard. She and Hannah were the same age. Hannah would never see her thirtieth birthday.

Trevor's serum must not be working. She closed her eyes as the implications sank in. The numbers in Hannah's blood had been good. Every day as she entered data into the charts, Kate had silently cheered as Hannah's blood got stronger. She drifted toward the women's ward on legs that felt weak as balsa wood. Tick loitered in the doorway, twisting his cap in his hands.

"You heard?" he asked quietly.

Kate nodded. She dreaded stepping into the women's ward, but Nurse Ackerman might need help. She tied a mask over her face and stepped into the ward.

The privacy curtains had been pulled on

352

the rods above Hannah's bed. Nurse Ackerman stood on the other side of the room,
manipulating the rubber tubing for a steam
treatment to help loosen Blanche Groveland's lungs. Blanche's health had been
plummeting for weeks. Why had Hannah
died, while Blanche was able to hang on?

Nurse Ackerman's eyes widened in relief
when she spotted Kate. "I've sent for Dr.
Schrader, but someone will need to help
him with the autopsy. Can you do it? Three
nurses are out sick with the flu, and the
autopsy needs to be done within the next
hour."

"I wouldn't know what to do." Her stomach cringed at the very idea. She wasn't
strong enough to stand by while a girl who'd
been her friend was opened up and poked
and prodded. She wanted to run.

"There's nothing to it," Nurse Ackerman
said. "You just write the data on the chart
as Dr. Schrader dictates it to you. Not much
different from what you've already been doing for Dr. Kendall, just a lot more detail."

And the lifeless body of her friend only a
few feet away.

Trevor needed to learn why Hannah had
died, and the autopsy had to be done
quickly. They needed to understand exactly
what had failed, and why Hannah's blood

looked good and yet she still died.

She straightened her back in resolve. "I can do it."

The final stages of tuberculosis were never easy, nor was it possible to predict how long it would last. Trevor had already been at Mrs. Kendall's bedside for three days, and it could easily be another three before it was finally over. Her hair had come undone from the tidy coronet she'd worn for decades. Her daughter had tried to comb the scraggly mess into some semblance of order this morning, but she was crying too hard to have much success.

A handful of the old servants from Senator Campbell's house came to pay their respects. Trevor had a generous supply of cotton masks he handed each of them before he allowed them through the door.

"Don't get too close," he cautioned. "Even though she's sleeping, a fit of coughing may seize her and be dangerous for you."

On the third day, a batch of messages from Nurse Ackerman was delivered. Hannah Wexler died, and two more were likely to pass within the next week. Trevor stood, preparing to leave. Kate was going to need help with this. She had cracked when Ephraim Montgomery died, and she barely knew the man. Hannah's death was going to hit her hard.

It hit *him* hard. Patient 27F had good blood. Her lungs were in decent condition, but one of her organs must have failed. The note indicated Dr. Schrader would be performing the autopsy, so he would soon learn exactly what had brought her down.

His lips thinned as he reached for his coat. This was why he'd warned Kate not to become friendly with the patients. She was too tenderhearted for this sort of work, and she would need someone to comfort her. If he hurried, he could get to the hospital within the hour and be back at Mrs. Kendall's side by lunchtime.

His hand stilled. Kate could not be his responsibility anymore. He wanted to hold her as she cried and prop her up until she was ready to rejoin the living. He sought her out last spring because she was fierce and relentless; he never knew how soft she was beneath that fiery exterior.

It made him love her all the more.

For all he knew, she was already gone from the hospital, and a replacement had been hired. He set his coat over the back of the chair and resumed his seat beside Mrs. Kendall, listening to the rattle in her lungs and wishing he were a better doctor.

■ ■ ■ ■

Kate blanched at the sight of Hannah's dead body stretched out on the metal autopsy table. Hannah's face was contorted in a grimace of pain, her naked skin purple, her lips blue. *Oh, sweet Jesus, please let me have the strength to do this.*

She accepted the paper forms from Dr. Schrader, his kindly face giving her a sympathetic smile. He thanked her for filling in and assured her she didn't need to watch as he performed the autopsy, but merely record his notes.

Dr. Schrader gave her a dab of camphor to rub under her nose, which was supposed to mask the smell. It didn't work. She kept her eyes averted during the procedure, but the clicking of instruments and the terrible stench never let her forget exactly where she was. She made it through the two-hour procedure without fainting or crying, which was more than she could say for when Ephraim Montgomery died.

She ran outside when it was over, sucking in huge gulps of fresh air and wondering how long the smell would linger in her hair and clothes. Clinging to the banister on the front steps of the hospital, the magnitude of what she just did sank in. She wanted to rush home and take a bath and get the stench off her, but several applicants were coming today to interview for her job, and she needed to be there. It hurt just thinking about turning her position over to someone else. Although it was the most frustrating, challenging, and grueling job she'd ever had, still she loved it here.

A whimper at her feet grabbed her attention. The golden-haired dog looked up at her.

"Hello, Princess." Kate sank onto the steps and rubbed the dog behind both ears. The dog whimpered again and nudged closer to Kate. "I'm okay, Princess."

How strange that this mangy old mutt was offering her comfort, but she must have sensed Kate's distress. In the aftermath of the autopsy, her legs trembled and she couldn't get the smell out of her nose. But soon a sense of accomplishment began replacing the fear. Kate looked up at the hospital, looming five stories above her, a grand building filled with people who did such heroic work every day. Kate never imagined she'd have the fortitude to stand a few feet away while an autopsy was performed. She never wanted to do it again, but she hadn't given in to the impulse to run away. Trevor would be proud of her.

She pushed the thought away. It was going to be hard, but she needed to train herself to quit thinking about Trevor.

Princess laid her head on Kate's lap. How nice the weight of the dog felt. After being starved of physical affection for so many years, it was soothing to have someone to cuddle with, even if it was only a dog.

"I wish I could take you home with me." But a boardinghouse was no place for a dog, and she had an applicant coming for an interview within the hour. She marched up the staircase, determined to see this through.

Tick was waiting for her when she entered the clinic. "You survived?"

The worry on his face got to her, and she reached out to hug him, even though he was in uniform and she wasn't supposed to. "I'm still alive, yes."

Which was more than she could say for the first job applicant. Julius Hessman was a painfully thin man with a degree in mathematics and five years of experience as an actuary for the pension bureau. He had the mathematical ability to perform the job, but the way he clasped his hands as if he were reluctant to touch anything made her worry he might not be a good match.

"I would be required to share an office?" he asked as he hovered in the doorway of her office.

"Yes, but I can attest that Dr. Kendall is very professional. He will not disturb your concentration."

It was hard to coax Julius into the office. He fiddled with his tie and glanced at all four corners of the ceiling, the surface of both desks, and all along the filing cabinets. His mouth was pursed in disapproval. "I'm very particular about my space. This may be difficult for me."

A lifetime of serving demanding customers at her mother's boardinghouse made it easy for Kate to placate him.

"Perhaps you would be more comfortable at the table behind the nurses' station? It's where we take our meals and gather for meetings. We can discuss the position out there if you would be more comfortable."

Julius backed out of her office and followed her to the staff table. A few of the patients were playing checkers in the sitting area and watched the strange man with curiosity.

Kate outlined the position for him. When she tried to ask him about his work at the Pension Bureau, Julius was reluctant to talk. He set a stack of reports on the table and slid them toward her with a slender finger. "Examples of my reports," he said. "I prefer to let my work speak for itself."

This man was a walking disaster. When she asked if he had any questions, he looked around the space with trepidation and asked if this table was where the staff ate their meals.

"Yes, the hospital provides our lunch, and the food is excellent. We eat all our meals here."

"I don't like to hear other people chew," Julius said delicately.

From down the hallway Tick struggled to cover his laughter with a cough. Even some of the patients in the sitting area were trying not to laugh.

"I see," Kate said in a soothing tone. "Would you excuse me? Private Norton seems to be choking on something."

She kept a straight face until she was able to show Mr. Hessman out the door. An orderly arrived with the day's mail at the same time, and Kate flipped through the letters, scanning the return addresses and holding her breath against another anonymous, hate-filled letter. Her gaze landed on a bold scrawl in the corner of an envelope, and she gasped.

"What's wrong?" Tick asked, moving to

360

her side. Kate's mind was racing so fast it was hard to answer him.

"Mark Twain wrote us back!"

It was hard to believe, but the letter was there in her hands. Everyone within the range of her voice clustered around, eager to see the letter. Leonard Wilkes wheezed as he pushed himself to his feet and staggered over. Kate's fingers trembled while opening the envelope and reading it to the group. It was impossible not to laugh as she read. Mr. Twain did indeed plan to write another novel featuring Tom Sawyer, and he would happily send them an autographed copy upon publication.

A smile spread across her face until she remembered that Hannah Wexler, the one who so eagerly awaited any book by Mark Twain, wasn't here to celebrate the news. The laughter fled as a wave of grief settled over her.

Kate remained in the sitting area to wait for the next job applicant. Nurse Ackerman wasn't available to welcome him, as Blanche Groveland was continuing to deteriorate, and one of the men was critically ill as well.

Would it be possible for three people to die in a single day? On her first day, Trevor warned her that all the patients in the ward would be dead within a year. So many of the patients seemed to be hobbling along fine, and she hadn't believed him. She should have.

She rested her forehead in the palm of her hand and prayed the next applicant would be suitable for the position. Philip Walsh was much older and had plenty of experience at the Naval Hospital, so hopefully he would be capable of listening to people chew without suffering a case of the vapors.

The door opened, and a handsome gentleman strode through the door. Kate rose to greet the next applicant, but when she saw the man's face, she gasped. He looked so much like Trevor it took her breath away.

"I'm looking for Trevor McDonough," the man announced in a heavy Scottish brogue. "Excuse me," he amended. "I believe he's calling himself Trevor *Kendall* these days. Please fetch him for me."

It had to be Trevor's father. He had the same lean face and firm, unsmiling mouth. Aside from the threads of silver in his dark hair, it was as if she were staring at Trevor himself.

"I'm sorry, but he isn't here," she finally replied.

The older man looked around the clinic, stepping forward to peer around the corner into the staff area and behind the nurses' station. "Are you certain? The boy likes to avoid me when he can, but he must be here somewhere. I've already confirmed he's not at his home."

Nurse Ackerman came hustling into the front to grab a file from her desk. "You're looking for the doctor?" she asked. "He's still over with Mrs. Kendall, and we aren't sure when he'll be back. Kate can send a message to him if you need."

A round of coughing came from the women's ward, and Nurse Ackerman hurried back.

Mr. McDonough looked amused. "He still sees old Mrs. Kendall then? The boy always liked mingling with the servants. I gather some things never change." Then a transformation came over his face, and his dark eyes zeroed in on her, noting her red hair. "Kate? You wouldn't be Kate Norton, would you?"

She felt a niggling sense of unease. How would he know that? "That was my maiden name. I'm Kate Livingston now."

A grin spread across the man's face. It was disconcerting to see an identical dimple to Trevor's appear on the older man's cheek. "Well, well," he drawled. "The famous Kate, the redheaded genius who kept Trevor on his toes all those years in school."

"I did my best."

"Excellent. He needed someone like you to give him a little competition." Mr. Mc-Donough began strolling down the aisle of the clinic as if he owned the place. He wore a handsome set of clothes with a fine wool jacket that looked tailored to fit him to perfection. A ruby-encrusted gold watch was pinned to his vest.

"So Trevor is in charge of the entire floor of this hospital, I take it?" Mr. McDonough scanned the walls and the furniture. He went to a nearby window and looked outside. "Very fine view." When he started walking down the hallway toward the wards, Kate stepped in front of him.

"What can I do for you, sir?" she asked.

"You can fetch my son. I'm sure he's hiding here somewhere."

Kate didn't want him in the wards. "Private Norton," she called, "I need help."

Tick quickly appeared in the hallway, blocking Mr. McDonough's advance. "This is a private clinic, sir."

"Yes, paid for by money I provided my son. It looks as though the boy has done very well for himself." It irked her that he called Trevor a boy. Trevor was one of the finest men she'd ever met.

Tick didn't back down. "This clinic is not

open to members of the public. You'll have to return with Dr. Kendall if you want access to the floor." Tick rested his hand on the service revolver strapped to his hip, which seemed to amuse the older man.

"Easy, lad. I merely wish to see what my money paid for." He turned back to Kate. "Now, tell me how I may get in contact with my son. I've come all the way from Scotland, and our meeting is long overdue."

"If you would like to leave a message," Kate said, "I'll be sure that he receives it."

A hint of a smile passed over the older man's mouth, but it didn't linger long. "Tell him I won't allow him to continue to ignore me."

Trevor wasn't going to welcome her presence at Mrs. Kendall's bedside, but he needed to know about his father's sudden appearance at the hospital. Could it be true that the funding for the hospital came from the elder McDonough? Something about his presence made her uneasy. What kind of man would send his son to another continent to be raised? Trevor seemed to have no affection for the man. *"I despise my father and I want nothing to do with him,"* he'd told her. Despise him enough to drop his given name and take another from a housekeeper who had been kind to him?

The thoughts swirled in her mind as she took the streetcar to the Georgetown neighborhood where Mrs. Kendall lived. The days were getting shorter, and it was dark by the time she stepped off the car. Fallen leaves and acorns crunched beneath her feet as she walked toward the town house where Mrs. Kendall lived. She was tired and hungry, and the scent of the roast beef sandwich she'd brought for Trevor was tempting her. She had no idea if he'd been eating properly over the past few days, so she'd wrapped up a sandwich from the dinner cart to bring to him.

She knocked softly on Mrs. Kendall's door, and it was promptly opened by Nellie, Mrs. Kendall's frazzled-looking daughter. Exhaustion radiated from the woman's pale face. She looked confused to see Kate.

"Is Trevor here?" Kate asked.

The door opened wider, and Trevor moved into view. His shirt was rumpled. It looked like he hadn't shaved in several days, nor slept much either. "What do you need, Kate?"

She held up the sack. "I brought you a sandwich and a bottle of your cod liver oil. I know how much you enjoy it."

A wry grin twisted his lips. "Come on in,"

he said, taking the sack from her.

It was warm inside. The bedroom door was open, revealing Mrs. Kendall's motionless form on the bed.

"She's asleep," Trevor said. He motioned to the small dining table on the other side of the room. "Tell me why you've come. It can't be to deliver a sandwich, as much as I'm going to enjoy eating it."

Kate sat at the table, Trevor across from her. Nellie donned a mask and returned to her mother's bedside in the next room. Trevor had been ferociously angry the last time they were together, and there was caution lurking in his eyes, almost as if he was afraid she was here to renew their argument.

"Trevor, your father came by the clinic this afternoon."

His response was electric. "Stay away from him," he snapped.

"He didn't stay long. He looked around the lobby area and asked to see you."

"What did he say? Tell me *exactly* what he said."

Kate scrambled to remember the details, but she'd been so stunned by the man's startling resemblance to Trevor that she couldn't remember much. "I told him you weren't there, but he didn't believe me. He said he came all the way from Scotland to see you."

Trevor gave a harsh laugh. "He came all the way from Scotland to marry an American heiress. I hear she's worth twelve million dollars. A soap fortune. What else did he say?"

He'd said she was the "famous Kate" and made snide remarks about Trevor's habit of mingling with the servants, but both those things would be awkward to say with Nellie in the next room. Trevor sensed her hesitation.

"Nell, I want to go for a little walk with Kate. Will you be all right for a spell?"

Nellie half rose from her seat and waved him away. "Go on. We'll be fine."

Cold air surrounded Trevor once they stepped outside. He glowered at Kate's thin cloak. "Don't you have a decent coat? You'll catch your death in that scrap of nothing."

It was easier to grouse at her than look at the weary exhaustion on her face. She didn't look good, and he knew she must have had an awful day. He cocked an elbow out for her to hold, then set off down the street.

"Nurse Ackerman sent a message this morning about Hannah Wexler," he said. "I know the two of you were friends, and her loss must have been hard. I'm sorry." When they were fifteen, he remembered Kate getting misty-eyed when their class's pet hamster died. She was always too tender-hearted for this sort of work.

"Dr. Schrader said there was tubercular scarring in her heart. That was why she went down so quickly and with no warning."

"You saw the lab report?" he asked.

There was a slight hesitation as she walked alongside him. "A bunch of nurses are out with the flu. I took the notes during the autopsy."

He sucked in a breath, then turned to face her. No wonder she looked so overwhelmed. Without thinking he drew her into his arms, holding her tight against him. "Oh, Kate, I'm sorry you had to do that."

"I'm not." Her voice was muffled against his shoulder. "It made me really respect what you do — what all of you doctors do in trying to help people."

He squeezed his eyes shut, his heart beginning to split. Reaching out to hold her was stupid and he was bound to pay for it, but sometimes he needed her so badly. He simply *needed.* Needed to know he wasn't alone. Needed the solid warmth of another person who cared.

His hand moved up to cup the back of her head, stroking her hair. Her arms tightened around his back, and he didn't care that they stood in the middle of a public walk. He just needed a few seconds of comfort, holding on to another human being who was a friend and a partner. He might never hold Kate Livingston in his arms again, but at this moment they both needed this.

He opened his eyes and drew a steadying breath. "You're freezing. There's a coffee shop at the end of the street where we can talk."

She drew back, and they both started walking again, her slim hand clasped in his. The warm glow of gaslights illuminated the interior of the coffee shop on the corner. He almost regretted when they arrived and he had to release her hand. But it was warm inside the shop, with a booth in the front where they could sit side by side and look out the large window. He waited until two steaming mugs of coffee were placed in front of them before speaking.

"Tell me again what my father said."

"It happened very quickly," Kate said as she held the warm mug between her hands. "He seemed to believe you were hiding somewhere on the floor, but Tick wouldn't let him get any farther down the hall than the nurses' station. He got a little angry and said that he'd paid for the clinic."

Trevor choked on his coffee, making a mess. He reached for a napkin to wipe it up and had to clear his throat several times until he could breathe properly again.

"Are you all right? Shall I ask for a glass of water?"

He shook his head. "I'm fine," he said, his voice a little scratchy. "My father never fails to amaze me."

"He is a rather imposing man, isn't he?"

"That's one word for him."

As a boy, Trevor had been in awe of him. Neill McDonough rarely visited the cottage where Trevor lived with his mother, no more than once or twice a month. Trevor wasn't even sure who the strange man was, but his mother was always nervous before the visits and warned Trevor to be on his best behavior. For days she'd tutor him to memorize some Shakespearean poem or fancy mathematical equation.

"If Mr. McDonough sees what a smart boy you are, perhaps he will pay for you to go to college. Wouldn't that be fine, Trevor?"

Trevor wasn't even sure what college was, but he agreed it would be fine. All he knew was milking cows and spreading hay and running over to the neighboring crofter's cottage, where Deirdre Sinclair lived.

All of that came to an end when his mother died. He was only nine years old, and it seemed she'd been sick her whole life. One morning he awoke to find his mother dead in her bed. He didn't know what he was supposed to do. He sat on the corner of her mattress, certain that if he waited long enough, she would wake up. He prayed. He rubbed her hands and tried to slip water down her throat, but nothing happened. Finally he ran over to the Sinclair cottage for help. A few days later, Neill McDonough came to fetch him.

"You can live in my house, lad. I suppose it's only fitting."

He would never forget his amazement when the carriage drew closer to Mr. McDonough's house, which was in fact a mansion. A massive building of imposing granite blocks, it was four stories high with mullioned windows that sparkled in the sunlight and towers at the corners that soared even higher. The sprawling house looked like it had been built for a king.

A room was found for Trevor in the servants' wing. He took all his meals there, and it was the only place he felt comfortable. It was obvious to everyone who his father was. There was his last name for one thing, but even as a child, people noticed the stunning resemblance he bore to the master of the grand estate. His father was a widower with no legitimate children, so Trevor was spared the embarrassment of encountering his half-siblings living abovestairs.

The one truly generous thing Neill Mc-Donough did for Trevor was to provide him with an excellent education. A tutor came to live at the house, and Trevor latched on to the education like a hungry wolf, eager to lap up every drop of knowledge. Instead of sheep and cows, he learned about math and science and chemistry. He discovered whole new worlds living beneath tiny glass slides he put under a microscope. He learned about Aristotle and Beethoven and the rotation of the planets around the sun.

His father never paid him much attention, which made it possible for Trevor to run the three miles back to the Sinclair cottage, where he smuggled treats from the kitchen to Deirdre and stole kisses behind the sheep pen.

It all came crashing to an end his thirteenth year.

"I came by my sense of competition honestly," he told Kate, who pressed tightly to his side on the coffee-shop bench. "My father is the most competitive person on the planet, but what he seeks to win is money and power. He inherited a fortune and amassed another through a series of strategic business arrangements and marriages. His first wife generated millions from overseas plantations in India and Africa, but she died in childbirth. When I was thirteen, my father became engaged to a German princess. Very rich and very conservative. It would not do to have a bastard son living below the stairs, so I needed to be sent off somewhere."

He would never forget the deal he struck with his father that year. Neill McDonough looked nervous and guilty as he took him for a walk through the peat field on a corner of his estate. "Look, boy, I have a cousin in America who is willing to take you in. Robert Campbell is a senator in Washington. Do you know what that means? He's a powerful man in the United States. I will provide for your allowance and a hefty settlement on your behalf. You will be a very rich man when you come of age, but you can't live here anymore."

The thought of leaving Scotland terrified him. The Sinclairs were the only people in the world who cared if he lived or died, and he was pretty certain he was in love with Deirdre. He wanted to marry her when they grew up.

"I don't want to leave," he told his father.

The man had no patience. "Your only other option is your mother's cousin, who lives in a frozen fishing village in the Orkney Islands. It's a barren wasteland, and you'll freeze your hide off up there."

"There's a girl . . ." he said hesitantly.

His father gave an impatient wave of his hand. "The sheepherder's daughter. Trust me, lad, you can do better than that. I'll send you to America with a fortune in your back pocket, and you won't ever think of her again. Or you can live with strangers in a sod hut on an island in the North Sea. What's your pleasure?"

He took the money. To this day he felt as if he'd struck a deal with the devil. The Sinclairs would have taken him in, but he already had a taste of his father's life and didn't know if he could go back. The years with a private tutor opened up a glimpse of a dazzling new world, and he hungered for more — for science and chemistry and the chance to keep learning about the fantastic universe he'd discovered under his microscope. Living with the Sinclairs would mean cutting sod and herding sheep.

"I hated myself for what I did," Trevor said. "Deirdre sent me letters at Senator

Campbell's house, but I never answered them. I knew I couldn't go back to her. I knew the money from my father was sitting in a bank account, and the senator saw to it that it was wisely invested. But I didn't want to touch it; that money had the stink of betrayal on it."

He turned to face Kate, sitting beside him and quietly listening. He didn't want to broach the subject, but it was one that had been eating at her for the past twelve years, and she deserved an honest explanation.

"You know where this is leading, right?"

"The scholarship," she said.

He nodded. "I wanted to become a man. I wanted to support myself on my own merit and without the tainted money I took from my father. Winning the scholarship would set me free of that godforsaken deal. It would prove I was capable of making my own way in the world. I'm sorry, Kate. I knew you had hopes for college, but I was too selfish to step away from the chance to win it." Every ounce of energy drained from his muscles, leaving him unspeakably weary and ashamed. "I was wrong. I should have been strong enough to use my father's money if it meant clearing the way for you. I hope you can forgive me."

Kate stared blankly at the lukewarm mug

of coffee before her. It was impossible to tell if she was seething in resentment, yet the last thing he expected was the fear in her voice.

"Is that why you hired me? Because you felt guilty about the scholarship?" She held her breath, as though learning his job offer had been based on pity rather than merit would sink her.

He wished he'd been so kind, but it had never even occurred to him.

"I hired you because I needed a fighter on my team." He tried to find her when he first arrived in Washington, but there was no sign of Kate Norton. It took him months to realize she'd been married, but within twenty-four hours of learning her new name and where she worked, he penned a letter to lure her to the hospital. There was neither pity nor romantic motives in his intent. He simply knew she would be the best person in the world to have at his side as he geared up one more time to fight the dragon that had plagued him for most of his life.

"Okay," she said softly. "That makes sense to me."

"It does?"

"I still want to smack you for it, but at least I understand now." A reluctant smile tugged at the corner of her mouth. She reached out to squeeze his hand. "Trevor McDonough," she muttered. The way she said his name carried a whole world of frustration and annoyance, and a sliver of grudging respect.

"I used the money from my father to fund my research and pay for the medicine I give away to the poor. Yes, it pays for the clinic, and there's plenty more where that came from. I've never touched any of it for my own support. I never will."

He rarely confided his personal life with anyone, but Kate was . . . well, Kate was like the other half of his soul. Talking with her felt as natural as a sunrise turning into the bright light of day.

Not that he had much longer with her. He never knew until now how the sweetness of love could be mingled with the ache of despair. It was a blend of joy and longing so intense that he wanted to suspend this moment in time and make it last forever. Tomorrow might be riddled with fear and heartache, but right now in this perfect, fleeting God-given moment, he knew joy and was grateful for it.

Kate walked back with Trevor to Mrs. Kendall's town house, savoring the feel of his hand clasped with hers. She could have gone directly to the streetcar stop, but she wanted a few more minutes with him.

Memories of the scholarship contest and the gangly, graceless Trevor were etched so clearly in her mind, it was as if it had happened yesterday. At the time she thought Trevor had everything because he was driven to school in a fancy carriage and had nice clothes, but it was *she* who had everything. She had parents who loved her. She had a classroom full of friends. She had a pair of healthy lungs she always took for granted. Trevor had none of those things. Instead, he had a towering sense of ambition and a need to escape the shame of the bargain he'd made with his father. She couldn't hold on to her resentment any longer. She admired him too much to wallow in trivial old grievances.

Trevor unlocked the door to Mrs. Kendall's house, motioning for Kate to be quiet lest the old woman was still asleep. The moment the door opened, he paused, cocking his ear to listen.

Nellie Kendall rose, struggling against tears. "Thank God you've come! I think she's gone, Trevor."

The color disappeared from Trevor's face as he raced to Mrs. Kendall's side. He stroked a strand of white hair away from the woman's forehead, still damp with sweat. He grabbed the stethoscope from the table, his fingers clumsy as he fit the rubber tubes into his ears. He pressed the disk to her chest and froze, his eyes closed as he listened.

Then he removed the stethoscope, sat down on the bed, and grasped Mrs. Kendall's hand. "Dear God, please speed her journey," he said softly. "She was a good woman, the very finest. She was like my mother, my father, and my North Star." His voice became hollow, as if it were too painful to continue speaking.

Kate's vision blurred, and her throat hurt. She stood behind Trevor, her hands resting on his shoulders. "It's okay, Trevor. It was her time."

He nodded but didn't look up. Then the strangest sound, like that of a strangled animal, came from deep inside his chest, and Kate realized he was trying not to cry. "I hate this!" he finally said. "I hate failing. I would have given anything to cure her."

She sat on the bed behind him and clung to his back, feeling the uneven breaths he struggled to contain, but he lost the battle. She held him while he wept, wishing she could carry some of his burden.

Later that night, Trevor walked her home.

He needed to talk and had been babbling nonstop ever since leaving the town house. Even in the weak moonlight, she could still see the tracks of tears on his face.

"I know the patients think I'm cold," he said. "I can't let myself get close to them. It hurts too much. The logical portion of my brain knows I can't be responsible for people who die from tuberculosis, but something inside me rages each time I lose a patient, spurring me forward to keep working harder, to try something else. Sometimes I want to run away and never think of this horrible disease again."

She sucked in a breath, and he must have heard it because he shot her a glare.

"Don't start," he warned. "This is what I meant that first day when I interviewed you. Anyone who works with this disease will get beaten down over and over. Hammered and smashed and broken, but tomorrow morning I will get back up and carry on. I know that isn't what you want to hear, but I won't give up. Even if it kills me — and I accept that it may — I won't quit."

Whatever weakness Trevor showed at Mrs. Kendall's bedside was fading. As he spoke, she could sense the energy and confidence trickling back into his spirit, even as it drained from her. She could never live this life. She couldn't turn her emotions on and off the way Trevor did. She could not quietly stand by his side as he battled with a disease until it killed him.

They arrived at the front porch of the boardinghouse.

"Thank you for walking me home," she said.

He touched the side of her face. "Thank you for everything."

His smile was sad as she turned her face into his palm, pressing a kiss to his warm skin. He turned away and started walking back to the streetcar stop. She watched until he disappeared.

Tonight confirmed her need to disentangle herself from Trevor as quickly as possible. She loved him too much to stay.

Tick was waiting for her in the parlor. The house was quiet, and only a single gas lamp illuminated the front room.

"I was worried about you," he said. "Did you tell Trevor about his father?"

"Yes." She peeled off her cloak and set it on the sofa.

"And?"

She knew Tick was anxious to learn more about the mysterious Neill McDonough, but her spirit was too battered and weary to recount the discussion.

"Mrs. Kendall died tonight." She was barely able to get the sentence out before the muscles of her face crumpled, and tears pooled in the bottoms of her eyes.

Tick pulled her into a hug. "I'm sorry."

At his words, the floodgates released. She sobbed into his shoulder. If he wasn't holding her so tightly she would have collapsed to the floor.

"It'll be okay, Kate. You're tough. The toughest person I know."

No, she was a weakling. She wanted to run after Trevor and beg him to let her stay at the hospital. She wanted to hold him and comfort him through this terrible night. At the same time she wanted to shake him for being so stubborn! She cried harder.

"If you don't knock it off, I'm going to start bawling too." Tick's voice was strangled, as though he was already there, and she gave a gulping laugh against his shoulder. He squeezed tighter.

This had been the longest day of her life. She thanked God for Tick's strong shoulder to weep on, but her heart ached for Trevor. As long as he was walking the earth, a piece of her would always long for Trevor.

21

The morning after Mrs. Kendall's passing, Trevor strode to the hospital with renewed determination to smoke out the lowlife rat who was trying to ruin him. His private investigator in Baltimore had finally tracked down the last of the people associated with the Baltimore study, and he needed to follow those leads immediately. He wanted to get to the clinic, address whatever urgent needs arose while he was tending Mrs. Kendall, and then be on his way to Baltimore. The first thing he saw upon returning to the ward was that Frederick Lambrecht had the gall to change the locks on the fifth-floor clinic without his permission.

It took Trevor less than three minutes to grab a wrench and pull the offending doorknob from the unit. The superintendent was counting the hours until Trevor's eviction, but as long as Trevor was in charge of the fifth floor, he'd tolerate no changes. He barged into the superintendent's office without knocking, tossing the entire door-knob and lock mechanism onto Mr. Lambrecht's fancy walnut desk, where they landed with a clatter.

"That's what I think of your new lock," Trevor snapped.

Mr. Lambrecht rose. "You've got the blasted marines standing guard. Do you really need your own lock and key?"

"Until I know who's been sniffing around my clinic, yes, I do. And I'll rip out anything else you try to install without talking to me first."

"You've got only ten more days. After that, I'll finally see the last of you."

"I can see you're devastated at the prospect," Trevor said dryly.

He left without a backward glance and bumped into a man about to enter the superintendent's office. Michael Wells. The puppy hired to take over his tuberculosis study. The young man took a step back, brushing a swath of curly brown hair back from his forehead.

"Mr. Wells," Trevor said. "Or is it *Dr.* Wells?"

Michael took another step back and swallowed hard, his Adam's apple bobbing in his thin neck. "Dr. Kendall," he said weakly.

"I . . . uh, I was just going in to meet with Mr. Lambrecht about some . . . some business."

"Well, is it Dr. Wells now?" Trevor pressed.

"Not quite. I've yet to pass the licensing exam. I'm taking it next week."

"Right before you start your new job," Trevor said. "That's convenient." A kinder person would have put the young man at ease, but Trevor wasn't feeling particularly kind at the moment. Michael Wells was the man handpicked by the surgeon general to take over Trevor's study. If the study was to be turned over to anyone, Trevor wanted it to be his former assistant from Baltimore, but Andrew Doyle was still attending medical school at Harvard. Andrew had more experience with tuberculosis than the youth standing before him.

"I feel lousy about what's happening," Michael said. "You know I've always admired your work, but Barrow seems determined to find new blood for the study."

"Yes, *very* new," Trevor said. He turned and left the soon-to-be doctor standing in front of the superintendent's office.

The moment he returned to the clinic, Trevor pulled Tick aside. "I'm leaving tomorrow morning to follow a lead in Baltimore, and I'll need you to keep an eye on Michael Wells while I'm gone," Trevor said. "He's a young man, curly brown hair, here to take over my job. And I don't trust him."

"Do you think he could be our man?" Tick asked.

Could a twenty-two-year-old medical student engineer this reign of terror? It seemed outrageous, but Trevor's downfall would vault Michael Wells into one of the few positions in the country performing a controlled tuberculosis study.

"I've not sensed that level of cunning in him," Trevor said. "He's entering the field because he wants to find a cure. He seems to care. It's hard to believe he'd launch an attack like this, but then again, I didn't think he'd get in line for my job either."

"Professional jealousy?" Tick asked.

"Maybe. And keep an eye on Henry Harris." He didn't want to imagine that his jovial lab assistant could have anything to do with this, but Henry was a logical suspect. Henry had worked with him in Baltimore and was the only person who had complete insight into both the Baltimore study and the current activities in the lab. For the life of him, Trevor couldn't see a motive for Henry to destroy him and felt guilty even asking Tick to spy on the man.

The only thing Trevor knew for sure was that there were few things more demoralizing than sorting through his short list of friends to determine who hated him enough to engineer his downfall.

Kate spread out a newspaper on the staff table, scanning the job advertisements that interested her. She needed to find a job, and fast. Her mother had recently pawned a bracelet to pay the bank note this month, and the new hot water heater was acting up again.

"I need to go to Baltimore."

She startled and sat upright. Trevor had been standing behind her, his face somber and aloof. He nodded toward the nurses' station. "I'll be gone for several days, and I need to go over some details before I leave."

She followed him to the front counter, where he laid out a stack of papers. "The architect will be here tomorrow with two proposals for an elevator to the roof. I need you to meet with him. Don't let him scrimp on the size of the elevator."

"Naturally."

"I also want the statistics on the blood work for the past month. I want it graphed against the preceding four months."

"Certainly."

He continued rapping out orders, demanding someone make a trip to the surgeon general's library and pull the latest research on iron metabolism in blood.

"Of course."

"I want it here by the time I return, with a summary of each article."

"All right."

There was a pause, and she looked over at him, surprised that he stopped barking out orders long enough to draw a breath.

"Don't go," he whispered. "Please don't go, Kate."

The plea was so soft she barely heard it, but it sliced her to shreds. If Nurse Ackerman hadn't been standing a few feet away, Kate would have wept. Instead, she swallowed hard so that the tears wouldn't leak into her voice.

"Hold it together, McDonough," she said softly.

Never had she seen a man keep a volcanic flood of emotion so tightly locked inside, yet any attempt to comfort him would merely prolong their agony. Trevor knew exactly what he needed to do to keep her with him.

And it broke her heart to know he never would.

The clinic door banged open, and Neill

McDonough came walking into the clinic. "There you are, Trevor. No escape this time, my boy."

Trevor's father wore a greatcoat that flared out behind him in an impressive sweep of black wool and expensive cologne.

Trevor took a step back. "Good morning, Mr. McDonough," he said. "I'm heading out of town on business, so I'm afraid I have limited time to meet with you."

Before Trevor could retreat to his office, his father's gold-tipped walking stick shot out to block Trevor's escape. "Nonsense. I've come to invite you to my wedding. My boy, surely you will be interested in renewing the family connections. Oh, and I have a business proposition for you." He paused and glanced at Kate. "The famous Kate," he said in a silky tone. "You seem to be a constant presence in my son's life." His eyes narrowed as he observed the close proximity between her and Trevor. "Perhaps there's to be another wedding in the family? Now, you're the daughter of people who run a boardinghouse, correct?"

"Yes," she said stiffly. "But you may rest assured there are no wedding bells in my future. Your son's virtue is safe from me."

"Thank heaven for small favors," the elder McDonough said.

Trevor snapped. "There's the door. I'm unable to attend your wedding, so please show yourself out."

"No need to be hasty —"

"This clinic is full of working-class people who have dirt under their nails and who grew up in boardinghouses and tenements and crofters' huts. We have no interest in high-society weddings or business propositions."

Nurse Ackerman stopped her filing, and the patients gathered nearby set down their playing cards. Everyone held their breath while Mr. McDonough raised his chin, smiling faintly down at Trevor.

"On Saturday morning I'll be marrying Miss Fannie Bates of Nutter Hollow, West Virginia. Her father was a hog farmer until he found a very clever means of making soap that softens the skin and smells like roses. Women all over the world are clamoring to get their hands on it. Virgil Bates is one of the finest men I've ever met. One of the cleverest too, if I take my son out of the equation, so I'm not quite the snob you assume I am. And, Trevor, you really *do* want to hear the business proposition I have on the table."

Kate watched in fascination. The two men were so close in appearance they could be twins were it not for the silver strands in the older man's hair. Their eyes were locked in a battle to see who would falter first.

Trevor did. A bit of the ice thawed, and he unclenched his fingers. "My office," Trevor said bluntly and then stalked back to the room, his father trailing close behind.

The door slammed, and those there in the clinic stared at the closed door. Kate wanted to dash inside and fling herself in front of Trevor to protect him from a man who had no business polluting their clinic with whatever schemes he had up his sleeve. Instead, she whirled to the people who were staring at Trevor's door.

"Go back to your card game," she said nervously, then tiptoed toward Trevor's office. Tick was at his post and looked at her with a quizzical expression, but she ignored him as she pressed her ear to the door. Trevor's father was speaking.

". . . a backwater compared to Edinburgh. You can be the director of the most prestigious medical center in all of Europe. You'll do far better than operating a clinic on the fifth floor of a city hospital."

Kate froze. The medical centers in Edinburgh were so exalted, even she had heard of them, and Trevor did seem to put a lot of stock into such things. Would he leave?

Never had she imagined he could be tempted away from his work here.

Trevor mumbled a reply she couldn't hear, and then his father started in again.

"You could get away from all this nonsense in the press. I don't know how you can live in a country where rabble-rousing journalists have access to barrels of ink. That sort of thing won't happen in Scotland, no matter how unpopular your research."

And then Trevor's father moved in with the heavy guns.

"Fannie is a wonderful woman, but there's no guarantee she will produce a male child. Until she does, I'm prepared to acknowledge you as my heir. I've always felt bad about the way things ended before, but the princess, God rest her soul, was old-fashioned about such things. Come back to Scotland, lad. I'm very impressed with your work, and any man would be proud to call you his son."

Kate's mouth went dry. There was a long silence, and she pressed her ear closer to the door. She heard Trevor asking after some of the people from back home. The butler. The housekeeper. Yes, they were both still there, and Trevor laughed when his father recounted how the butler persuaded him to buy a newfangled open-carriage

393

motorcar from the Benz company and was learning to drive it around the estate.

Unbelievable! She couldn't continue to listen to this. She straightened and looked over at Tick, who was pretending to stand at attention but was really watching every move she made. She hurried over to him.

"I can't believe he's listening to that snake," she said in a harsh whisper.

Tick raised a brow. "Maybe his father came to offer an olive branch?"

"More like a poisoned apple." As quietly as possible, she told him Mr. McDonough's offer to make Trevor his heir.

Tick didn't share her sense of outrage. "It doesn't sound so bad to me."

That was because Tick didn't know what happened to Trevor when he was only thirteen and ill equipped to make life-altering decisions. Shaking her head, she took her statistics back to the table, stewing as the conversation behind Trevor's door continued.

Almost an hour later, Trevor and his father emerged. Both men looked relaxed, and they shook hands before the older man left the clinic, smiling and nodding to the peasants as he strode out the door.

Trevor returned to his office, and she didn't wait long to pounce.

"Well?" she said, leaning against the door-frame of their office. Trevor sat in his chair, staring out the window with his hands steepled before him.

"He had some interesting offers," Trevor finally said.

"You're not entertaining them, are you?"

"I'd have a lot more influence over there." He swiveled in his chair to look at her. "And there's nothing holding me in Washington, is there, Kate?"

She looked away, hating that there was a tiny bit of hope in Trevor's eyes. Would he never give this up? He knew precisely what he needed to do if he wanted her to stay with him.

"I guess not," she said quietly.

He spun around and returned to his work.

Trevor's trip to Baltimore was going to be difficult. Rose O'Grady was the only patient from the ill-fated mercury study whose family he had yet to interview. Rose's death had been especially tragic, given the doomed love affair she had in her final months with his former assistant, Andrew Doyle. At the time, Andrew was supposed to leave for medical school at Harvard, but he refused to leave Rose's bedside during those terrible last few weeks. After her death, Rose's parents moved several times, which was why it took so long for his investigator to find them. The O'Gradys were kind, hardworking people, and it was difficult to envision them orchestrating this campaign, but he couldn't afford to overlook them.

"My husband couldn't take the noise at the cannery," Mrs. O'Grady said as she filled Trevor's teacup for a second time. The snug parlor overlooked the harbor, where gulls wheeled and swooped on chilly gusts blowing in from the east. "It wasn't safe working there with his almost going deaf, so we moved to the other side of town. My father has a tobacco-rolling company here, and George went to work for him."

George O'Grady sat stiffly in the upholstered armchair before the fireplace, holding a cup of tea but refusing to drink it. Maybe his hearing loss made him reluctant to talk, or perhaps there was a more sinister reason.

Trevor barely knew the O'Gradys, and this conversation was exquisitely awkward. How, precisely, did you ask a pair of strangers if they were trying to destroy your medical career? At least Mrs. O'Grady seemed welcoming enough, showing him a photograph of Rose on her sixteenth birthday. The fresh-faced girl was unrecognizable compared to the emaciated wraith admitted into Trevor's study in a desperate effort to save her life.

He took another sip of tea. "You have been happy in your new home?"

"Oh yes," Mrs. O'Grady said. "As much as possible, I suppose. Our other daughter, Margaret, married last year and is already expecting our first grandchild. We're all so happy about it." She leaned forward and whispered, "Poor, dear Andrew Doyle came to the wedding, and we couldn't help but wonder what he would have become if not for . . ." Her voice trembled, and she fumbled with her teacup. Setting the cup down, she added, "That boy was like a son to us. He would have made such a fine doctor. Such a shame . . ."

Trevor stiffened. "What do you mean? Has some sort of harm come to him?"

Mrs. O'Grady shifted in her seat. "Well," she said uneasily, "it's not as if there's anything wrong with becoming an undertaker; it just seems a step down from being a doctor."

"An *undertaker*?" It was inconceivable. He'd visited Andrew only two years ago at Harvard, where he was flying through his classes in medical school. Andrew Doyle working as an undertaker was a colossal waste of talent, like having Michelangelo paint houses.

Mrs. O'Grady nodded. "His poor mother was shattered by it. I spoke with her at the wedding, and she said he couldn't bring himself to treat patients. Such a tragedy. He spent a fortune going to Harvard, and now he can't even practice medicine. He had to move in with his mother, and they built the mortuary onto the back of her house. Poor woman. She had to go back to work just to keep their heads above water, although I gather Andrew's business is doing quite well now."

Trevor had stopped paying attention. Like Kate, Andrew was too tenderhearted. Of course, it was difficult to begin treating actual people, but that didn't mean he should abandon medicine to become an undertaker. Trevor would find him and talk some sense into him.

"Where does the mother live?" Trevor asked abruptly.

"Somewhere in northern Virginia, right near the border," she replied. "She works as a nurse somewhere. Do you remember where, George?"

Mr. O'Grady merely shrugged.

Hard-of-hearing people often responded that way. Trevor crossed the room and spoke in a loud, distinct voice. "Andrew Doyle," he said. "Do you know where his mother lives?"

George O'Grady cupped his hand behind his ear but still gave a noncommittal shrug.

His wife stood and leaned over her husband. "Where does Andrew Doyle's mother live?" she shouted. "Dr. Kendall wants to know."

"She's at a hospital in Washington," he shouted back. "Ackerman, that's her name."

A barrage of unholy thoughts tormented Trevor as he dashed to the train depot. How could he have been so blind to the parasite living in his midst? He never knew of Nurse Ackerman's connection to Andrew Doyle, but she still wore the two gold wedding rings around her neck, so it made sense that they didn't share a last name.

During the two-hour train ride back to Washington, Trevor sorted through with clinical precision all that he knew so far. It was Nurse Ackerman who'd spilled the mercury while he and Kate were on the roof. She would have known every scrap of gossip that happened at the clinic, most likely funneling that information to journalists and the hospital superintendent. When Nurse Ackerman suspected what Kate meant to him, she spread her venom further by tormenting Kate with mortuary photographs of his patients and planting evidence at her parents' boardinghouse. Nurse Ackerman had been poisoning the well all along, and he had never once questioned her.

Was Nurse Ackerman acting alone, or was her son also involved in the scheme? It was hard for Trevor to believe that Andrew had played a part in this. Rose's death was five years ago, and he and Andrew had met several times in the intervening years. Andrew seemed *fine.* Why would Andrew wait five years to take his revenge?

But Trevor could think of no other way for Nurse Ackerman to get the photographs of his former patients without Andrew's cooperation. He scrambled, racking his brain for a scenario in which Andrew could be innocent.

It would take some time to determine if Andrew was indeed involved in his mother's scheme, and that meant Trevor was going to have to walk into the clinic and act as if nothing had changed in his attitude toward Nurse Ackerman. Because the moment she sensed his suspicion, she would begin covering her tracks.

But now that Trevor knew the identity of the person he was battling, he'd have a web

spun around Nurse Ackerman before she
even knew what was happening.

22

Kate was a little miffed when Trevor arrived home and abruptly kicked her out of their office. Quite frankly, he'd been acting odd ever since returning from his business yesterday. First, he had asked Dr. Schrader to perform his morning rounds, and now he was locked in a closed-door meeting with Tick in his office.

She had to use the staff table to interview their latest candidate, but thank heavens Mr. Philip Walsh appeared ideally suited to fill her position. With a mathematics degree from the University of Virginia and years of experience at the Naval Hospital, he was an outstanding candidate.

At long last, Trevor and Tick emerged from the office and headed toward the front of the clinic.

Kate stood. "Dr. Kendall, this is Philip Walsh, an applicant for the statistical analyst position. His credentials are excellent.

Perhaps you would like to discuss the position with him?"

"That's what I'm paying you for," Trevor said. "Please don't start shirking your responsibilities until you're no longer employed here."

So, the charm lessons at her mother's dining table failed to take root in the frozen tundra surrounding Trevor's heart. For heaven's sake, how was she to convince Mr. Walsh this was a fine opportunity if Trevor kept scowling at their best candidate?

She pasted on her friendliest smile and skirted around the reception counter to say in a fierce whisper, "Please stop barking at our best candidate. I've interviewed six men, and Mr. Walsh is the only one who passes all our criteria with flying colors. Try to pretend you can be trusted in polite company."

Trevor only glared at her. She held her breath as he took a few steps toward the candidate. "Mr. Walsh, I apologize for Kate's excitable nature. She sometimes forgets her responsibilities in the face of needless anxieties. Women, you know. I assure you, I would welcome a man of common sense who won't be subject to the overly emotional whims that send some women fleeing for the hills at the first sign of difficulty."

She stiffened but kept a serene look plastered on her face as she turned to Mr. Walsh, who looked like a rabbit frozen on the field of battle.

"Dr. Kendall could certainly use a man of your sound common sense," she said calmly. "Sometimes he gets carried away and thinks he can single-handedly save the world. Men, you know."

Trevor ignored her comment. Turning to Tick, he gestured to a spot at the front of the sitting area. "I think your line of sight from this position will be suitable, don't you?"

Tick moved to stand near the front of the clinic, glancing up and down the corridor and nodding his assent. "This will work fine. I can't see the back door, but the hinges are so loud I'll be able to hear if anyone goes in or out."

"Why are you changing the position of the guard?" Nurse Ackerman asked.

"Standard procedure, ma'am," Tick answered. "It allows the men guarding the facility to have a fresh perspective on operations."

Nurse Ackerman seemed to bristle at that. "I don't think the patients will like it. That sitting area is one of the few places they can feel like they're at home. They shouldn't have a guard looming over them. They won't be able to relax." It was a valid point, even though Nurse Ackerman had never shown such concern for the patients' feelings in the past.

"I prefer to follow Private Norton's recommendation regarding the rotation of the guards," Trevor said dismissively, then proceeded back to his office, slamming the door so loudly they all jumped a little.

It would be a challenge to convince Mr. Walsh this was a delightful place to work — with Nurse Ackerman scowling at Tick, and Trevor acting like a bear with a thorn in its paw.

But after listening to Mr. Walsh outline his former position, and hearing a few of his suggestions for alternative forms of collecting data, she knew he'd be an ideal match. Due to his work at the Naval Hospital, he already understood the dangers of tuberculosis and was willing to accept the risk.

An hour later, Kate offered the position to Mr. Walsh, and he accepted. He would need time to resign at the Naval Hospital but would then begin work at the clinic, one week from today.

Her mission accomplished, she would be

free to leave soon, which made the hollow ache in her chest hurt even more.

Trevor acted frosty when he heard the news. Standing in the doorway of their office, she spoke to his back, because he continued staring out the window as she outlined her plans for leaving. His shoulders stiffened but he made no comment.

"Did you hear me?" she finally asked.

He turned from the window. "I heard you. I'm disappointed you don't have the gumption to stick this out, but I've got no time for rehashing old arguments. I've informed the orderlies to install an additional bed in both of the wards. Please start a file for two new patients. They will be arriving tomorrow morning."

Trevor's strange demand sent the hospital administration into a tizzy. Superintendent Lambrecht made an uncharacteristic appearance within minutes of learning the news.

"Why is he doing this?" he asked while looking at Kate. "A new doctor will be taking over the study next week, and this sort of disruption is entirely unwarranted. Each ward was designed for sixteen beds, not seventeen. I want to know what he's up to. I don't trust him."

Kate had no answer for him. Neither did Henry nor Nurse Ackerman.

Trevor had left the clinic after making his demand and apparently was still gone. Meanwhile, a pair of orderlies carried in metal bedsteads, bumping and clanging as they navigated around tight corners. The patients were forced to rise so that their beds could be moved closer together. Space was so tight they needed to remove the chairs that had been placed between each bed.

"It seems mean to take the chairs away," Henry said. "How will they visit one another without a proper chair? Some of them are too weak to make it out to the sitting area."

Kate glanced over at Tick, who had spent an inordinate amount of time closeted alone with Trevor in the past few days.

Tick shrugged. "I expect Dr. Kendall knows what he's doing."

Strangest of all were the two new patients who arrived the following morning as Kate was making the rounds with Trevor. Both patients seemed much healthier than the typical ones being treated at the clinic. In the men's ward, Oskar Holtzmann greeted them with a cheerful smile and a thick German accent, complimenting her on her dazzling red hair.

Oskar's cheerfulness was in contrast to their new patient in the women's ward. Marlene Chester was a frazzled woman riddled with anxiety over the well-being of her son.

"Luke has never been on his own," she said.

"He's in good hands," Trevor replied in an unusually kind voice. "The Quaker school will provide him with a solid education during the day, and he'll have a clean, safe place to live in the children's dormitory. You understand that, right?"

The tension seemed to ease as she quit twisting the sheet in her hands. "I trust you," she finally said. "I just want what's right for Saint Luke."

For the first time in days, Kate saw a faint smile on Trevor's mouth. "He'll have it. No matter what happens, you can be sure of that, Marlene."

His voice was soothing, and how nice that he used her name instead of a patient number. Everything seemed a little odd, but nothing so much as when Henry provided her with the laboratory reports later in the day. Kate sat at her desk, staring at the reports for their two new patients, certain that Henry must have made an error. She showed the reports to Trevor.

"Neither of the new patients have tuberculosis in their blood," she said.

He swiveled around. "They have it in their lungs."

"Yes, but the criteria for your study require their blood to have a heavy tubercular count. Neither patient qualifies."

Without a word, Trevor crossed the office and took the two curious lab reports from her hands. "You're not to mention a word of this to anyone. I know what I'm doing, Kate."

Maybe Trevor knew what he was doing, but something was going on. After months of having the marine guard stationed at the rear of the clinic, it was disconcerting to have him up front near the nurses' station. And the two new patients didn't quite fit in with the rest of the group. Marlene and Oskar were both healthier than the others but never rose from their beds or visited with the others in the sitting area.

In fact, the only time Kate could recall seeing them leave the ward was when Trevor called them in to a private meeting each morning in his office. He never met alone with any of the other patients, and he always made Kate leave the office during those morning meetings with Oskar and Marlene.

Trevor was up to something, and Tick knew what it was.

When she pestered him about it, Tick remained tight-lipped. "Just hang on. It won't be much longer," he said.

Trevor had gathered the evidence he needed, all the players were in place, and it was time to close the chapter on this sordid affair.

It was sleeting by the time Trevor reached the neighborhood where Nurse Ackerman lived with her son in one of the modest eighteenth-century clapboard homes that were common in this part of town. It was a little after lunchtime, though the cloud-covered sky made it seem later. The barren branches of elm trees appeared black against the leaden sky, and the slate tiles were slick as he walked to the back of the home, where the mortuary had been added to the house.

The addition to the house jutted out awkwardly, but it was well constructed and had a professional-looking sign advertising mortuary services. A little bell rang as he opened the door, and Trevor had to dip his head while stepping inside. His nose twitched at the acrid scent of embalming fluid. The spacious room was dominated by three mortuary tables, two of which held cloth-draped corpses, and the third was empty. The single window in the room was open, a chilly breeze lifting the filmy drapes and easing the stench of the room.

Andrew was busy rinsing a number of beakers in a washbasin. "I'll be with you in a moment," he said over his shoulder.

"Hello, Andrew."

His former assistant whirled around, and Trevor almost gasped at the change in Andrew's appearance. He had lost weight, and his gaunt face was haunted with shadows. His thinning black hair was carefully combed and his mustache clipped, but despite the careful grooming there was an unsteadiness about him.

Andrew's surprise was quickly masked as he grabbed a towel and dried his hands. "What can I do for you, Dr. Kendall?" His voice was like sandpaper, thin and raspy.

Trevor walked farther into the room. The front was furnished like a parlor, a cozy space for Andrew to meet with grieving family members, far more comfortable than the dingy facilities typical among undertakers.

"You have a nice place here," Trevor said, "but it's a long way from Harvard. It seems an odd choice for a man of your qualifications."

Andrew cocked his head in curiosity. "Why? I respect the bodies of the people I care for. Each one of them is someone's father or son or friend. I care for them with the respect they deserve."

"And the photograph of Mabel Berkin's naked corpse stretched out on a mortuary slab? Did you send that to me because you respected her?" Trevor's heart sank. Despite the overwhelming evidence he and Tick had amassed over the past week, Trevor still harbored a tiny flame of hope that Andrew might have no part in the crimes his mother was waging. That flame flickered and then vanished as venom crept into Andrew's eyes.

"I sent it so you would *remember*," Andrew said tightly. "Remember what mercury does to a woman's body."

"Trust me, Andrew, I've never been able to forget it. Why are you trying to ruin me?"

"Because you turned me into a murderer. Someone like you shouldn't be allowed to tamper with people's lives. They were *people*, Trevor, not laboratory rats. I helped mix up that mercury solution and stood at your side as you injected it into Rose's body. I smiled and held her hand while you did that to her. I helped kill her."

The despair in Andrew's voice sliced through Trevor's anger. His tormentor wasn't some ignorant fool afraid of a disease he didn't understand, but a colleague who once respected him.

"You aren't responsible for Rose's death," he said.

Andrew acted as though he hadn't heard him. "Do you have any idea of how much I loved Rose O'Grady? We had such dreams for a life together after she was cured. She trusted me to make it happen. Do you know what it feels like to have every hope for tomorrow rest on the decisions you make?"

Trevor wished he didn't, but no doctor alive was free of that curse. Andrew braced his hands on the empty mortuary table, his shoulders sagging. "I quit medical school because I can't treat patients. What if the patient is allergic to a drug I prescribe? Or gets an infection at an injection site? Or maybe a patient had a simple headache, but I misdiagnosed it and did more harm than good? All these things can happen." He uncurled his fists, and the tension in his voice eased. "So I care for the dead," he continued. "You doctors look at undertakers like we're little better than the janitors who scrub your floors. I treat the dead with reverence. Each person I care for is a beautiful, perfect creation of God. Not a corpse! Not a body! It makes me sick the way you

413

research doctors shuffle them off to an undertaker when you have no more use for them. You shoot them full of poison and study them like animals in a cage. You poke and prod and measure them, and then when they die you open them up and do it all again." Andrew's voice turned cold now. "You even call them by a *number* instead of their given names."

Trevor winced. The barb had found its mark, but if he hadn't developed that means of protecting himself, he might have cracked like Andrew. "Yes, I do," he said calmly. "And I will continue to refer to them by their numbers, because it's the only way I can maintain my sanity in this job."

"If using patient numbers robs you of simple human compassion, you shouldn't be allowed to touch another patient as long as you live."

Trevor hated this. Had it not been for Andrew's disastrous introduction to medicine in Trevor's laboratory, he would have finished medical school and learned to treat patients like a normal doctor.

"What is it you want from me?" Trevor asked.

"I want you to quit medicine."

"That will never happen," he replied swiftly.

Andrew pushed away from the mortuary table, pacing around the room, weaving between the tables like a tiger in a cage that was too small. "Then I won't stop trying to destroy you in the press. If you move, I'll follow. I'll drive you out of business in whatever city you try to practice. There's no law against speaking the truth, and everything I've told to the press about you is the truth. You can't hide from me."

"Rose O'Grady would have died anyway," Trevor said. "Tuberculosis had gotten in her blood, and there's never been a case on record where someone has survived that. She was searching for a last desperate shot at a cure. I tried to give her that chance, and I failed. That's what usually happens with tuberculosis."

"Is that the lie you tell yourself? Rose died from mercury poisoning, not tuberculosis. She was shaking so hard at the end she couldn't even swallow. That was *your* fault."

The snapping of a twig outside the window caused Andrew to startle. "What was that?"

"Probably just a squirrel," Trevor said, moving quickly to divert Andrew's attention. "Why did you plant falsified records in Kate's boardinghouse?"

Andrew shook his head, a smug look on

his face. "Who said I planted those records? I wouldn't put it past you to indulge in medical fraud to prop up your tarnished reputation."

Trevor rocked back on his heels and folded his arms. Andrew was clever. Of all the chaos he'd unleashed over the past months, breaking into Kate's house was the only actual crime he committed. It was perfectly legal to talk to journalists and to send angry letters through the mail. Even spilling mercury on his desk could be attributed to a simple accident, and creating a set of falsified records wasn't a crime until he tried to use them in a legal case. But breaking into Kate's boardinghouse? That was a crime, and Andrew wasn't going to own up to it.

"Why don't you just quit medicine?" Andrew pressed. "I don't need to see you dragged through the mud and convicted of fraud. Just quit. That's all I want. Rose will be able to rest in peace if I make sure the man who engineered her death is no longer conducting his sick trials on desperate people as if they're rats in a laboratory."

Andrew stopped pacing, and Trevor heard more footsteps slicing through the overgrown grass outside the window. He held his breath, hoping for more time.

"I understand your concerns," Trevor said.

Surprise lit Andrew's expression. "Then you'll quit?"

Medicine would never advance unless someone was able to step into the arena, armed with knowledge, hope, and the fortitude to make tough decisions. It was a grueling road to walk and very few people could do it. Trevor had been slogging toward a cure for years, and the weight of the responsibility pressed down on him, sapping his energy.

"No. I won't quit," Trevor said in a tired voice. "The cure for tuberculosis won't be found in a mortuary or a university library. It's going to be found in a laboratory, and I won't let anything stop me from that work. Not a hostile press or threats of professional sanctions." *Or the tears of a woman he loved more than life itself.*

"Then I won't stop trying to take you down," Andrew said, his voice vibrating with quiet intensity.

Behind Andrew's back there was a movement in the window. Tick peered through an opening in the flimsy cotton drapes, a question in his eyes. Trevor sent him an infinitesimal shake of his head, warning him to keep his distance. Given enough time, perhaps Trevor could still find the spark of scientific reason inside the young man who wanted to destroy him.

"Andrew, we want the same thing. The Baltimore study was the biggest failure of my career. It's a regret I will carry for the rest of my life, but at least we know mercury is not the answer. I published the results of that study, and now all the physicians studying this disease can turn their efforts to the next possible solution. It wasn't a pointless test. Rose's death was not in vain."

"Six human beings died a miserable death because of you."

They would have died anyway, but they gave their lives to help better understand a disease that was almost always fatal.

"Andrew, you and I are brothers in arms. I understand the stress you've been under. The avalanche of hope and doubt and fear. But if you choose to fight me in this . . ."

The memory of carrying Amy Collison to the top of that mountain flashed in his mind. The weight of her on his back as he carried her those final steps, her brother beside them, and hope surging in the air as they reached the crest of the mountaintop was as clear as if it had happened just yesterday. Amy and her brother had been dead for nine years, but that memory would shine forever. He'd been diverted for too long by a mentally unstable man. He gave the signal.

"Andrew, I'm sorry, but I'm taking you out of the battle."

"What's that supposed to mean?"

Footsteps sounded outside the door, and then a second later Tick led half a dozen men inside, their booted feet thudding heavily on the wooden floor. A sharply dressed man in a formal suit loitered in the doorway while three policemen took position at the corners of the room and Tick stepped forward, astounding maturity on his eighteen-year-old face. "Sir, I'm Private Timothy Norton, and I've been standing guard at the hospital. I have authorization to detain anyone who has breached the hospital's security. I've brought the metropolitan police to search the premises."

Dumbstruck, Andrew looked at Trevor. Finally he found his voice and stepped closer to Tick. "You can't invade the privacy of my business. I haven't done anything illegal."

"We have a warrant, sir." Tick produced the document, and Andrew's eyes narrowed in contempt. "We have evidence you are creating a duplicate set of records in an attempt to frame Dr. Kendall. A judge has agreed with our proof."

"You won't find anything. Everything I've done is perfectly legal."

Two police officers headed to Andrew's desk and began pulling out drawers and rifling though papers. Tick went and stood over them, scanning every document as it was pulled out. It didn't take long to find what they were looking for.

Tick flipped through a stack of papers, lifting the top page for everyone to see. "Do you have any explanation for this form, sir?"

It was a blank laboratory form, identical to the one Trevor and Kate used in their study. There was no reason for Andrew to have hundreds of blank forms unless he was using them to forge a second set of documents like the ones planted in Kate's house.

"It's no crime to have blank medical forms," Andrew said.

"Perhaps not," Tick said. "But these didn't come from Washington Memorial Hospital. They were commissioned at Steigler's shop on Twenty-Third Street. The owner verified you ordered five hundred blank copies based on a single blank form your mother took from the hospital. He made copies of the forms used in the Baltimore study too. There's no reason for you to order those forms unless you were creating a second set of records that would imply Dr. Kendall was falsifying his research."

Despite the chill, a sheen of perspiration gleamed on Andrew's skin as he glanced back at Trevor. "You know this is playing into my hands, don't you? The publicity I'll garner from this will put everything else I've accomplished in the shade."

Trevor motioned to one of the nattily dressed gentlemen standing in the corner. "I asked Dr. Josiah Mason to be here today. I could tell from the newspaper articles you sent me that your ultimate aim was the revocation of my medical license. Dr. Mason oversees the board of physician licensure for the state of Virginia. He will be a witness to your campaign to manufacture a record of medical fraud to use against me."

In all the years of watching his patients succumb to disease, the pain of watching Andrew Doyle being handcuffed was a unique sort of misery. The victims of tuberculosis could not help their condition, but Andrew chose to walk this path. He'd once been a kind and sensitive man, before he was driven over the edge by witnessing the death of a woman he loved. And Trevor had played a part in that downfall.

The Baltimore study had just claimed its final victim.

Kate sat at the staff table, anxiously scanning the newspaper advertisements for available positions. Perhaps she'd been foolish to quit her hospital job before securing another position, but the faster she could get away from Trevor, the better. She loved him too much to linger.

The door banged open, and the midday brigade of attendants wheeled in meal carts loaded down with covered trays, the metal wheels squeaking in steady rhythm as the carts rolled forward. She wasn't hungry but should force herself to eat something. Pushing the newspaper to the side of the table, she glanced up at Nurse Ackerman.

"Do you know of any decent job prospects?" she asked. "I shudder at the thought of another clerical job. Or worse, getting stuck in my mother's kitchen slinging out meals three times a day. I want to do something *meaningful* with my life."

Bridget Kelly, the Irish attendant who once flirted with Trevor about milking cows, stopped her cart in its tracks. "Are you suggesting my work isn't meaningful?" she asked in her pretty Irish lilt.

Kate straightened. "Of course not." But

the other two attendants looked at Kate with similar wounded expressions.

Bridget put her hands on her hips and raised her chin. "Because I think what I do is very meaningful. And what about the cooks who trudge in at four o'clock every morning to make sure the sick people get their breakfast on time? Or Howard Radowitz, who mops the floors of the hospital every night without fail when you're safe at home in your bed? This hospital would grind to a halt if we weren't here to do our *meaningless* work."

Kate was speechless, but every one of Bridget's words struck home. After all, weren't her parents the sort of people who worked with their hands so that others in Washington could pursue more glamorous work? She stood to apologize, but Nurse Ackerman beat her to the punch.

"How dare you go mouthing off like that," the nurse said. "Mrs. Livingston is a valued professional, and we could get any Irish girl fresh off the boat to take your place if you can't show proper respect."

Bridget grabbed a plate off the cart and plunked it in front of Kate, the metal cover clanging on the table. "Here's your lunch, ma'am. I'm sure you'll show it proper respect, since I haven't got any left."

A group of the male patients were playing cards in the sitting area. One of them hid an amused smile behind his hand of cards, but Kate was mortified. Most of the patients in this clinic came from gritty working-class neighborhoods, and she wanted to sink into the floor and disappear.

Bridget was about to push her cart into motion again when the door swung open and Trevor marched inside. Tick and three police officers followed.

"Nurse Ackerman, you're fired," Trevor said.

The nurse gasped. "For speaking harshly to Bridget? The girl deserved it!"

Kate stepped forward, ready to defend Nurse Ackerman, but Tick's firm shake of his head made her think better of it.

"No, it's for siphoning off hospital supplies, leaking information to the press, manufacturing fraudulent records, and spilling mercury across my desk. For a start."

"I don't know what you're talking about," Nurse Ackerman sputtered. "I've only been doing my job." But the color dropped from her face, and her lips quivered and turned white.

Kate was in shock, unable to comprehend the scene unfolding before her.

Trevor's eyes glittered with anger. "The

424

new patients have been making a careful observation of your behavior in the wards," he continued. He nodded to the other side of the room, where Oskar Holtzmann emerged from the men's ward. A housecoat hung from his thin frame, but a look of anticipation lit up his face.

"You replace each patient's bar of soap with a fresh one every day," Oskar said. "The patients all think this is for cleanliness, but Dr. Kendall didn't know anything about it until I told him. He says it's a waste of money. You told the attendants to throw away everyone's bedsheets each week for fear of contamination and ordered up new ones instead of washing them." He folded his arms across his chest. It looked as though he was enjoying this.

"Nonsense!" Nurse Ackerman cried.

"You've been running through supplies like a madwoman, and then reporting the waste to Superintendent Lambrecht," Trevor said. "No wonder he was suspicious of all our expenditures."

"Are you begrudging dying people a bar of soap? Or fresh sheets?" Nurse Ackerman's voice was outraged, but her hands twitched and fluttered like a moth trapped in a corner. She stilled as Trevor moved to the supply closet, a fat ring of keys jangling in his hand.

"You can't go in there!" Nurse Ackerman said in a panicked voice.

It always seemed odd how territorial she was about the supply closet, but Kate thought it was a sign of her frugal diligence. Apparently there was more to the story. It didn't take Trevor long to emerge from the supply closet with a raft of papers in his hands.

"And what are these?" he asked coldly.

"All I did was make a second copy of the reports," she said. Nurse Ackerman sent a heated glare at Kate. "I didn't trust that woman to keep accurate statistics. You hired Mrs. Livingston because you fancied her, no other reason."

Kate sucked in a breath at the insult, but there was no time to voice her outrage. Trevor remained impassive as he handed the forms to one of the policemen.

"Both Oskar and Marlene have watched you come into the wards each morning after Kate and I leave. You make duplicate copies of what's on the charts hanging from the patient beds. I expect those will be used to manufacture a set of fraudulent records to accuse me of falsifying my research."

Kate turned to see how Nurse Ackerman would respond. The look of offended innocence was gone now, replaced by steely-eyed resolve.

"You killed all those people in Baltimore with an unproven cure. What right do you have to use human patients like that?"

Before Trevor could reply, Oskar said, "I want those unproven cures! Every day I feel my lungs fill with more fluid. I am *drowning* for want of an unproven cure! I won't let you try to stop doctors who are searching for those cures."

His voice choked off in a fit of coughing. Tick stepped back, reaching for his mask. The others did the same. The horror of this disease was that men like Oskar were probably going to die before the cure could be found, and it was going to take an army of doctors willing to undertake the demoralizing quest, year after year. Perhaps decade after decade.

Nurse Ackerman refused to back down. "Maybe the people who died in Baltimore were willing to run the risk, but you destroyed my son! He would have been a good doctor if you hadn't made him feel like a murderer."

Without warning she stepped toward Trevor and slapped him across the face. "You ruined my son. Ruined him!"

Two policemen pulled her away, but not

427

before she spat at Trevor. Nurse Ackerman was pressed against the wall and handcuffed while Trevor wiped his jacket with a handkerchief. The red imprint of the nurse's hand was already appearing on his face.

Kate saw a combination of anger and regret simmering in Trevor's dark eyes as the policemen hustled Nurse Ackerman out the door of the clinic.

The news of Nurse Ackerman's arrest spread like wildfire through the hospital wards. All the patients were stunned, and those healthy enough to leave their beds gathered around Tick in the sitting area as he recounted what happened.

"They probably won't get more than a slap on the wrist, since everything is considered a misdemeanor," he said.

Kate stared at the empty nurses' station. It was hard to believe Nurse Ackerman's grumpy attitude masked such seething hatred. In addition to training a new statistical assistant, Trevor now needed to hire another receiving nurse.

Henry was even more upset than Kate. "I can't believe it," Henry said as he scrubbed his hand across his face. "Andrew Doyle and I were a team. He was one of the nicest men I ever met. How could he attack Dr.

Kendall like that?"

Kate never met Andrew Doyle, but given Henry's bewildered expression, it was obvious the sense of betrayal ran deep. She could only imagine how unnerved Trevor must be feeling. He'd been alone in his office ever since the police took Nurse Ackerman away over an hour ago. When he finally emerged, he was unreadable as he walked toward her in the sitting area.

"I need to see you," he said. "Up on the roof."

The roof was their sanctuary, a haven where they shared their innermost dreams during those wonderful stolen hours. She followed him up the narrow staircase onto the flat of the roof. Trevor walked toward the far wall, bracing his hands on the ledge to look out over the city. It was breezy, and she tugged the folds of her cloak tighter.

"I never saw it coming," Trevor said. "I've always been so careful about guarding myself against getting too close to the patients, but I never realized the people around me might blame themselves for the decisions I made."

His hands were clenched into fists. They were shaking. It hurt to see him so miserable, but Kate held her tongue, knowing the best thing for Trevor was to unload the turmoil he'd kept bottled inside.

"He's gone insane, Kate. If you could have seen the look in his eyes. Sheer revulsion and hatred."

"Don't blame yourself for this. It wasn't your fault."

"It's *entirely* my fault," Trevor countered. "Andrew would have been a good doctor, but what happened in Baltimore so traumatized him, he can't lay a finger on a patient for fear of making a mistake. He was fine in medical school. I saw him every time I was in Boston and I never sensed anything wrong. But when it came time to work with real people, the old memories came to the surface and he couldn't do it. He blamed me for involving him in that study, and that blame is not entirely misplaced." She hated the hollow, hopeless look in Trevor's eyes, and she laid a hand over his trembling fist.

"Generals on the battlefield make mistakes, and some men die," she said softly. "Doctors make mistakes and the same thing happens. You're human, Trevor. If you can't forgive yourself for making a mistake, you'll start floundering like Andrew Doyle, and that would be a terrible waste of your God-given talents."

Trevor took a deep breath, refusing to meet her eyes. "I don't know what's going to happen to him. I don't want to press charges, but Andrew can't be allowed to run loose."

"Aren't there places for people with that sort of sickness?"

"An insane asylum? I think he'd rather go to prison."

"Tick said he doesn't think the charges will amount to much."

"Maybe not." Trevor turned and grasped her hand. "Thanks for listening to me ramble. I needed to talk, and you're the only person who really understands."

He drew her into the circle of his arms, squeezing tightly as he buried his face against her neck. She sensed a weakness in him, like a mighty oak that was growing weary of battling the storm and was in danger of toppling in the face of relentless winds. She'd never seen Trevor this needy before, and now she was about to walk out on him as well.

All she could do was return his embrace and pray he would find the strength to continue the battle on his own, because it was time for her to leave.

23

How do you say goodbye to a woman you know will die before you see her again? It was Kate's last day at the hospital. She'd already said goodbye to each patient in the men's ward and was exhausted from the task. Her cotton mask hid her trembling lips as she said goodbye to each woman, but several times she had to dab her eyes with the cuff of her sleeve.

"God bless you, Margaret," she said. "I'll be keeping you in my prayers."

"Good luck, Kate," Margaret said, barely having the energy to turn her head on the pillow. "Where are you off to next?"

"I'm not quite sure. I'll help at my parents' boardinghouse until I can find a paying job."

It was a conversation she repeated countless times as she spoke to each woman, clasping the patient's hands and smiling directly into her eyes. On her first day at the hospital, Kate had been afraid to even stand close to these people. Many of the attendants who brought the meals had the same reluctance, and yet this simple bit of human contact meant so much to the people in this ward.

She moved on to the next bed. "God bless you, Ethel," she continued. "I'll always remember sharing in your sweet grand-daughter's baptism."

Trevor hovered in the open doorway, glowering at her as she said these final good-byes, which was insane. If he wanted her to stay, he knew how he could make it happen. After saying goodbye to the last of the women, she walked on shaking legs to the door. She mustn't look back; she had to keep walking. Trevor remained planted in the doorway as she approached.

"I need to pack up my desk," she said. He still didn't budge, so she angled her body to slip past him. Once in the hallway, she tugged her mask down to blow her nose. She shoved the handkerchief into her pocket, then pressed her fingers to her swollen eyes.

The box Kate brought to pack her belongings filled quickly as she emptied her desk. A couple of framed family photographs and a fancy pen Charlie Davis gave her when she graduated from school. A dish for lemon drops, and her paperweight with a daisy blossom that would remain forever frozen in silent perfection inside the glass. She cleared away an empty flower vase and used a rag to wipe up a few dried curls of chrysanthemum petals from the corner of her desk. Mr. Walsh was beginning next Monday, and it was only fair to leave him a clean desk.

"So this is the end." Trevor's voice was flat as he leaned against the doorframe.

"I suppose so." She tipped the dead flower petals into the wastebasket and brushed the grit from her hands.

"I went looking for you when I got back to Washington because I thought you would never surrender. I thought you were up for any challenge and would rather go down fighting than quit before you got to the finish line."

How typical for Trevor to pick a fight before she left. "I have no interest in the finish line for the race you are on. You will *die*, Trevor."

"Maybe. Maybe not."

She emptied the last of the pencils from a drawer and slammed it shut. How could she have fallen in love with such an iron-hearted man? All she wanted to do was finish her business and get out of here, but there was one final thing she needed from Trevor. She swallowed and composed herself.

"You once said you would write a letter for Tick's application to the Naval Academy. I hope you're still willing to do that. The applications are due at the end of January."

There was a long pause, and she turned to look at him. With his arms folded across his chest and his faultless posture, he looked so handsome it almost hurt. His features were somber as he stared at her.

"Kate, you need to lay off Tick."

She blinked. "What?"

"He doesn't want to go to the Naval Academy. Let him make his own decisions for his life."

"I raised Tick. I know exactly what he wants out of life."

Trevor shook his head. "I see him as the man he is today, and you still see the boy you raised. You don't understand the hold you have over him. Tick would do *anything* for you, but it's time to let him go." A reluctant smile tugged at the corner of his mouth. "Tick won't let you down. You raised a smart and strong man and have every right to be proud of him. I won't write him a letter of recommendation unless he asks for one and, Kate . . . I don't think he will."

"I think you're wrong."

She scanned the room, looking for any final belongings. Now that the office was stripped of the frilly feminine touches, it looked as blank as a monk's cell.

Except for a fancy box sitting on the edge of Trevor's desk. Covered in Italian marbled paper, it looked out of place in the barren office. She pointed to the box. "What's that?"

"A crystal vase," he said. "My father is getting married this weekend, and I thought it would be a suitable gift."

"Are you going?"

"Yes."

She let out a sigh. "I can't believe you're putting yourself back into that man's orbit."

"He's my only living relative. Perhaps you have an abundance of family and friends, but I do not."

"He sent his child to the other side of the planet because you were an embarrassment and he wanted a rich wife."

"He's my *father*, Kate. He's not perfect. And this may come as a stunning surprise, but neither are you."

She turned away from the condemnation in his eyes, forcibly checking each of her desk drawers to be sure they were clear. "You changed your name because you despised him."

"I was eighteen. It was a stupid and impulsive thing to do, but I've built a reputation on my new name, and it's too late to go back now. I want to establish some kind of relationship with him, because the rift between us was as much my fault as his. He's not a bad man, but I painted him as one because it eased my conscience."

Trevor's face remained emotionless. She once mistook that look for apathy, but now she knew it to be the look he hid behind when his emotions threatened to get the better of him. Trevor always hid rather than confront problems head on. How could she expect him to know how to handle normal human emotions when he never had any friends or family to speak of?

She knelt on the floor beside her paltry box of possessions, her hands on the rim. "Trevor, if you would find another type of medicine to pursue, I would follow you anywhere. To a rural practice on the Dakota plains. To China. The North Pole. Anything but this."

Trevor came to kneel beside her, and for a fraction of a second her heart leapt in hope. He closed the flaps of the box and pushed it toward her.

"Kate, go home."

Then he stood and left the room.

Kate trudged up the stairs to the boarding-house and fumbled at the knob, using her shoulder to nudge open the door. She dumped the box onto the sofa in the parlor and plopped down beside it.

For the first time in twelve years she had no job and no purpose. The boardinghouse was going under, and her heart had just been smashed beneath Trevor's will of iron. She had lost Trevor. In the most important battle she ever had with him, she had lost.

Pans clattered in the kitchen, but she couldn't face her mother yet. Her mother would rally to Kate's defense, but if she said one negative thing about Trevor, Kate would snap. The back door slammed, and her father came up the hallway, wiping his hands on an oily rag. That new hot water heater required more tending than any of them anticipated. And it still needed to be paid for.

"The mail arrived," her father said. "A letter for you."

Kate took the letter, her breath catching at the sight of Trevor's distinctive handwriting across the front of the envelope. She clutched it and headed to the front stoop.

She didn't want anyone watching her as she read it.

She sat on the steps outside and ripped the envelope open.

Why had Trevor sent her a bank check for two thousand dollars? She unfolded the note.

Dear Kate,

The attached check should cover several months of the mortgage on your parents' boardinghouse and finish paying for the hot water heater. I hope this will compensate for the damage caused by Andrew Doyle.

I have never been good with difficult conversations, which is why a note is easier than speaking with you. Despite how it ended, your friendship has been the most meaningful of my life. I don't know if I will die next year or in fifty years, but I am quite certain the memory of our friendship will sustain me as long as I live.

In all our battles over the years, even when it seemed like I came out on top, you were always the best, Kate.

Trevor

Postscript: I believe in clean endings, so please consider this our final communication. Don't return to the hospital. You won't be welcome.

She wanted to weep. How typically Trevor. Even when he was trying to be nice, he had to spoil it at the end. But she loved him, blunt edges and all.

Should she treasure this letter or tear it to pieces? Her smile was sad as she folded the note and gently tucked it back into the envelope. Her parents would be overjoyed when she showed them this check. It would lift a burden that had been weighing on their spirits, but she couldn't face them quite yet.

She curled over, clasping the letter and pressing her forehead to her knees. There were plenty of battles in life she could never win, but she'd just lost the biggest.

24

Two weeks after Kate quit her job, Irene Bauman finally pushed her father over the edge. As the blustery December rain turned into sleet one afternoon, Justice Bauman left his work at the Supreme Court early to avoid an impending snowstorm. After shaking ice crystals from his overcoat, he followed the sound of his daughter's laughter back to the laundry room, where she had trapped one of the new boarders, an English professor from Georgetown.

With her bloomers pulled up, her stockings tugged down, and her skirts gathered up around her hips, Irene was boasting about the shapeliness of her knees, proudly displaying them from various angles and bragging how they weren't knobby like other girls' knees, and the professor should feel the smoothness of her skin, because she used cocoa butter every evening to soften it.

Kate could hear the bellows of outrage all

the way on the fourth floor. It was clear Irene could no longer be left alone during the day, so her father put her to work in his office. Even there it was dicey to trust her among the all-male staff without oversight. The clerks at the Supreme Court were lawyers with degrees from the best colleges in the land. They were intelligent young men, but they weren't blind, and that was where Kate came into play.

"You'd be a fine secretary to oversee the operations in the office," Justice Bauman said. "You could keep an eye on Irene too. If you can show her a woman can aspire to something more than hair ribbons or shapely knees, I will be forever in your debt."

"So I am to be a baby-sitter?" Kate asked.

Justice Bauman was a smart man, and he knew how to appeal to Kate's sense of challenge. "No, no. I need much more than that. You know how Washington operates, Kate. Half the people in this city have eaten at your mother's table, and you know what it takes to get things done. My office has never been very efficient. Government offices rarely are. If you have a quarter of your mother's skill for organization, I would be very grateful."

That clinched it. Kate began working at

Justice Bauman's office at the US Capitol, where the Supreme Court had been housed since 1810. There were plans to someday fund a grand new building for the Supreme Court, but for now it was tucked into a wing above the old senate chambers. Each day was a thrill as she walked toward the majestic building with the dome that could be seen for miles. Its gleaming white stone seemed to shimmer in the sunlight, the massive neoclassical lines an awesome sight of strength and stability.

The office where she worked was spacious, with four oversized desks for the clerks, Kate's secretarial desk, and a table in the corner for Irene. With no marketable skills, Irene had been charged with typing addresses onto the envelopes of office correspondence. The typewriter was a new and baffling piece of equipment for all of them, and Irene struggled to peck out the correct letters. She usually ruined about four envelopes before successfully banging out a correct address. The male population of the city was safe from the sight of Irene's knees, although the girl took complete credit for Kate's new position.

"Papa knew we would work well together, that's why he hired you," Irene said as she pulled another ruined envelope from beneath the rubber roller of the typewriter.

"No doubt," Kate muttered. Minding Irene wasn't as terrible as Kate feared. Now that the girl had something more meaningful to do, she spent less time obsessing over attracting a man to fill the void in her days.

The holidays passed, and afterward the city descended into its gray pattern of damp cold that blanketed everything and seeped into her bones. Every afternoon warmed just enough to begin melting the snow, only to have it freeze over into a layer of slick ice overnight.

As the months rolled by, Kate's hands began developing calluses from the amount of paper she proofread, sorted, stamped, and filed. It was wickedly dull work, but it paid a respectable wage. What did it matter if there were no patients she could try to help cheer? Or a fascinating, challenging, and darkly brooding man who made her heart speed up as he crossed her line of sight?

Trevor had turned down his father's offer to return to Scotland. She knew because the one time she worked up the courage to walk past the hospital, she saw construction workers on the roof and Trevor's dark figure leaning over a set of plans, the architect beside him. Kate scurried away, darting around piles of snow and melting puddles of slush in her haste to avoid being seen. What if he'd looked down and seen her lollygagging in the street like a heartsick fool?

She thought of him every day, but especially on Mondays when she knew he swabbed his throat and smeared the results onto a glass slide that Henry checked for tuberculosis. On Monday mornings she always said an extra prayer for Trevor.

The last time he contracted tuberculosis, he went to a sanitarium in the Himalayas. Surely he would do the same if he contracted it again. Throughout the winter Kate suffered a constant fear of learning Trevor had disappeared from the hospital, for she knew what such an abrupt absence would mean. As winter loosened its grip on the city, bright green tips of grass nudged through the barren soil. Gray skies gave way to crystal blue, and the damp air dissolved into the fresh breezes of April. The walkways were clear again, making movement throughout the city easier, and Kate finally landed on the perfect solution to keep an eye on Trevor's whereabouts.

Irene Bauman had a nose for gossip that rivaled any bloodhound, and she loved her new role in supplying Kate with information.

"I think this machine is faulty," Irene said as she tugged an envelope from beneath the roller of the typewriting machine. "I'm sure I've been hitting the key for *S,* but sometimes it comes out with other letters. Maybe I should go to the stationer's to buy more envelopes?"

Heat flooded Kate's cheeks at the code word. Irene spoiled so many envelopes they needed to regularly replenish their stock. It just so happened the best stationery shop in the city was across the street from Washington Memorial Hospital, and Irene had proven herself to be an enthusiastic spy for Kate.

"If you wait a moment, I have another batch of letters to deliver." Kate reached for the box beneath her desk, pulling out the pile of note cards she regularly penned to the patients in the clinic. Having seen the eagerness with which the patients greeted the daily mail, and the subtle disappointment on their faces when the mail clerk passed them by, Kate made sure each of them got a note from her at least once per week. Sometimes it was hard to think of things to write, so she passed along Washington gossip or even amusing pictures she clipped from newspaper stories.

Nine more of the patients Kate once knew

had died. Irene always got the names of the new patients, and Kate proceeded to pen notes to them as well. Even a cheerful note from a stranger was welcome to people who were trapped in a bed all day.

Delivering mail to the patients was a perfect excuse for Irene to go up to the fifth-floor clinic. All Kate needed to know was if Trevor was still at the hospital. If he was, that meant his lungs were clear and he was still a healthy man. If he disappeared on her . . .

She passed the stash of mail to Irene. "Say hello to Nurse Augusta for me." After Nurse Ackerman had been fired, a cheerful woman named Augusta Jones had been hired as the new receiving nurse.

Once Irene had left, Roger Moreno approached her desk. The young lawyer looked about eighteen, although Kate knew he had to be at least twenty-five. She suspected his bushy mustache was an attempt to make himself look more mature.

"I'm hoping you can proofread this for me," Mr. Moreno said. "My last brief had three spelling errors in it, and I can't afford that kind of lapse again."

Kate flashed a sympathetic smile and held out her hand for the papers. "And what is it this time?"

"Real estate taxation."

Kate winced, but Mr. Moreno launched into the topic with enthusiasm. "I think you'll find it fascinating. Did you know it's legal to use variable accounting techniques for assessing the value of property? If this case is upheld, it will turn the whole world of municipal accounting on its head."

Mr. Moreno continued to ramble on about taxation law while Kate thumbed through six pages of dense legal text. She looked up and tried to smile brightly.

"Heavens, don't give away the ending," she said. "I'll read this and let you know if there's anything that needs correcting."

His smile could have lit the room. "Thanks, Mrs. Livingston. You're the best!" Mr. Moreno returned to his desk, and Kate began reading the brief.

She had never been so unhappy in her life. She'd lost the man she loved, walked away from a wonderful job, the likes of which she was unlikely to ever find again, and now she had six pages of real estate taxation to proofread.

At least Tick's future was set, having finally been accepted into the Naval Academy. The day after hearing the news, her parents hosted a huge celebration at the boardinghouse. For that one night they hired a cook and left the meal preparation to someone else, as a hundred people flooded their home for a party that shook the rafters. Tick's letter of acceptance had been framed and displayed above the mantelpiece. He would leave for Annapolis next August, and Kate had never been so proud.

Except . . . why hadn't he contacted her yet about getting fitted for his new uniforms? She wanted to accompany him to the tailor's, so she could see him in his smart new midshipman's uniform. If he got fitted without her . . . well, that would be okay, but she had better be sure it hadn't slipped his mind.

Something about this didn't sit right. Tick's visits to the boardinghouse had been scarce lately, and paying a visit to ensure he was on track would be her first order of business after work today.

The guard at the Marine Barracks told her that Tick had gone to the shooting range at the Navy Yard. She'd never been to the shooting range before, but given the steady blasts sounding every few moments, it was easy to let her ears be the guide. The shooting range bordered the Anacostia River, and a handful of men were taking careful aim at

449

targets placed on the opposite side of the field.

Standing at the base of the wharf, she shielded her eyes from the glare of the afternoon sun and waved. "Private Norton!"

Tick looked at her and grinned, motioning her closer.

"Very impressive," she remarked at the smattering of bullet holes in the center of the concentric rings.

"I've been training hard," he said. "What can I do for you, Kate?"

"Have you gotten fitted for your uniforms yet? It should be done before the end of the month."

A steady wind blew in from the river, and Kate swatted a strand of blowing hair out of her eyes. Tick's mouth twisted in apprehension. He shifted his weight and bit his lip, staring somewhere over her shoulder.

"I'm not going, Kate. I sent in my refusal of the appointment last week."

Instantly she became dizzy. If the other soldiers weren't standing only a few yards away, she would have let out a screech in protest. "So you're going to be an enlisted soldier for the rest of your life? Anyone can be cannon fodder, and you're worth more than that."

Tick crouched down to open a box of bullets, feeding them into the revolver's chamber and snapping it closed. He stood and fired off six quick rounds, the burst of noise echoing across the field and the scent of gunpowder heavy in the air. He hit the target each time. He lowered the gun and looked at her. "Not just anyone can do that! I'm not officer material, Kate . . . and I want something else."

"What is it?"

He knelt down to reload again. His fingers were methodical as he slid each bullet into the chamber with a click. Then he stood and looked her in the eyes. "You're not going to like it."

"Please, just say it, Tick."

"I want to join the Secret Service. I've already been approached by folks at the Treasury who oversee the agency. I'm going to be transferred at the end of the month."

She let out a huge breath, tilting her head toward the sky. "Flinging yourself in front of an assassin's bullet? You can do better."

"Doing what? Paper work? Performance reviews? That's what officers do, and I'd rather clear dishes from Mother's table than be stuck at a desk like that." Tick had never been so angry with her, and it hurt deeply.

"You don't understand what you're passing up," she said. "I want to protect you from a life of bowing and scraping along when you can be so much more."

The anger faded from Tick's face. He set the revolver down, then turned and pulled her into a hug. Her chin didn't even reach his shoulder. When he pulled back, he placed a kiss on her forehead, and a hand on each shoulder, and forced her to look at him.

"Now, listen carefully because I'm only going to say this once, and I'll go to my grave denying I ever said it at all, so pay attention." He drew a breath and looked her straight in the eyes. "I know you raised me. You were more a mother and father to me than either of our parents, and I'm grateful for that. I know you want what's best for me. But, Kate, I don't want to go to college. That's never going to change."

She looked away. Hadn't Trevor tried to tell her the same thing last November? She refused to believe it, but apparently it was true. Tick hadn't stopped talking.

"When I was standing guard at the hospital, I felt like I had a purpose. I was protecting you and the patients from someone trying to ruin Trevor. It was hard work. Some people might say any mindless fool could stand guard all day, but you have to pay attention every minute. Notice things. Never get tired and be on alert at all times. It's hard work and I'm good at it, Kate. Protecting and serving people is what I'm meant to do. Not sit at a desk."

It hurt too much to look at him, so she stared at a pair of mallards that had drifted in front of the wharf, bobbing on the choppy waves. Why couldn't Tick take after their father and be happy fixing gutters and arguing with plumbers?

But that wasn't what God intended for Tick. He and Trevor were both warriors. Trevor fought his battles in the laboratory, and Tick wanted to work on behalf of the government. Both required the heart and soul of a hero, and suddenly she'd never been so proud of her baby brother.

"Okay, Tick, I get it."

The relief that crossed his face shamed her. Did her opinion really matter that much to him?

"I live in terror of telling Mom. She's almost as bad as you when it comes to college."

"If you can face down Maude Norton, you'll be fine up against any assassin."

The look he gave her was part amusement, part skepticism. "You sure about that? She can be pretty tough."

"So can I. And I'll be standing behind you

453

if she gives you any trouble."

Tick swallowed hard. Oh, good heavens, he wasn't getting misty-eyed on her, was he?

She reached up to give him a hug. "Everything will be okay, Tick." She loved this boy who was now a man. It was time to let him find his own way.

25

Trevor was used to worrying about his patients, but getting an ulcer from worrying over a dog was a new experience for him. After Kate left the hospital, he caved in and finally adopted the stray dog she used to feed on the hospital steps.

At first he wasn't quite sure why he started letting Princess follow him home in the evenings. He didn't want to admit it, but he liked the way she shook with excitement when she saw him coming down the steps at the end of the day, yelping and eager for a quick rub. It didn't take long to become attached, even though Princess made a mess of his room above the train station. He purchased a grooming comb, but no matter how much he combed her, there were always fine strands of dog hair littering his room. She also had a habit of planting her huge paws on his chest to lick his face with her sloppy tongue. His laundry bill soared, and he had to pay for regular visits from a cleaning woman to mop up the dog hair, but it was worth it. The absolute loyalty and boundless affection that dog gave him was beyond price.

Except there was something wrong with her. She hadn't eaten in days and had been too tired to follow him home in the evenings. This morning he saved some bacon from his breakfast tray to bring down for her. He found the dog lying on her side under a chestnut tree behind the hospital. She lifted her head when he approached, but then set it back down again.

"Come on, Princess. It's bacon! Can't you smell it?" He beckoned again, and the dog pushed herself up, lumbering over slowly. She nosed the bacon, her pale tongue flicking at it. She lapped up a crispy piece, her jaws pumping, and then whimpered as most of the bacon fell from her mouth.

Princess turned her big liquid eyes to look up at him. He rubbed the fur on the top of her head, wishing the dog could speak and tell him what was wrong. Why wasn't she eating or drinking when she must be starving by now?

There was only one thing left to try. He would catch grief over it, but he wasn't going to let his dog die because he was too shy to ask for a favor. The new field of veterinary science was beginning to turn out doctors for animals, but they lived in rural areas and only treated farm animals. If Trevor wanted his dog cured, it was going to be by a human doctor.

"You want me to operate on a dog?" Dr. Schrader asked, disbelief in his eyes. With his white beard and pale-blue eyes, Dr. Schrader was washing his hands in the washbasin outside the operating room. He spoke loudly enough for some of the nurses laying out the day's supply of bandages to hear. The nurses exchanged glances and giggled.

"I'll operate, but I need you to administer the anesthesia," Trevor said. "I think there's something wrong in her throat or esophagus. She can't eat or drink. I nearly lost a finger the one time I tried to get a better look."

"I've never operated on a dog," Dr. Schrader said.

"Neither have I, but I'm guessing we should use the same amount of anesthesia we'd give a child. I need to get in and look without getting my fingers bitten off."

Dr. Schrader reached for a towel, drying his hands briskly and refusing to make eye contact. "Neither one of us know what

457

we're doing. We could lose the dog."

"I'll lose her if we do nothing," Trevor said. "And I really care about that dog. I'll try anything."

"That's so sweet," one of the nurses cooed. She was looking at him with calf's eyes, and the other looked a little flushed as well. Trevor turned back to Dr. Schrader.

"I'll pay for all the expenses and use of the operating room. We'll have to do it after business hours. Are you willing?"

Dr. Schrader tossed the towel into the laundry bin. "I'll meet you at five o'clock. Just don't blame me if the mutt dies on the table."

Relief flooded through him. How pathetic that he allowed a mangy old dog to become his most precious companion, but there it was. It had never been easy for him to make friends.

Except for Kate. His friendship with Kate had been easy. He never had to pretend to be somebody else or feign interest in fashionable things when he was with her. Kate accepted him as he was, blunt edges and all.

He still wondered if he'd done the right thing in letting her go. What if he never found a cure for tuberculosis? Would his sacrifice have been worth it? His need to cure tuberculosis was more than just ambition or an award to hang on the wall. It was a calling. Why else would God have spared him from an early death if he were not to use his insight to join the fight?

He walked up to his office. "Good morning, Philip," he said as he crossed the room to his desk.

It still seemed strange to see Philip Walsh sitting at Kate's desk every morning. Kate had worked here for only six months, but in that time she'd ingrained herself into every square inch of this clinic. He couldn't look at the daily statistical reports without remembering how Kate would hold her breath and wait for his reaction. The stolen hours up on the roof or how they'd share a meal at the staff table. Even how she nagged him about his manners and bickered with him in such amiable familiarity. Most of all he remembered her laughter. It felt like a shower of gold coins raining down in the midst of a gloomy day. Kate had always had that effect on him. He would never find another woman who suited him so well.

Not that it mattered anymore. He collected his chart and glanced over at Philip. "Let's make the rounds."

It only took a minute to locate the problem.

As soon as Princess was anesthetized, Trevor used a long pair of tweezers to extract the three-inch fish bone lodged in the back of his dog's throat. No wonder she'd been too miserable to swallow anything.

"What have you been feeding this dog?" Dr. Schrader asked as he examined the bone.

"I gave her a second serving of whatever I had for dinner. She always seemed to like it."

"You can't feed a dog the way you feed a human. No wonder she got sick."

A wave of guilt swept over him. How was he supposed to know? He'd never had a pet before! He'd get some veterinary books and read up on the proper diet for a dog, so he wouldn't do something so foolish again.

Both men began washing up in the sink. The surgery had taken less than ten minutes, and it was still early in the evening.

"Can I take you out for a drink to thank you for saving my dog's life?" Trevor asked. It was the polite thing to do. Kate had drilled that much into him, and perhaps if he worked a little harder at making friends, he wouldn't be so dependent on the companionship of a dog.

"Thanks for the offer, but my wife is probably keeping dinner warm," Dr. Schrader said as he shrugged into his suit coat and left the room. Trevor met Mrs. Schrader once, and given that woman's open adoration of her husband, it was little wonder he was eager to return home to her.

The thought made Trevor even lonelier.

It wasn't until after Dr. Schrader left that Trevor realized he had a sixty-pound problem lying on the operating table. Princess was going to be groggy for hours, and there was no way she could walk all the way home to his apartment. He squatted down to slide her off the operating table, carefully draping her head and forelegs over his shoulder. It was awkward angling out the door with a slumbering dog weighing him down, but he got her up the stairs to the clinic.

Marlene nearly had a fit when she saw him lugging the massive dog through the clinic's front doors. After helping monitor Nurse Ackerman's nefarious activities in the wards, Trevor offered both Oskar and Marlene positions at the hospital. Oskar had no interest in staying, but Marlene was desperate to quit working as a prostitute. She wouldn't always be healthy enough to work, but he'd take care of her for as long as necessary. For now, she covered the overnight shift at the clinic, drank his cod liver oil daily, and seemed to be maintaining her health.

"Will you open my office?" he asked her. "I'll be staying the night with my patient."

It wouldn't be the first time he spent the night on the floor of his office. On nights he had to work late, it was easier to grab a pillow and a blanket from the supply closet and stretch out on the floor. It wasn't like there was anyone at home who would miss him.

Could it be that his only friend in the world was really a dog?

After getting Princess settled on the floor, he darted downstairs to slip a few dollars to a janitor with instructions to do an extra-thorough job cleaning the operating room. Trevor knew better than anyone how that dog could shed.

It was too early to sleep, and the isolation in his office held no appeal. He walked the floors to shake the hollow ache of loneliness expanding in his chest. How could he be in a building full of people and still feel so alone?

The hospital always seemed different at night when the bustle of the daytime had faded. His footsteps echoed off the cold tile as he walked the dim corridors. He paused when he came to a wall with framed photographs of former employees of the hospital. Three nurses and a doctor, with a small bronze nameplate beneath each photograph. All of them had died because of their work here. Two of the nurses contracted diphtheria and one caught typhoid, all from treating infected patients. Dr. Edwin Jones cut himself during surgery, contracted septicemia, and died two days later. For all Trevor knew, someday he would finally fall victim to tuberculosis, and then his photograph would hang on this wall as well.

He braced a hand against the wall, hanging his head to stare at the floor. Was it worth it? He had lost the only woman he would ever love because he wouldn't walk away from this exhausting and demoralizing work.

He squeezed his eyes shut as the knot of anguish expanded. *Kate.* Sometimes the regret was a physical pain that threatened to swamp him. Right now she was probably sitting at that brightly lit dining table in the boardinghouse, surrounded by dozens of people. Dinner would have wound down, and everyone would be drinking coffee and gossiping about the latest happenings on Capitol Hill. The temptation to run across town and join her clawed at him. Was he destined to live out the rest of his life alone?

"Dr. Kendall?"

He straightened, embarrassed to be caught off guard. A pretty young attendant with kind eyes was standing beside him. "Are you all right?" she asked. "You look ill."

There was concern in her face, as though she were truly worried about him. He wasn't used to being on the receiving end of sympathy, and it unsettled him. He straightened his coat and smoothed his tie.

"I'll be fine, thank you," he said. He glanced at the soiled mess she held, the stink of vomit rising from the wadded-up sheets. "It looks like you haven't had an easy night either."

She gave him a weary nod. "The patient at the end of the hall hasn't been able to keep anything down in days. He's got a gall-bladder infection, poor man. I'm going to fetch clean linens."

"It's not an easy task, is it?"

Her shoulders sagged a bit, but she gave a resigned smile. "It's not so bad."

"He's lucky to have you looking after him. Hang in there. You're doing a good job."

Her eyes widened in surprise. He didn't exactly have a reputation for being chatty with the staff, but he meant what he said. The nurses and attendants did heroic duty here, bathing patients, wiping up vomit, carrying bedpans.

She smiled back at him. In that split second when he met her eyes, a silent message hummed between them. A message of comfort, of empathy.

"Thank you, sir." The nurse walked toward the laundry with the foul mess in her hands.

Only the people who worked under this roof could truly understand the toll caused by caring for the sick, and not everyone was cut out for it. He thought Kate would be up to the challenge, but he'd been wrong.

He hung his head as he continued walking the halls. That wasn't true. Kate could handle the work; she just couldn't tolerate *him* working here.

It was time to get back and check on the dog. He grabbed a bowl of water for Princess, but when he returned to his office, she was still slumbering. He tossed a pillow and a blanket on the floor. The tile was hard beneath his shoulder blades as he lay down beside the dog. A glance to his side showed she was drooling on his floor, and he smiled a little. Another mess to clean up in the morning, but he didn't mind. If nothing else, Princess taught him the value of patience.

He wondered what Kate would think if

she knew he had adopted Princess. He turned his face up to stare at the ceiling.

He needed to quit thinking about Kate so much. She had made her choice, and he was a distant second to her fears. He didn't like it, but he needed to accept the way things were.

The next morning, Princess downed a plate of cooked barley and two full bowls of water. Trevor monitored each mouthful as it went down. She ate slowly, as though the back of her throat still ached. But she got it down, and Trevor smiled in satisfaction. Afterward he walked Princess down the stairs and tied her to a tree in the back of the hospital, where he could keep an eye on her from his office window.

When he returned to the clinic, he froze at the sight of the last person he expected to see in a tubercular ward.

"What is *she* doing here?" he snapped to Nurse Augusta.

Irene Bauman flashed him a coy smile as she turned away from the nurses' station to face him. "Dr. Kendall! We miss you at the dinner table. Everyone who stays at the boardinghouse is so old and boring. I wish you would come back."

He looked impatiently at Nurse Augusta.

"What is she doing here?" he repeated.

"Kate Livingston sends letters to the patients every week," the nurse replied.

"I know. That still doesn't explain why Miss Bauman is here."

"You don't have to sound so scary," the girl replied. He wondered if that pout worked with her father. It didn't work with him.

He glared at the stack of letters on the nurses' counter. Clearly the girl brought them along and had probably been doing so for some time. He lowered his voice and pointed to his office.

"Follow me," he snapped. "I need to speak with you."

26

How could a man as young and healthy as Roger Moreno suffer from such a bizarre assortment of ailments? Aside from spelling errors, the young law clerk also suffered from a severe case of hypochondria.

Kate sat at her desk and tried to block out Mr. Moreno's voice as he shouted into the telephone mounted on the wall in the corner of the office. There was no need to shout into a telephone to be heard on the other end, but Mr. Moreno apparently didn't know this as he recounted his medical plight to his mother, who lived ten miles away in Alexandria.

"My gums are turning white," he shouted into the telephone. "They hurt when I eat, and I don't know what to do."

Kate continued proofreading a legal brief on insurance law and tried not to think about Mr. Moreno's sore gums. The man was likely to live to be ninety, but the past five months of sharing an office with him had been torture.

One good year with Trevor would beat fifty with Mr. Moreno.

She set her pencil down, surprised at the truth of the thought that flitted into her mind. What if Trevor never caught tuberculosis and he lived to be ninety? Her fear would have cost her the joy of sharing her life with the one man on the planet who challenged and thrilled her every moment she worked alongside him. Yes, he could catch tuberculosis and die within a year, but he might *never* get the disease and the effect would be the same. He would be lost to her because she was too cowardly to face her fears.

As soon as Mr. Moreno hung up the telephone, Irene pounced. "You should use a toothpick after meals," she said helpfully. "I can show you."

Kate intervened before Irene could embarrass herself any further. "Irene, why don't you go down the hall and pick up today's mail. It ought to be here by now."

Mr. Moreno sent Kate a relieved smile as Irene flounced out of the office. No clerk wanted to be caught tampering with the boss's daughter.

The postal delivery to Justice Bauman's

office usually filled an oversized bin, and today was no exception. Legal journals, official correspondence, and letters written from all over the country flooded the office every day. She quickly pulled all the fat legal journals into a stack, then began flipping through the letters to pull out government correspondence that needed quick attention.

A small, square envelope plopped onto her lap. She would recognize that handwriting anywhere.

Why was Trevor writing to her? Her name was boldly scrawled across the front of the envelope, and her mouth went dry as she tore it open. In typical Trevor fashion, the note was short and brusque.

Kate,
  Tell Irene to stay away from the hospital. She is distracting the orderlies. Besides, you should not be coercing Irene to do your dirty work.
                                    Trevor

Kate bit her lip, knowing she had been caught. How was she going to learn what was going on with Trevor if Irene was banished from the hospital?

That last line caught her attention. Trevor

never misspoke. His words were chosen with the precision of a surgeon selecting the correct tool. He always meant *exactly* what he said, and he told her to quit using Irene to do her dirty work.

A thrill of excitement rippled through her.

Kate sensed a challenge in the words, and she never backed down from a challenge.

Kate used her lunch hour to go to the hospital.

This was a big gamble. Maybe she was reading too much into the note and Trevor would throw her out. As long as she lived, she would never forget those fleeting moments in the storage closet when Trevor's famous control snapped as he shouted at her, *"You're like sunlight and water and air to me. . . . I love you, but you don't know the meaning of the word. You only love when it's easy. . . ."*

He'd been right in his accusation. Her marriage to Nathan had been easy. Falling in love with Trevor had been easy too. It was living with him that would be hard. It had been five months since she'd seen him, but her feelings hadn't faded, and she doubted they ever would. She was going to need to accept the hard with the easy if she could ever share a life with Trevor. She wasn't ready to give up on him. Not yet.

Henry must have been absent today, for Trevor was in the laboratory and analyzing slide data when she arrived. His eye was to the microscope as he dictated his observations to Mr. Walsh, the man hired to replace her. The cool professionalism in Trevor's voice stirred her. How odd was it to get a thrill from simply listening to a man interpreting a slide sample?

"The presence of hemoglobin remains low, and borderline anemia is suspected," Trevor said, still looking through the eyepiece. "Please note I want additional serum given to her."

"Noted," Mr. Walsh said.

"What were the iron levels on 31F's sample last week?"

Mr. Walsh noticed Kate standing in the open doorway. "Mrs. Livingston," he said pleasantly. "How nice to see you again."

Trevor reared back from the microscope. A flush stained his face and he blinked at her, but he masked his surprise quickly. "Kate," he said coolly, then removed the specimen slide from beneath the lens. His face looked as if it were carved from stone, yet his eyes glittered with emotion. "You may leave for lunch, Philip. I'd like a word with Mrs. Livingston."

Mr. Walsh closed the laboratory door when he left. Trevor folded his arms across his chest and shot her a glare that could give her frostbite, but she refused to let him intimidate her.

"You once said I was your sunlight and air," she said. "Funny, because based on your chilly reception, it appears I'm your arctic blast."

The corner of his mouth twitched a little. He stifled it before it could break into a smile. "Why are you sending Irene to spy on me?"

"I like sending notes to the patients, and she offered to carry them. It saves on postage."

"Keep trying, Kate. I cornered her yesterday, and she said you gave her orders to ask Nurse Augusta about me. Where I was and what I had been up to. Why?"

He rapped out the questions like a prosecuting attorney. Like she had something to be ashamed about when he had no conception of the strangling fear she endured since learning of his condition.

"I sent her so I could be sure you were still here," she said in a rush. Her throat started to ache and close up, but she forced herself to continue. "Because I know one day you will simply disappear from this hospital without telling anyone why. And when that day happens, I'll know it's because you're on your way to some sanitarium in New York or Colorado or the Himalayas, because you're dying and wouldn't have the human decency to even tell me about it. *That* is why I sent Irene!"

Trevor looked absolutely speechless. He opened his mouth, but nothing came out. Did he really believe she was so heartless she wouldn't check up on him?

She planted a hand on his shoulder and shoved him. "You idiot! Don't you have any idea how terrified I am of you dying? Did you know I begin every Monday with a prayer because that's the day you get tested, and I pray to God the sample will come out clean?"

He dragged a hand through his hair and gestured to the door. "Come on," he said. "Let's take this outside."

She followed him out of the clinic, their footsteps echoing in the stairwell, where the dank concrete was an oddly comforting and familiar scent. They walked to the side of the hospital where benches had been placed beneath the chestnut trees. The ground was soft from spring rains, and puddles gathered in bare patches in the lawn. Kate was too nervous to sit, and Trevor didn't seem any more comfortable. He braced one foot on the bench and rested an elbow on his knee, staring off into the distance.

"Tuberculosis is a horrible disease," he said slowly. "It grinds you down and saps the spirit out of you, but it taught me something. It taught me that life is precious, and sometimes it's very short. I've always accepted that I may not live a long time, and I've vowed never to squander a single day. I can't promise I'll be here to grow old with you, but I know I will love you every day of whatever time I have left. I won't marry a woman I don't love. If I can't have you, I'll go to my grave alone."

"Why do we have to discuss your grave? Most normal couples don't even think about such things."

"You're the one who won't let it drop. I never talked about it until you went nosing through my files."

"If you would quit your job here, it would be a lot easier for me." There wasn't an ounce of softening in the steel of his eyes. Wouldn't a man who loved her be willing to make this concession? But no, this was Trevor McDonough, and he had to win everything. "You're the most arrogant, hardheaded, and inflexible man. I'm surprised you're able to walk around with the weight of that ego on your shoulders."

A little of the steel faded from his eyes, and he looked tired. "Kate, would you just stop? I know it isn't in you to give up, but I'm asking you to. You can't beat me into submission. I won't ever walk away from this disease. It's what I am called to do."

"You are 'called' to help yourself into an early grave?"

He sighed. "There you go again."

There was a yelping from somewhere in the distance. It wouldn't quit, and Kate turned her head to see a familiar golden dog chained to a tree at the far side of the hospital yard.

"Is that Princess?" The dog looked cleaner and healthier than she did before. Trevor smiled and pushed away from the bench.

"Come on," he said. "It looks like she wants to see you."

Sure enough, Princess looked happy and healthy, wagging her tail so vigorously her entire body rocked back and forth. She was also wearing a dog collar with her name etched on a brass nameplate. Kate knelt down to give Princess a good rubbing, smiling to herself. This had to be Trevor's doing, for who else would have known the proper name to engrave on the nameplate?

"She kept trying to follow me home every

day," Trevor said. "I finally gave up and took her with me. I bring her to the hospital when the weather is good."

Kate always wanted a dog, but it was impossible at the boardinghouse. Never in a million years would she have expected the fastidious Trevor to accept a dog into his home.

"Maybe there's hope for you after all," she said. "If you can welcome a dog into your life, where else might you be willing to change?"

He gave an exasperated sigh. "Kate, what if I went on a nonstop crusade to try to change something about you? What if I suggested your first husband's untimely death has warped your ability to function as a normal human being? Your fear of my catching tuberculosis, while I cannot say it's completely unfounded, is overblown and irrational. How would you feel if I belittled your fears and tried to brainwash you to become a different person?"

Her hands stilled on the dog's fur. She would give *anything* if she could just stop being so afraid. Other women were married to men with dangerous jobs, and they didn't collapse into blobs of insecurity.

She stood and faced him. "I think I would welcome it."

For the second time in one day, it appeared as though she'd rendered him speechless. The wind tugged at his jacket and ruffled his hair, but his face remained still as he looked at her, a combination of disbelief and hope in his eyes.

"It won't be easy," she warned. "Nathan's death wiped me out. I quit having nightmares about collapsing scaffolding, but now I have nightmares of a collapsing lung, which is just as bad. Quite frankly, I doubt you have it in you to be able to shake me out of it."

The dimple appeared on his cheek. "You know I've never backed down from a challenge."

She brushed the dog hair from her hands and stepped closer to him. "That's what I'm counting on." She moved even closer, until her nose was only inches from his and she could smell the pine-scented soap he used.

"Figure this out, Trevor. Use that awesome brain of yours to convince me you're worth the gamble." She turned and started walking away, throwing one last taunt over her shoulder. "I dare you!"

She wanted to run back and fling herself against him and never let go, but she forced herself to keep walking. She prayed Trevor could find a way to put her fears at ease, because she'd never willingly marry another man who was meant for an early death. She walked faster lest temptation send her fleeing back into his sheltering arms.

The boardinghouse dining room was packed, which included Tom Wilkerson from the Patent Office, who was caught up in a debate with Charlie Davis about the upcoming presidential election. Kate tried to stay out of the fray as she weaved between the men, balancing platters of glazed ham steaks with fried apples and parsley potatoes. A knock at the front door turned her head in that direction. She placed the last dish and wiped her hands on her apron as she made her way to the front hall.

It was Trevor. He held a bouquet of roses. "I've come for dinner."

She buried her nose in the velvety petals, inhaling their heady fragrance. It was embarrassing how thrilled the half smile on Trevor's face made her feel. It had been almost six months since Trevor had been at their dinner table, and she instantly felt a familiar rush of excitement. She tried to keep the giddiness out of her voice.

"I hope you like ham. And can hold your own while arguing if Grover Cleveland deserves to recapture the White House.

Everyone has very strong opinions about it."

Trevor stepped inside, his voice as warm and rough as woodsmoke as he smiled down at her. "We're going to have a delightful evening while I slaughter you in a friendly debate about presidential politics," he said with a gleam in his eyes. "I've decided that I may be the luckiest man alive. I have the chance to pursue the woman who was the wildest fantasy of my boyhood. She's beautiful, intelligent, and the finest statistician any man could hope for." He leaned in closer, and her heart raced when he kissed the curve of her jaw. His voice then lowered, and he whispered, "And if she mentions the words early grave, painful death, or sputum samples, I will stand up and walk out. Clear?"

Why did she always turn into putty when he was rude to her? He planted another kiss on her forehead and straightened to await her answer. She fought to keep herself from laughing. "You're stifling my favorite topics."

"Break it up over there," Tick called from the dinner table. "The food's getting cold."

It was a warm evening, and Trevor shed his suit jacket and pulled up a chair to the packed table. It took Kate a while to get the rest of the meals served, and then she joined the rollicking debate.

That evening set the tone for the rest of the spring. Trevor came to dinner at least three times a week. He was still more of a listener than a talker, but she loved having him at their table, especially after the meal was finished and they slipped into the walled garden behind the house to steal a few minutes alone. She obeyed his rules and never mentioned anything about his vulnerable health, and those stolen hours became magical. In the privacy of the garden, with fireflies twinkling in the dark and the air perfumed by gardenia blossoms, Trevor let down his guard and became a different person. He was softer out here. Shy people often came off as cold and aloof, but when she was with Trevor in the garden he was the most gentle and tender man she'd ever met.

Only in private, though. In public he could revert to the stern, uncompromising man she knew so well. At the end of May, Trevor got into a huge argument with her mother when he insisted another servant be hired so that Kate could have a few nights off each week.

"Kate has been working two jobs all her life, and you can afford to hire another girl to serve the meals," he said.

"Kate likes working at the boarding-house," her mother hollered back. "And I can't afford the expense."

"Try again," Trevor snapped. "All your rooms are rented, and a little basic math tells me exactly how much you're taking in every week."

"What makes you think that's any business of yours?"

"It's my business if I can't court the woman I have serious intentions toward because she's dropping on her feet from exhaustion!"

Trevor won. A new girl was hired, and with Kate's newly liberated evenings, she started spending time with Trevor at a cozy tavern near the Navy Yard, where the crab chowder was spicy and the fiddle music lively. She loved it there, and the sound of fiddle music no longer made her want to weep. Instead she wanted to dance. On Sunday mornings Trevor walked her to church, and in the afternoon they played badminton on the lawn.

But always in the back of Kate's mind was the fear for his health, lurking like a grinning demon. Trevor's moratorium on discussing his job effectively quelled the arguments between them, but it couldn't stop her brain from indulging in its regular obsession. She still prayed every Monday when he swabbed his throat for a test, and then heaved a sigh of relief when he came to dinner on Monday evenings, giving her a wink as he walked in the door and took his seat at the table.

They both knew what that wink meant. It was the only reference he ever made to the fact that he needed to be regularly tested to catch the first hint of a relapse into tuberculosis.

Kate only slipped once the whole summer. They were having dinner at her mother's table when Trevor mentioned that he and Oskar Holtzmann were meeting for a regular game of backgammon at a local pub. Although Trevor always knew which of his patients were in the contagious stage of their disease, that wasn't the case with Oskar. And he probably didn't wear a mask at the pub.

Kate stiffened. "Is that a good idea? If there isn't adequate ventilation in that pub and you're sitting close together . . ."

There were no angry looks or words. Trevor simply pushed back from the table and walked to the front door. She couldn't believe it! She'd been a saint all spring and most of the summer, and now he got prickly at her first little slip? The chair upended behind her as she dashed after him. She grabbed his arm just as he made it to the door.

"Don't leave."

He shook her arm off and walked out the door.

She was stunned. She stepped out onto the sidewalk to yell after him. "This isn't working for me!" she shouted at his retreating back.

Trevor lifted his hand in a wave but didn't turn around as he continued walking down the street. Why did Trevor have to be so touchy? Couldn't he understand her fears at all? For a solid three months she'd been a model of stoic deportment, and the one time she slipped, he had to flee without saying a word. She'd been letting Trevor win all summer by stifling her fears, but she doubted she could do it for the rest of her life.

Trevor once said he vowed to live every day to its fullest. He knew his life might be cut short and chose to proceed at full speed, never letting dark fears cloud his days. Why couldn't she be equally as trusting? She needed a sense of control over her life, but how could she surrender that to Trevor when he couldn't be bothered to protect his own health?

She was due to meet him at the hospital after work the following evening to see the new rooftop retreat that had finally been finished. Whenever he spoke of the roof Trevor burst with pride, and she was itching to see it. But after his abrupt departure, she couldn't be sure she would even be welcome.

And did she even want to go? Quite frankly, their little experiment wasn't working out so well for her. Trevor was happy as a clam since they'd stopped arguing about his chosen profession, but *she* was still roiling with anxiety whenever she thought about it.

She slammed the door and marched back into the house.

27

Kate still simmered with annoyance as she approached the hospital the next afternoon. He hadn't contacted her to say if she was still welcome to visit the rooftop, but she'd come this far and wasn't going to be turned back.

Barking in the distance snagged her attention. Princess strained at her collar from where she'd been tied to an elm tree. It was always like this with Princess. Whenever she saw Kate, she bellyached to follow, even though she ought to know by now that Kate couldn't take her into the hospital.

Kate knelt beside the dog, giving her a rousing scratch behind both ears. If she married Trevor, she would move out of the boardinghouse and could finally have her very own dog.

Not that Trevor had asked. To the bottom of her heart she wished he would quit this line of work, and perhaps he sensed that.

He made it plain he would tolerate no nagging from her on the subject, but she didn't know how much longer she could pretend not to care.

Princess whined when Kate tried to disengage. Princess was a smart, intuitive dog, but how could Kate make her understand that the patients upstairs had weakened lungs and couldn't have a dog nearby? Her fur carried tiny specks that made it hard for them to breathe.

Trevor told her that Princess fussed and bellyached every morning, which was ridiculous. Trevor was the most predictable man ever born, and Princess ought to have a little more faith in him.

Kate's hand stilled as she stroked the dog. How could she expect Princess to grasp the nature of the work Trevor left her for each morning? Or that he'd been thrilled to learn that his new stepmother in Scotland would present him with a little brother or sister by the end of the year. Did Princess even understand there was a place called Scotland? Or the moon? Or the Milky Way? There was no way a dog could grasp those places, but that didn't mean they didn't exist. It just meant that a dog's mind could have no perspective for knowing such things.

A startling thought broke through.

Just as Princess couldn't possibly understand human concerns, how could Kate
possibly understand what was in the mind
of God? God never asked her to understand
Him. He asked her to *trust* Him. She would
never comprehend why Trevor had been
struck with such a terrible disease, but
perhaps it was part of a plan no human
mind was equipped to understand. She lived
in a tiny corner of Washington in the final
decade of the nineteenth century, while God
ruled over a vast universe encompassing
past, present, and future. How could her
paltry human mind begin to grasp such
complexity?

Trevor believed he'd been *called* to help
find a cure for tuberculosis. That was the
word he used over and over.

And yet she doubted him.

Was she any better than Princess, whining
and straining at her collar every time Trevor
left for the hospital to pursue his calling?
Kate didn't know why terrible diseases like
tuberculosis existed or why some of the
heroic doctors who tried to cure it would
fall victim to the disease, but that was a
limitation of *her* mind, not God's plan.

She was tired of doubting and living in
fear. It was impossible to know if Trevor
would find a cure next week or in the next

decade, or maybe he would never find it. Maybe he would die an early death, but maybe not . . . and she didn't want to be like Princess, crying out every time she feared for the future. It was time to take a leap of faith.

Wasn't the willingness to believe despite uncertainty the very essence of faith? Even now, a pull of energy and a sense of purpose gathered momentum inside her. A life of great purpose and fulfillment lay before her, if she could just be bold enough to step through the door into the unknown.

She bowed her head, opening her heart to the call flowing through her with an indomitable surge of hope and energy. It was a beginning. A quest. This was the path she was meant to walk. She and Trevor were going to embark on this calling shoulder to shoulder, heart to heart. Whatever blessings or perils came their way would be faced together. She was ready to step forward in the confidence and conviction that she was doing the right thing.

She hugged Princess and looked up at the perfect blue sky, unspeakable in its beauty. At long last she was ready to step into the future, blindly but with absolute trust. It didn't matter that there were no guarantees to protect her, for her life was going to unfold exactly as God intended, and she was ready now to accept the challenge.

Trevor waited with growing impatience for Kate's arrival. Was she still going to come? He'd spent the afternoon installing the last of the planters on the rooftop. He wanted everything to be perfect the first time Kate saw the roof. Some of his fondest memories had been those afternoons last summer when he and Kate daydreamed on this roof. How different it looked now, and she had been a part of that. He returned to his desk to finish paying the last of the bills for the rooftop's newly delivered plants.

As he expected, the hospital superintendent thought the rooftop retreat was an absurd waste of funds, but tensions between them eased after Mr. Lambrecht learned of Nurse Ackerman's crimes. It didn't hurt that the surgeon general was back on Trevor's side. Andrew Doyle had been sentenced to three months in prison for breaking into the Norton Boardinghouse and planting "evidence of mischief." Given the fraudulent forms Andrew manufactured, Trevor could have brought additional charges for slander, but his lawyer drafted a document offering to drop the charges so long as Andrew and his mother ceased their vendetta. The document was signed, notarized, and the pair of them had left the city after Andrew's release from prison.

He was just finishing the bills when Kate finally arrived, her face glowing with good health as she leaned against his open office door. "Hello, Trevor."

He shot to his feet. By heaven, she looked pretty with her hair piled atop her head like that! The schoolboy in him wanted to yank the clip out and watch it come tumbling down, while the man in him wanted to bury his face in it and smell her clean feminine scent. But the best thing was the light in her eyes. It sparkled with that rare combination of humor and intelligence that always dazzled him.

"Kate," he said, nodding. "Running a little late, are we?"

"I was waylaid by Princess. Besides, I couldn't be certain you'd want to see me after my fall from grace last night."

It hadn't been easy to walk away from her like that, but it had to be done. Kate was going to make them both miserable unless she came to terms with his calling, and he couldn't afford to yield even an inch. She'd take a hundred miles if he did.

"I always want to see you," he admitted. "You're like a splinter beneath my skin I can't stop thinking about."

"Good heavens, is that the elevator? It's magnificent!" She brushed past him down the hallway to the oversized brass doors that had been installed beside the washrooms.

He grinned as he cranked open the doors and guided her inside. The space was large enough for two gurneys and an attendant. She watched as he turned the lever to direct the car up. The doors closed, and the floor beneath them lifted.

She gasped and clutched his arm. The elevator moved very steadily, but people were usually startled the first time they felt the floor beneath them shift into motion.

The elevator jerked to a halt, and he held his breath as he turned the lever to open the door. What would she think of the rooftop? Maybe it would be a disappointment compared to all the fancy parks that dotted the city. The doors slid open, and he tried to imagine seeing it through Kate's eyes. The cracked asphalt had been replaced with slate tiles, and the brick walls supported planters overflowing with flowering begonias, salvia, and trailing ivy. Rows of comfortable chaise lounges were propped up so that patients could look out over the treetops. The sun was beginning to set now, and the patients had been moved downstairs. They had the rooftop all to themselves.

"It's so peaceful up here," she breathed as she stepped out onto the tile. "You even added plants!"

"Someone once told me a little greenery was good for the spirit."

They moved to the far wall, where they could look out over the trees.

"The patients love it up here," he said quietly. "Up here they can have a tiny slice of normal life and can enjoy a sunny day. They say . . . they say . . ." His throat closed up, and he had to stop speaking. Where had this surge of emotion come from?

It was embarrassing to get choked up like this, but he had walked in the same shoes as his patients. He had lived their fear, endured their pain, and suffered their isolation. He knew how precious this retreat was for people who had only a few months left to live.

Kate stepped closer and clasped his hand. She probably knew exactly what he was feeling, but he still blinked a little faster so she wouldn't see his eyes misting up. He took a deep breath and started again.

"The patients say it's easier to feel at peace up here. And that is very important to me," he managed to choke out.

A breeze rustled the leaves, summoning fleeting memories of the mountaintop. It was easier to feel closer to God here. It was easier to accept death as a natural part of life, merely the final chapter of one adventure before another began. This rooftop haven might be the best thing he could ever offer his patients, but it was a gift worth having.

Kate slid her arms around him and laid her head against his chest. She was probably going to be deafened by the pounding of his heart. "I'm so proud of you," she said. "It's perfect."

They stayed on the rooftop long after the sun slipped below the horizon. Throughout the city the gas lamps were lit, and the stars emerged in the night sky. He felt like he could stay up here with Kate forever. She lay on a chaise beside him, her fingers casually linked with his.

"I had the strangest conversation with Princess this afternoon." He cocked his head at the outlandish comment, but Kate kept her gaze fastened on the starlit sky. "That dog has limitations in her understanding of how the universe operates," she continued. "The workings of the cosmos. I'm willing to accept that I share a similar limitation."

"Coming from you, that's quite a conces-sion."

Her little foot reached out to kick him, but when she rolled onto her side to look at him, her face glowed. "I don't understand what God has planned for either of us, but I know it's pointless to keep worrying about it. I think your life is going to unfold exactly as God intends. I think you are at the begin-ning of a grand, monumental quest, and God sees the bigger picture, even if I can't. I'm willing to trust what I cannot see, even if it's frightening and uncertain. I'm ready to accept that."

His breath caught. Was she saying what he hoped? Her countenance shone with happi-ness, and he wanted to lunge across the space between them and haul her into his arms. Instead, he reached out to touch her cheek, soft and velvety as a rose petal.

"You have no idea how badly I've wanted to hear you say that," he said in an aching voice.

"Your fingers are shaking."

He gave a little laugh. "You've had me quaking since we were thirteen years old. Come on. Let me walk you home."

He could tell she was disappointed, but if they lingered any longer he was liable to spoil things. He wanted to ask her to marry him, but other plans were already laid, and too many people had helped him along the way for him to lose his head now.

Kate loitered too long with Trevor on the rooftop. It was almost midnight before they arrived at her doorstep, and she was late for work the next morning. Everyone in the office stared at her as she scurried to her desk.

"Sorry," she mumbled, sliding into her chair and pulling a stack of papers toward her. It didn't take long before Roger Moreno sidled up to her desk.

"I was hoping you would proofread a brief for me." He seemed unusually nervous. Dots of perspiration broke out on his forehead, and he shifted his weight from foot to foot. "It's a very important brief."

Irene started giggling. It was impossible to know why Mr. Moreno was so anxious, but Irene's giggles weren't helpful. Kate sent her a glare across the office, and the girl went back to feeding an envelope into her typewriter.

"What's the topic?" Kate asked, holding her hand out for the pages.

"I'm afraid it's contract law," Mr. Moreno said, and Kate winced.

"Don't worry, it's a short one. Just a single page," he assured her before doubling over in a fit of coughing. It seemed like a few of the other lawyers in the office were snickering at him. She felt sympathy for Mr. Moreno. Obviously he'd been struggling with his work, but it wasn't right for his colleagues to laugh at him.

"I'll get to work on it right away," she said.

He gave her a wide smile. "Thank you, Mrs. Livingston."

He went back to his desk, but how strange that he kept staring at her. In fact, it seemed everyone was staring at her. Was it because she was late this morning? She set the paper on her desk and started reading, trying to wade through the dense legal language.

When a party of superior intellect consorts with a lesser party (in this case, someone weak in trigonometry, albeit superior in statistics, spelling, and chemistry) certain necessary obligations must ensue.

Her jaw dropped open.

What on earth was she reading? Her head shot up, and she looked over to Mr. Moreno, who grinned at her from across the office. So did Irene. So were all the other clerks and even Justice Bauman, who stood in the open doorway of his private office.

She swallowed hard, looking back at the

497

document, jumping to the end of the legal blather.

Pursuant to the first party's hopeless love for the second party, it is only fitting that a marriage should result. The court orders Dr. Trevor McDonough Kendall to make all necessary and proper arrangements to secure Katherine Livingston's consent in holy and legal matrimony.

It was signed by all nine justices of the Supreme Court.

Her eyes drifted closed. "Trevor McDonough," she muttered under her breath.

She looked up to see Trevor standing behind Justice Bauman, looking dangerously tall and handsome with that stern expression on his face — the same expression he always wore when he was nervous.

Kate rose, bracing her trembling hands against the surface of her desk. "Am I going to need a lawyer to draft a response?"

"Not unless you're going to be difficult about it." His voice was flat.

Irene started giggling, and Trevor shot her a poisonous look. "You said she would think it was funny!"

It was kind of funny, even though it was awkward with all these people staring at them. Trevor took quite a risk by proposing in such a public fashion. His face was pale beneath his tan, and it was hard to watch him fidget like this, but before she could put him out of his misery he sweetened the offer.

"We can continue having dinner at your mother's table at least twice a week," he said. "I'll find a new job for you at the hospital if you want. And I won't fuss if you want to bring flowers. I should have thought of that originally; I just don't have an irrational feminine streak in me." His voice got tighter like it always did when he was frustrated. "I even asked for your parents' blessing. Do you know what that was like for me? Your mother is the nosiest woman on the planet. She wanted to know my income! My desire for children. For pity's sake, she wanted to know why I wash my hands before and after meals."

"I've always wondered too," Irene piped in.

Trevor looked like he was about to burst with frustration. "It's just a habit, okay?" He turned his attention back to Kate. "Anyway, your mother said you would be an idiot if you didn't marry me." There was a little wiggling of his lips as he tried not to smile.

"She did?" Maude Norton had come a long way in learning to accept Trevor. The woman who'd wanted to boil Trevor in oil the day he eked out a victory over her precious daughter in a school contest now accepted that Trevor made Kate happy merely by walking into a room. Still, there was no doubt their lives would all be easier if she had her mother's blessing.

"An idiot?" Kate pressed.

"A 'howling idiot' was the term she used. And I'd hate for you to be sullied in your mother's eyes."

Trevor was the best friend she ever had, even if she once thought of him as "the horrible Trevor McDonough." He had plagued, challenged, and inspired her. He'd traveled the world and collected more experiences than she could ever dream of. He had so much to teach her, and she wanted every drop of it. Trevor didn't know the first thing about marriage or intimacy, one area where she really did know a lot more than him.

She dropped the legal brief and raced across the room. Before he could brace himself, she threw her arms around him and slammed into him with the full force of her body. She dragged his face down and planted a kiss on his mouth that threatened to incinerate the Capitol.

She pulled away and said, "Are you really brave enough to take me on?"

"I really am." His smile was confident.

"Do I get to keep the dog?"

"You do."

Her smile was so wide her face hurt. "Then I'll marry you. Gladly. Joyously. With no regrets and no fear."

The office burst into cheers.

EPILOGUE

Eight Years Later
New Year's Eve — 1899

Kate glanced at the grandfather clock in the corner of the grand drawing room. It was still five minutes before the bells would chime and signal the new year. Most of the McDonough clan was gathered in the palatial home where Trevor's father lived in the wilds of Scotland. A roaring fire crackled in the cavernous fireplace dominating one side of the great room, but the vaulted ceiling still made it chilly. Kate drew a tartan plaid tighter around her shoulders. This was the last time she was going to let Trevor drag her to Scotland in December until his father finally installed a decent heating system in this oversized castle.

It was still a lovely sight. Candles glowed from dozens of candelabras, and the air was scented with pine boughs and mulled cider. Before her, the dining table groaned under the weight of roasted goose, mincemeat pies, oysters, pastries, ginger cake, and plum pudding. Trevor's father worked at twisting the cork off a champagne bottle while a butler set out crystal flutes.

She glanced over at the fireplace, where Trevor's young brothers were sprawled on the floor before the fire. They were giddy with ginger cake and excitement as the midnight hour drew near.

Trevor's stepmother had been dutifully producing a slew of McDonough offspring, and he now had four little brothers who idolized him. As an only child, Trevor always longed for siblings, and now he insisted on regular visits to Scotland so he wouldn't be a stranger to his brothers. Every time they arrived, the boys came barreling out of the house and tackled Trevor with all the might in their sturdy little bodies. Trevor would obligingly roll onto the grass as they climbed all over him and proclaimed victory in toppling their American brother. The McDonough sense of competition flowed strongly in the veins of those boys. All Trevor had to do was ask who was the strongest of the group to carry the bags in, and he was greeted with a chorus of "Me, me, me!" as each of the boys struggled to prove their strength.

Relations with Trevor's father had improved too. Trevor accepted that while his father had an inbred weakness for amassing a staggering fortune, he wasn't a bad man at heart, and Trevor accepted responsibility for needlessly prolonging their rift. Now that the elder McDonough had his legitimate male heir, he gladly welcomed Kate into the family despite her working-class roots.

The annual trips to Scotland weren't only about visits to the family. Trevor always called on the medical laboratories in Edinburgh, where research proceeded at an astounding pace. Scientists were experimenting with mold and fungus in an effort to cure diseases, which Kate thought was insane. She spent too many years battling mold in the boardinghouse washrooms to view it as anything other than a menace, but Trevor thought the research fascinating, and it wasn't the first time he'd put his faith in an unconventional theory. After all, no one was laughing at his suggestion of a sunlight cure anymore.

No quick and easy cure for tuberculosis was on the horizon, but Trevor's regimen was beginning to show real promise, and the patients who came to them now had a slim hope for a cure. Their survival rate was now twenty percent and rivaled those of the expensive mountain sanitariums. Trevor credited it to the sunlight. If it proved true, it would be a boon for working-class patients all over the world, as anyone could afford sunlight. Trevor had mended ties with the young doctor Michael Wells, who proved to be a dedicated physician capable of covering for him at the clinic during Trevor's annual trips to Scotland.

She glanced across the table at Trevor, whose head was tilted to listen to his stepmother chatter about their plans to install a new heating system in the house next year. He nodded while listening with one ear, but Kate followed his gaze to see that most of his attention was fixed on their two children slumbering on a bearskin rug on the far side of the room. Carl was six, Amy only four, and they appeared to be the only sensible people in the room by curling up in the warmest spot to sleep.

She rose to her feet and caught Trevor's attention. "Shall we wake the little ones? It's almost time."

Trevor came around the table to walk her over to the children. Before she could reach down and jostle them awake, he stopped her. He had a misty, faraway look as he gazed down at their children.

"I'll never tire of watching them sleep," he murmured.

She gave thanks to God every day for giving her the courage to marry Trevor. His health continued to hold strong, and now they had two beautiful children to complete their family. She still said an extra prayer every Monday when he tested himself for a recurrence of tuberculosis. She couldn't be certain what the future held for them, but they had built a beautiful life together, and she would carry on no matter what happened. Even if Trevor crossed over before her, she would never truly be alone, for the Lord promised He would be with her always, even to the end of the world.

Trevor handed Amy to her, then leaned over to shake Carl awake. They carried the children to the space before the grandfather clock, where everyone gathered to await the stroke of midnight. Dozens of servants poured in to join in the festivities. Glasses of champagne and cider were circulated, and people held their breath to listen to the ticking of the big grandfather clock.

Kate watched as the heavy brass pendulum ticked away the final seconds of the nineteenth century. Soon the anticipation became too much, and everyone started counting down the final moments.

"Three, two, one . . . Happy New Year!" The bells began chiming, and there were kisses, hugs, and glasses raised in celebration.

Trevor leaned over to kiss her cheek. "Welcome to the twentieth century, love."

Amy was confused by all the excitement and reached out for Trevor to hold her. Kate passed her over. "I still don't understand what all this means," Amy said, rubbing sleep from her eyes.

"It means you're going to see many amazing things," Trevor said as he hoisted their daughter higher in his arms, his face flushed with excitement.

And Kate knew it was true. They lived in an era when it wasn't so strange for girls to aspire to an education, and if their daughter wanted to go to college, it was going to happen. Every day the newspapers touted new discoveries and inventions. Automobiles were beginning to appear on the streets of Washington, and the race to create the first flying machine was well under way. Medical discoveries would continue to progress and make life better for everyone. Someday there would be a cure for tuberculosis, and she prayed Trevor would be there to witness it.

She stepped into Trevor's arms and dreamed of the world to come.

HISTORICAL NOTE

Tuberculosis was the leading cause of death in American cities in the late nineteenth century. In a desperate search for a cure, research doctors experimented with injections of mercury, arsenic, creosote, copper, and lime in an attempt to kill the disease without harming the patient. Barbaric surgeries removed sections of lung or immobilized the patients for months or even years. None of these treatments proved effective. From the 1880s through the 1930s, the best hope for tubercular patients was a lengthy stay at rural sanitariums in mountain climates. Patients were encouraged to lie outside, even in frigid winter conditions, and breathe in as much of the high, dry air as possible. Medical historians now believe the success achieved at sanitariums was a combination of fresh air, improved nutrition, and, to a certain extent, the benefits of vitamin D derived from exposure to sunlight.

Tuberculosis wasn't cured until the mid-1940s with the creation of streptomycin, an antibiotic developed in the medical laboratories at Rutgers University. Antibiotics proved highly effective against tuberculosis, curing the disease quickly, effectively, and inexpensively. For decades the menace of tuberculosis was considered a scourge of the past. Sadly, the miracle of antibiotics led to a sense of complacency, so that by the 1980s a resurgence in new cases of tuberculosis began spreading throughout the world. Many of these cases indicate resistance to traditional antibiotic treatments. Increased awareness, better drug combinations, and follow-up care are helping to turn the tide once again.

I was inspired to write this book after reading a fascinating memoir by Edward Livingston Trudeau (1848–1915), a doctor who contracted tuberculosis while treating his dying brother. Dr. Trudeau was the first to pioneer the concept of sanitarium care in America, and he lived with tuberculosis for over forty years before finally dying of the disease. In the closing pages of his memoir, when he knew he had only a few weeks to live, he wrote: "The struggle with tuberculosis has brought me experiences and left me recollections which I never could have known otherwise, and I would not exchange it for all the wealth of the Indies! While struggling to save others, it has enabled me to make the best friends a man ever had. . . . I have learned that the conquest of Fate is not by struggling against it, but by acquiescence; that it is often through men that we come to know God; that spiritual courage is of a higher type than physical courage; and that it takes a higher type of courage to fight a losing rather than a winning fight."

DISCUSSION QUESTIONS

1. When Trevor first arrived to America, Mrs. Kendall taught him to hide his disease, as she knew they would both be turned out of the house if her employer realized they had tuberculosis. Was this an immoral thing for her to do? Why or why not?

2. As is often the case with shy or introverted people, Trevor is perceived as aloof and unfriendly. Is there anyone in your life whom you might be making a similar assumption about?

3. Dinner at the boardinghouse was a major factor that drew people to live at the Norton Boardinghouse due to the networking and friendships that could be formed around the dining room table. What role does the dinner table play in your family?

4. People often wonder how a loving God could permit tragedies to befall innocent victims. Kate finally accepts she doesn't

understand everything in God's plan and decides to stop fretting about things beyond her ability to comprehend. How do you grapple with this question?

5. Kate is scolded by an attendant who overhears her remark about "meaningful work." How often throughout a typical day do you accept service from people in thankless tasks? How might you infuse that brief interaction with a sign that you respect and are grateful for their work?

6. Tick accuses Kate of smothering him, but isn't the proper role for a parent or mentor to provide guidance to young people, who often don't know enough to spot the problems around the corner? At what point should you retreat and let them make mistakes?

7. Do you agree with Trevor's insistence on staying in a job that carries unique physical dangers for him? Should he have chosen a safer field, especially after he married and had children of his own?

8. This book was inspired by doctors and nurses who risk their lives to treat people with lethally contagious diseases. Dr. Edward Trudeau (1848–1915), a physician who contracted tuberculosis during the course of his work, wrote that "spiritual courage is of a higher type than physi-

cal courage; and that it takes a higher type of courage to fight a losing rather than a winning fight." Do you agree with these statements? Have you undertaken losing battles in your life that were still worth the fight?

ABOUT THE AUTHOR

Elizabeth Camden is the award-winning author of five novels, including *Against the Tide* (2012), winner of a RITA Award, Christy Award, and Daphne du Maurier Award. With a master's in History and a master's in Library Science, she is a research librarian by day and scribbles away on her next novel by night. Elizabeth lives with her husband in Florida. Learn more at ElizabethCamden.com.

The employees of Thorndike Press hope you have enjoyed this Large Print book. All our Thorndike, Wheeler, and Kennebec Large Print titles are designed for easy reading, and all our books are made to last. Other Thorndike Press Large Print books are available at your library, through selected bookstores, or directly from us.

For information about titles, please call:
  (800) 223-1244

or visit our Web site at:
  http://gale.cengage.com/thorndike

To share your comments, please write:
  Publisher
  Thorndike Press
  10 Water St., Suite 310
  Waterville, ME 04901